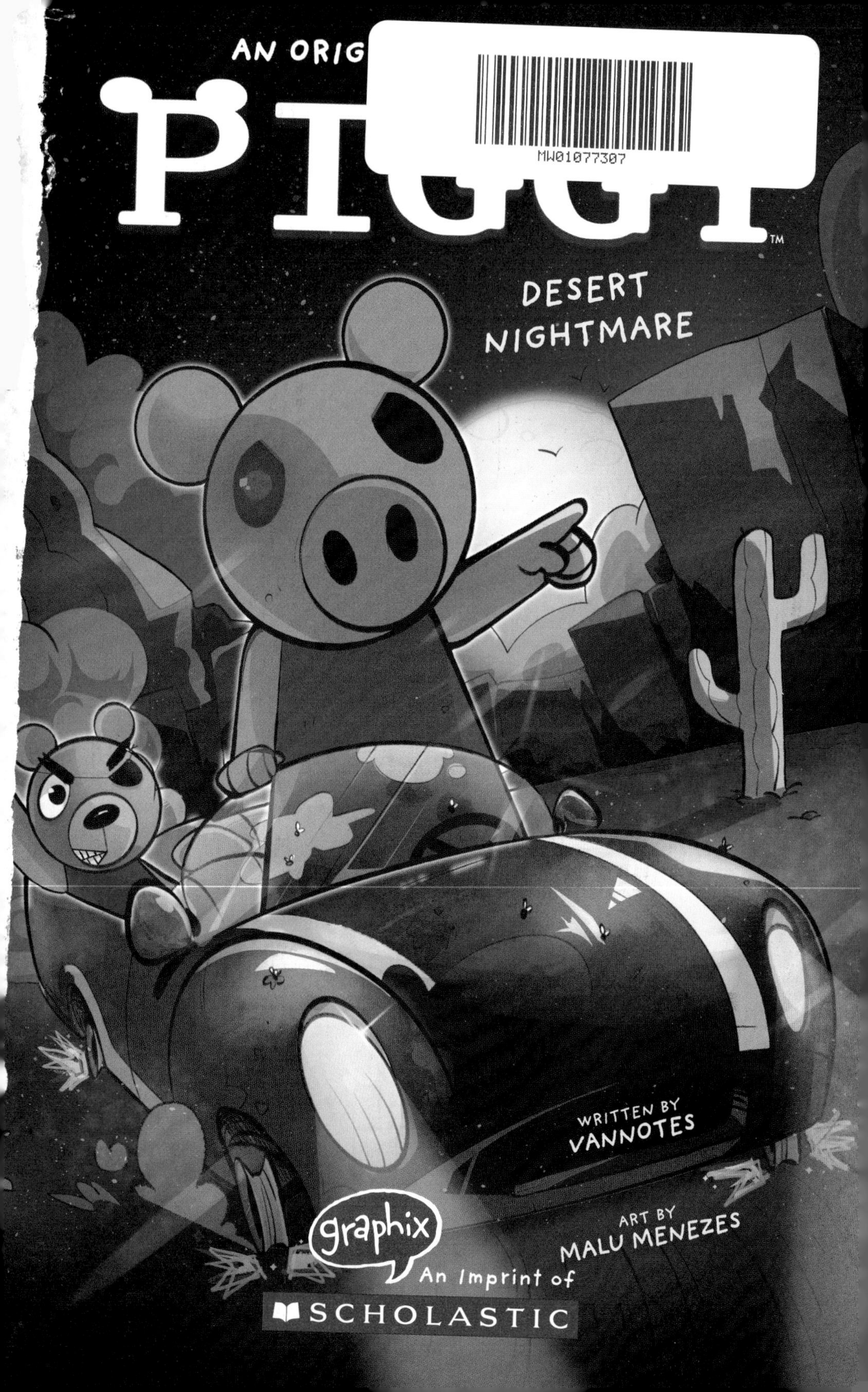
AN ORIG
PIGGY™
DESERT NIGHTMARE
WRITTEN BY VANNOTES
ART BY MALU MENEZES
graphix
An Imprint of
SCHOLASTIC

All rights reserved. Published by Graphix, an imprint of Scholastic Inc., *Publishers since 1920*. SCHOLASTIC,
GRAPHIX, and associated logos are trademarks and/or registered trademarks of Scholastic Inc.

The publisher does not have any control over and does not assume any responsibility
for author or third-party websites or their content.

ISBN 978-1-339-04240-4

10 9 8 7 6 5 4 3 2 1        24 25 26 27 28

Printed in the U.S.A.        40

First edition, September 2024

Edited by Michael Petranek

Lettering by Patrick Brosseau

Book design by Jeff Shake

Color by Astronym

Layouts by Dawn Guzzo

# CHAPTER: 1

AFTER AN OUTBREAK THAT'S TURNED THE WORLD UPSIDE DOWN, WILLOW AND HER MYSTERIOUS TEAM, THE SILVER PAW, HAVE DONE ALL THEY CAN TO STAY ALIVE. AFTER BEING TRAPPED IN HER OLD ELEMENTARY SCHOOL, WILLOW ESCAPED WITH THE HELP OF HER NEW FRIEND CAMI.

STAYING SAFE FROM THE INFECTED IS EASY WHEN YOU'RE INSIDE A SECRET HIDEOUT, BUT WHAT IF YOU'RE FORCED TO HIT THE OPEN ROAD?

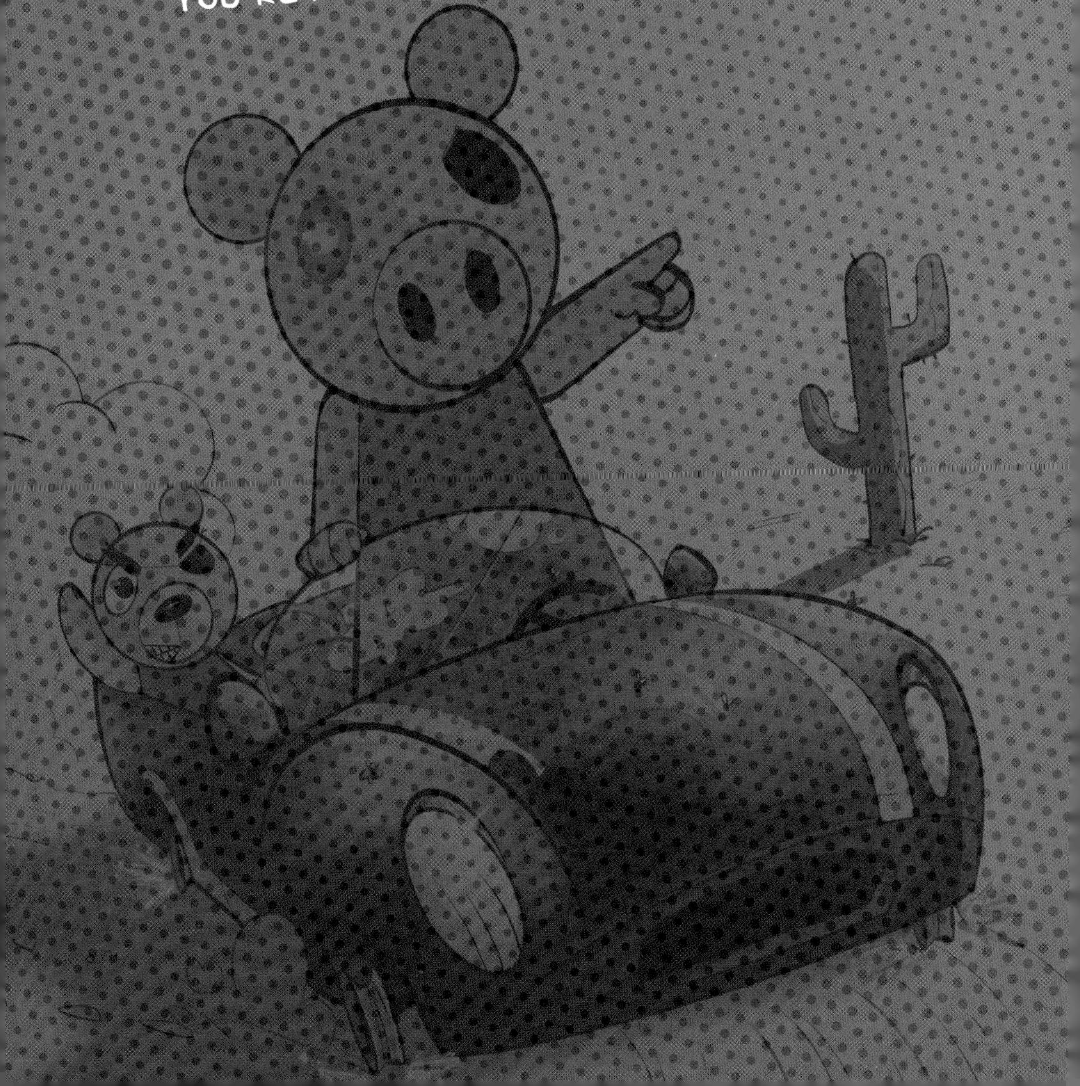

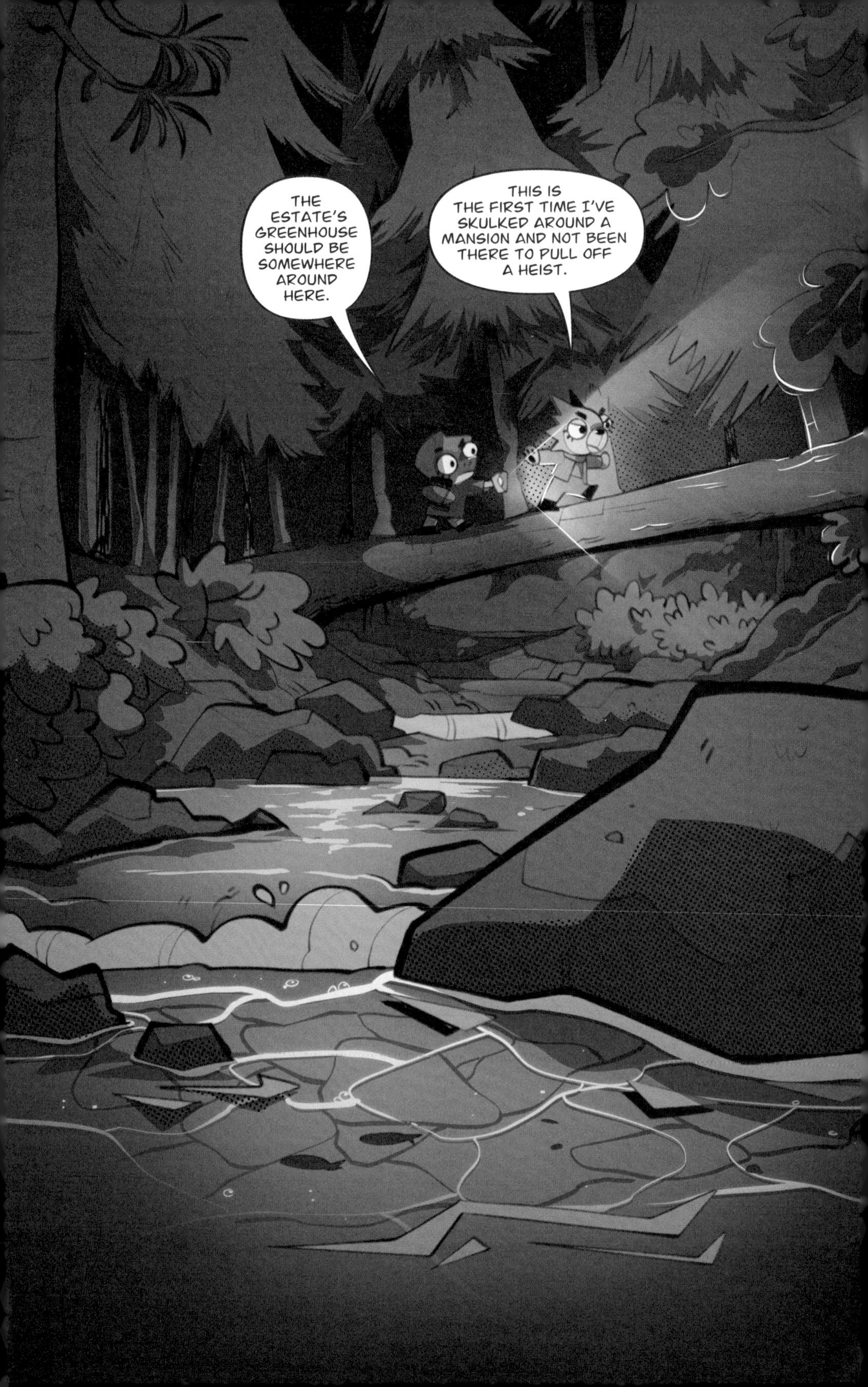
THE ESTATE'S GREENHOUSE SHOULD BE SOMEWHERE AROUND HERE.
THIS IS THE FIRST TIME I'VE SKULKED AROUND A MANSION AND NOT BEEN THERE TO PULL OFF A HEIST.

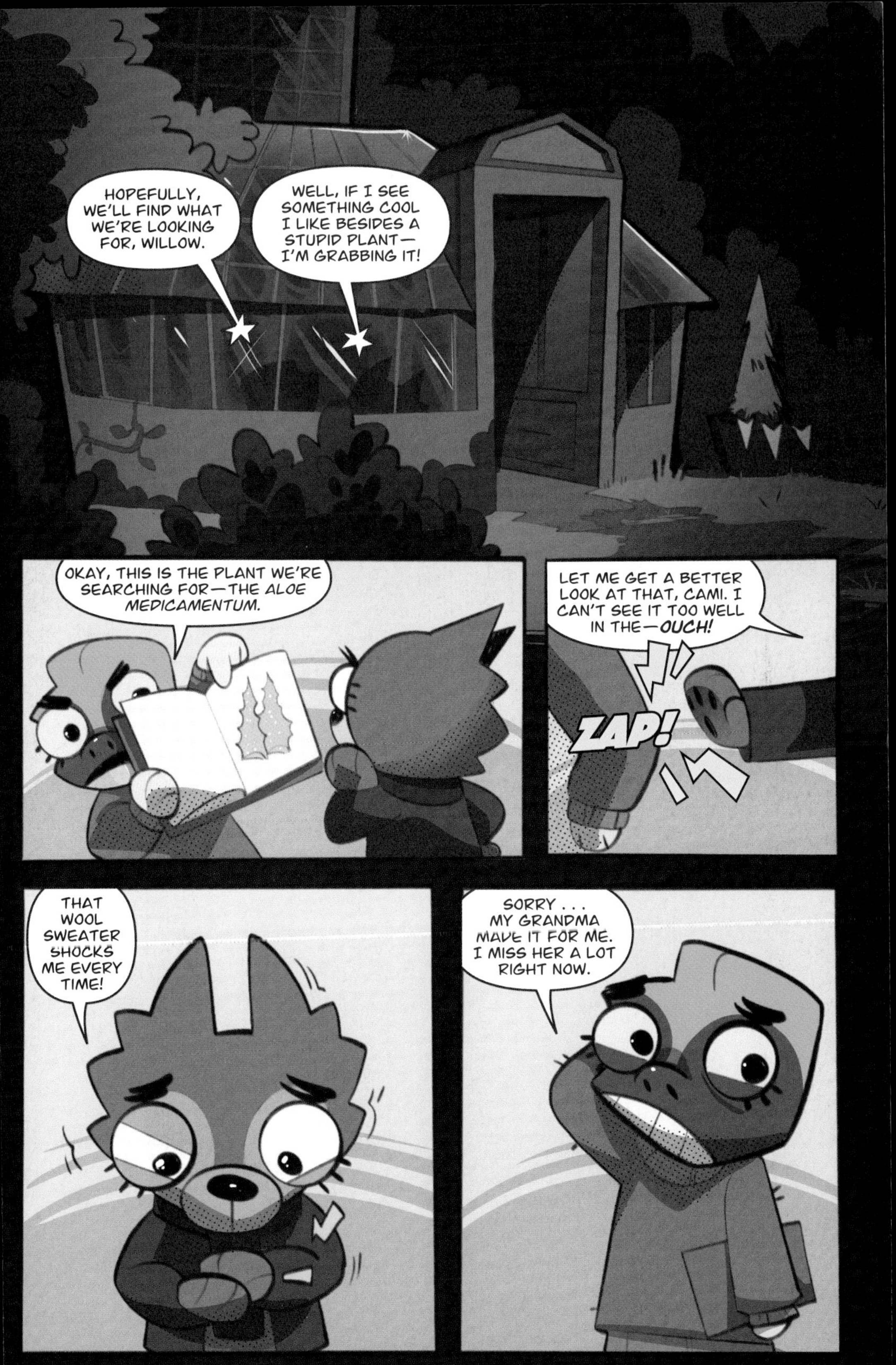
HOPEFULLY, WE'LL FIND WHAT WE'RE LOOKING FOR, WILLOW.
WELL, IF I SEE SOMETHING COOL I LIKE BESIDES A STUPID PLANT— I'M GRABBING IT!
OKAY, THIS IS THE PLANT WE'RE SEARCHING FOR—THE *ALOE MEDICAMENTUM.*
LET ME GET A BETTER LOOK AT THAT, CAMI. I CAN'T SEE IT TOO WELL IN THE—*OUCH!*
ZAP!
THAT WOOL SWEATER SHOCKS ME EVERY TIME!
SORRY . . . MY GRANDMA MADE IT FOR ME. I MISS HER A LOT RIGHT NOW.

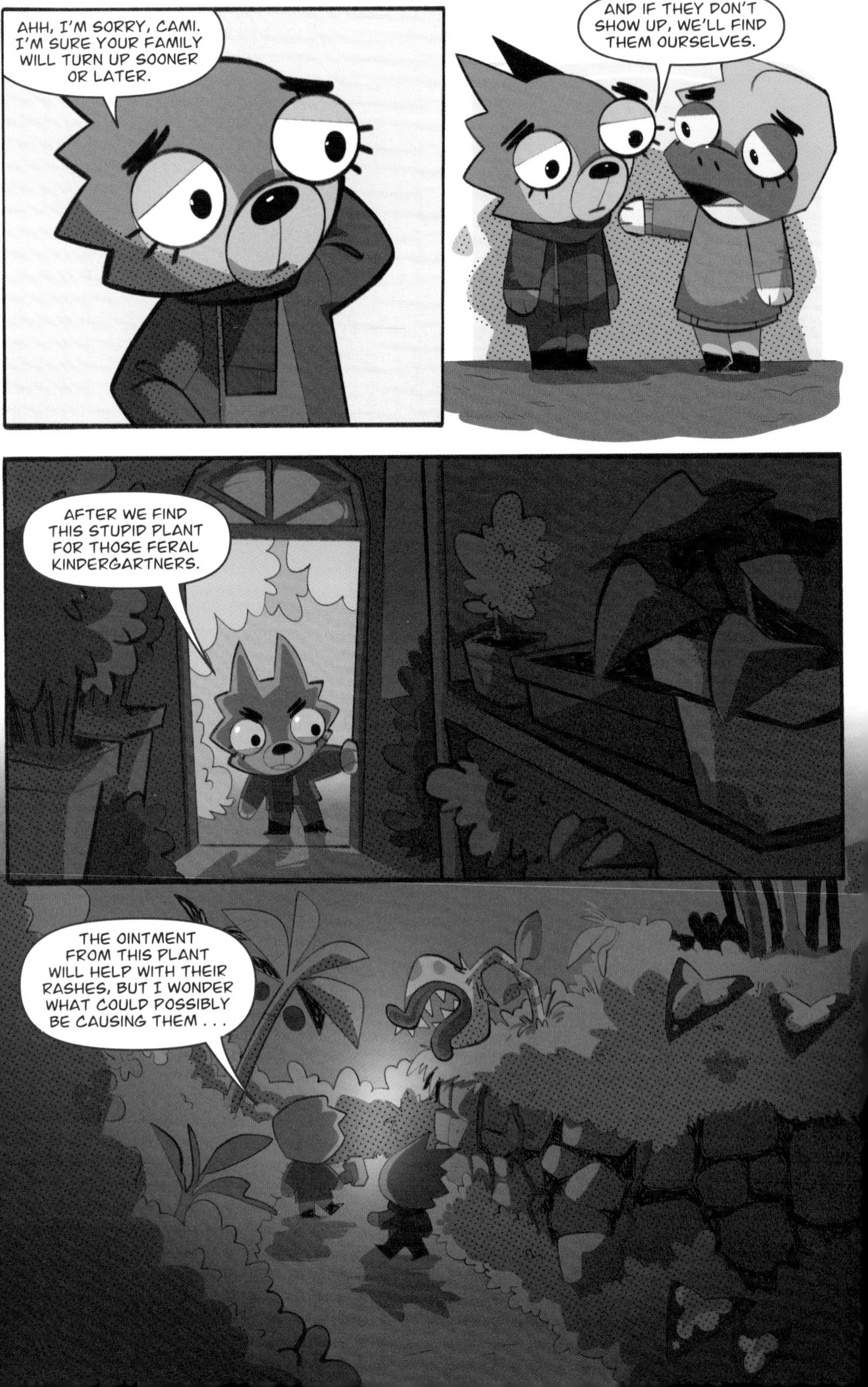
AHH, I'M SORRY, CAMI. I'M SURE YOUR FAMILY WILL TURN UP SOONER OR LATER.
AND IF THEY DON'T SHOW UP, WE'LL FIND THEM OURSELVES.
AFTER WE FIND THIS STUPID PLANT FOR THOSE FERAL KINDERGARTNERS.
THE OINTMENT FROM THIS PLANT WILL HELP WITH THEIR RASHES, BUT I WONDER WHAT COULD POSSIBLY BE CAUSING THEM . . .

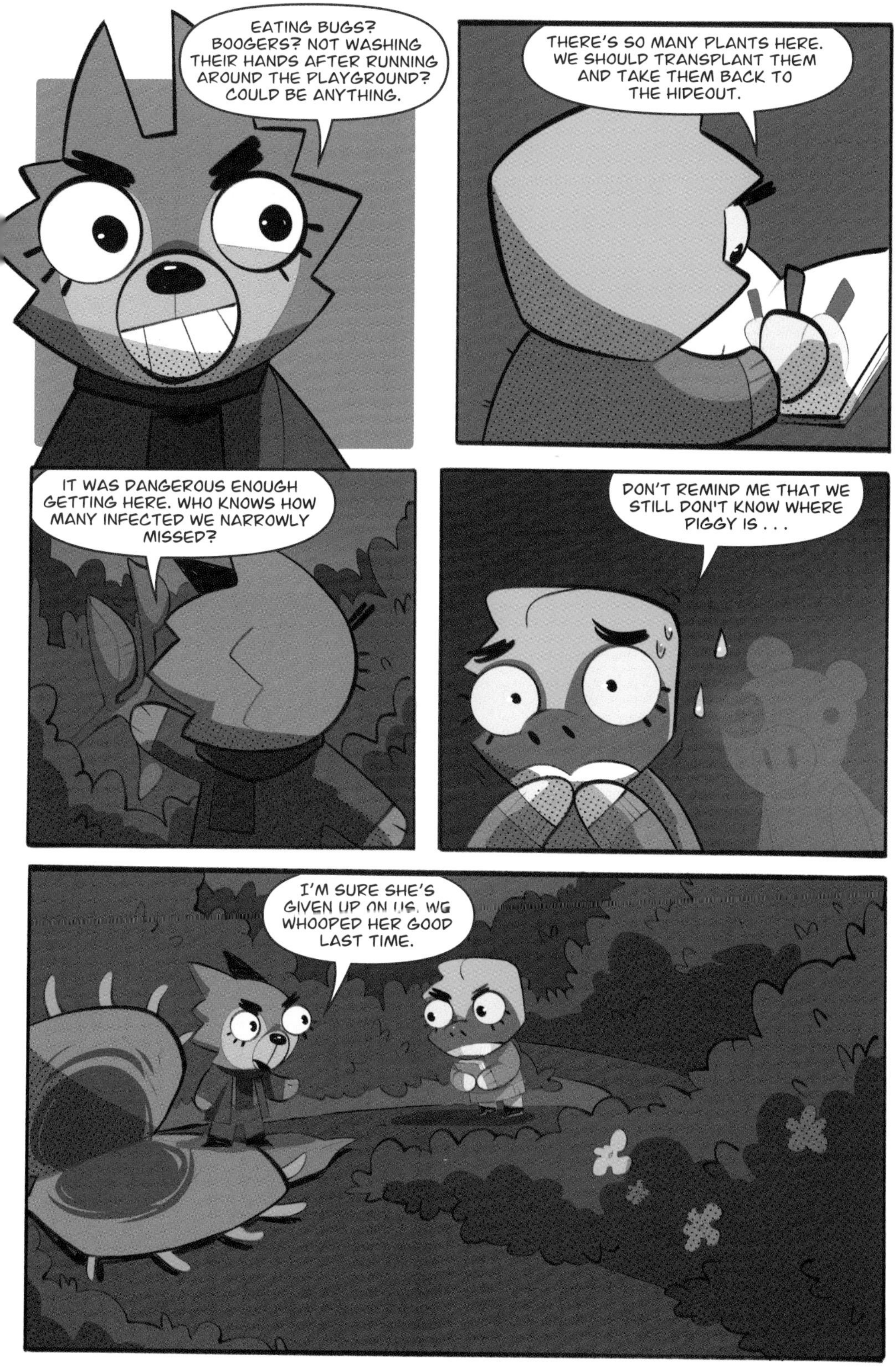

EATING BUGS? BOOGERS? NOT WASHING THEIR HANDS AFTER RUNNING AROUND THE PLAYGROUND? COULD BE ANYTHING.
THERE'S SO MANY PLANTS HERE. WE SHOULD TRANSPLANT THEM AND TAKE THEM BACK TO THE HIDEOUT.
IT WAS DANGEROUS ENOUGH GETTING HERE. WHO KNOWS HOW MANY INFECTED WE NARROWLY MISSED?
DON'T REMIND ME THAT WE STILL DON'T KNOW WHERE PIGGY IS . . .
I'M SURE SHE'S GIVEN UP ON US. WE WHOOPED HER GOOD LAST TIME.

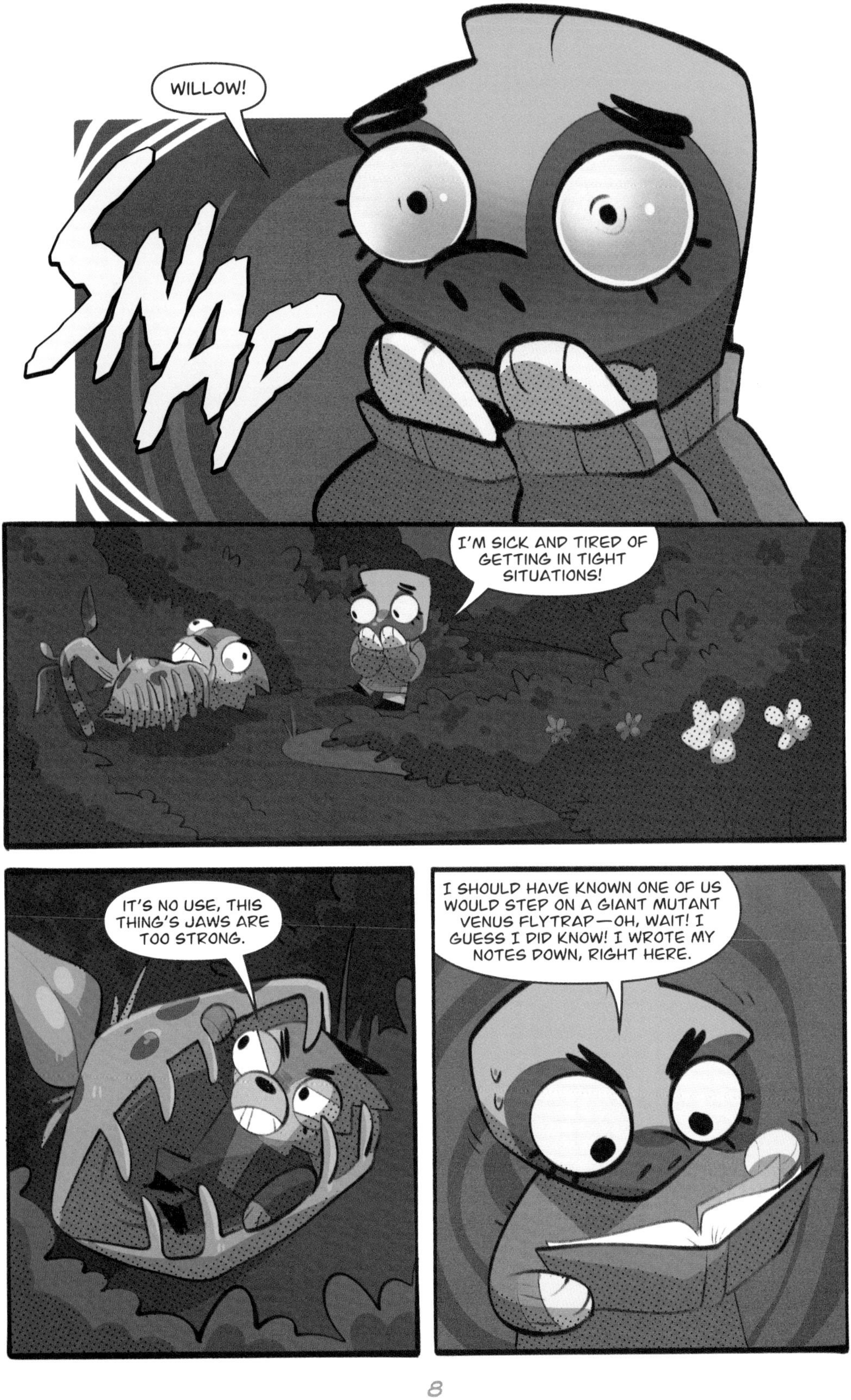
WILLOW!
SNAP
I'M SICK AND TIRED OF GETTING IN TIGHT SITUATIONS!
IT'S NO USE, THIS THING'S JAWS ARE TOO STRONG.
I SHOULD HAVE KNOWN ONE OF US WOULD STEP ON A GIANT MUTANT VENUS FLYTRAP—OH, WAIT! I GUESS I DID KNOW! I WROTE MY NOTES DOWN, RIGHT HERE.

# The Silver Paw Survival Tips-Carnivorous Plants

**Tip 1** - There are many kinds of carnivorous plants, but the most famous one is the Venus flytrap.

**Tip 2** - These plants have little hairs that signal whether the leaves should snap closed when they are touched.

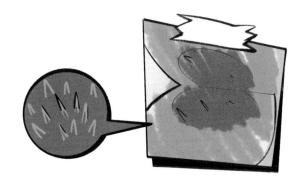

**Tip 3** - If carnivorous plants closed every time something touched them, they'd be opening and closing all the time.

**Tip 4** - So their sensory hairs wait until something's been standing there for a while before they enclose their prey.

**Tip 5** - Since snap trap plants don't have muscles the same way animals do, carnivorous plants use hydraulics to open and close themselves. This involves water and electric impulses from the hairs.

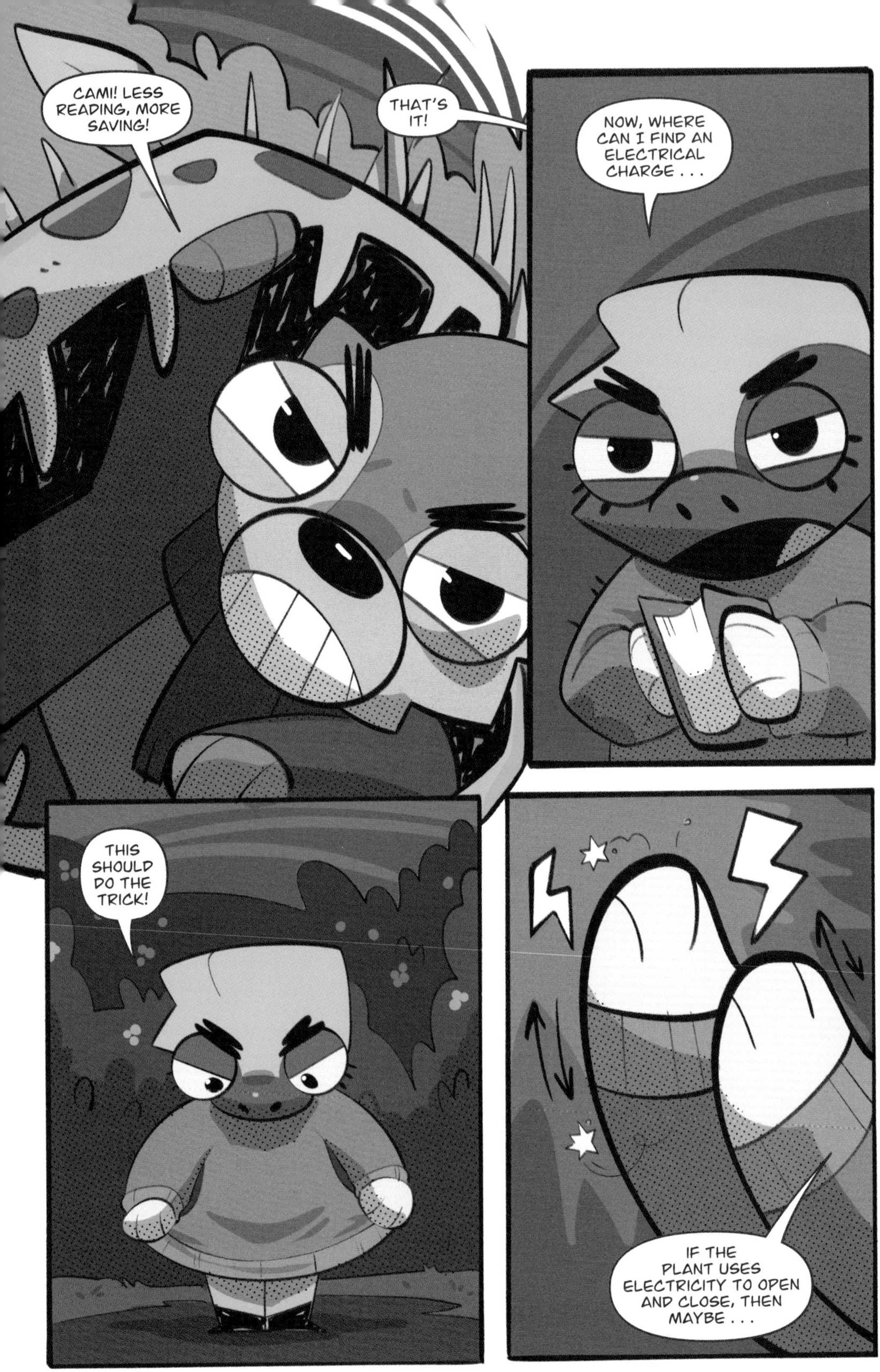
CAMI! LESS READING, MORE SAVING!
THAT'S IT!
NOW, WHERE CAN I FIND AN ELECTRICAL CHARGE . . .
THIS SHOULD DO THE TRICK!
IF THE PLANT USES ELECTRICITY TO OPEN AND CLOSE, THEN MAYBE . . .

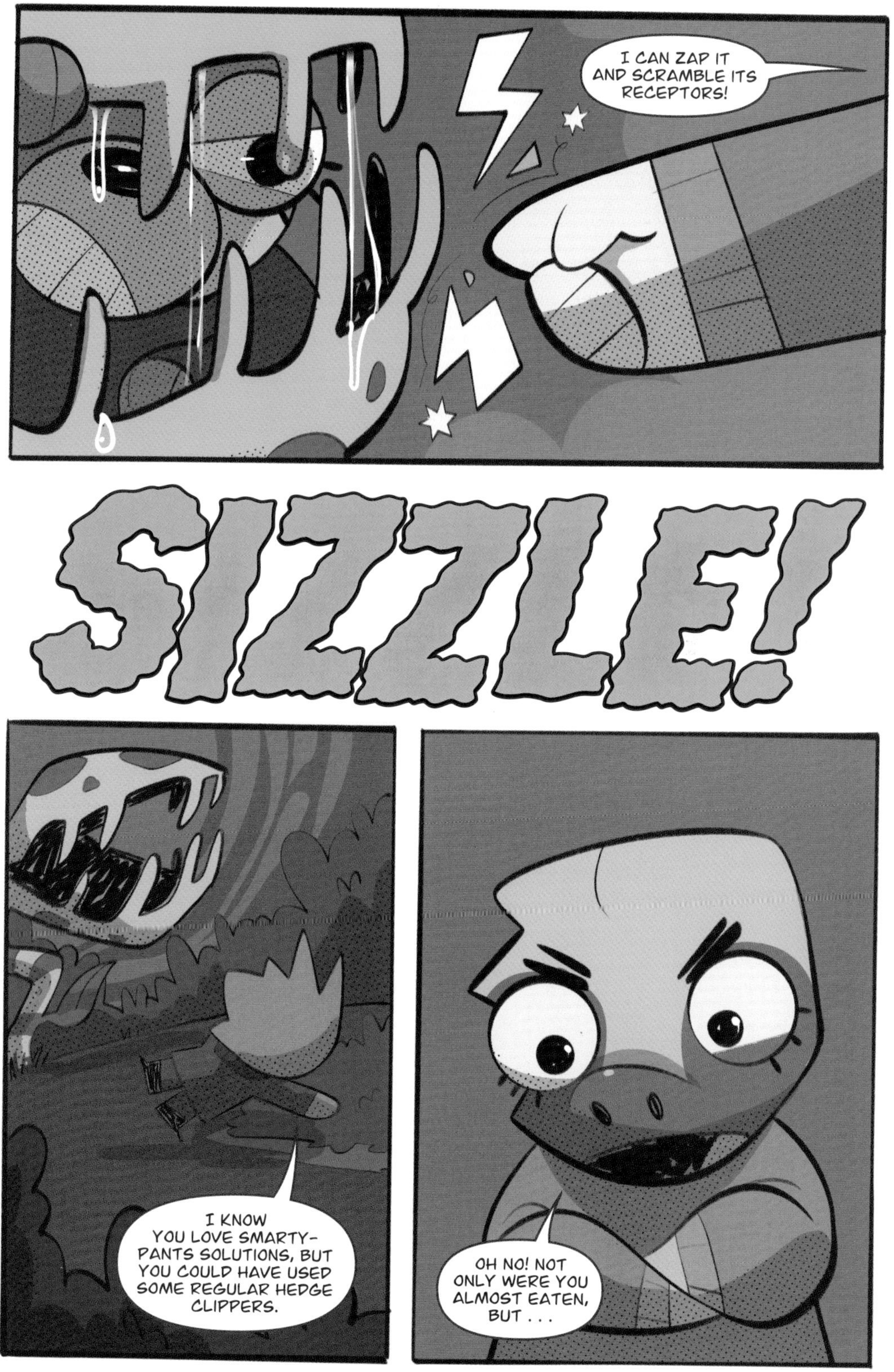

I CAN ZAP IT AND SCRAMBLE ITS RECEPTORS!
SIZZLE!
I KNOW YOU LOVE SMARTY-PANTS SOLUTIONS, BUT YOU COULD HAVE USED SOME REGULAR HEDGE CLIPPERS.
OH NO! NOT ONLY WERE YOU ALMOST EATEN, BUT . . .

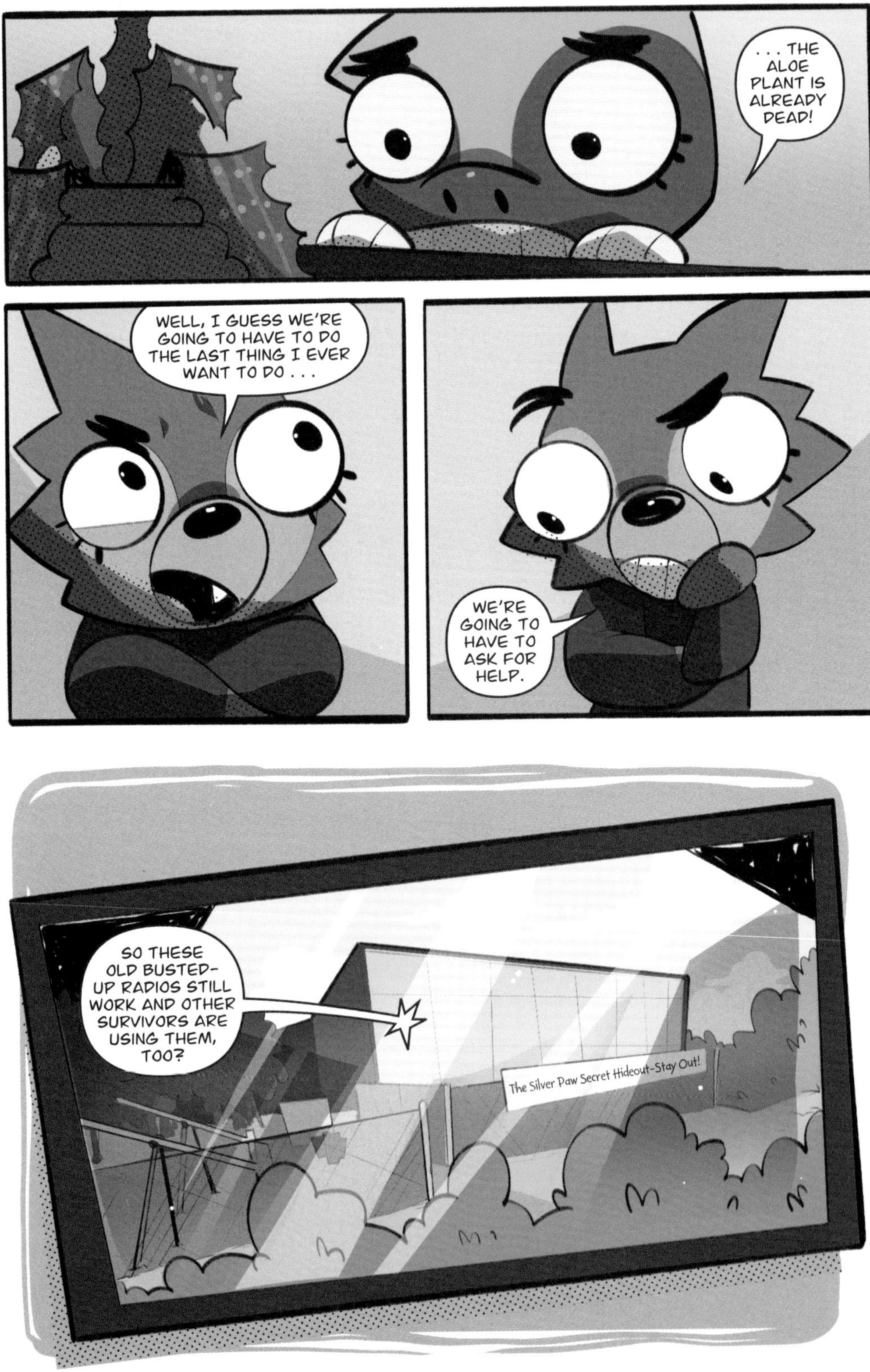
. . . THE ALOE PLANT IS ALREADY DEAD!
WELL, I GUESS WE'RE GOING TO HAVE TO DO THE LAST THING I EVER WANT TO DO . . .
WE'RE GOING TO HAVE TO ASK FOR HELP.
SO THESE OLD BUSTED-UP RADIOS STILL WORK AND OTHER SURVIVORS ARE USING THEM, TOO?
The Silver Paw Secret Hideout-Stay Out!

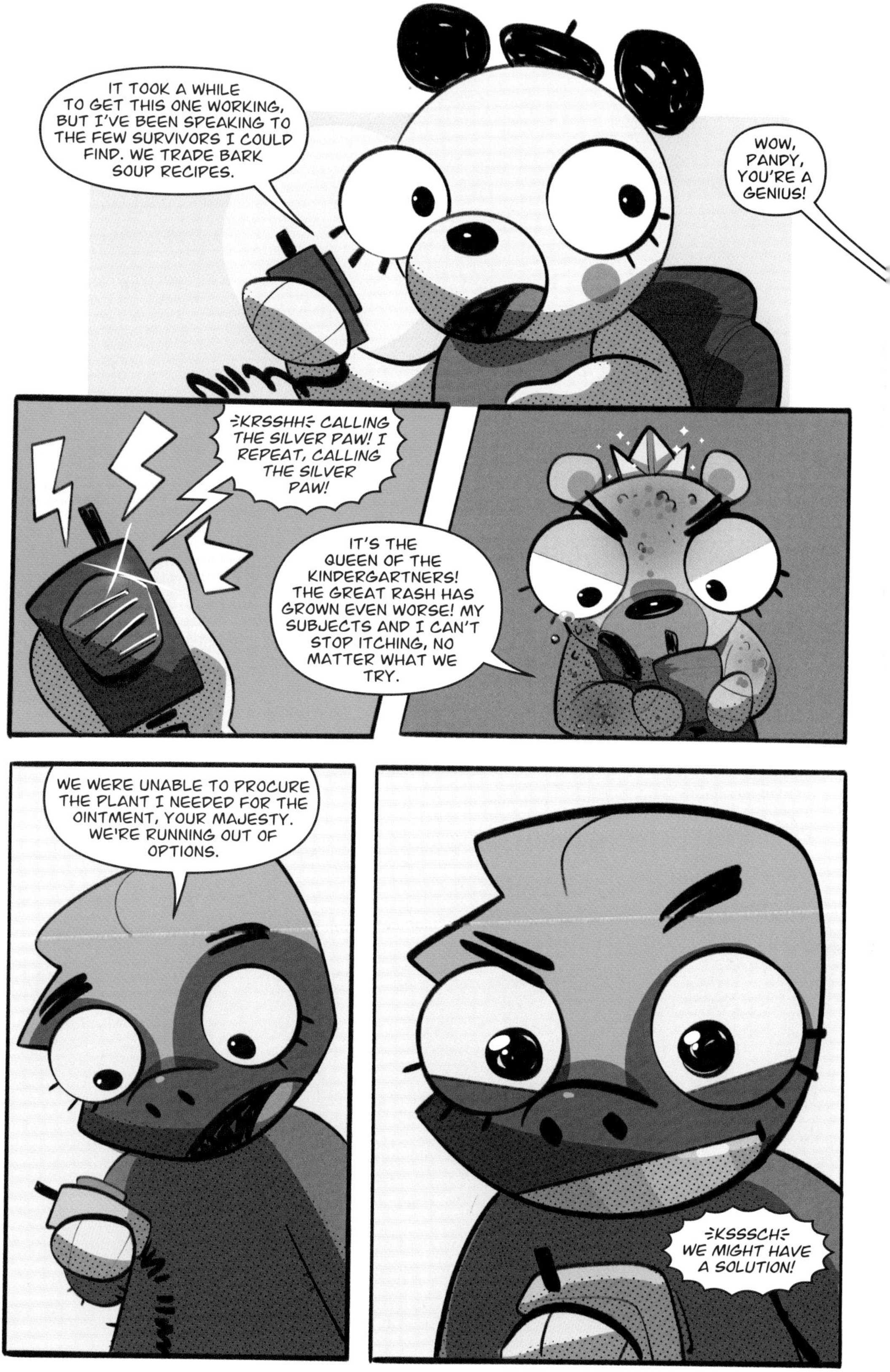
IT TOOK A WHILE TO GET THIS ONE WORKING, BUT I'VE BEEN SPEAKING TO THE FEW SURVIVORS I COULD FIND. WE TRADE BARK SOUP RECIPES.
WOW, PANDY, YOU'RE A GENIUS!
=KRSSHH= CALLING THE SILVER PAW! I REPEAT, CALLING THE SILVER PAW!
IT'S THE QUEEN OF THE KINDERGARTNERS! THE GREAT RASH HAS GROWN EVEN WORSE! MY SUBJECTS AND I CAN'T STOP ITCHING, NO MATTER WHAT WE TRY.
WE WERE UNABLE TO PROCURE THE PLANT I NEEDED FOR THE OINTMENT, YOUR MAJESTY. WE'RE RUNNING OUT OF OPTIONS.
=KSSSCH= WE MIGHT HAVE A SOLUTION!

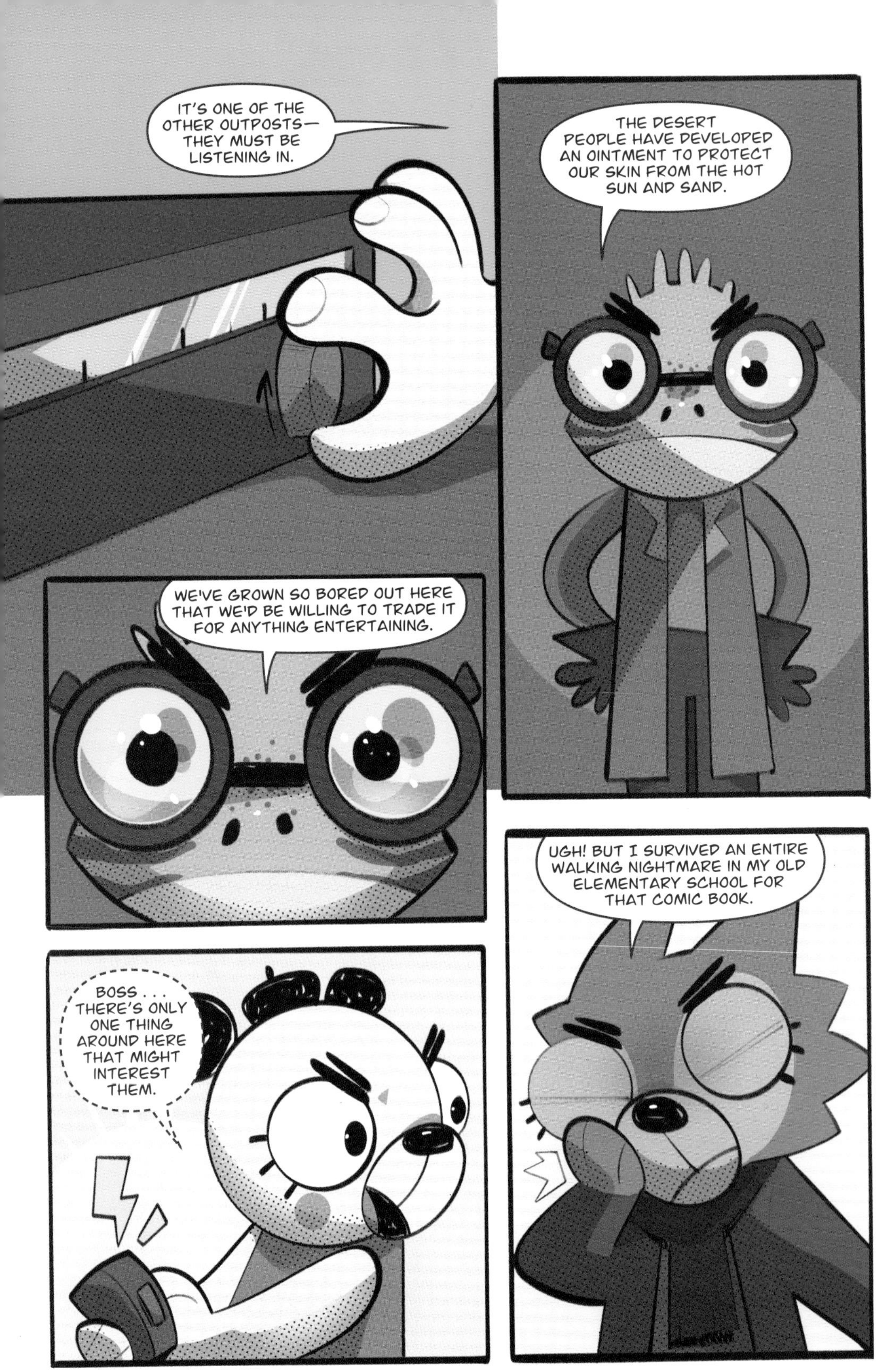
IT'S ONE OF THE OTHER OUTPOSTS— THEY MUST BE LISTENING IN.
THE DESERT PEOPLE HAVE DEVELOPED AN OINTMENT TO PROTECT OUR SKIN FROM THE HOT SUN AND SAND.
WE'VE GROWN SO BORED OUT HERE THAT WE'D BE WILLING TO TRADE IT FOR ANYTHING ENTERTAINING.
BOSS . . . THERE'S ONLY ONE THING AROUND HERE THAT MIGHT INTEREST THEM.
UGH! BUT I SURVIVED AN ENTIRE WALKING NIGHTMARE IN MY OLD ELEMENTARY SCHOOL FOR THAT COMIC BOOK.

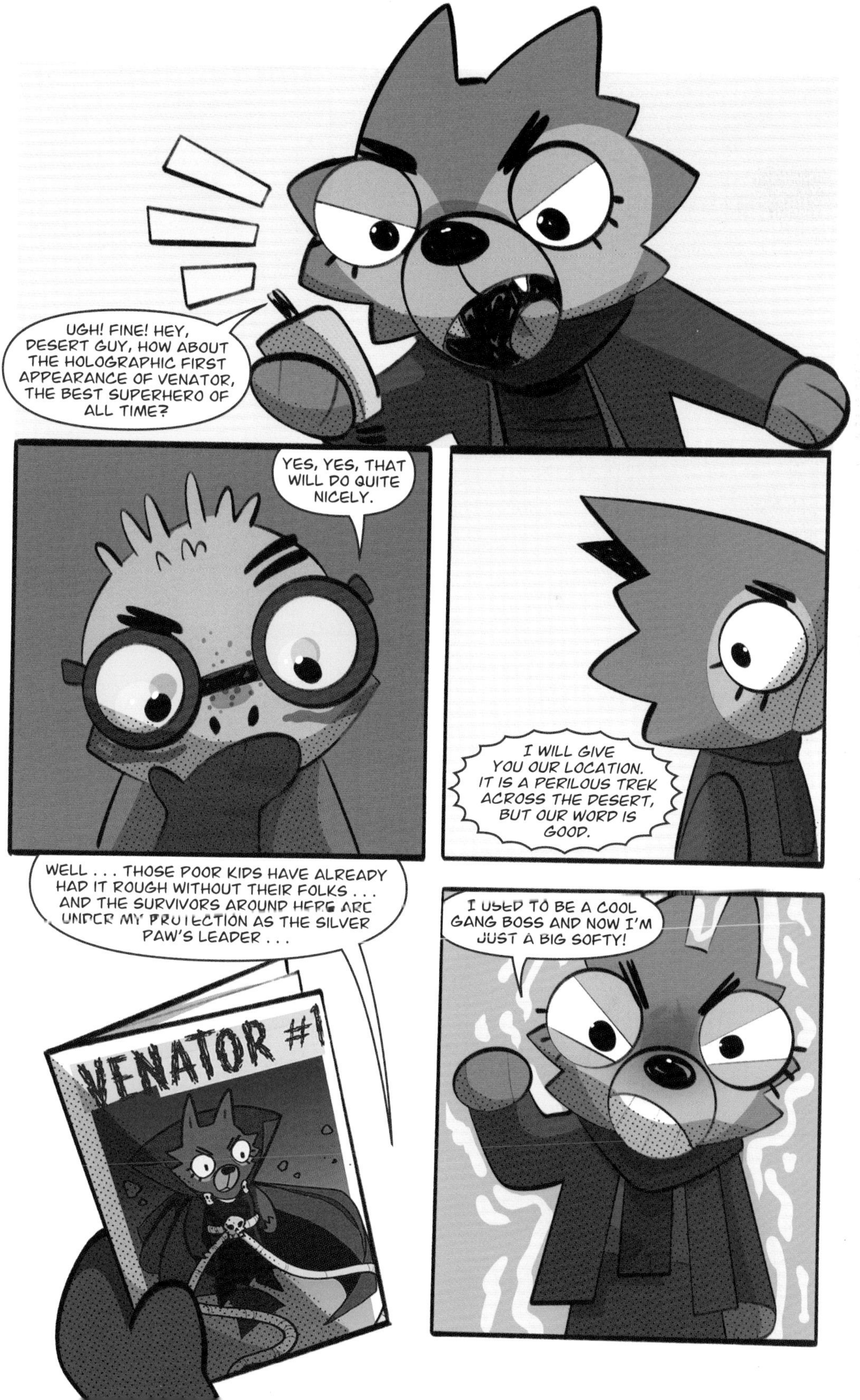
UGH! FINE! HEY, DESERT GUY, HOW ABOUT THE HOLOGRAPHIC FIRST APPEARANCE OF VENATOR, THE BEST SUPERHERO OF ALL TIME?
YES, YES, THAT WILL DO QUITE NICELY.
I WILL GIVE YOU OUR LOCATION. IT IS A PERILOUS TREK ACROSS THE DESERT, BUT OUR WORD IS GOOD.
WELL . . . THOSE POOR KIDS HAVE ALREADY HAD IT ROUGH WITHOUT THEIR FOLKS . . . AND THE SURVIVORS AROUND HERE ARE UNDER MY PROTECTION AS THE SILVER PAW'S LEADER . . .
VENATOR #1
I USED TO BE A COOL GANG BOSS AND NOW I'M JUST A BIG SOFTY!

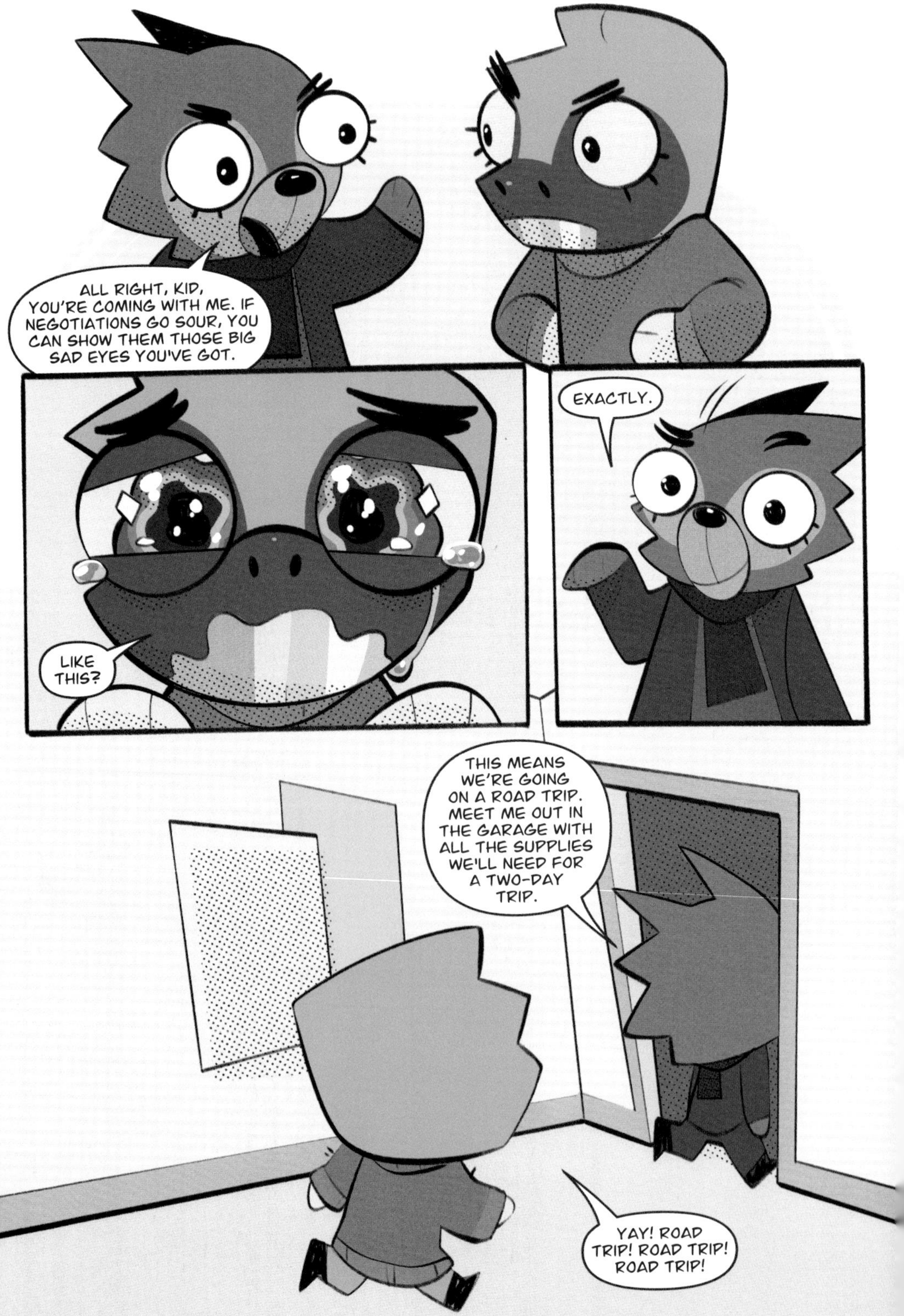
ALL RIGHT, KID, YOU'RE COMING WITH ME. IF NEGOTIATIONS GO SOUR, YOU CAN SHOW THEM THOSE BIG SAD EYES YOU'VE GOT.
LIKE THIS?
EXACTLY.
THIS MEANS WE'RE GOING ON A ROAD TRIP. MEET ME OUT IN THE GARAGE WITH ALL THE SUPPLIES WE'LL NEED FOR A TWO-DAY TRIP.
YAY! ROAD TRIP! ROAD TRIP! ROAD TRIP!

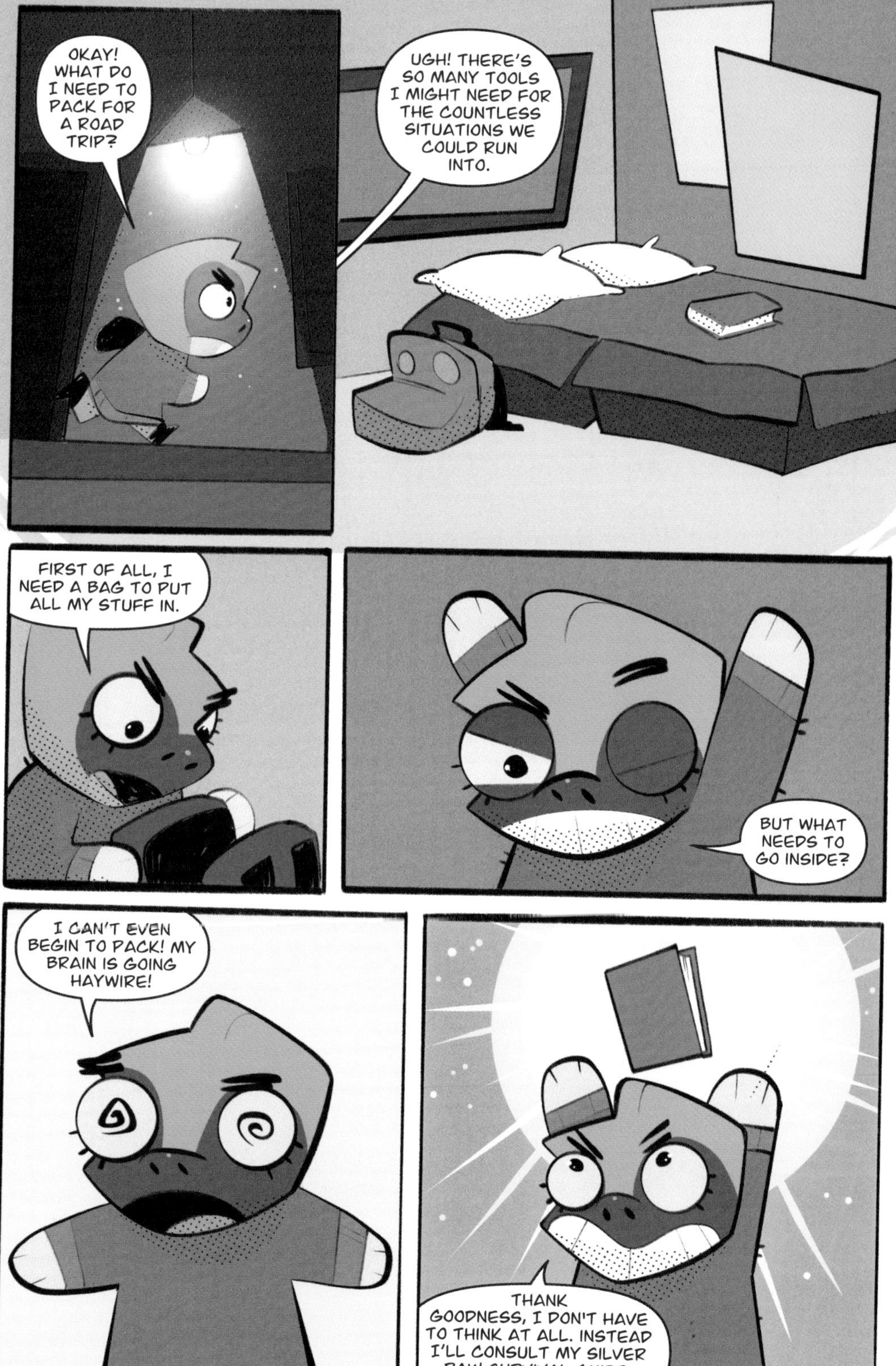
OKAY! WHAT DO I NEED TO PACK FOR A ROAD TRIP?
UGH! THERE'S SO MANY TOOLS I MIGHT NEED FOR THE COUNTLESS SITUATIONS WE COULD RUN INTO.
FIRST OF ALL, I NEED A BAG TO PUT ALL MY STUFF IN.
BUT WHAT NEEDS TO GO INSIDE?
I CAN'T EVEN BEGIN TO PACK! MY BRAIN IS GOING HAYWIRE!
THANK GOODNESS, I DON'T HAVE TO THINK AT ALL. INSTEAD I'LL CONSULT MY SILVER PAW SURVIVAL GUIDE.

# The Silver Paw Survival Tips- Everything You Need To Survive a Long Road Trip

**Tip 1** - Snacks and Water - You'll want to stay nourished and hydrated so you don't get cranky.

**Tip 2** - Pillow and Blanket - In case you get tired along the way.

**Tip 3** - Comics and Books - Unless reading in the car makes you queasy.

**Tip 4** - Puzzle Books and a Pen - Because they can't run out of batteries.

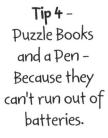

**Tip 5** - Binoculars - In case you see something cool in the distance.

\* Please see pages 77 through 326 for all other possible contingency safety supplies.

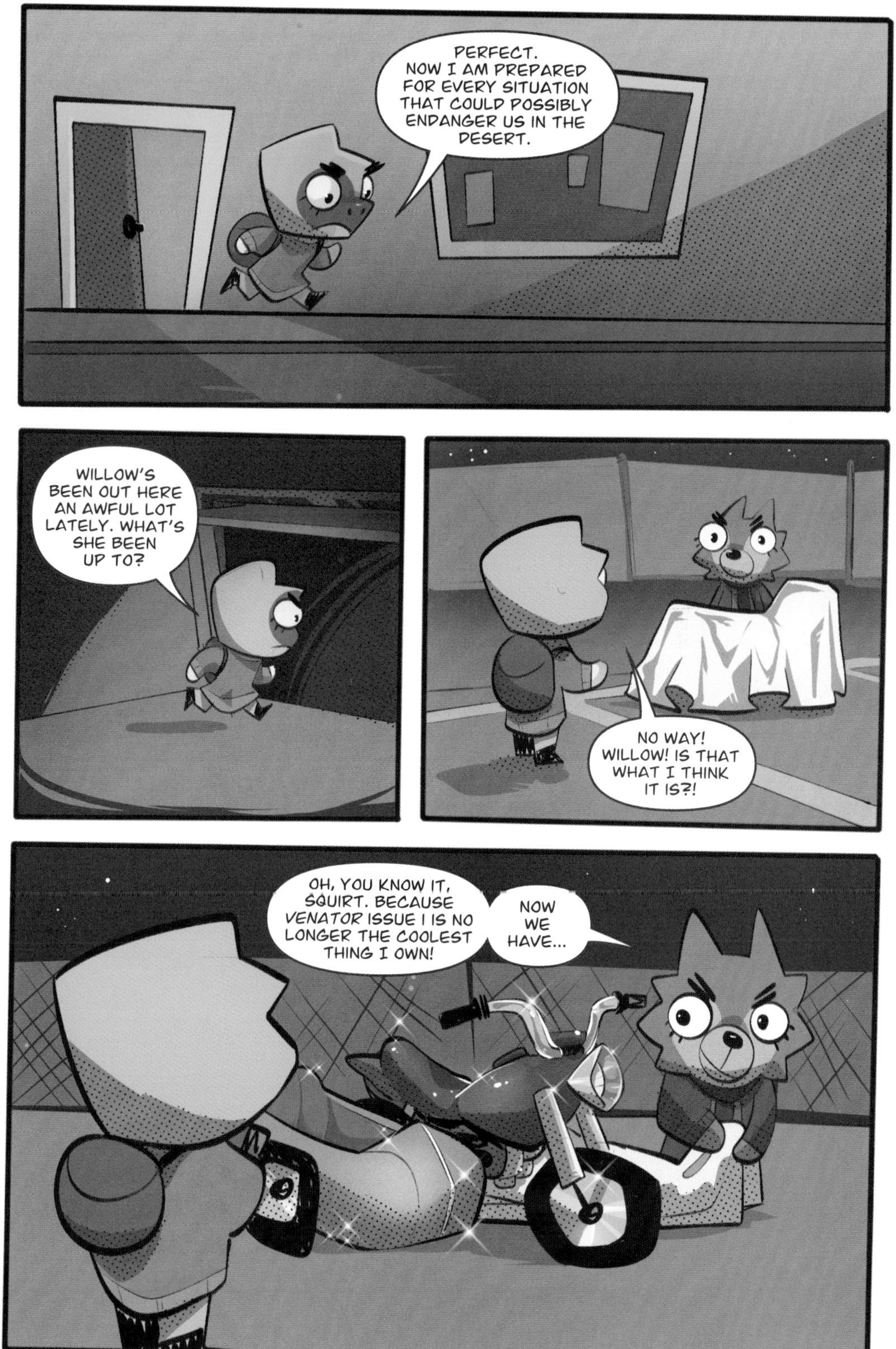
PERFECT. NOW I AM PREPARED FOR EVERY SITUATION THAT COULD POSSIBLY ENDANGER US IN THE DESERT.
WILLOW'S BEEN OUT HERE AN AWFUL LOT LATELY. WHAT'S SHE BEEN UP TO?
NO WAY! WILLOW! IS THAT WHAT I THINK IT IS?!
OH, YOU KNOW IT, SQUIRT. BECAUSE VENATOR ISSUE I IS NO LONGER THE COOLEST THING I OWN!
NOW WE HAVE...

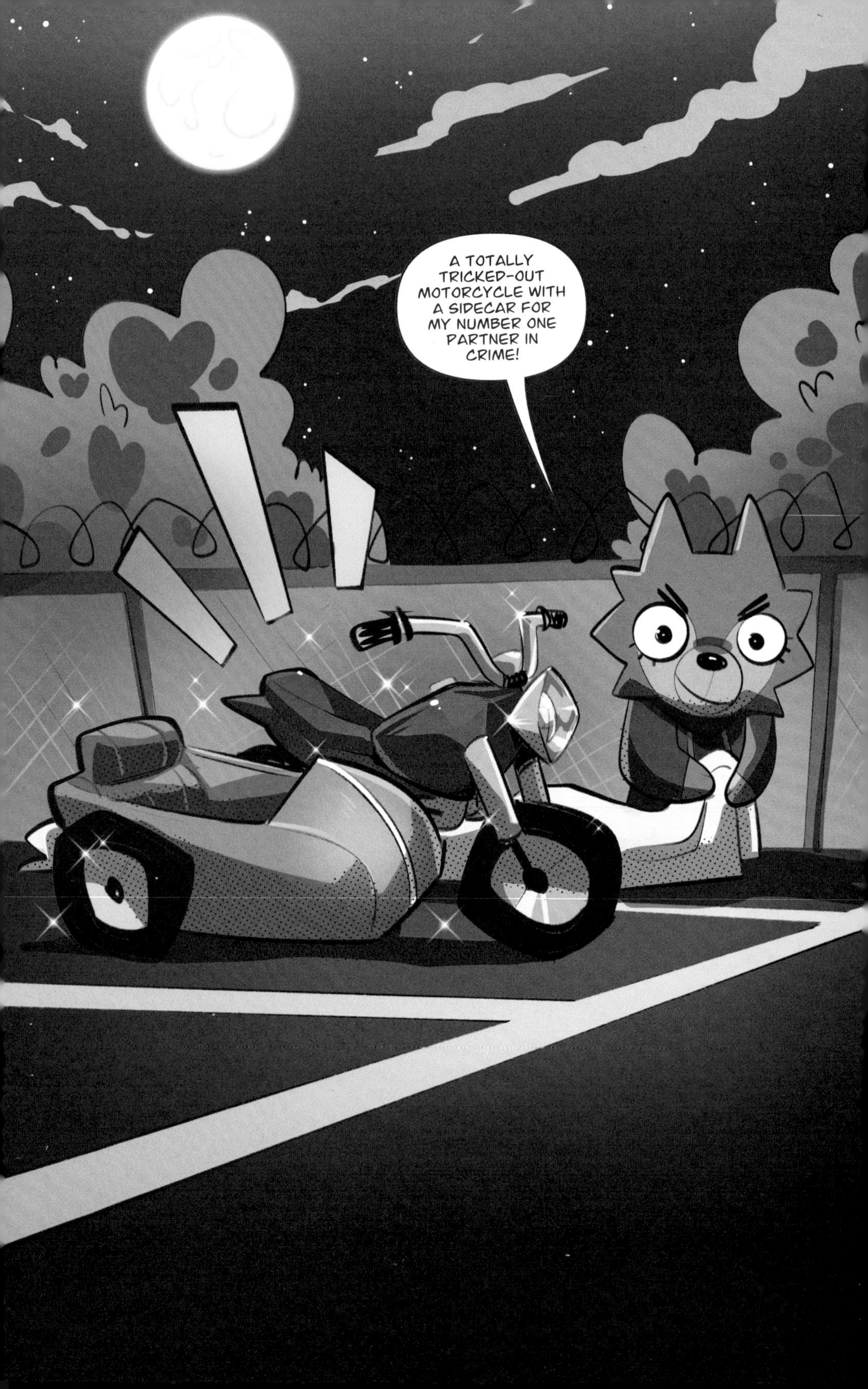
A TOTALLY TRICKED-OUT MOTORCYCLE WITH A SIDECAR FOR MY NUMBER ONE PARTNER IN CRIME!

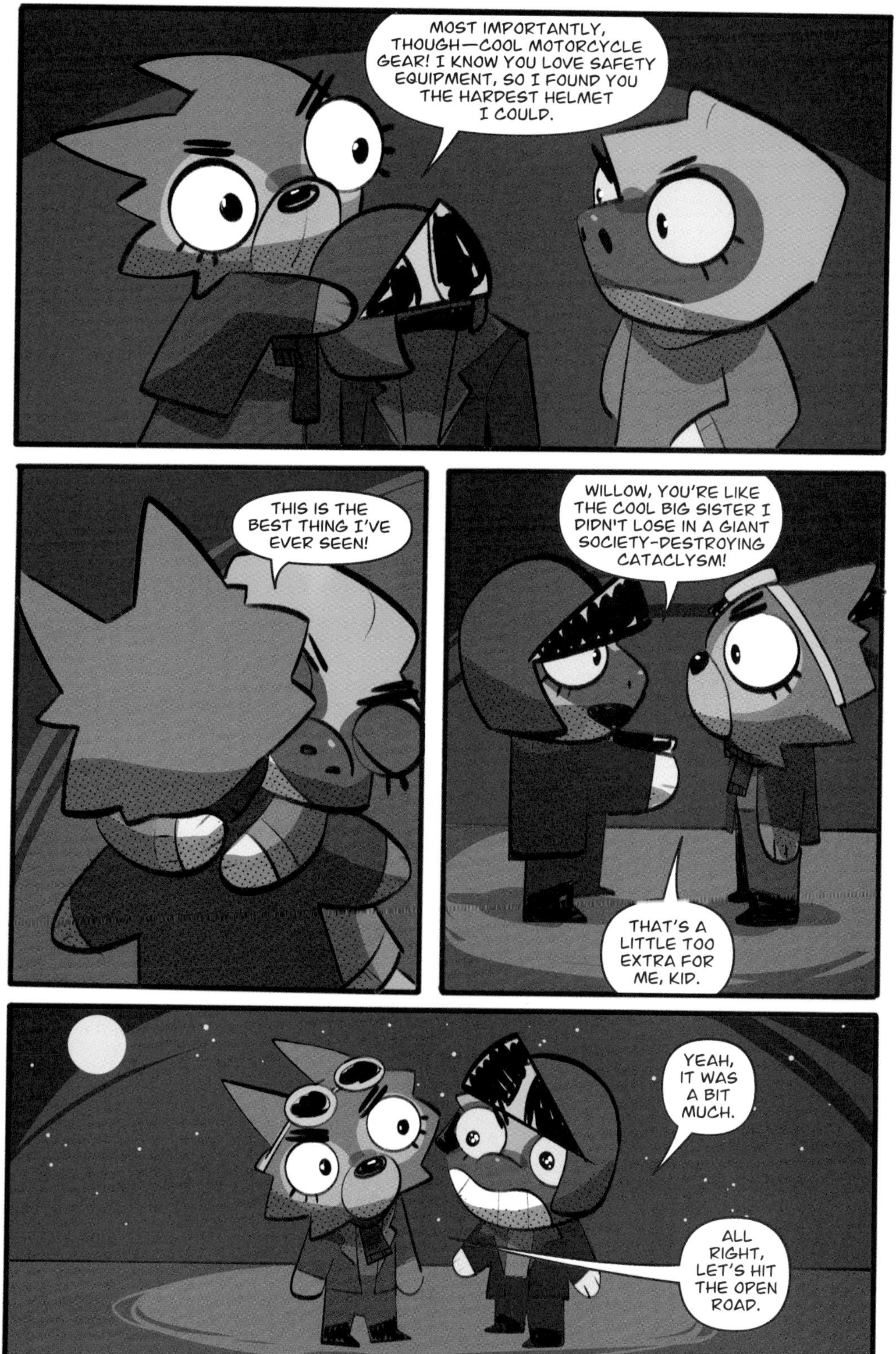
MOST IMPORTANTLY, THOUGH—COOL MOTORCYCLE GEAR! I KNOW YOU LOVE SAFETY EQUIPMENT, SO I FOUND YOU THE HARDEST HELMET I COULD.
THIS IS THE BEST THING I'VE EVER SEEN!
WILLOW, YOU'RE LIKE THE COOL BIG SISTER I DIDN'T LOSE IN A GIANT SOCIETY-DESTROYING CATACLYSM!
THAT'S A LITTLE TOO EXTRA FOR ME, KID.
YEAH, IT WAS A BIT MUCH.
ALL RIGHT, LET'S HIT THE OPEN ROAD.

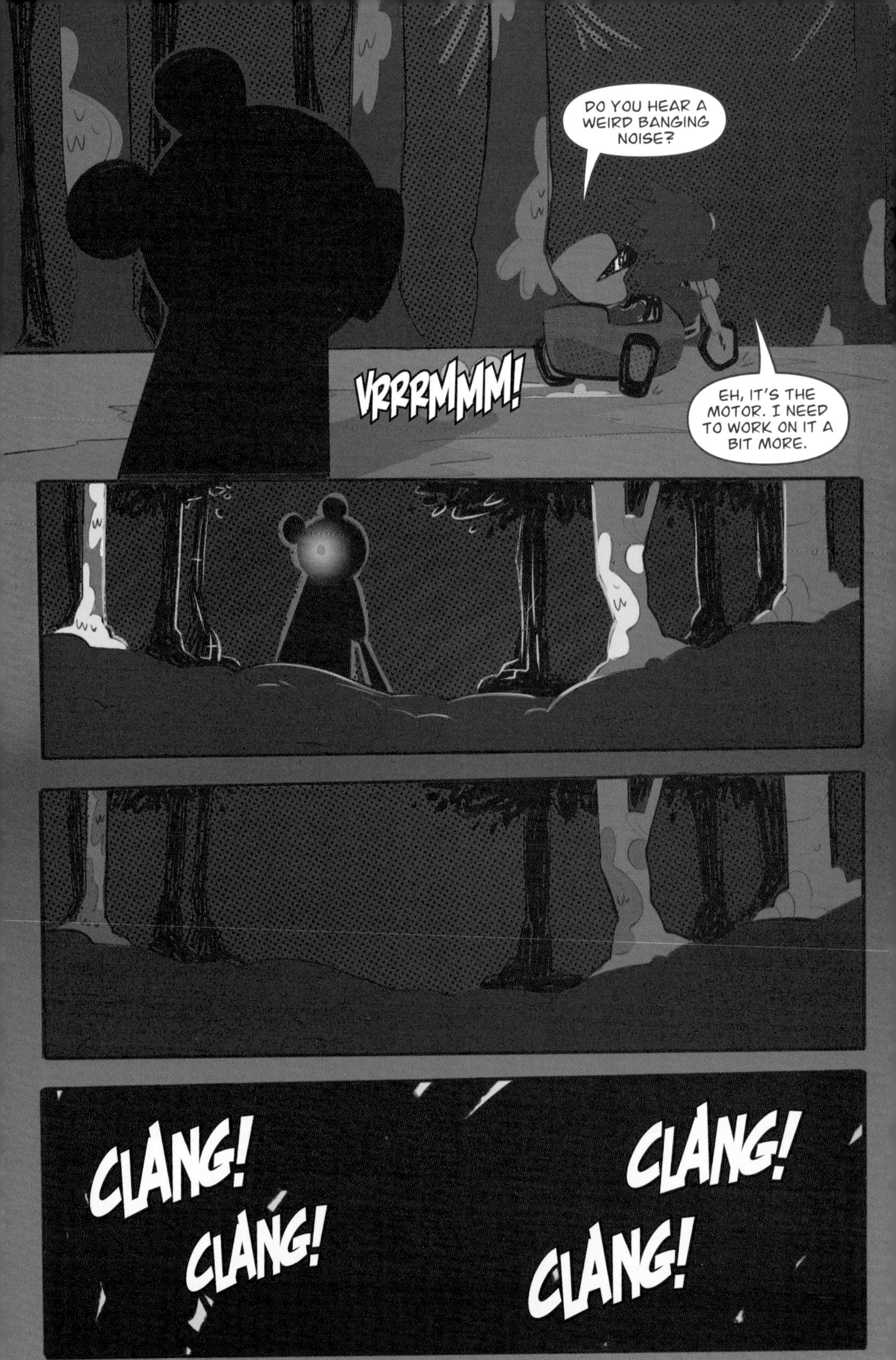
DO YOU HEAR A WEIRD BANGING NOISE?
VRRRMMM!
EH, IT'S THE MOTOR. I NEED TO WORK ON IT A BIT MORE.
CLANG!
CLANG!
CLANG!
CLANG!

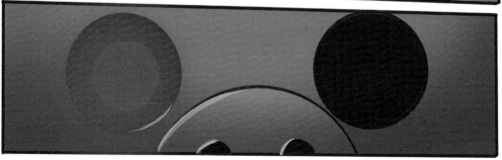

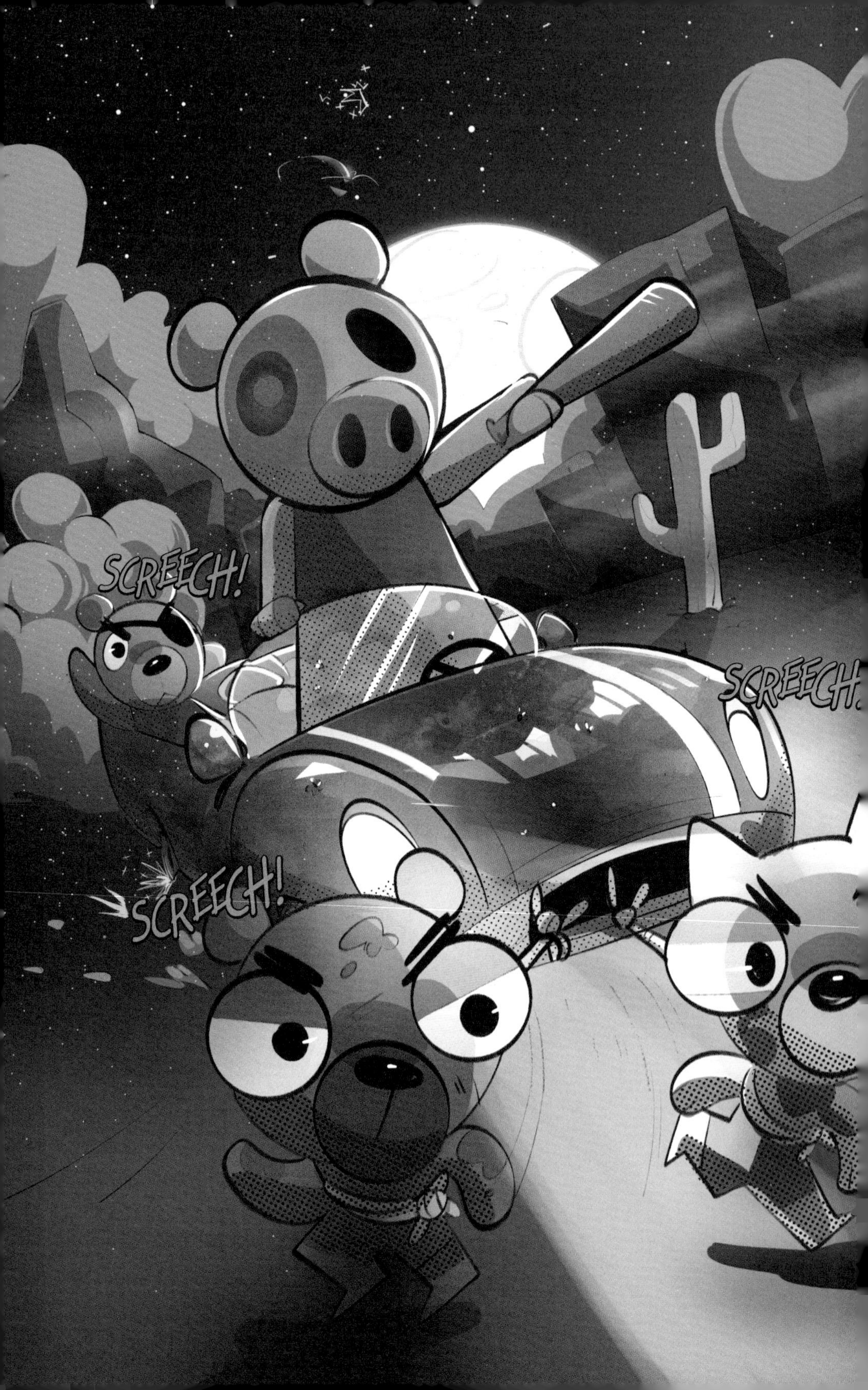
SCREECH!
SCREECH!
SCREECH!

# CHAPTER: 2

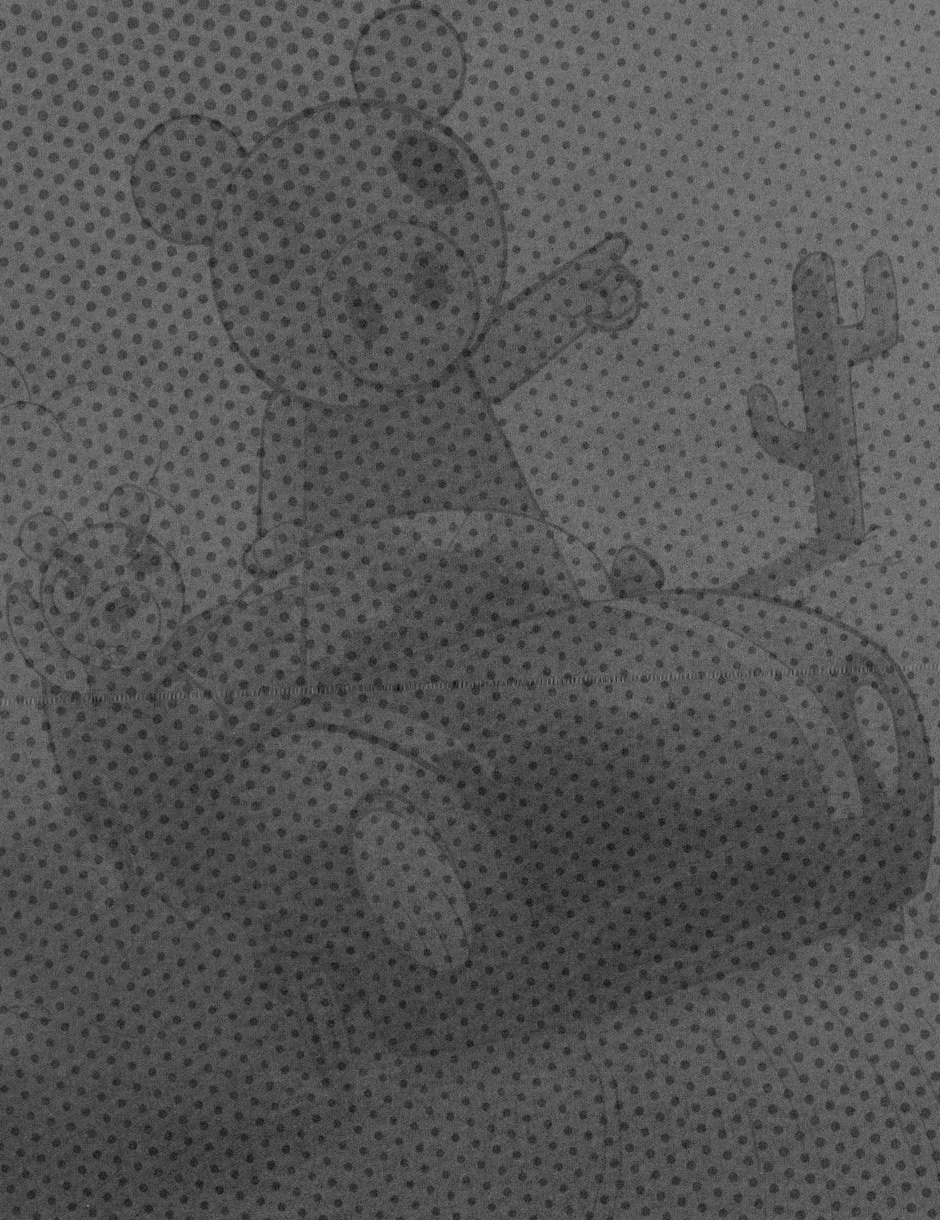

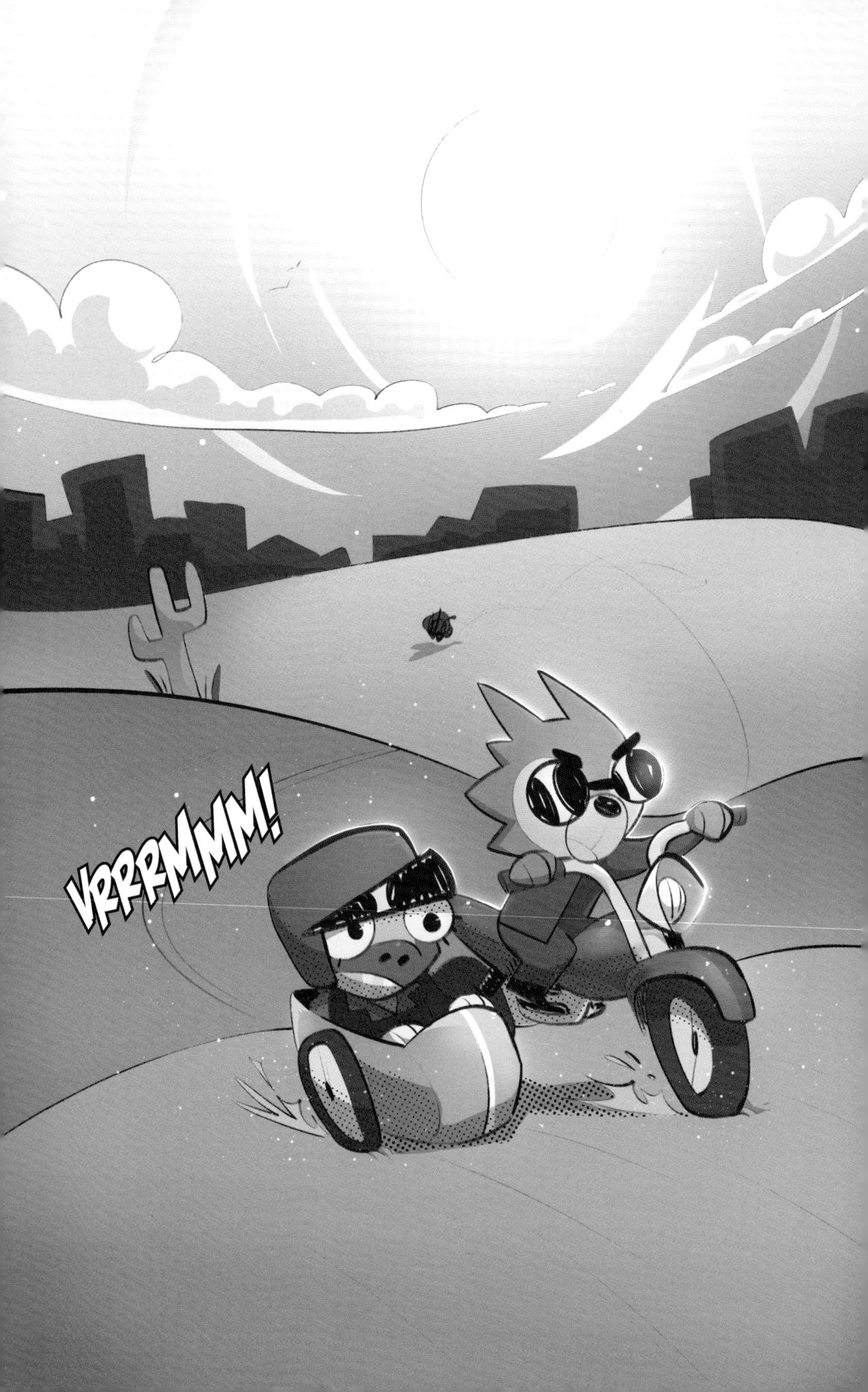
VRRRMMM!

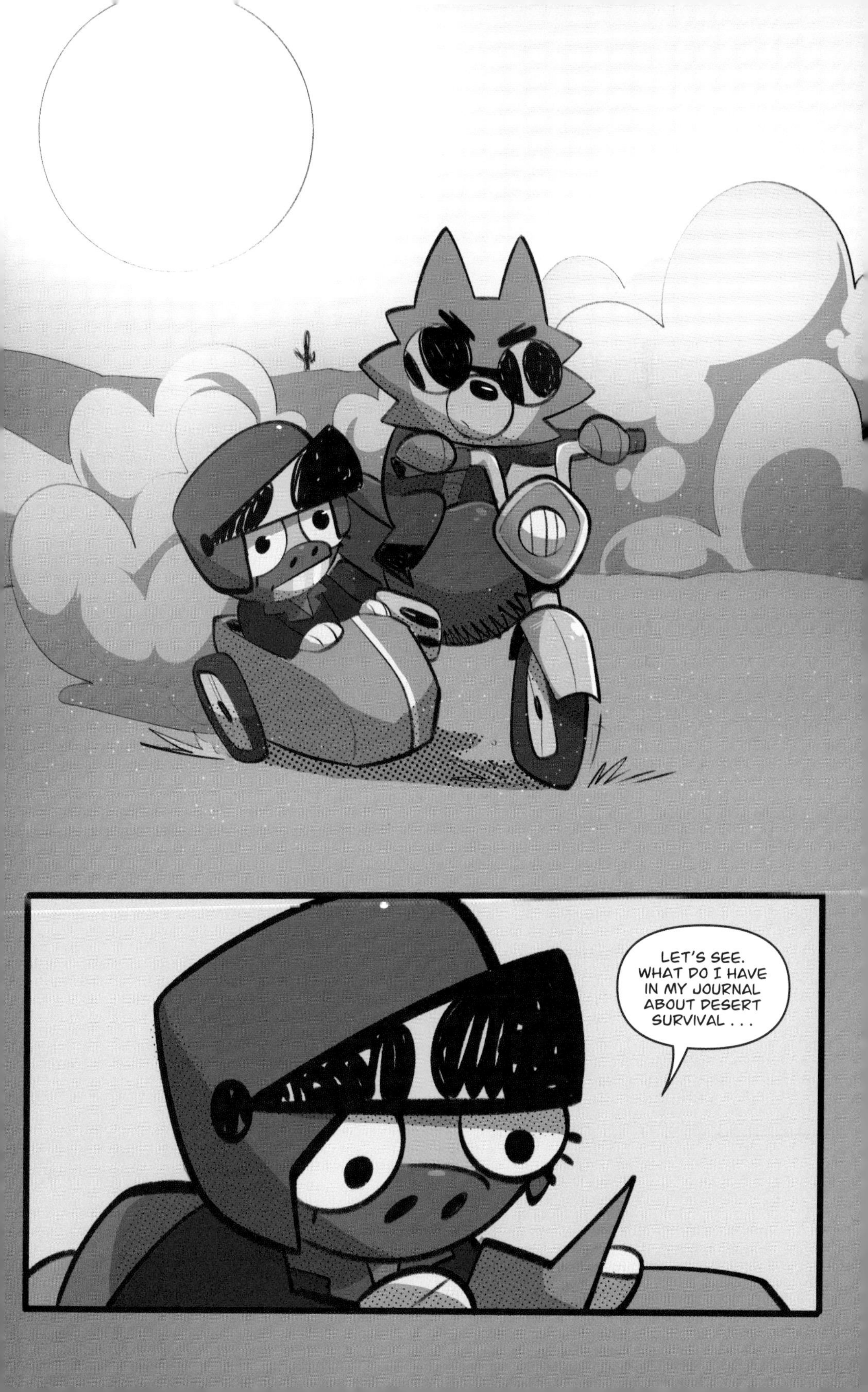
LET'S SEE. WHAT DO I HAVE IN MY JOURNAL ABOUT DESERT SURVIVAL . . .

# The Silver Paw Survival Tips – Desert Basics

**Tip 1** – Deserts are places with little rainfall. This can be due to things like wind, elevation, and even polar ice caps where rain hardly appears.

**Tip 2** – Staying hydrated is essential. Drinking plenty of water is important, but we lose a lot of water through sweat.

**Tip 3** – Wearing cotton and linen clothes that cover the body to protect it from UV rays may be less comfortable, but it helps preserve that sweat.

Deserts can also get very cold, so it's important to have a jacket on hand when the temperature drops.

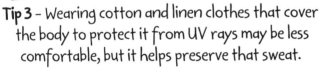

**Tip 4** – The ground can be even hotter than the air! So if you sit on the ground, make sure to put something underneath you first.

**Tip 5** – The best part of desert safety? Sunglasses look cool and protect your eyes from harsh sunlight.

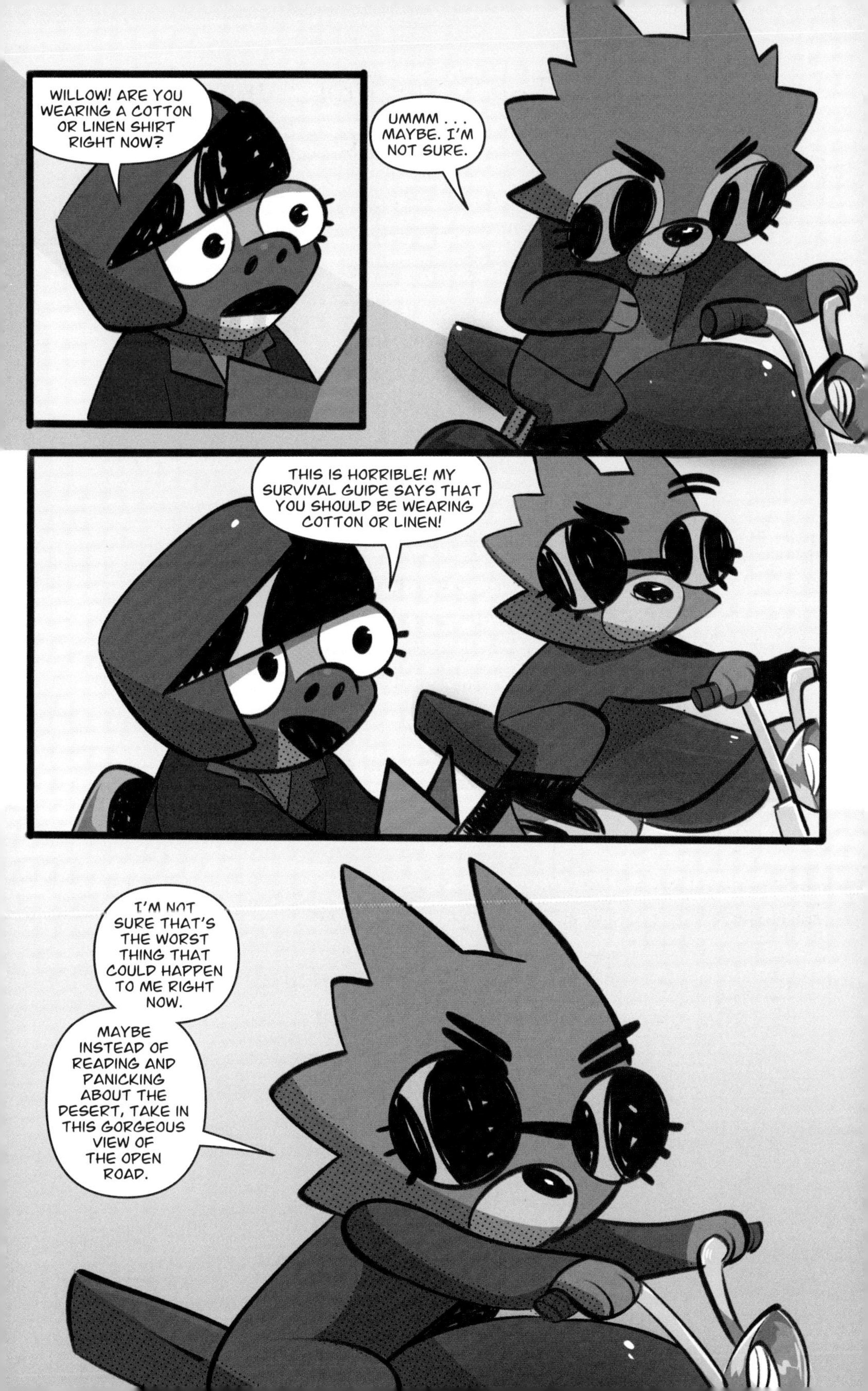
WILLOW! ARE YOU WEARING A COTTON OR LINEN SHIRT RIGHT NOW?
UMMM . . . MAYBE. I'M NOT SURE.
THIS IS HORRIBLE! MY SURVIVAL GUIDE SAYS THAT YOU SHOULD BE WEARING COTTON OR LINEN!
I'M NOT SURE THAT'S THE WORST THING THAT COULD HAPPEN TO ME RIGHT NOW.
MAYBE INSTEAD OF READING AND PANICKING ABOUT THE DESERT, TAKE IN THIS GORGEOUS VIEW OF THE OPEN ROAD.

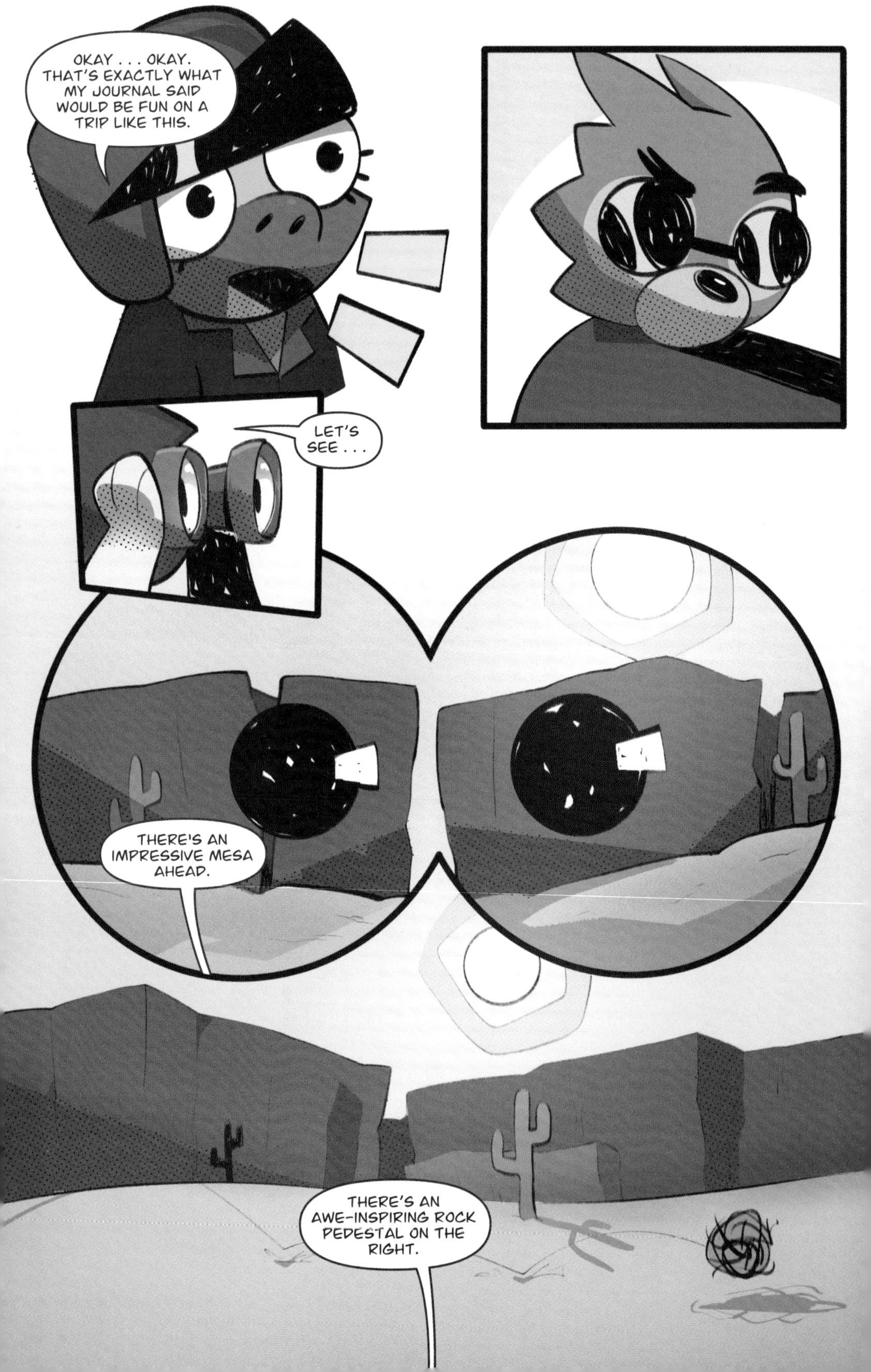
OKAY . . . OKAY. THAT'S EXACTLY WHAT MY JOURNAL SAID WOULD BE FUN ON A TRIP LIKE THIS.
LET'S SEE . . .
THERE'S AN IMPRESSIVE MESA AHEAD.
THERE'S AN AWE-INSPIRING ROCK PEDESTAL ON THE RIGHT.

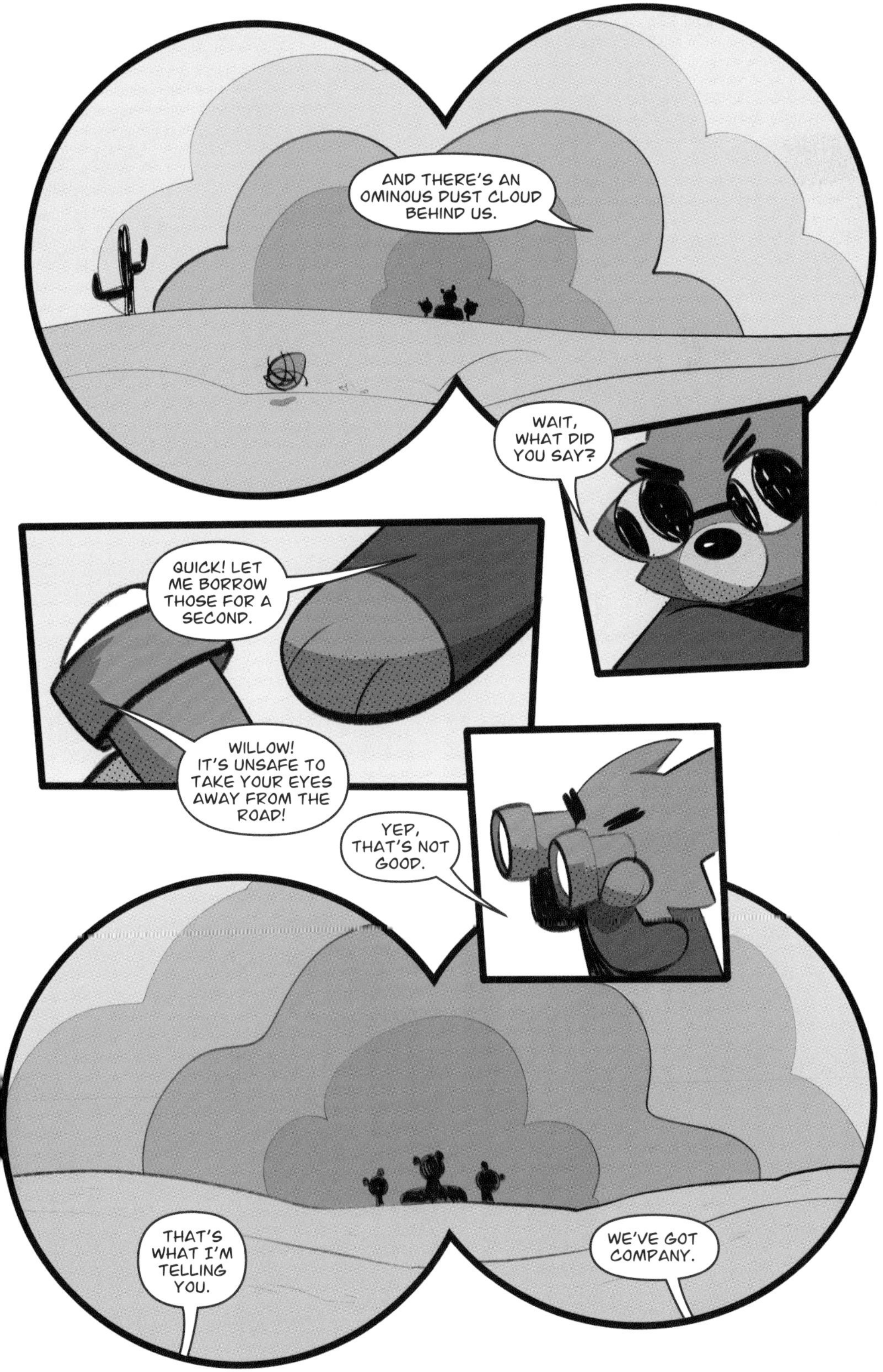
AND THERE'S AN OMINOUS DUST CLOUD BEHIND US.
WAIT, WHAT DID YOU SAY?
QUICK! LET ME BORROW THOSE FOR A SECOND.
WILLOW! IT'S UNSAFE TO TAKE YOUR EYES AWAY FROM THE ROAD!
YEP, THAT'S NOT GOOD.
THAT'S WHAT I'M TELLING YOU.
WE'VE GOT COMPANY.

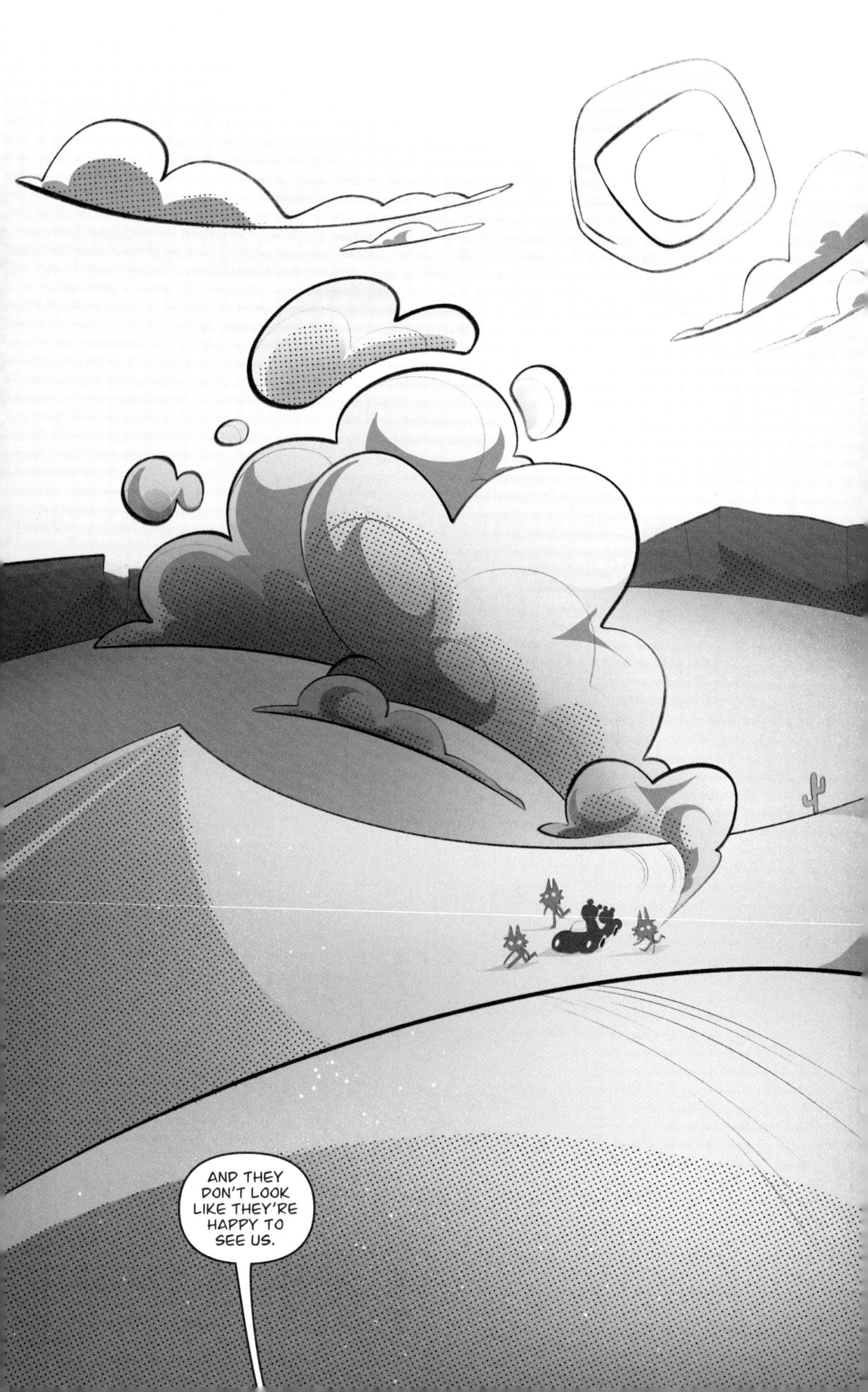
AND THEY DON'T LOOK LIKE THEY'RE HAPPY TO SEE US.

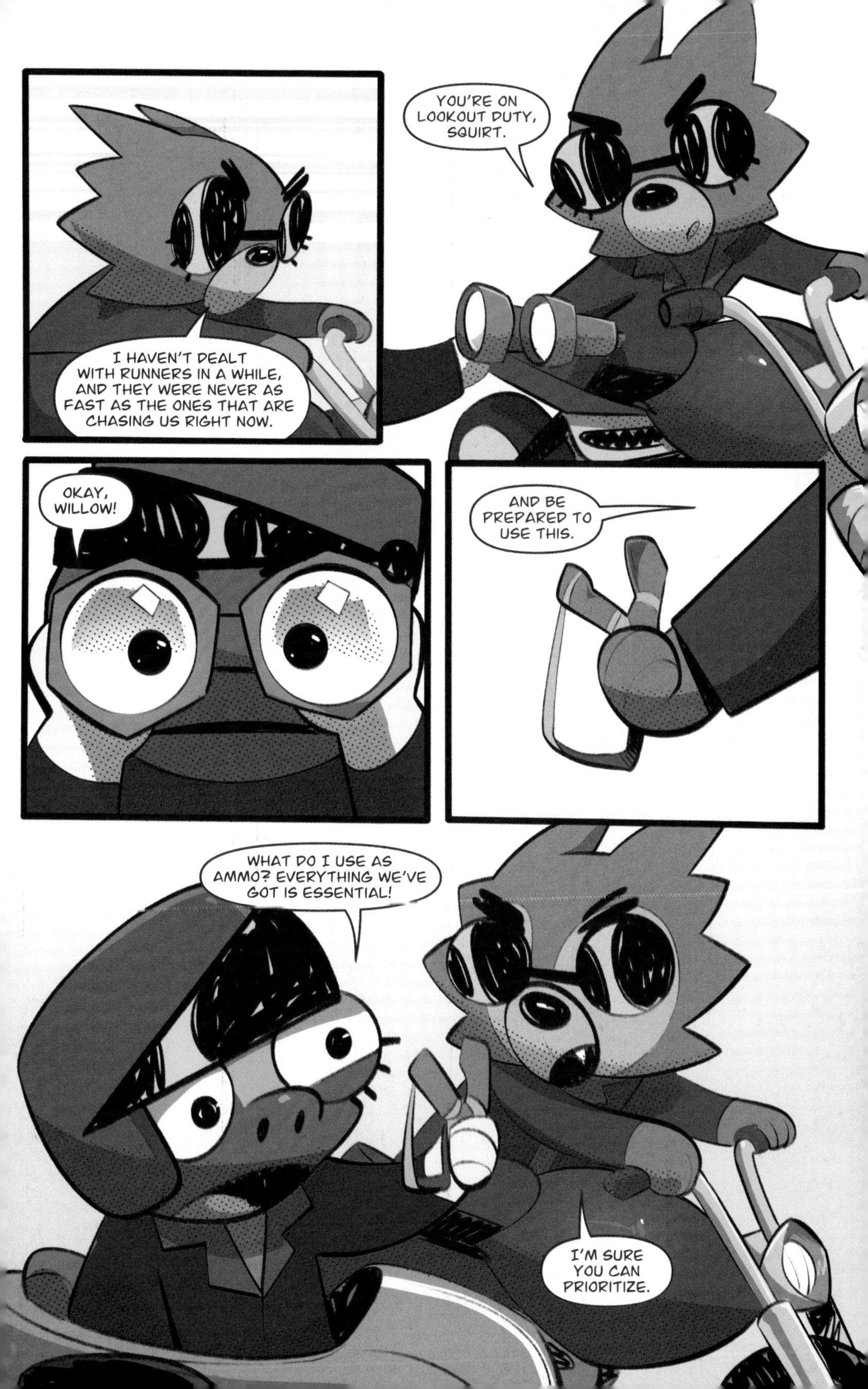
YOU'RE ON LOOKOUT DUTY, SQUIRT.
I HAVEN'T DEALT WITH RUNNERS IN A WHILE, AND THEY WERE NEVER AS FAST AS THE ONES THAT ARE CHASING US RIGHT NOW.
OKAY, WILLOW!
AND BE PREPARED TO USE THIS.
WHAT DO I USE AS AMMO? EVERYTHING WE'VE GOT IS ESSENTIAL!
I'M SURE YOU CAN PRIORITIZE.

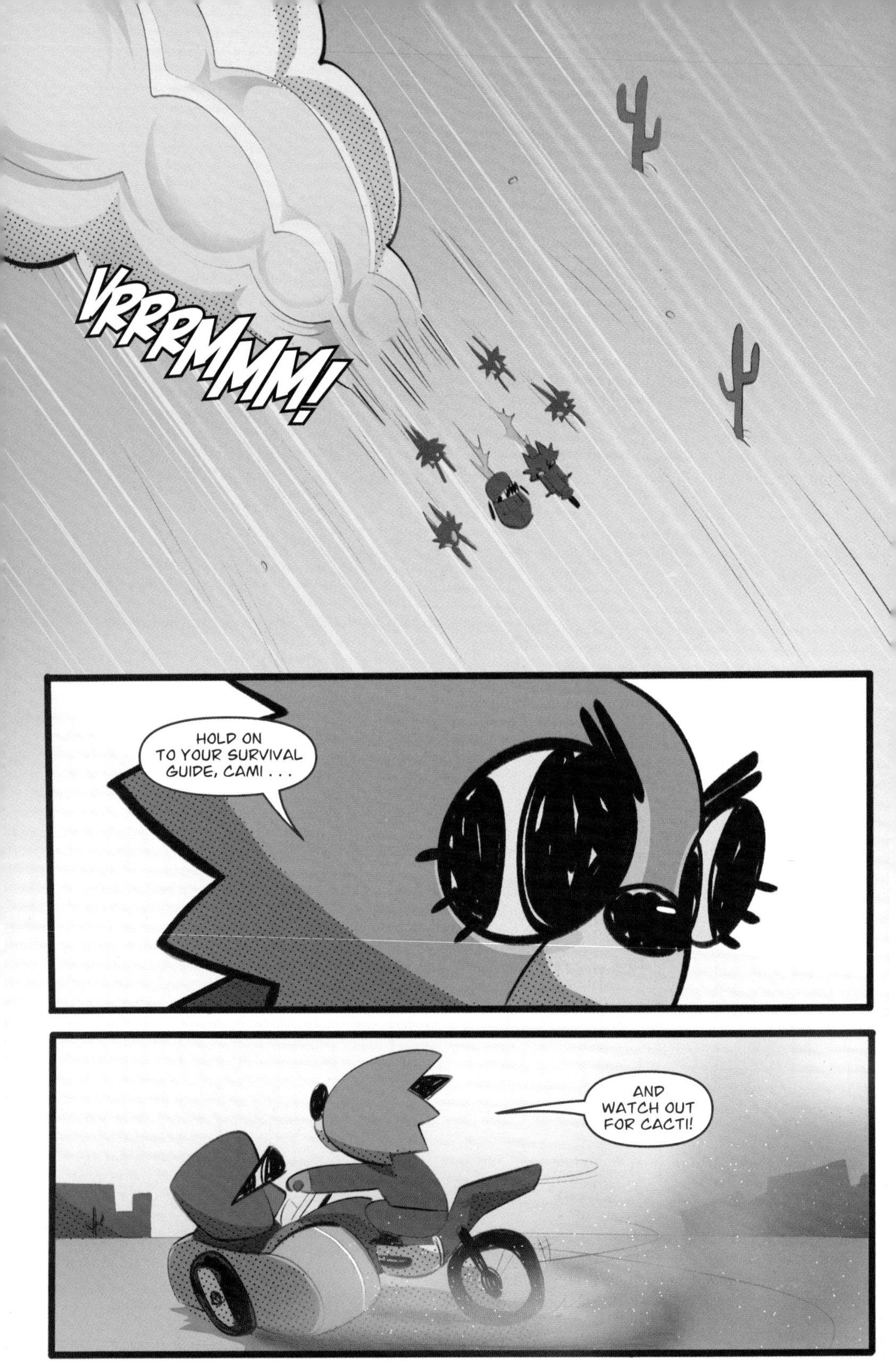
VRRRMMMM!
HOLD ON TO YOUR SURVIVAL GUIDE, CAMI . . .
AND WATCH OUT FOR CACTI!

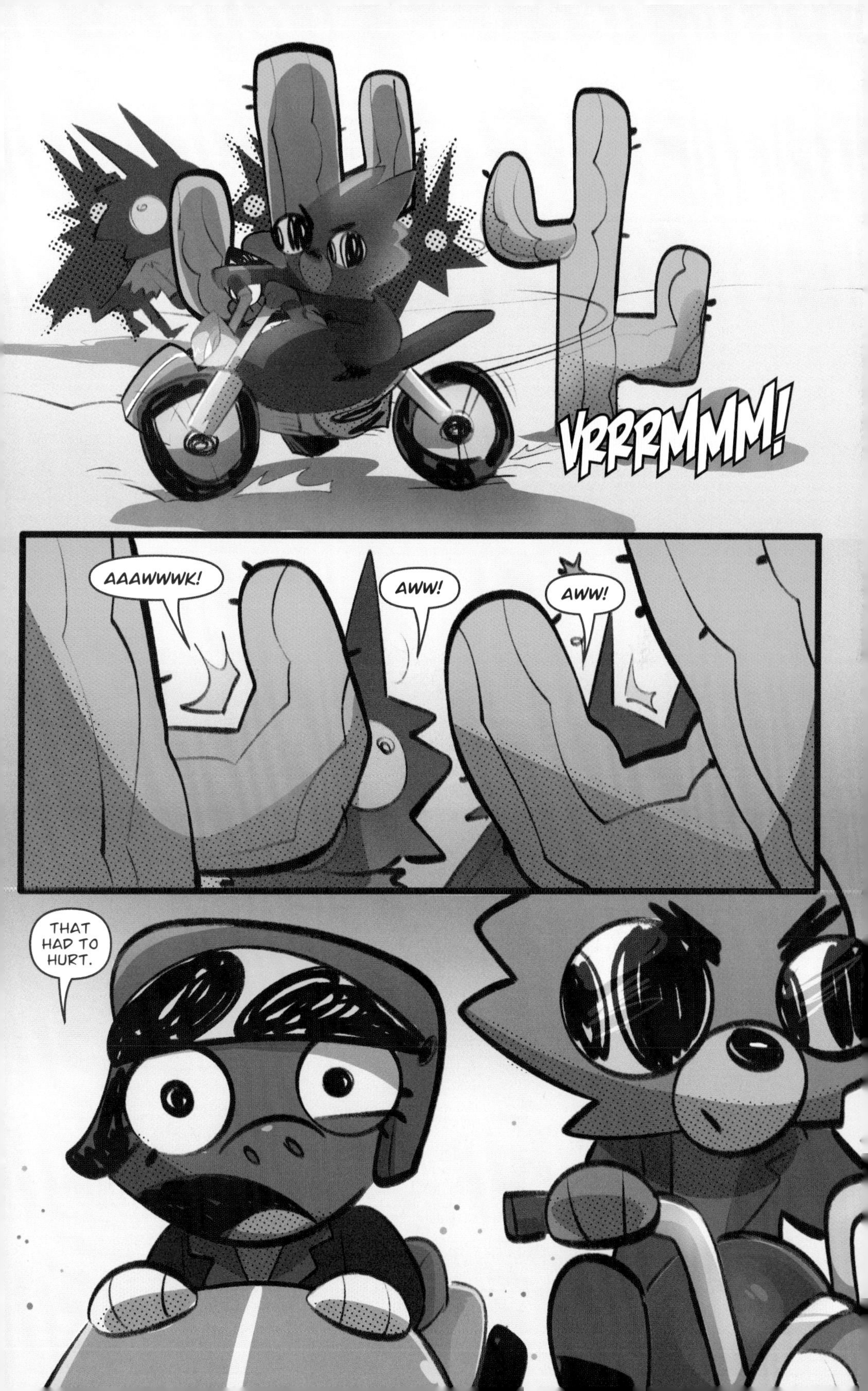
VRRRMMMM!
AAAWWWK!
AWW!
AWW!
THAT HAD TO HURT.

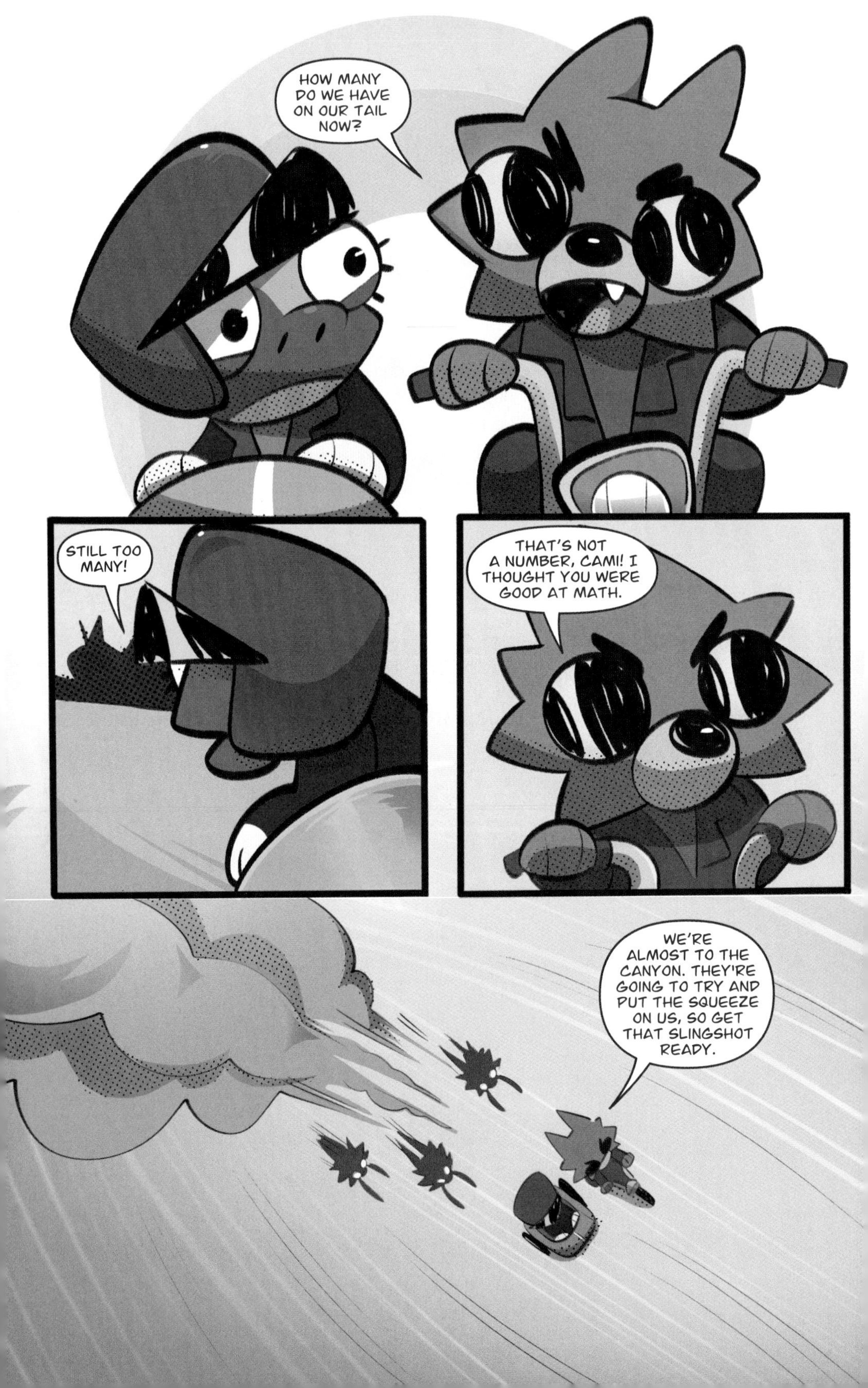
HOW MANY DO WE HAVE ON OUR TAIL NOW?
STILL TOO MANY!
THAT'S NOT A NUMBER, CAMI! I THOUGHT YOU WERE GOOD AT MATH.
WE'RE ALMOST TO THE CANYON. THEY'RE GOING TO TRY AND PUT THE SQUEEZE ON US, SO GET THAT SLINGSHOT READY.

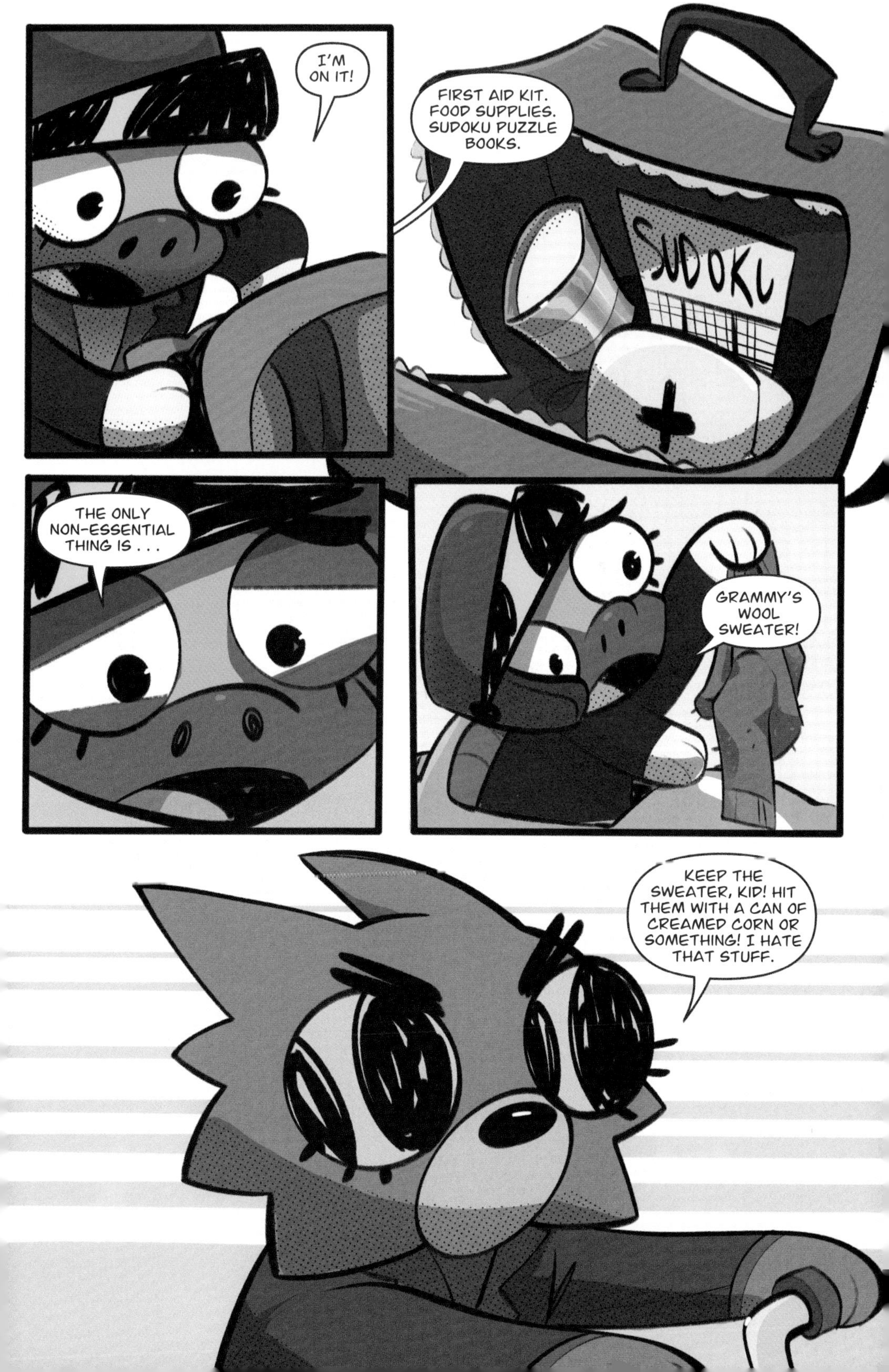
I'M ON IT!
FIRST AID KIT. FOOD SUPPLIES. SUDOKU PUZZLE BOOKS.
SUDOKU
THE ONLY NON-ESSENTIAL THING IS . . .
GRAMMY'S WOOL SWEATER!
KEEP THE SWEATER, KID! HIT THEM WITH A CAN OF CREAMED CORN OR SOMETHING! I HATE THAT STUFF.

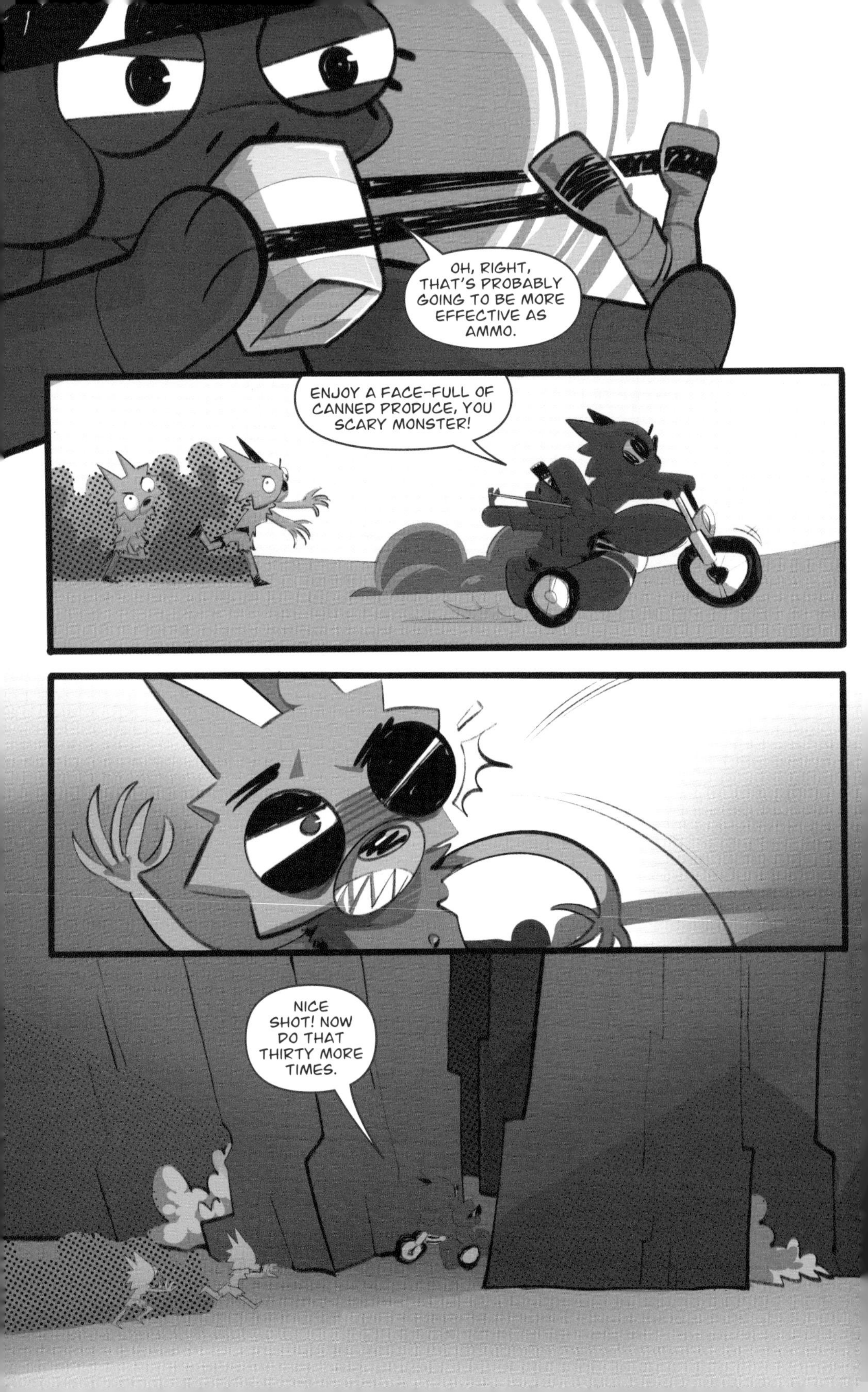
OH, RIGHT, THAT'S PROBABLY GOING TO BE MORE EFFECTIVE AS AMMO.
ENJOY A FACE-FULL OF CANNED PRODUCE, YOU SCARY MONSTER!
NICE SHOT! NOW DO THAT THIRTY MORE TIMES.

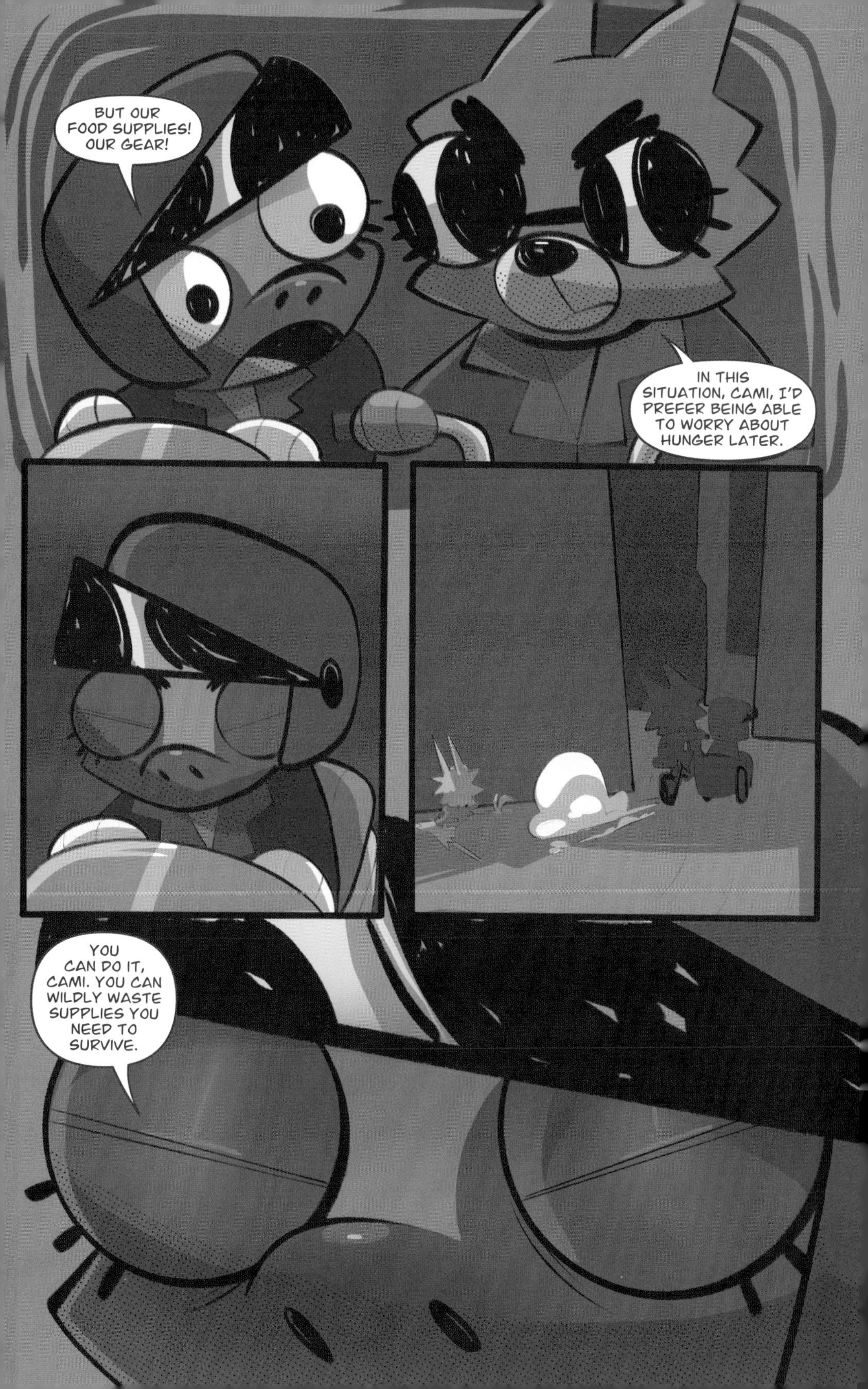
BUT OUR FOOD SUPPLIES! OUR GEAR!
IN THIS SITUATION, CAMI, I'D PREFER BEING ABLE TO WORRY ABOUT HUNGER LATER.
YOU CAN DO IT, CAMI. YOU CAN WILDLY WASTE SUPPLIES YOU NEED TO SURVIVE.

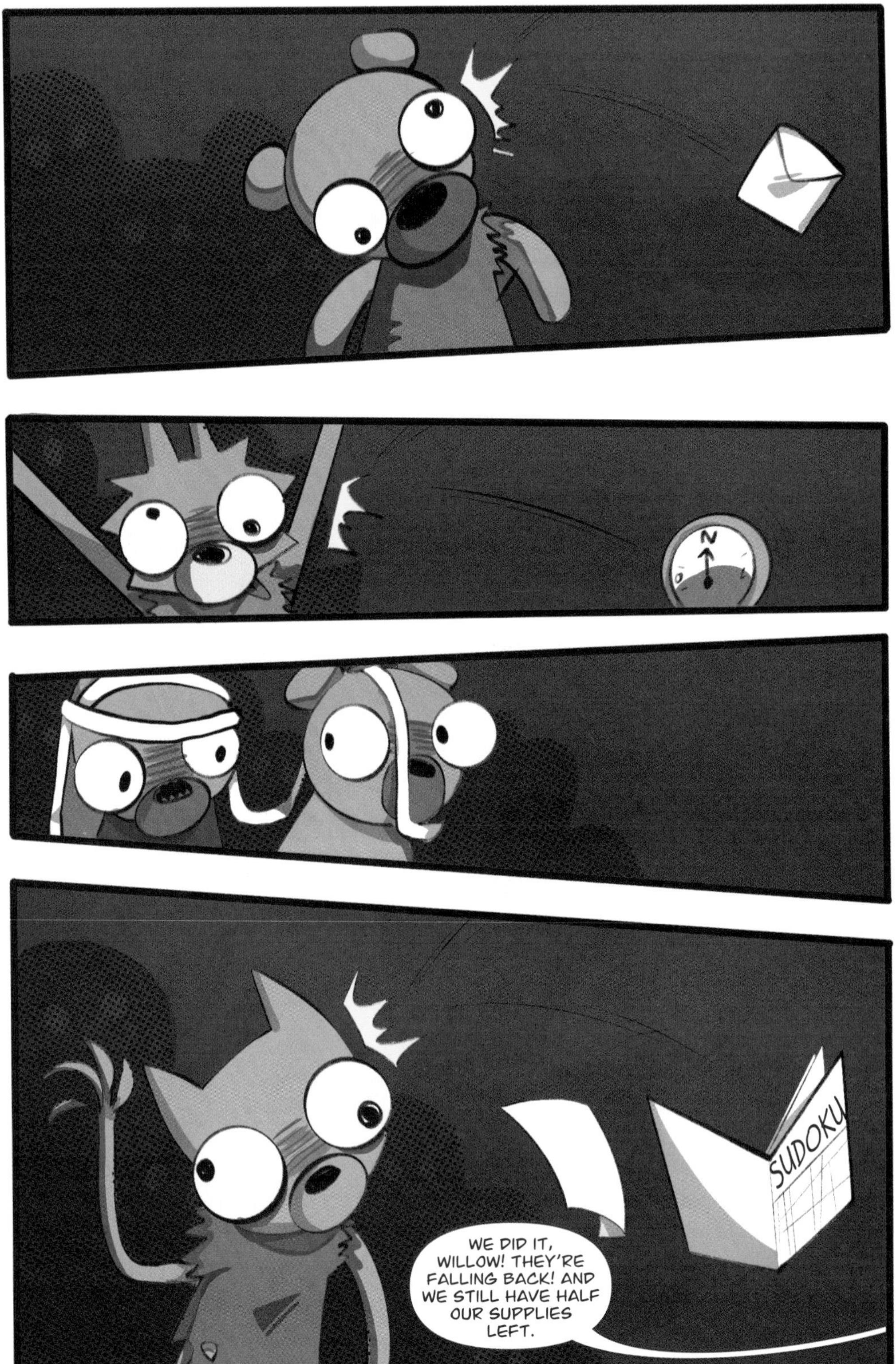
N
SUDOKU
WE DID IT, WILLOW! THEY'RE FALLING BACK! AND WE STILL HAVE HALF OUR SUPPLIES LEFT.

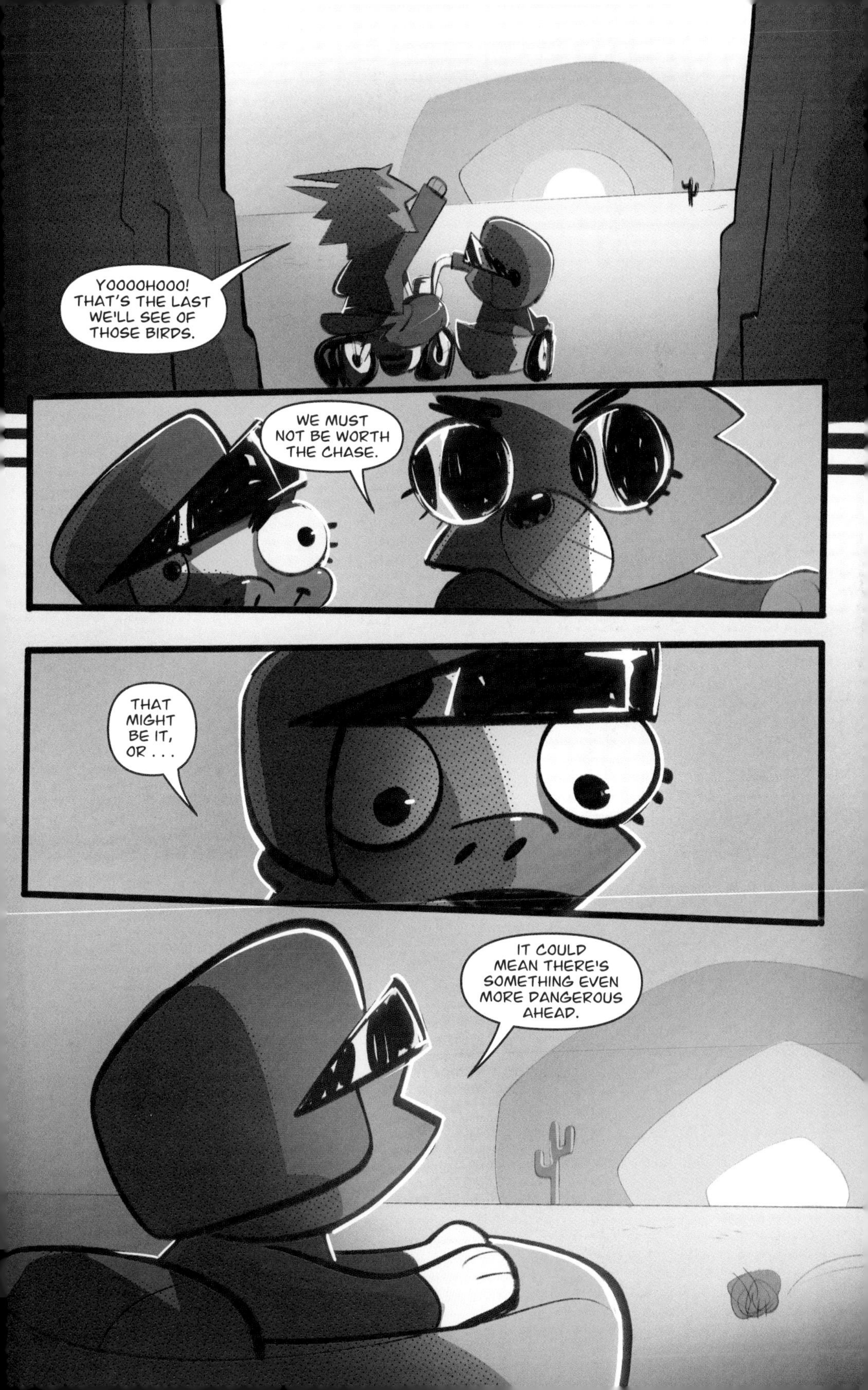
YOOOOHOOO! THAT'S THE LAST WE'LL SEE OF THOSE BIRDS.
WE MUST NOT BE WORTH THE CHASE.
THAT MIGHT BE IT, OR . . .
IT COULD MEAN THERE'S SOMETHING EVEN MORE DANGEROUS AHEAD.

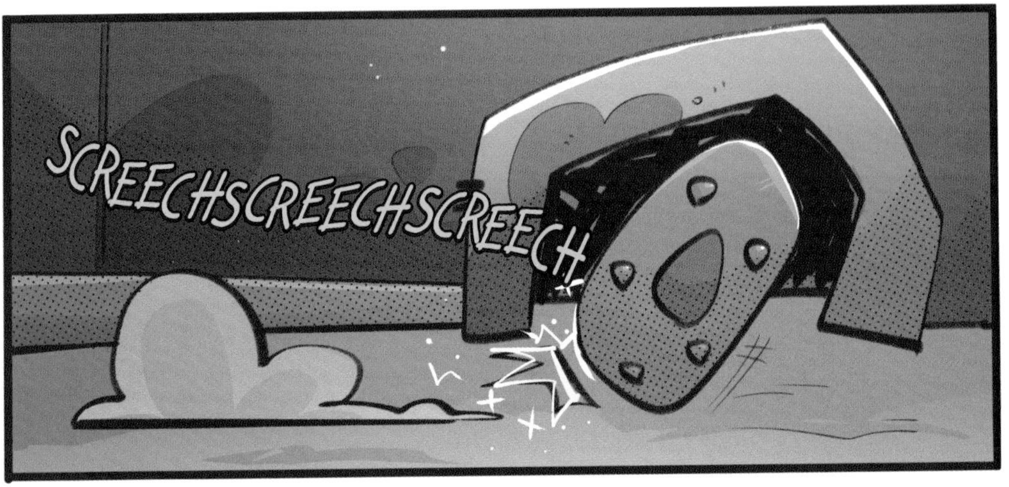
SCREECHSCREECHSCREECH

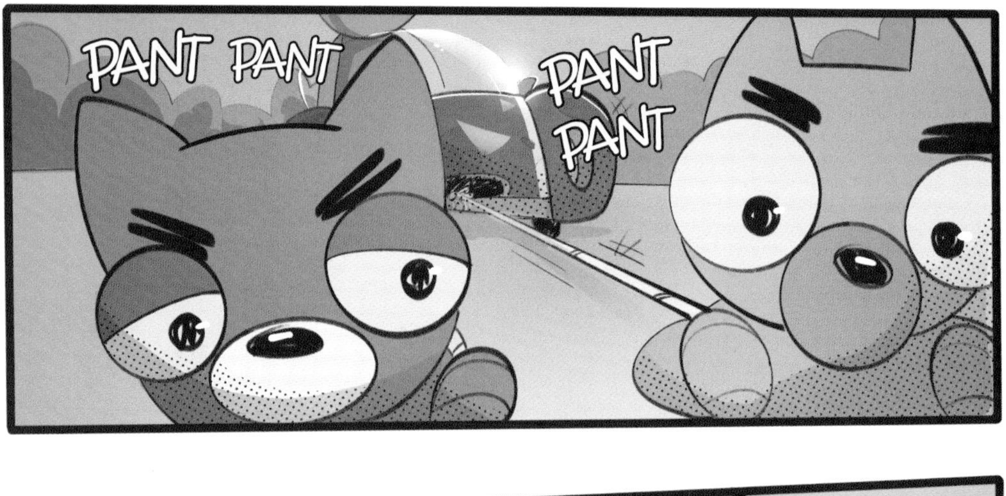
PANT PANT
PANT PANT

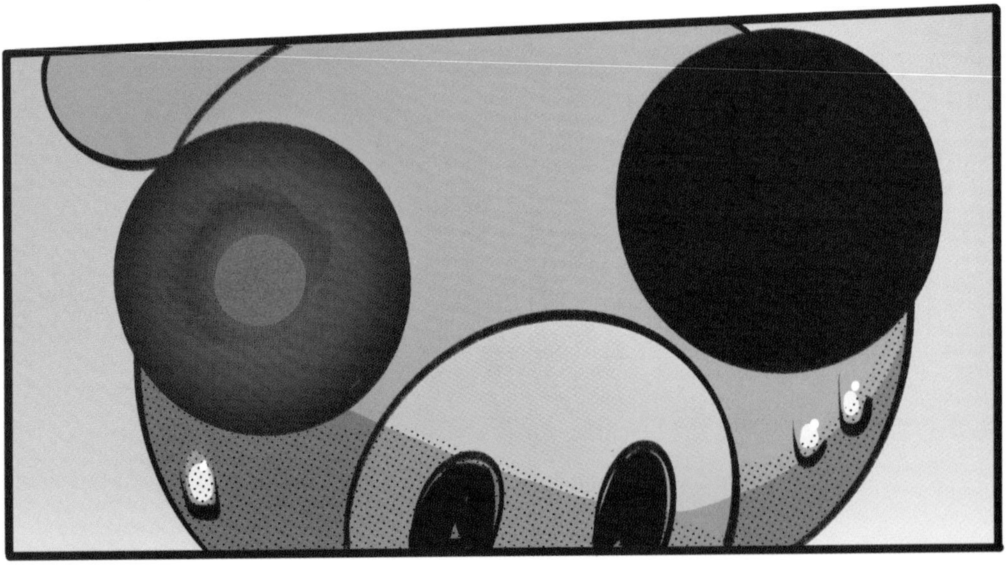

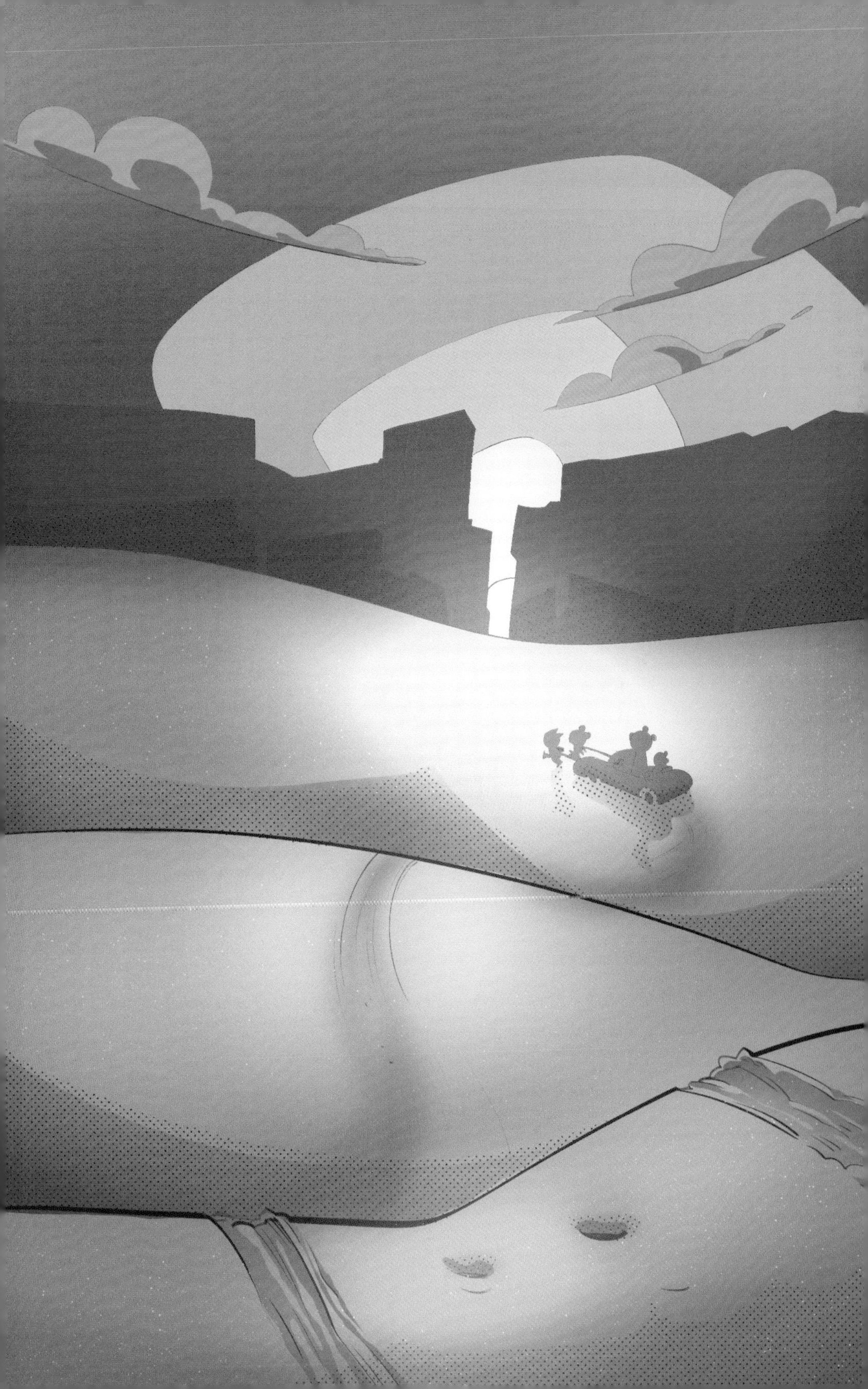

# CHAPTER: 3

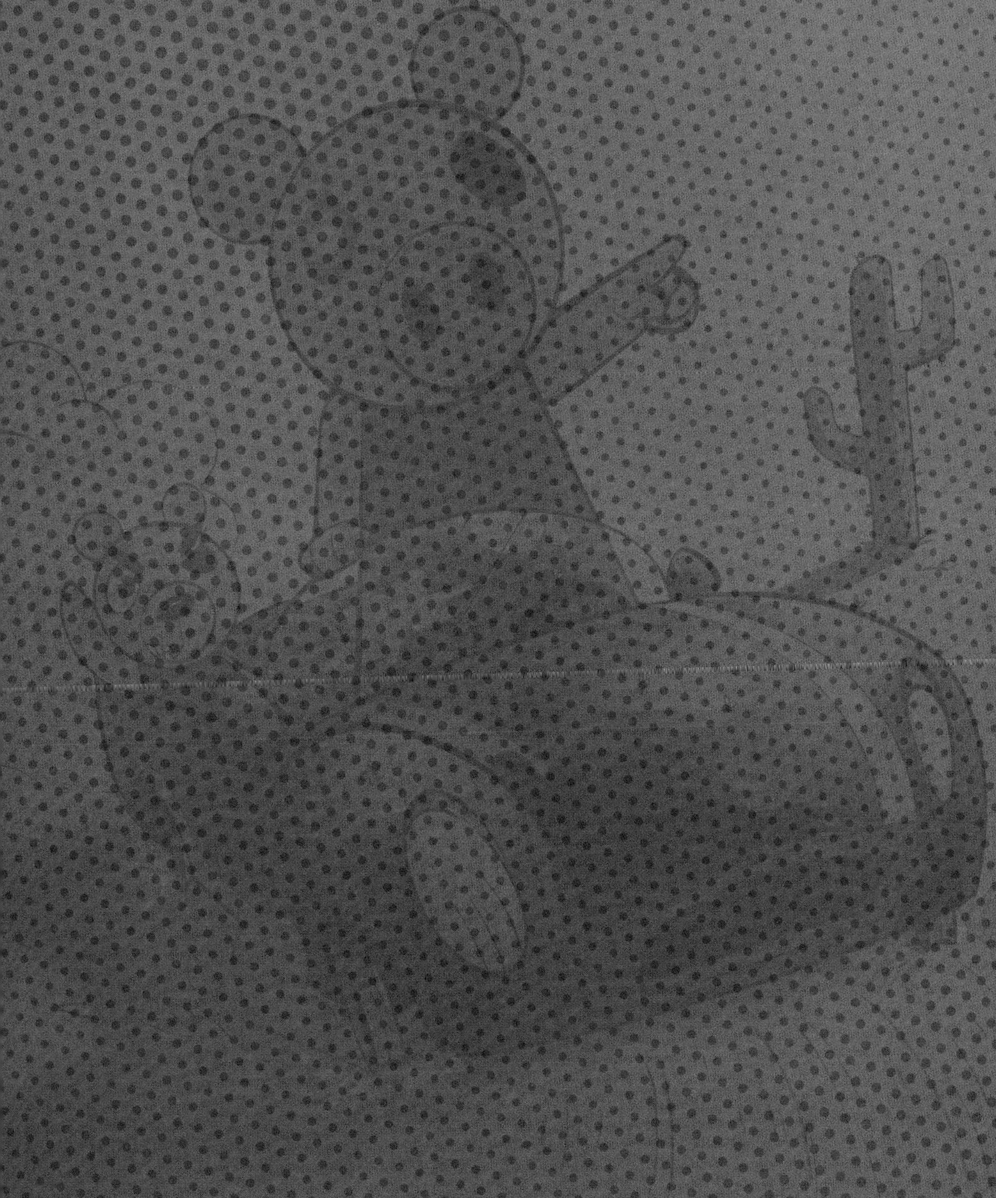

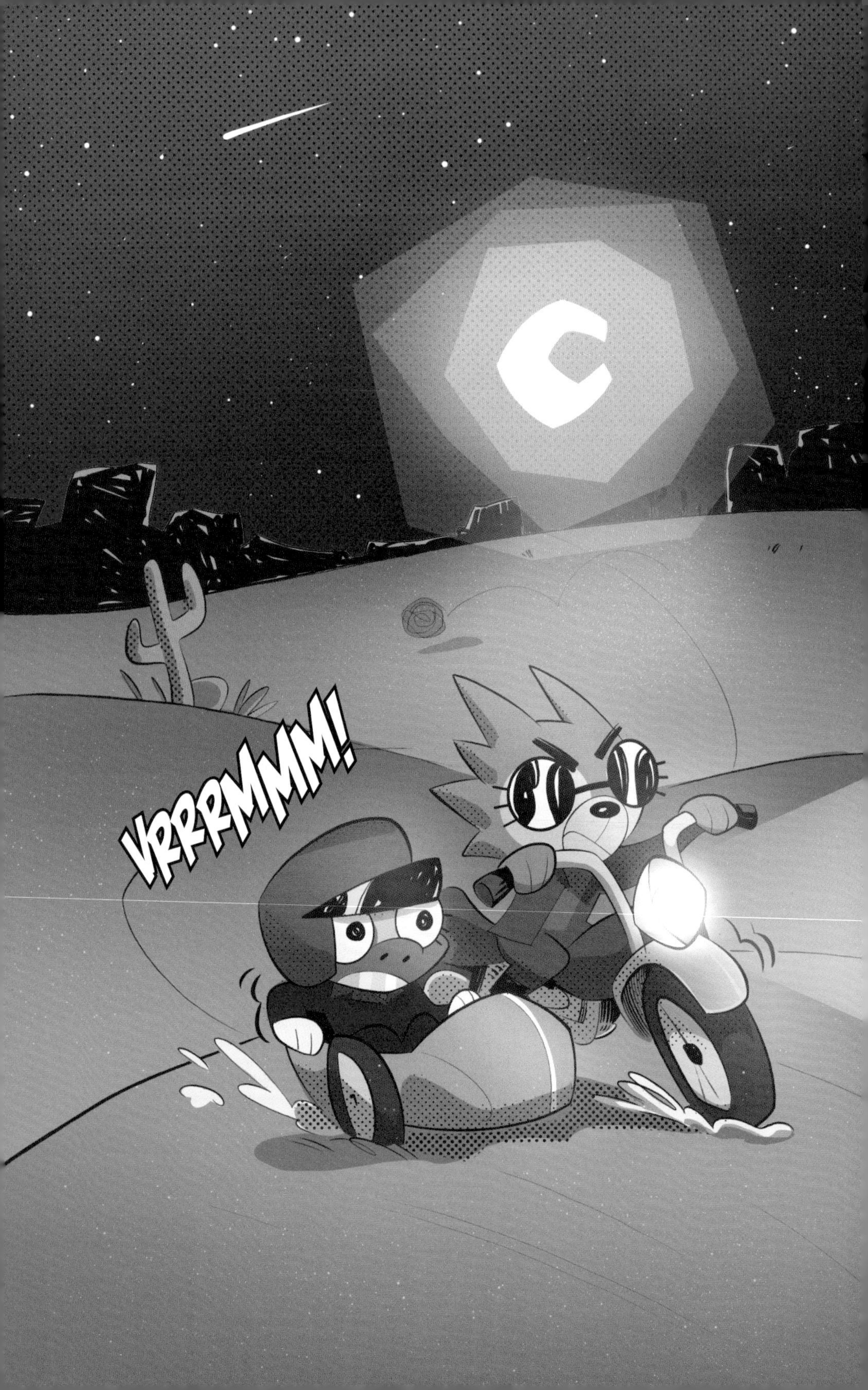
VRRRMMM!

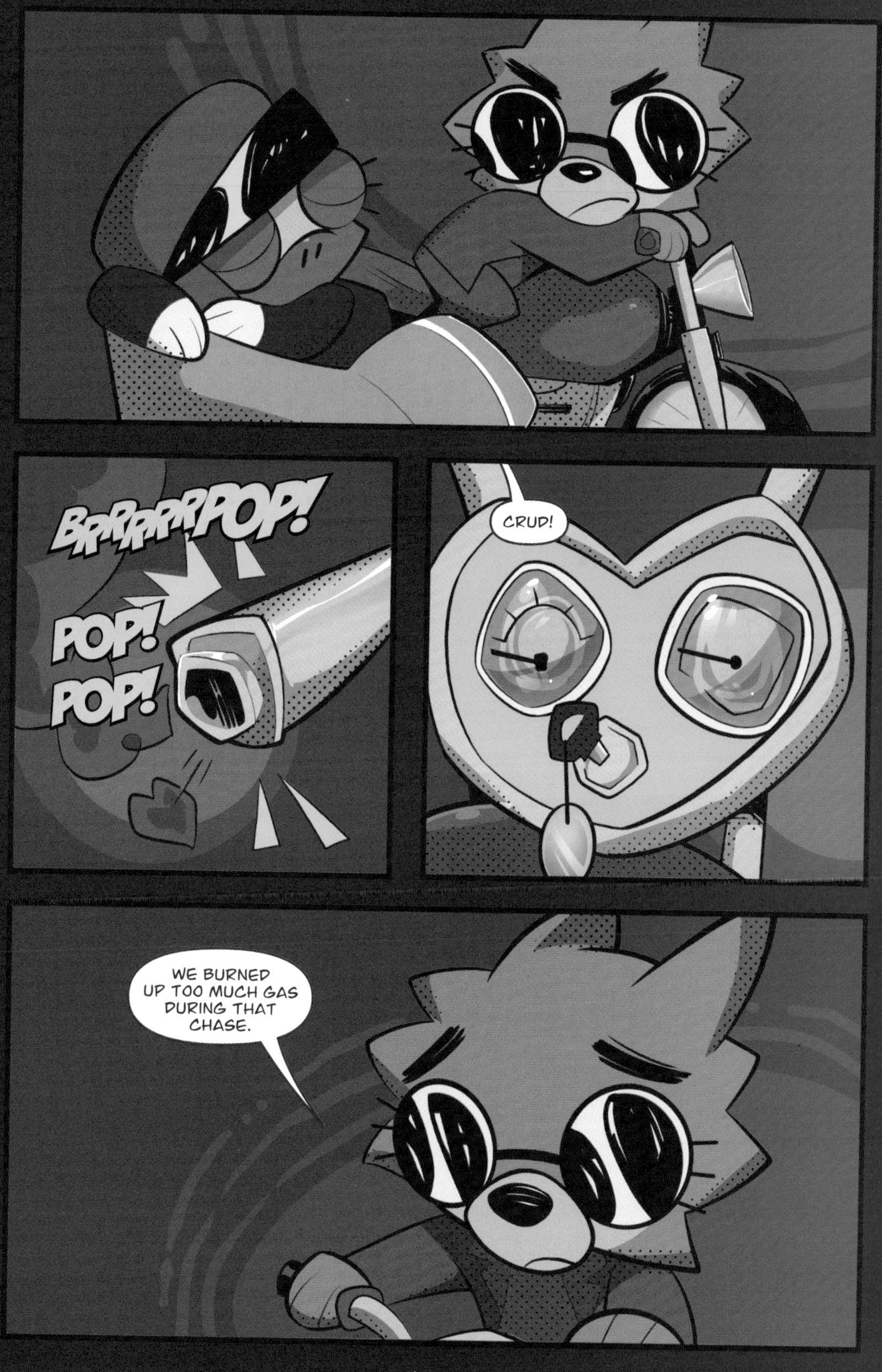
BRRRRRPOP!
POP!
POP!
CRUD!
WE BURNED UP TOO MUCH GAS DURING THAT CHASE.

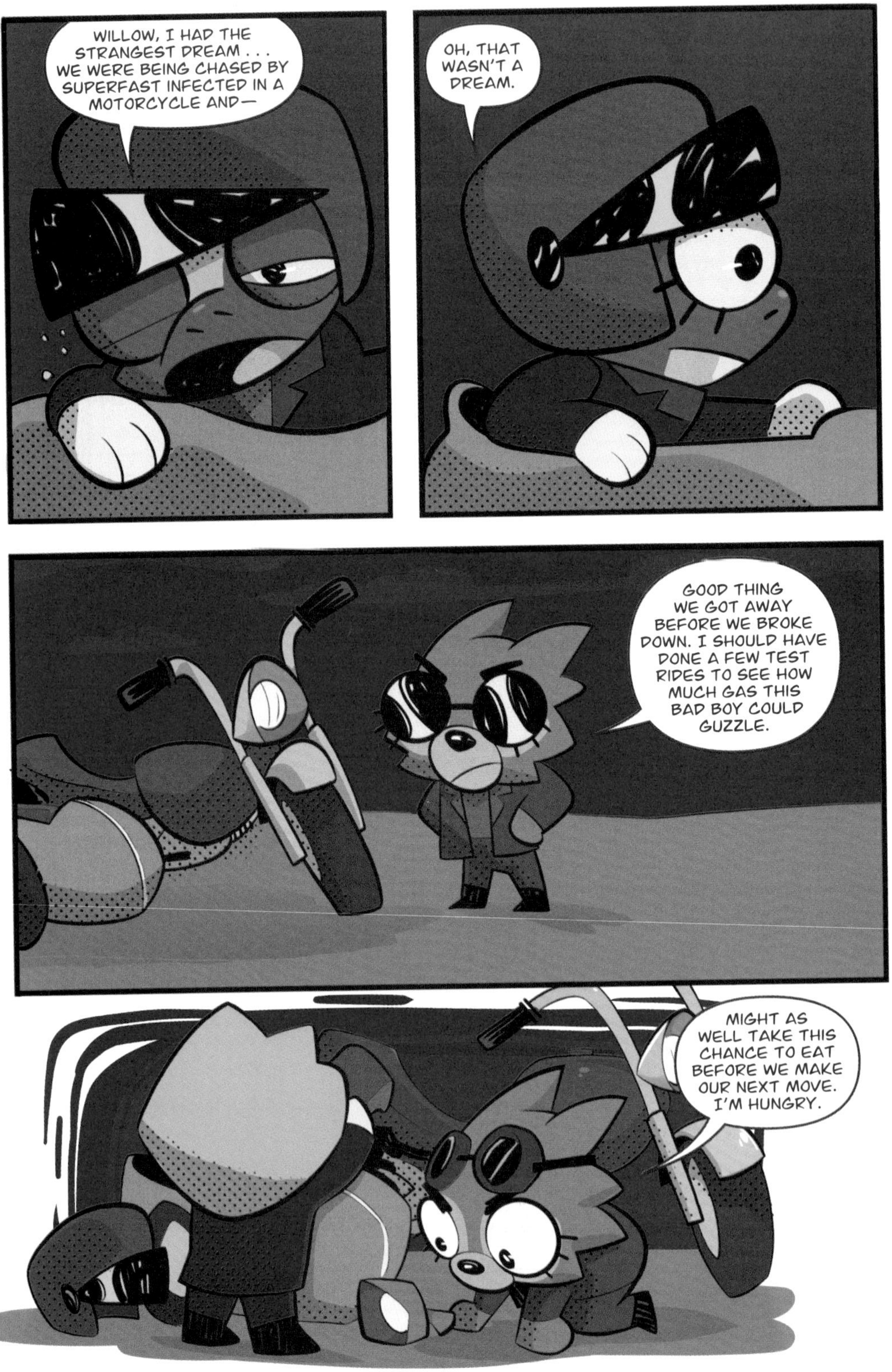
WILLOW, I HAD THE STRANGEST DREAM . . . WE WERE BEING CHASED BY SUPERFAST INFECTED IN A MOTORCYCLE AND—
OH, THAT WASN'T A DREAM.
GOOD THING WE GOT AWAY BEFORE WE BROKE DOWN. I SHOULD HAVE DONE A FEW TEST RIDES TO SEE HOW MUCH GAS THIS BAD BOY COULD GUZZLE.
MIGHT AS WELL TAKE THIS CHANCE TO EAT BEFORE WE MAKE OUR NEXT MOVE. I'M HUNGRY.

# The Silver Paw Survival Tips– Nutrition in the Desert

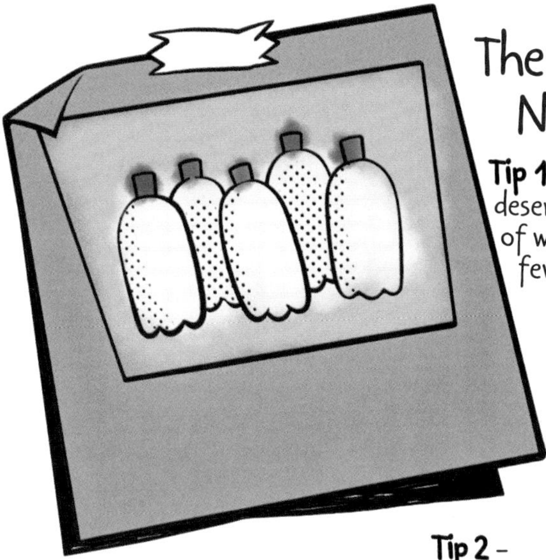

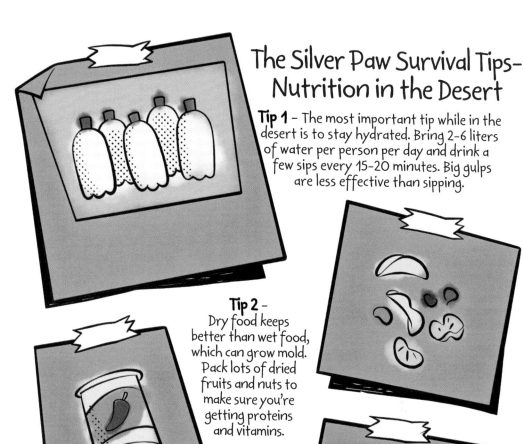

**Tip 1** – The most important tip while in the desert is to stay hydrated. Bring 2-6 liters of water per person per day and drink a few sips every 15-20 minutes. Big gulps are less effective than sipping.

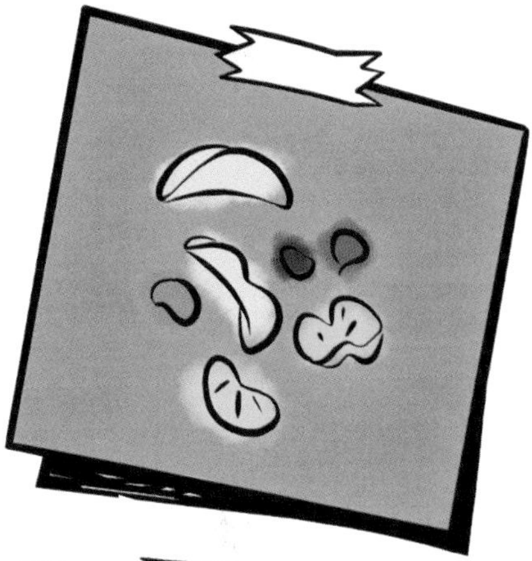

**Tip 2** – Dry food keeps better than wet food, which can grow mold. Pack lots of dried fruits and nuts to make sure you're getting proteins and vitamins.

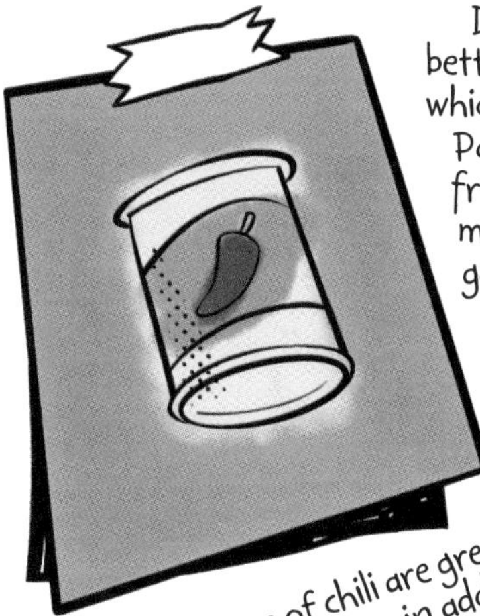

**Tip 3** – Cans of chili are great at providing sodium, in addition to nutrients, which helps you store water and proteins from beans. They're also easy to cook over a campfire.

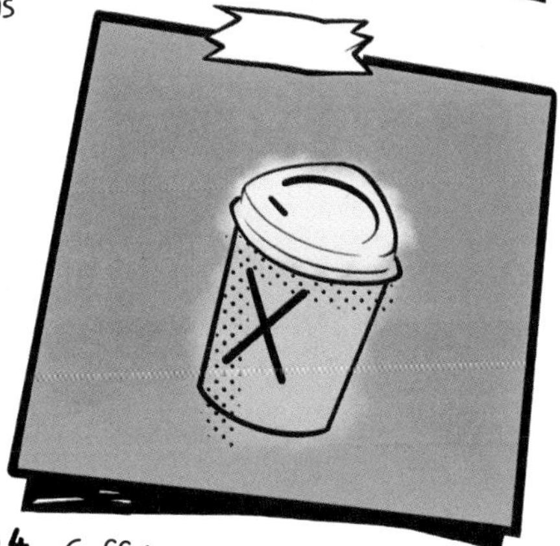

**Tip 4** – Caffeine is a big NO while in the desert! Avoid soda, iced tea, and coffee!

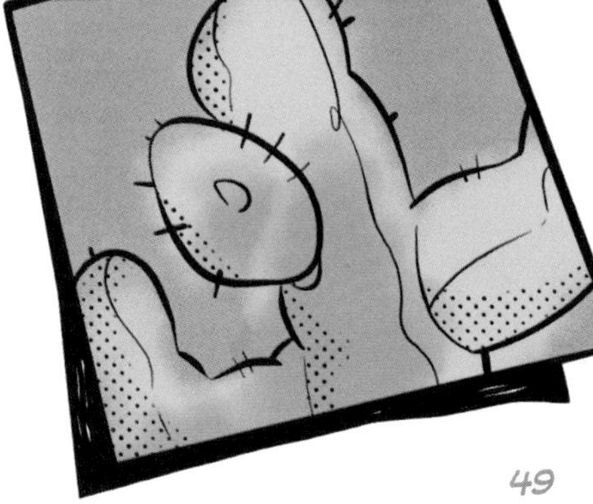

**Tip 5** – There are edible plants in the desert like prickly pear cactus, certain kinds of agave, and wild berries, but harvesting wild plants should be done under the supervision of a knowledgeable adult.

Willow is *not* a knowledgeable adult.

CAN'T RISK A FIRE, SO COLD CHILI IT IS.

I LIKE COLD CHILI BETTER, ANYWAY.

YOU'RE A WEIRD ONE, KID.

BUT THAT'S WHY YOU LIKE ME SO MUCH.

ALL RIGHT, THE MOON'S PRETTY BRIGHT SO LET'S SEE IF I CAN MAKE ANYTHING OUT. THERE HAS TO BE A GAS STATION SOMEWHERE ALONG THIS HIGHWAY.

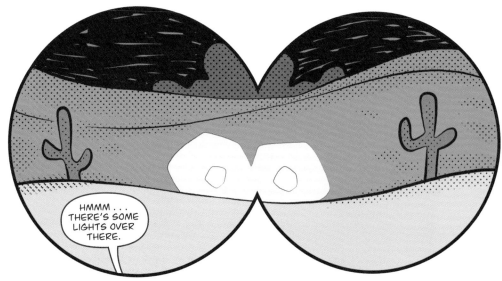

HMMM . . . THERE'S SOME LIGHTS OVER THERE.

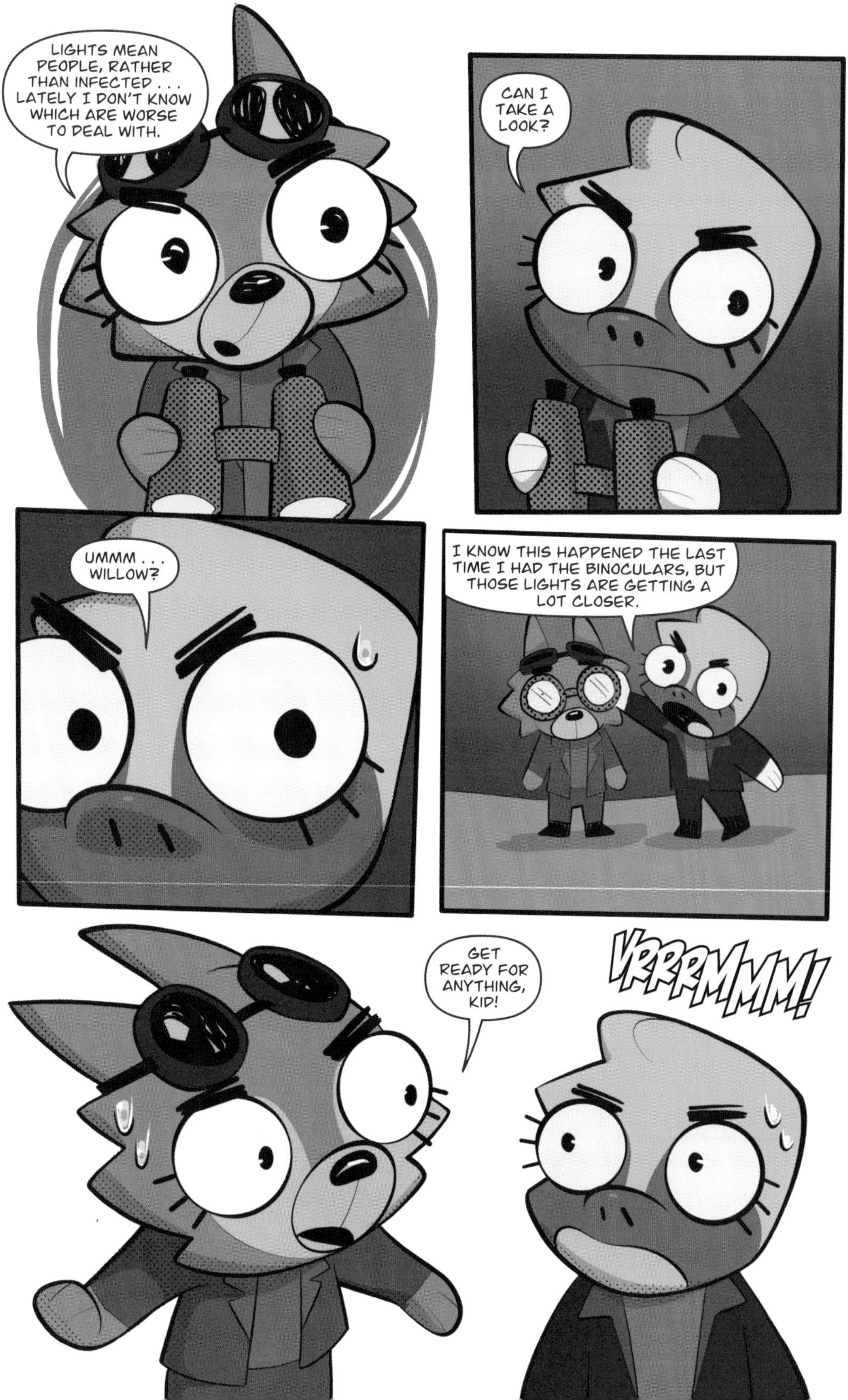
LIGHTS MEAN PEOPLE, RATHER THAN INFECTED . . . LATELY I DON'T KNOW WHICH ARE WORSE TO DEAL WITH.
CAN I TAKE A LOOK?
UMMM . . . WILLOW?
I KNOW THIS HAPPENED THE LAST TIME I HAD THE BINOCULARS, BUT THOSE LIGHTS ARE GETTING A LOT CLOSER.
GET READY FOR ANYTHING, KID!
VRRRMMMM!

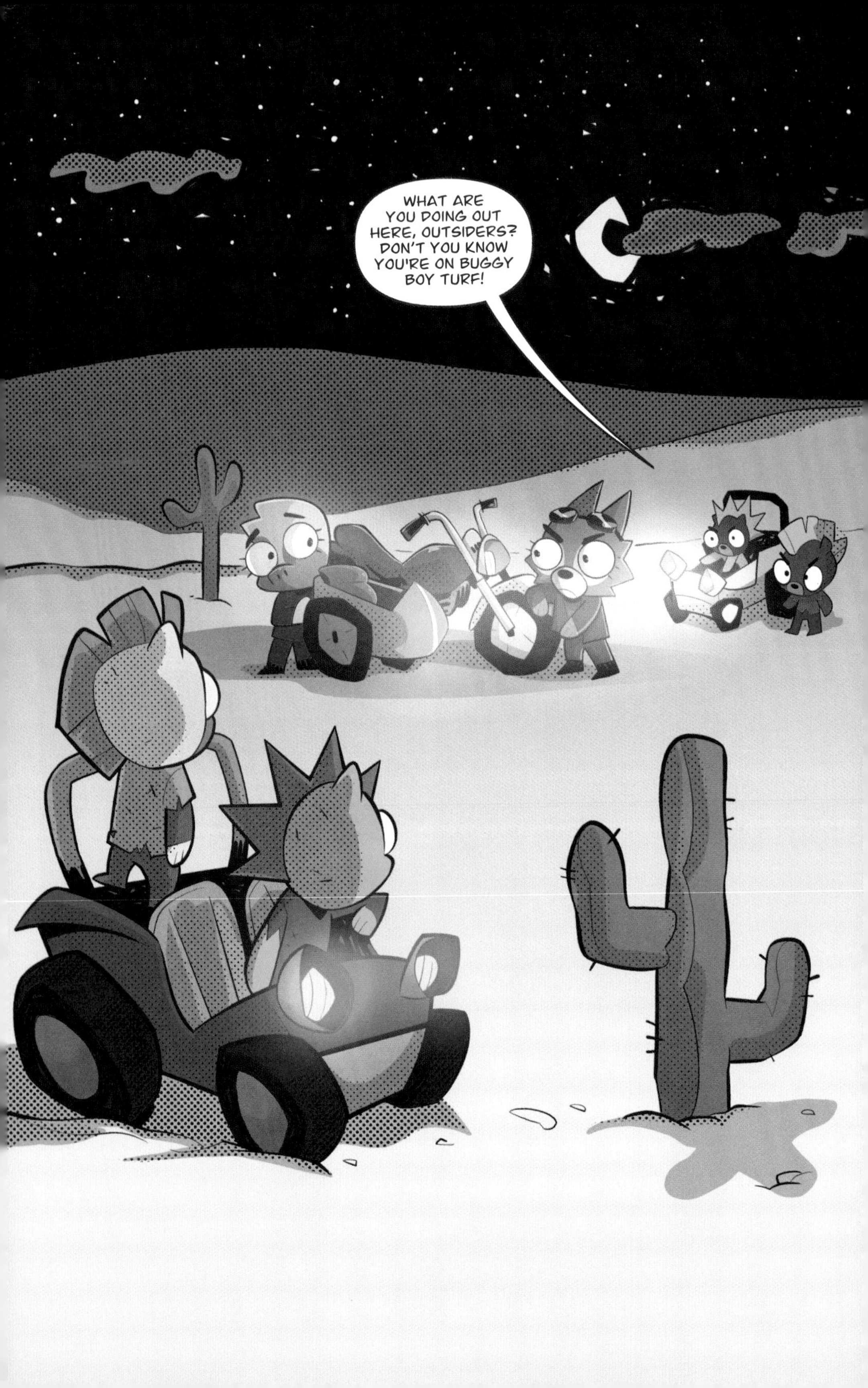
WHAT ARE YOU DOING OUT HERE, OUTSIDERS? DON'T YOU KNOW YOU'RE ON BUGGY BOY TURF!

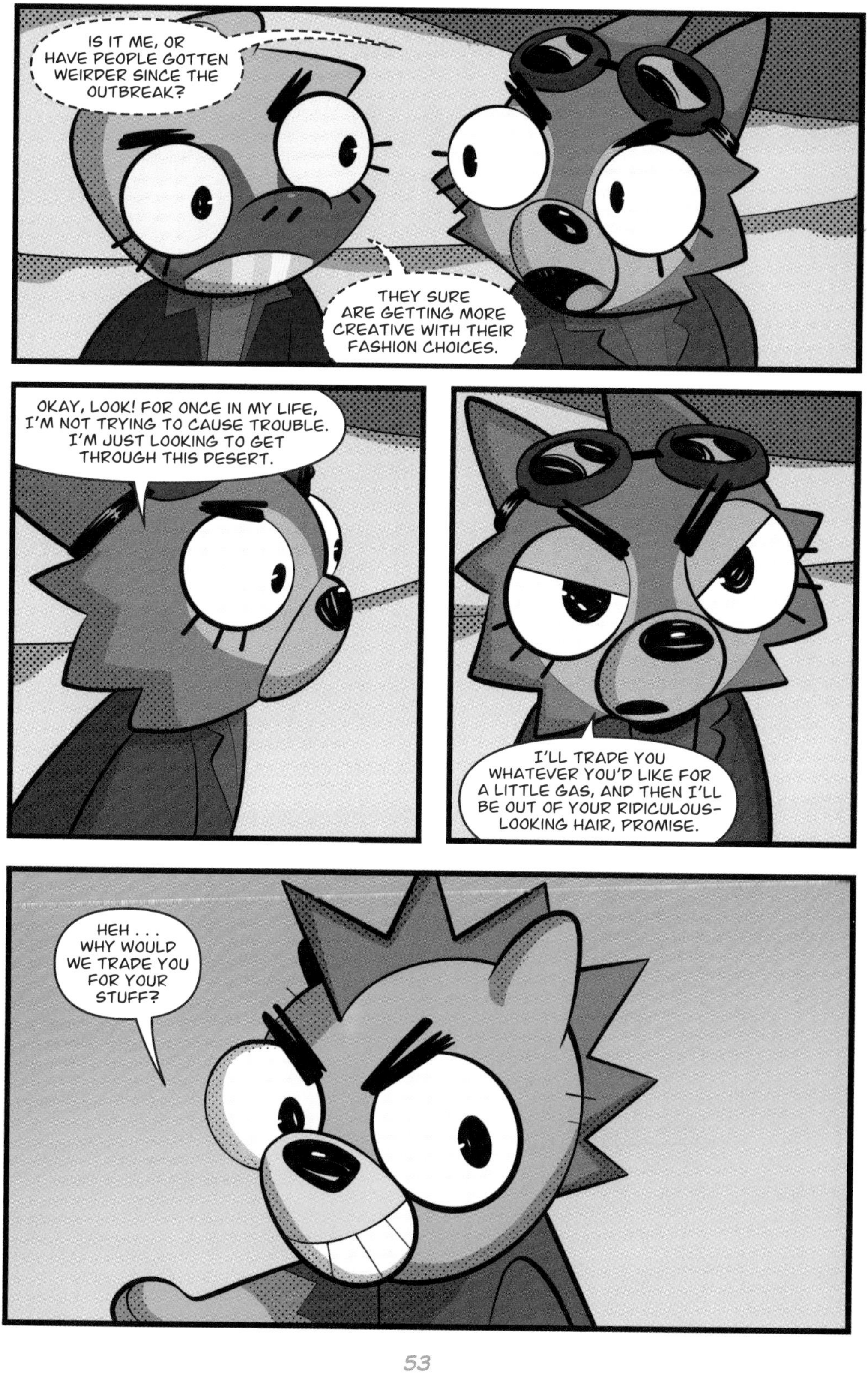

IS IT ME, OR HAVE PEOPLE GOTTEN WEIRDER SINCE THE OUTBREAK?
THEY SURE ARE GETTING MORE CREATIVE WITH THEIR FASHION CHOICES.
OKAY, LOOK! FOR ONCE IN MY LIFE, I'M NOT TRYING TO CAUSE TROUBLE. I'M JUST LOOKING TO GET THROUGH THIS DESERT.
I'LL TRADE YOU WHATEVER YOU'D LIKE FOR A LITTLE GAS, AND THEN I'LL BE OUT OF YOUR RIDICULOUS-LOOKING HAIR, PROMISE.
HEH . . . WHY WOULD WE TRADE YOU FOR YOUR STUFF?

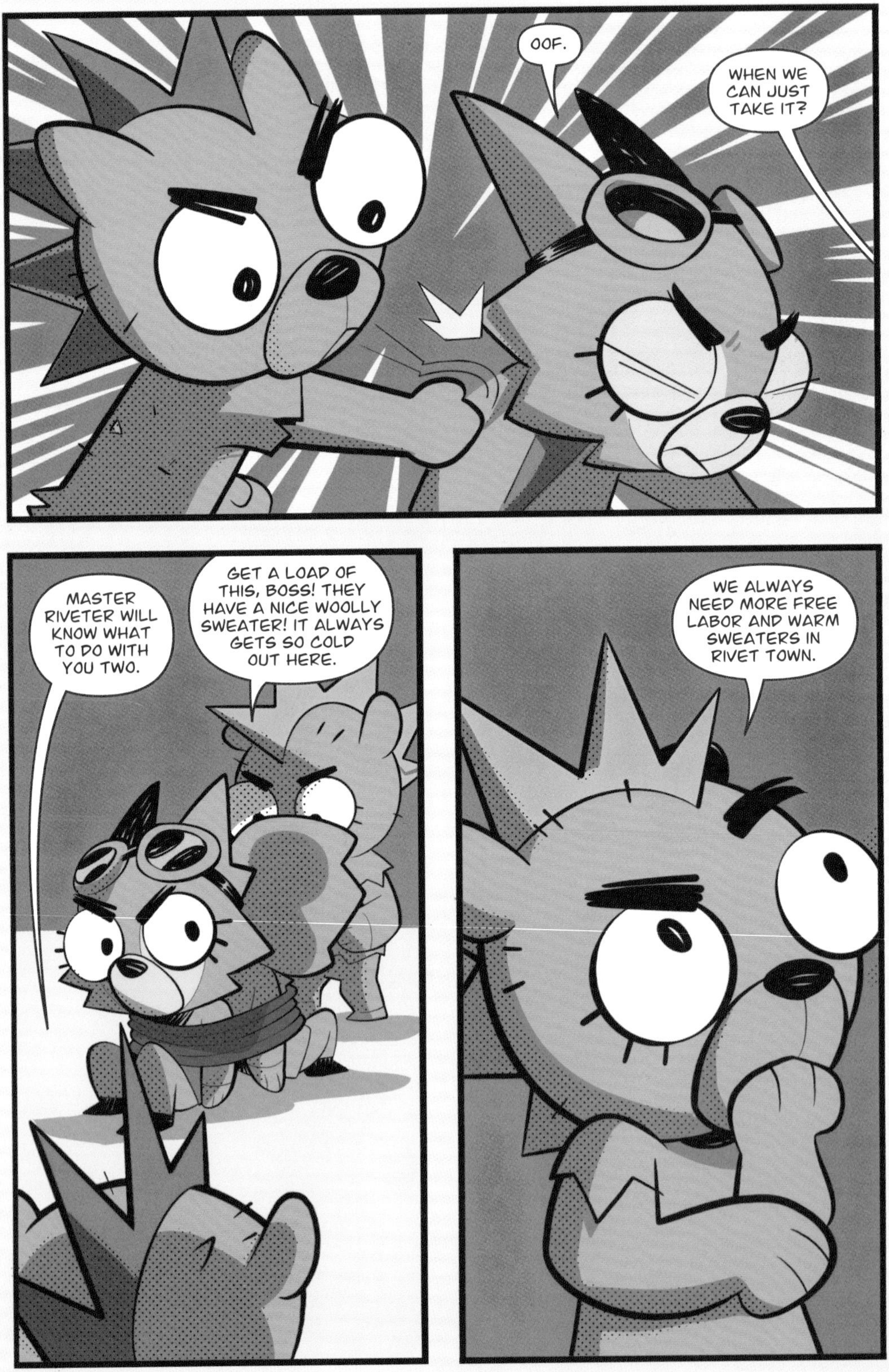
OOF.
WHEN WE CAN JUST TAKE IT?
MASTER RIVETER WILL KNOW WHAT TO DO WITH YOU TWO.
GET A LOAD OF THIS, BOSS! THEY HAVE A NICE WOOLLY SWEATER! IT ALWAYS GETS SO COLD OUT HERE.
WE ALWAYS NEED MORE FREE LABOR AND WARM SWEATERS IN RIVET TOWN.

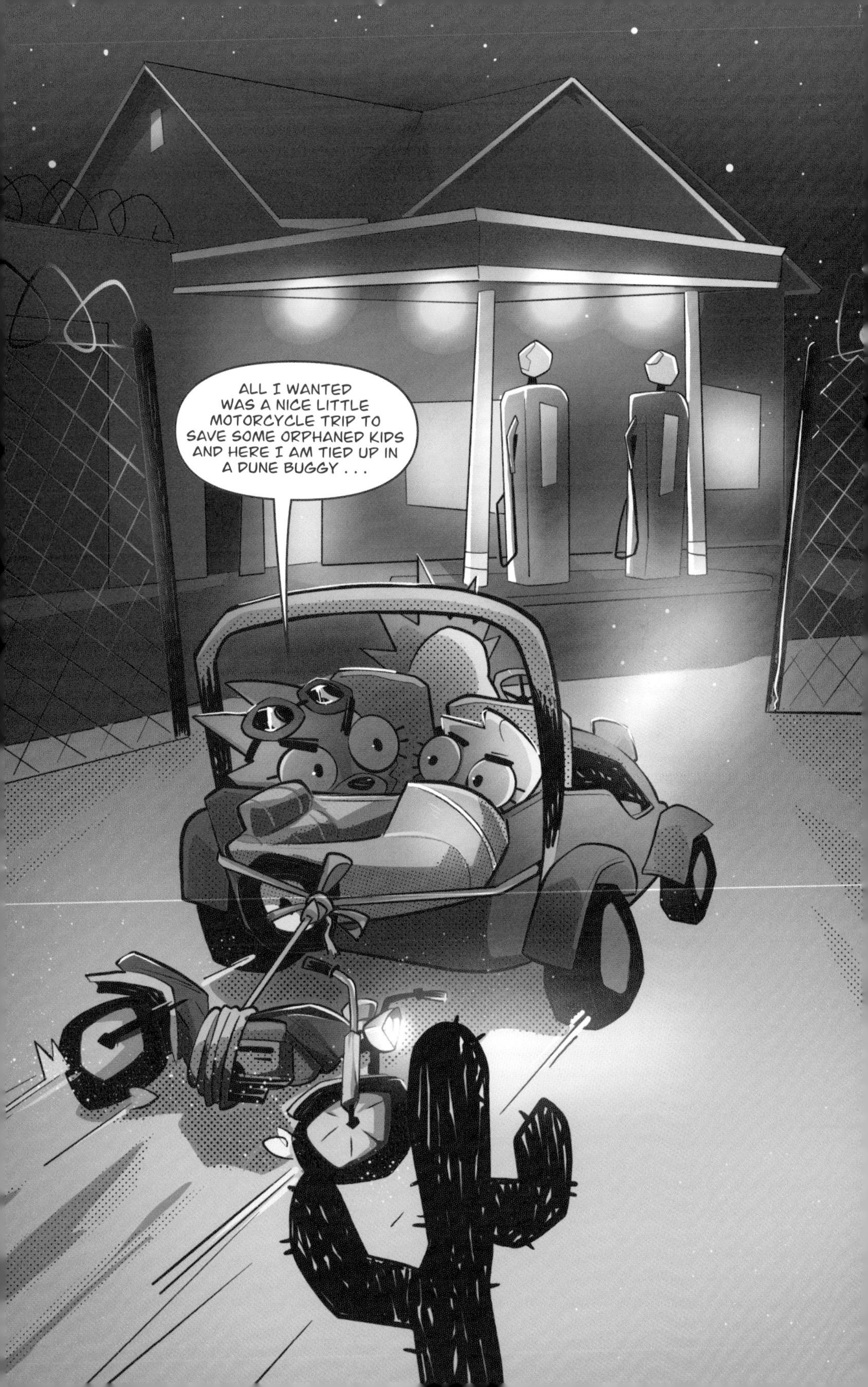
ALL I WANTED WAS A NICE LITTLE MOTORCYCLE TRIP TO SAVE SOME ORPHANED KIDS AND HERE I AM TIED UP IN A DUNE BUGGY . . .

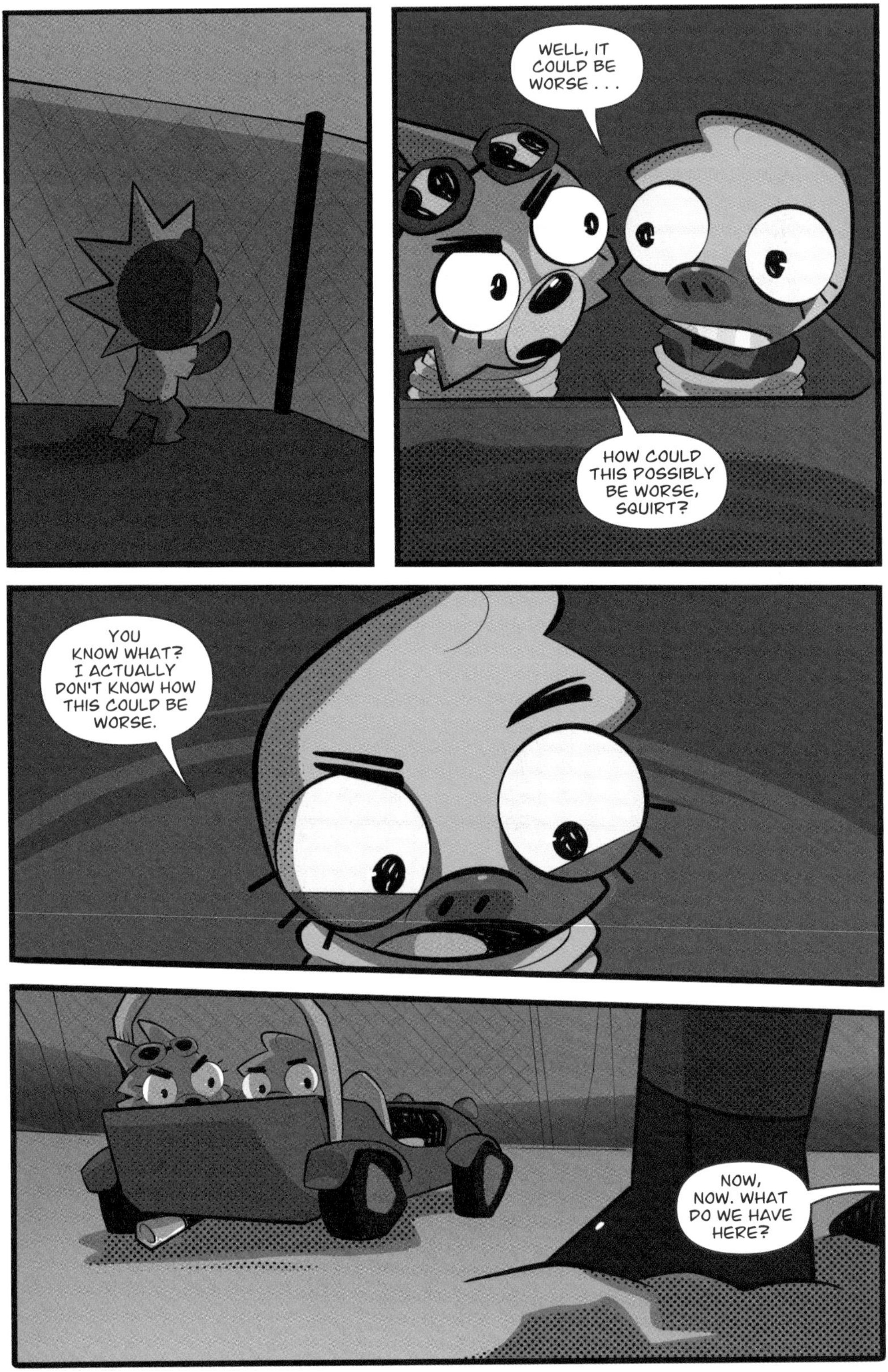
WELL, IT COULD BE WORSE . . .
HOW COULD THIS POSSIBLY BE WORSE, SQUIRT?
YOU KNOW WHAT? I ACTUALLY DON'T KNOW HOW THIS COULD BE WORSE.
NOW, NOW. WHAT DO WE HAVE HERE?

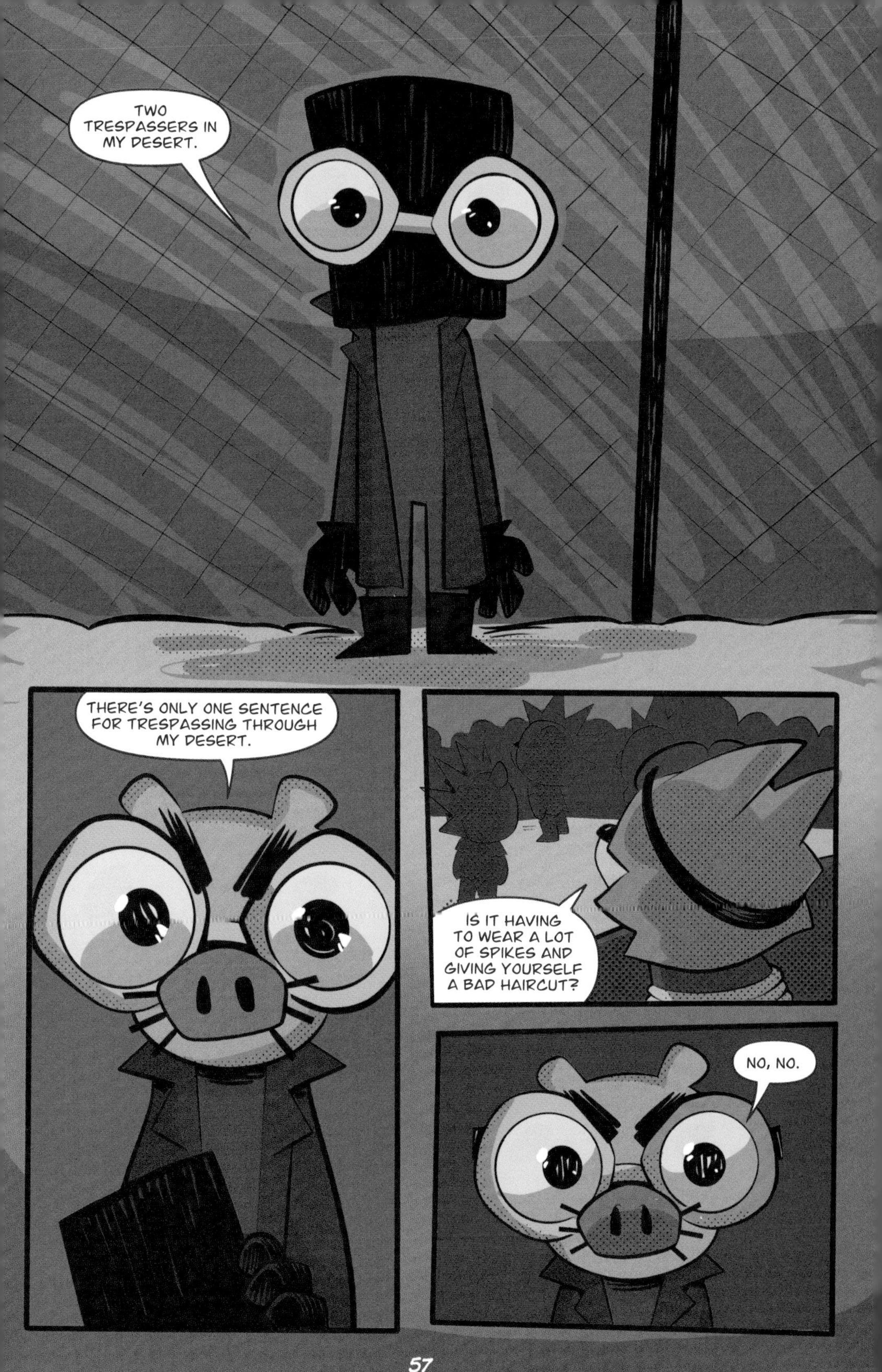
TWO TRESPASSERS IN MY DESERT.
THERE'S ONLY ONE SENTENCE FOR TRESPASSING THROUGH MY DESERT.
IS IT HAVING TO WEAR A LOT OF SPIKES AND GIVING YOURSELF A BAD HAIRCUT?
NO, NO.

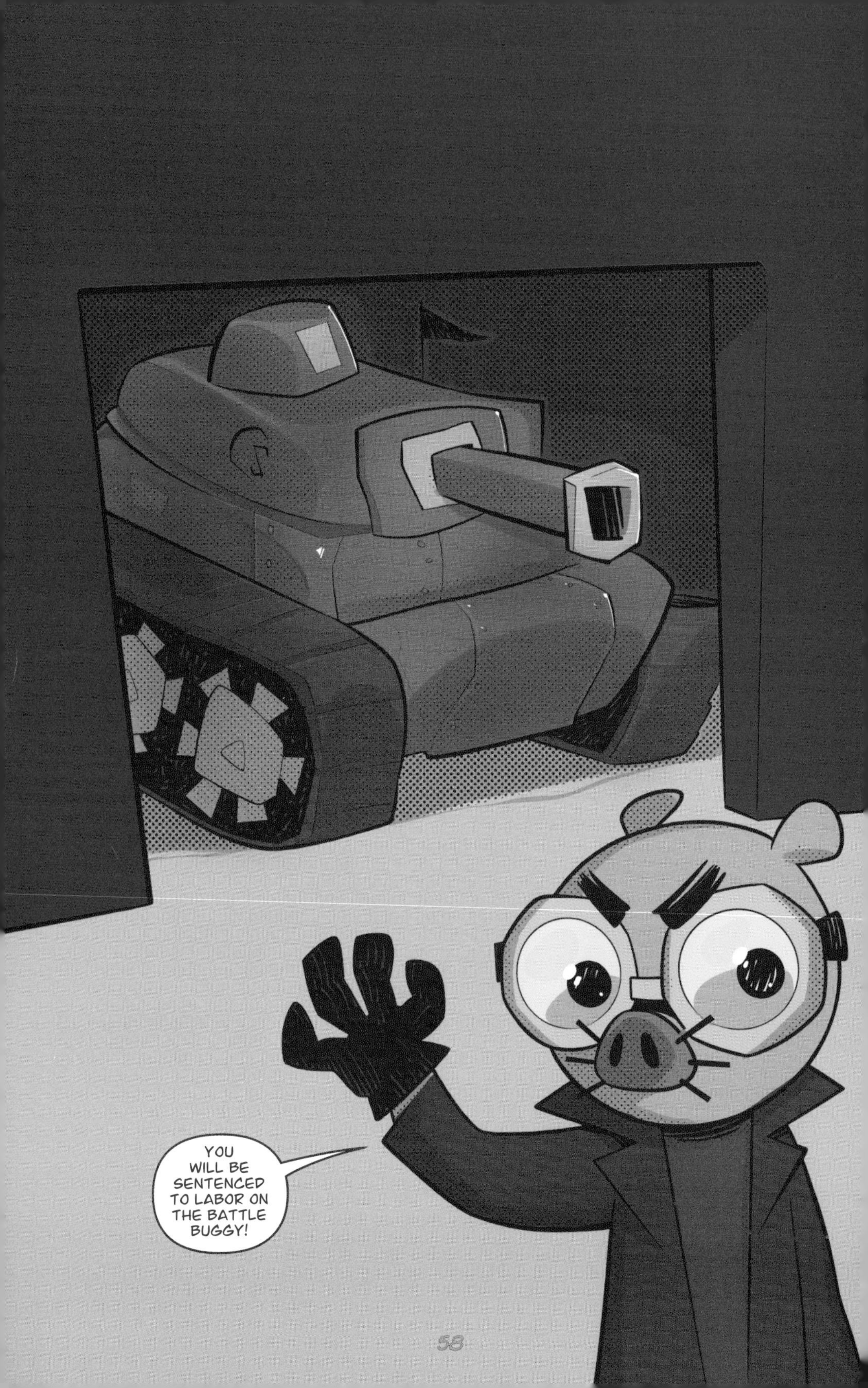
YOU WILL BE SENTENCED TO LABOR ON THE BATTLE BUGGY!

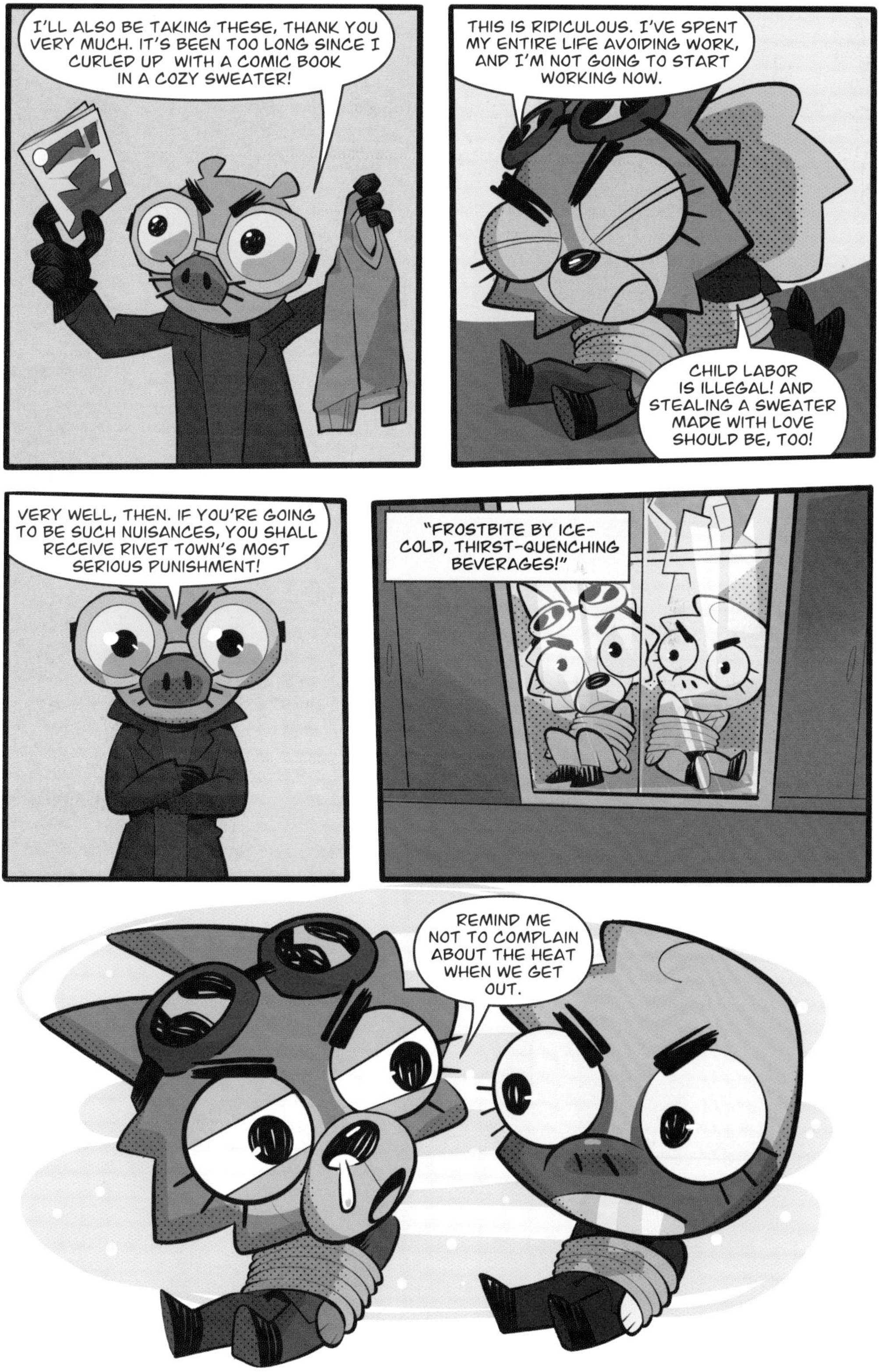
I'LL ALSO BE TAKING THESE, THANK YOU VERY MUCH. IT'S BEEN TOO LONG SINCE I CURLED UP WITH A COMIC BOOK IN A COZY SWEATER!
THIS IS RIDICULOUS. I'VE SPENT MY ENTIRE LIFE AVOIDING WORK, AND I'M NOT GOING TO START WORKING NOW.
CHILD LABOR IS ILLEGAL! AND STEALING A SWEATER MADE WITH LOVE SHOULD BE, TOO!
VERY WELL, THEN. IF YOU'RE GOING TO BE SUCH NUISANCES, YOU SHALL RECEIVE RIVET TOWN'S MOST SERIOUS PUNISHMENT!
"FROSTBITE BY ICE-COLD, THIRST-QUENCHING BEVERAGES!"
REMIND ME NOT TO COMPLAIN ABOUT THE HEAT WHEN WE GET OUT.

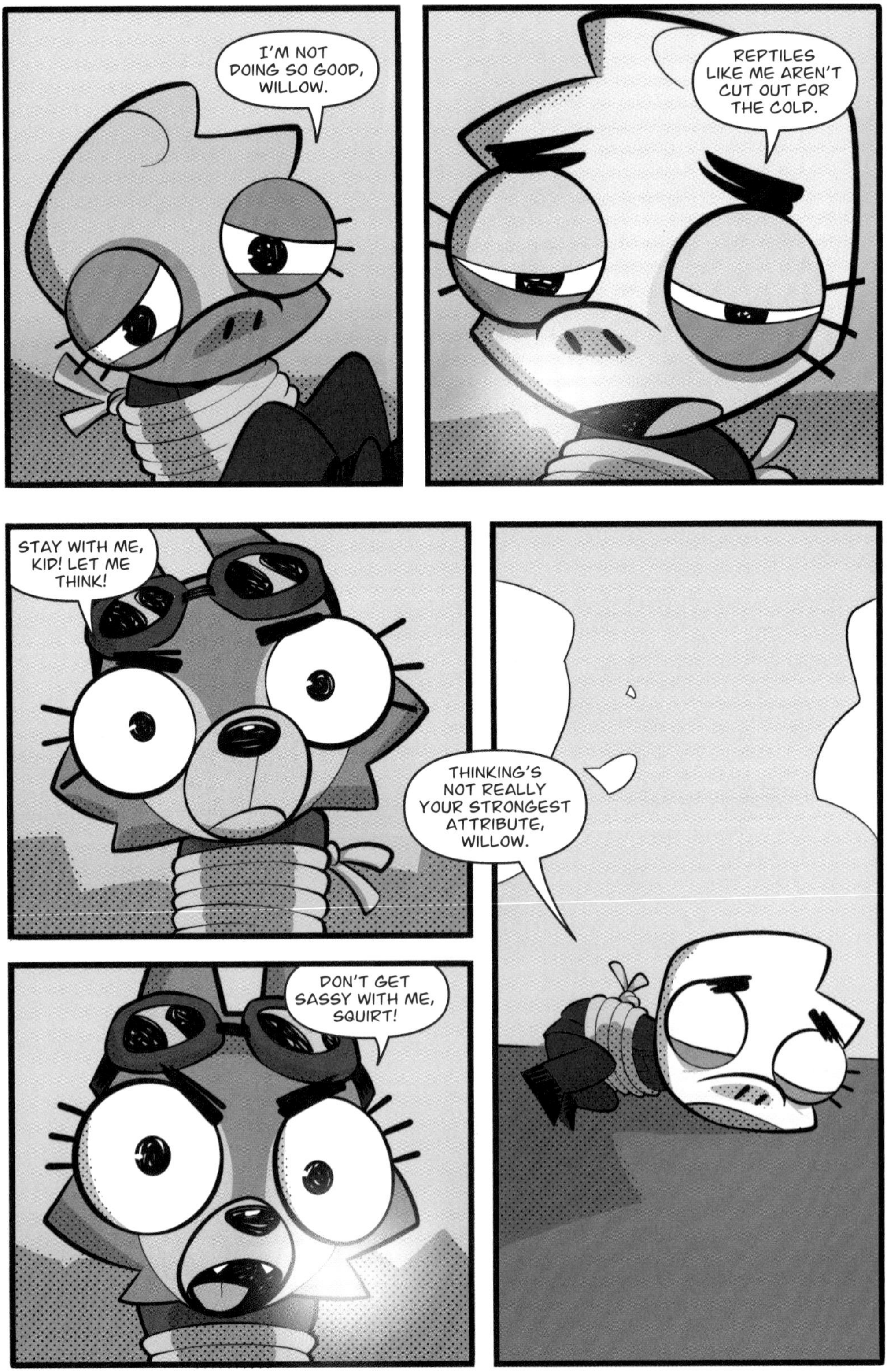
I'M NOT DOING SO GOOD, WILLOW.
REPTILES LIKE ME AREN'T CUT OUT FOR THE COLD.
STAY WITH ME, KID! LET ME THINK!
THINKING'S NOT REALLY YOUR STRONGEST ATTRIBUTE, WILLOW.
DON'T GET SASSY WITH ME, SQUIRT!

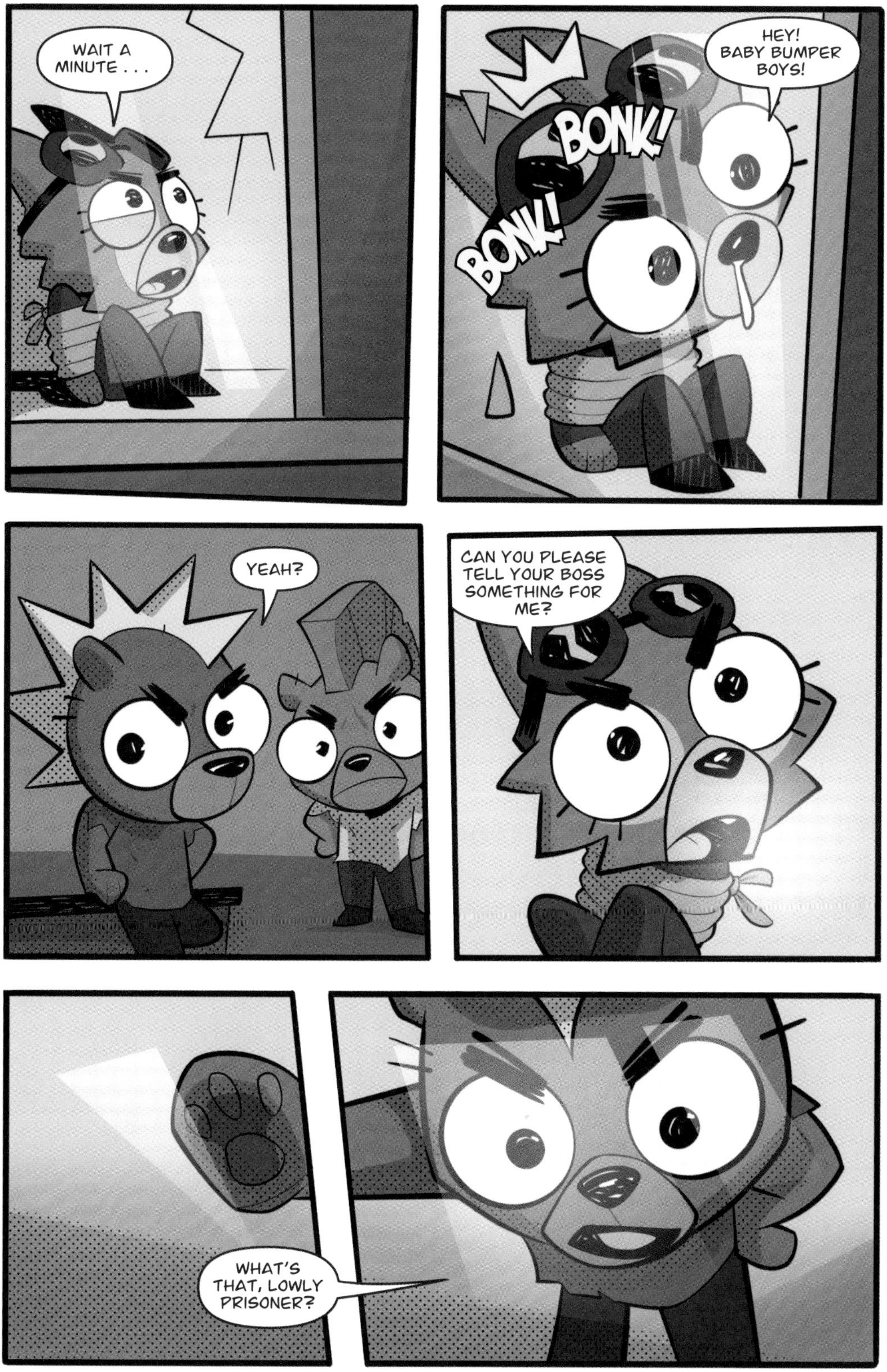
WAIT A MINUTE . . .
HEY! BABY BUMPER BOYS!
BONK!
BONK!
YEAH?
CAN YOU PLEASE TELL YOUR BOSS SOMETHING FOR ME?
WHAT'S THAT, LOWLY PRISONER?

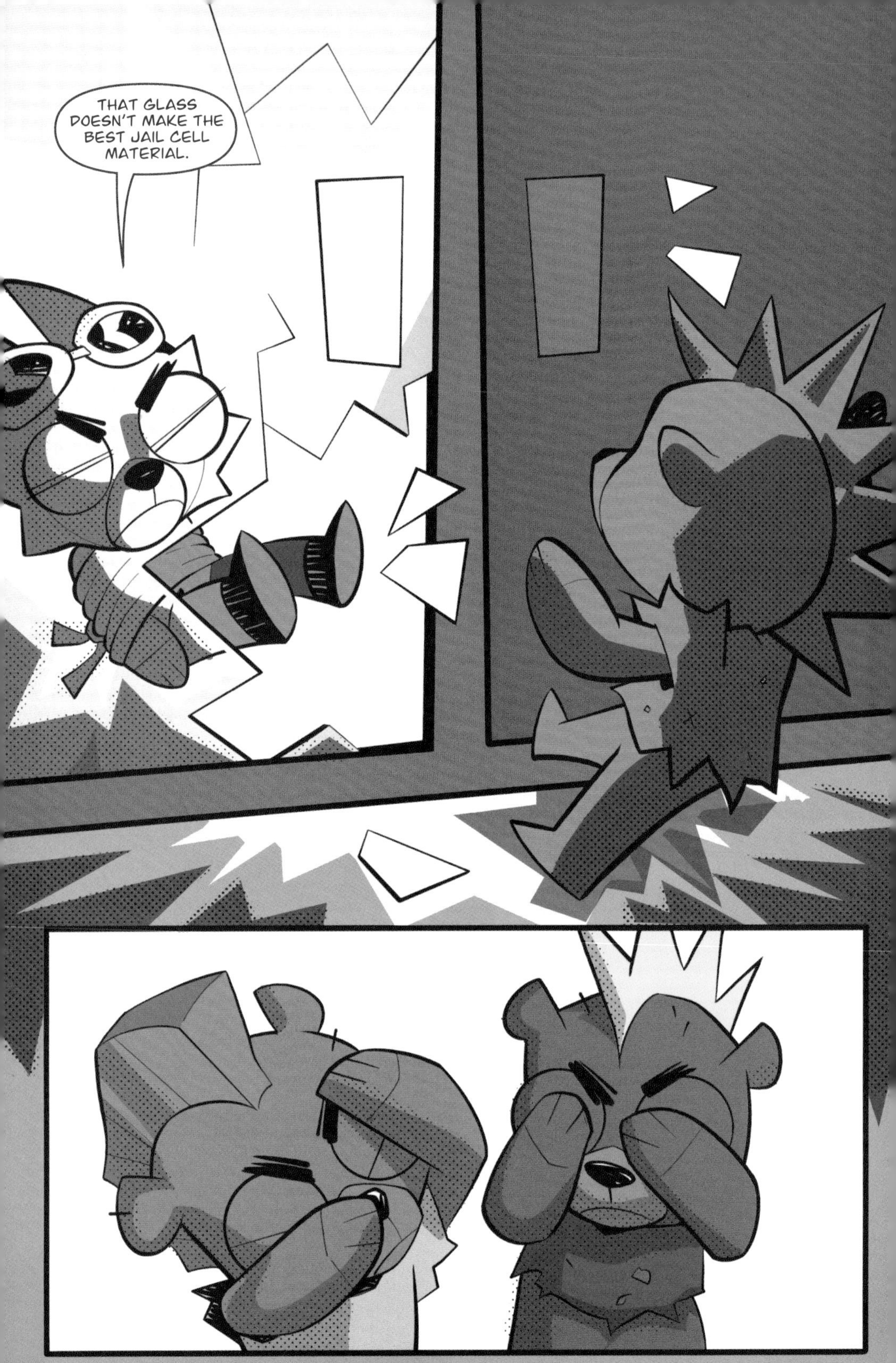
THAT GLASS DOESN'T MAKE THE BEST JAIL CELL MATERIAL.

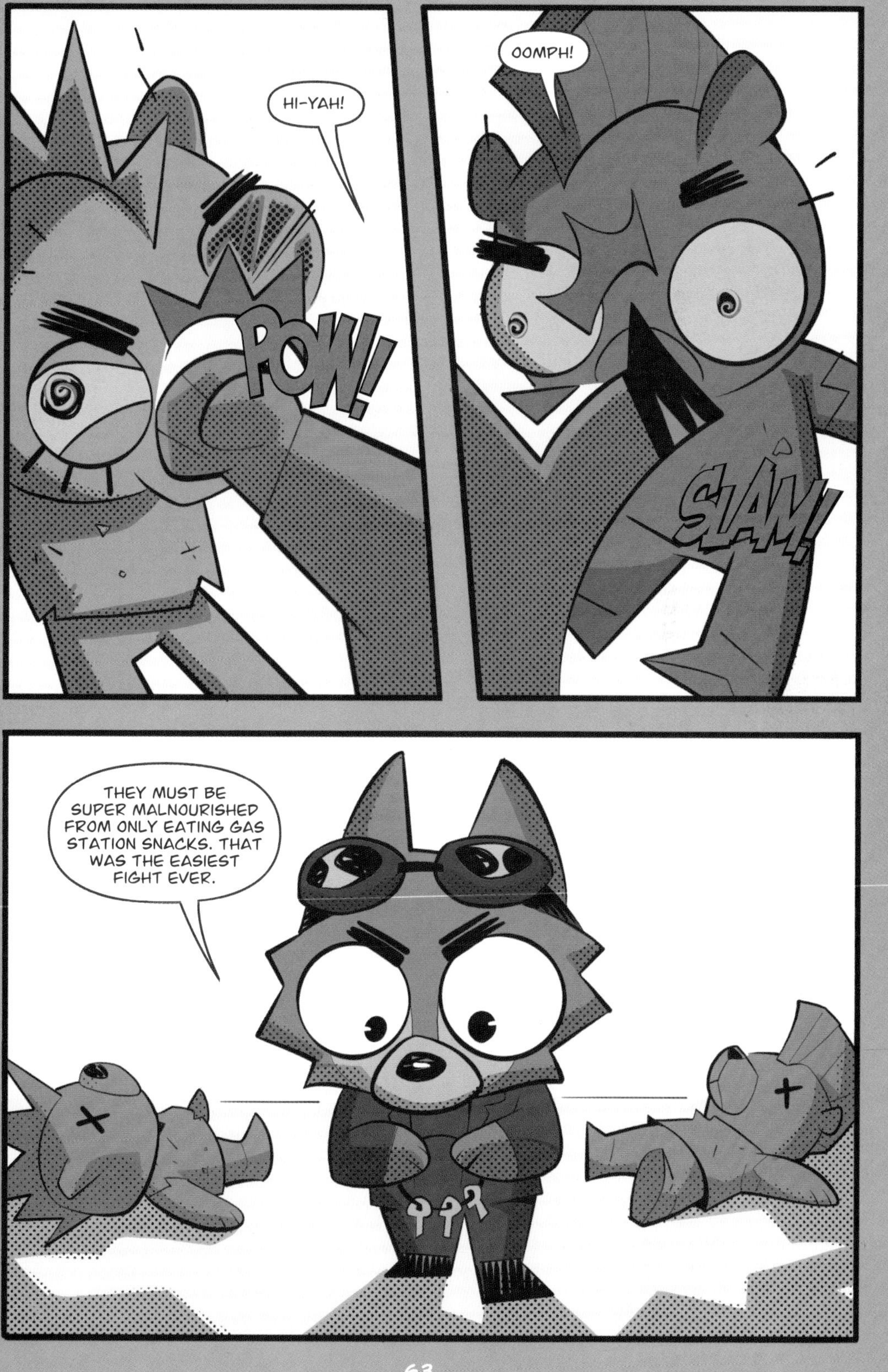
HI-YAH!
POW!
OOMPH!
SLAM!
THEY MUST BE SUPER MALNOURISHED FROM ONLY EATING GAS STATION SNACKS. THAT WAS THE EASIEST FIGHT EVER.

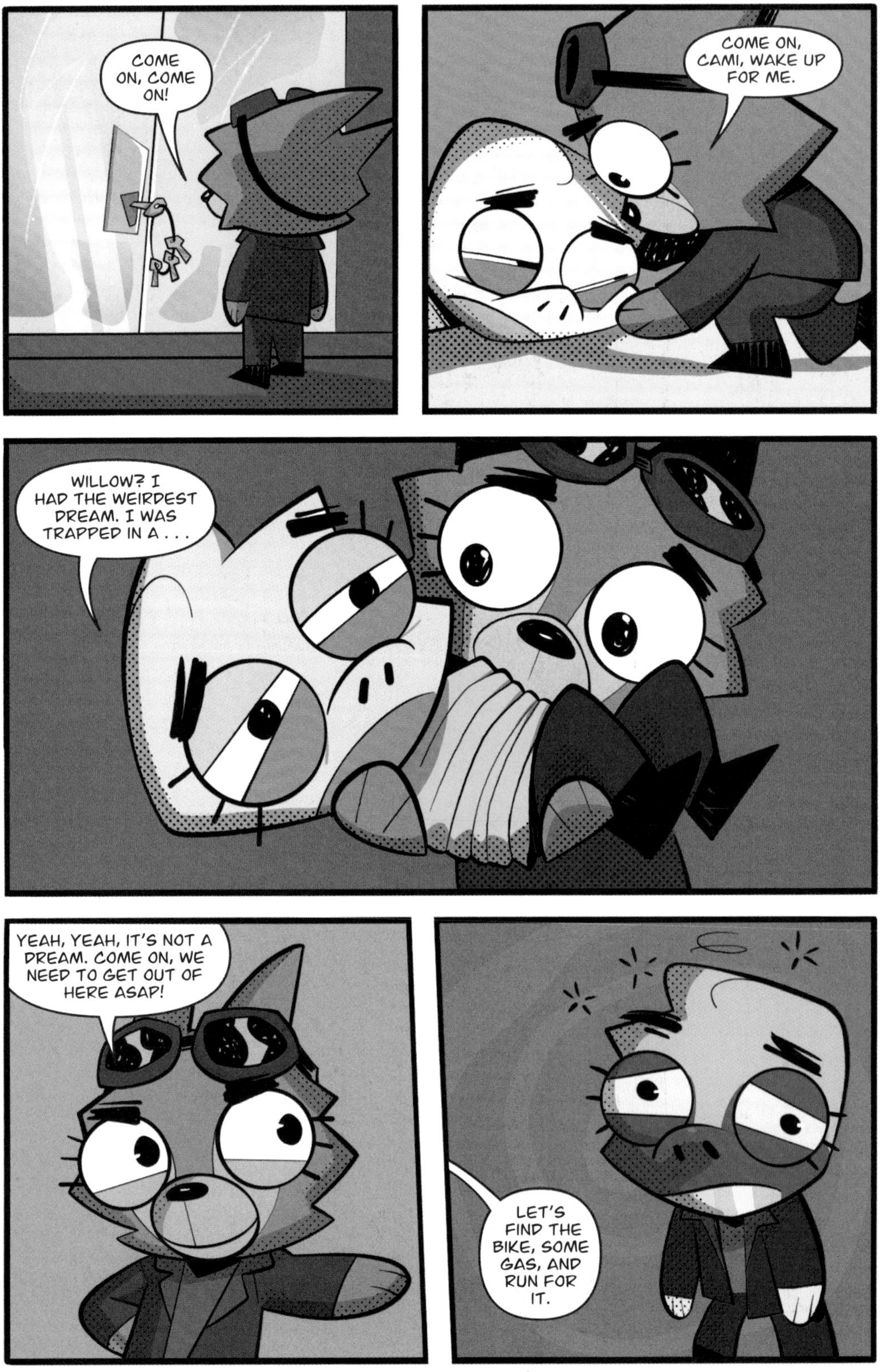
COME ON, COME ON!
COME ON, CAMI, WAKE UP FOR ME.
WILLOW? I HAD THE WEIRDEST DREAM. I WAS TRAPPED IN A . . .
YEAH, YEAH, IT'S NOT A DREAM. COME ON, WE NEED TO GET OUT OF HERE ASAP!
LET'S FIND THE BIKE, SOME GAS, AND RUN FOR IT.

BZZZT!

WHIRRRRR!

BANG!

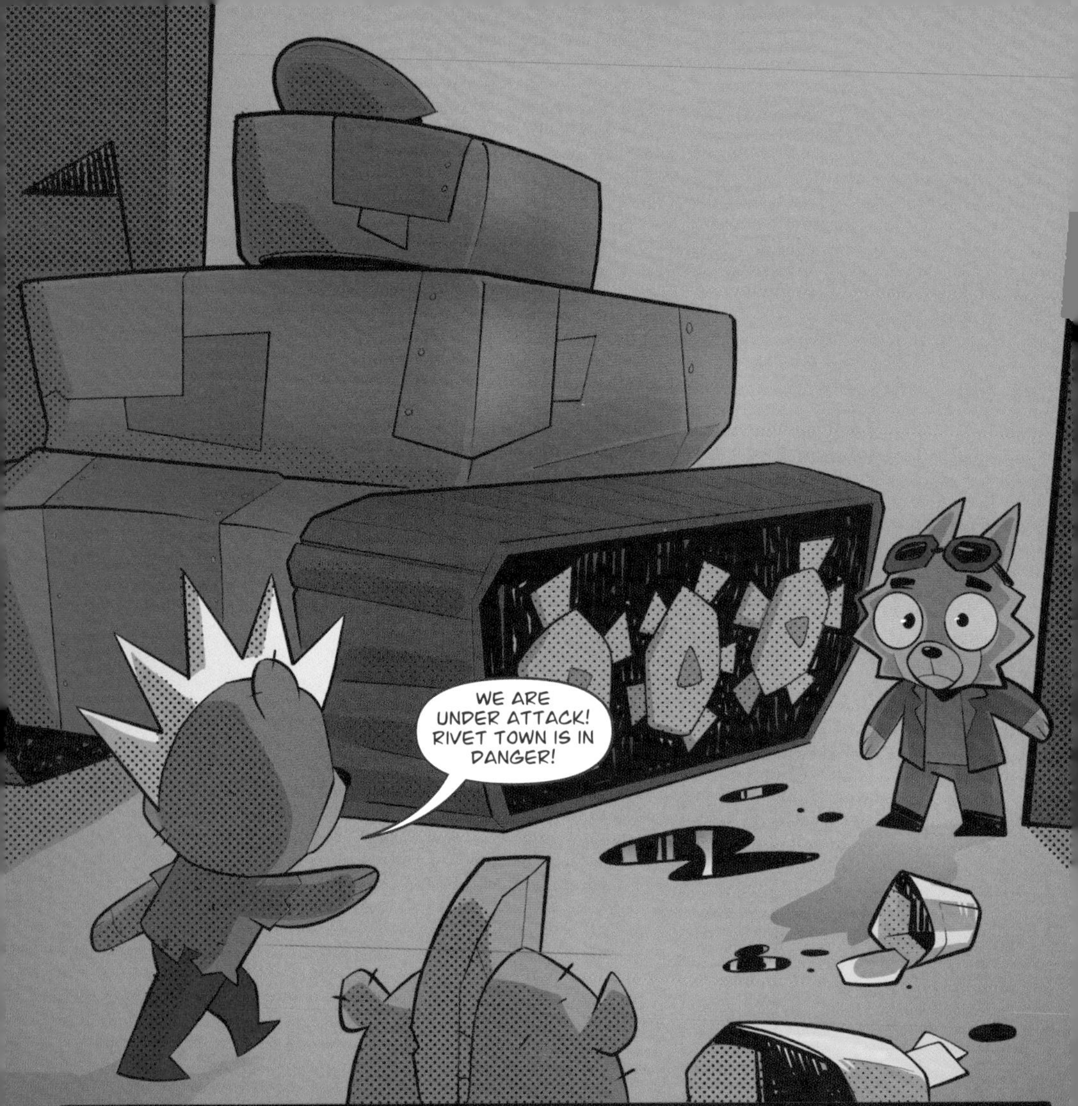
WE ARE UNDER ATTACK! RIVET TOWN IS IN DANGER!

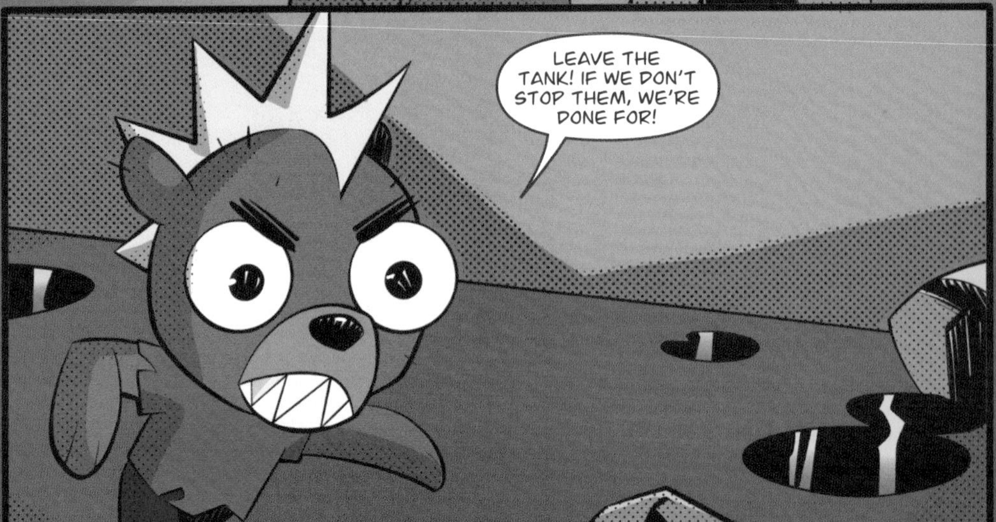
LEAVE THE TANK! IF WE DON'T STOP THEM, WE'RE DONE FOR!

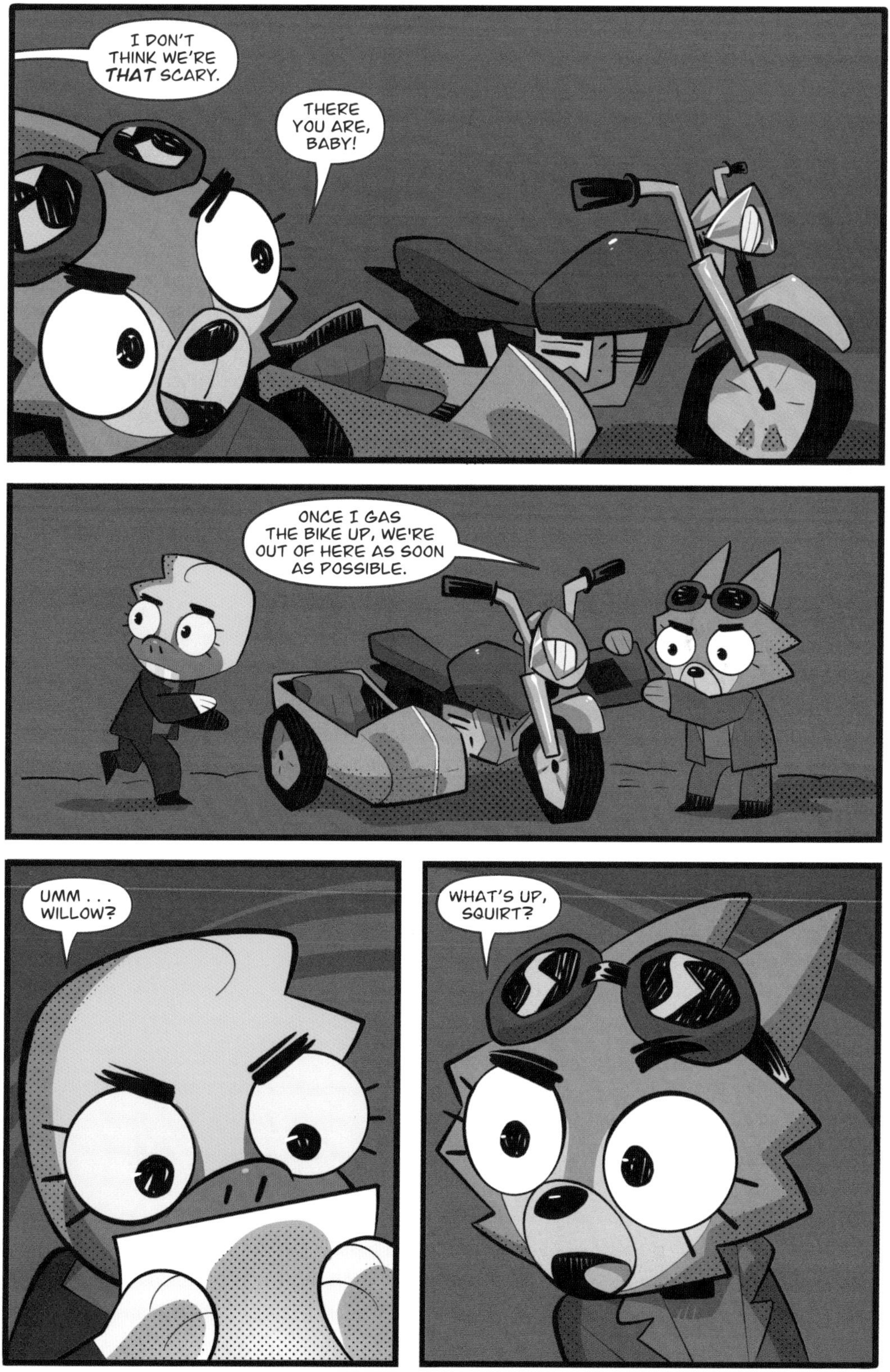

I DON'T THINK WE'RE *THAT* SCARY.
THERE YOU ARE, BABY!
ONCE I GAS THE BIKE UP, WE'RE OUT OF HERE AS SOON AS POSSIBLE.
UMM . . . WILLOW?
WHAT'S UP, SQUIRT?

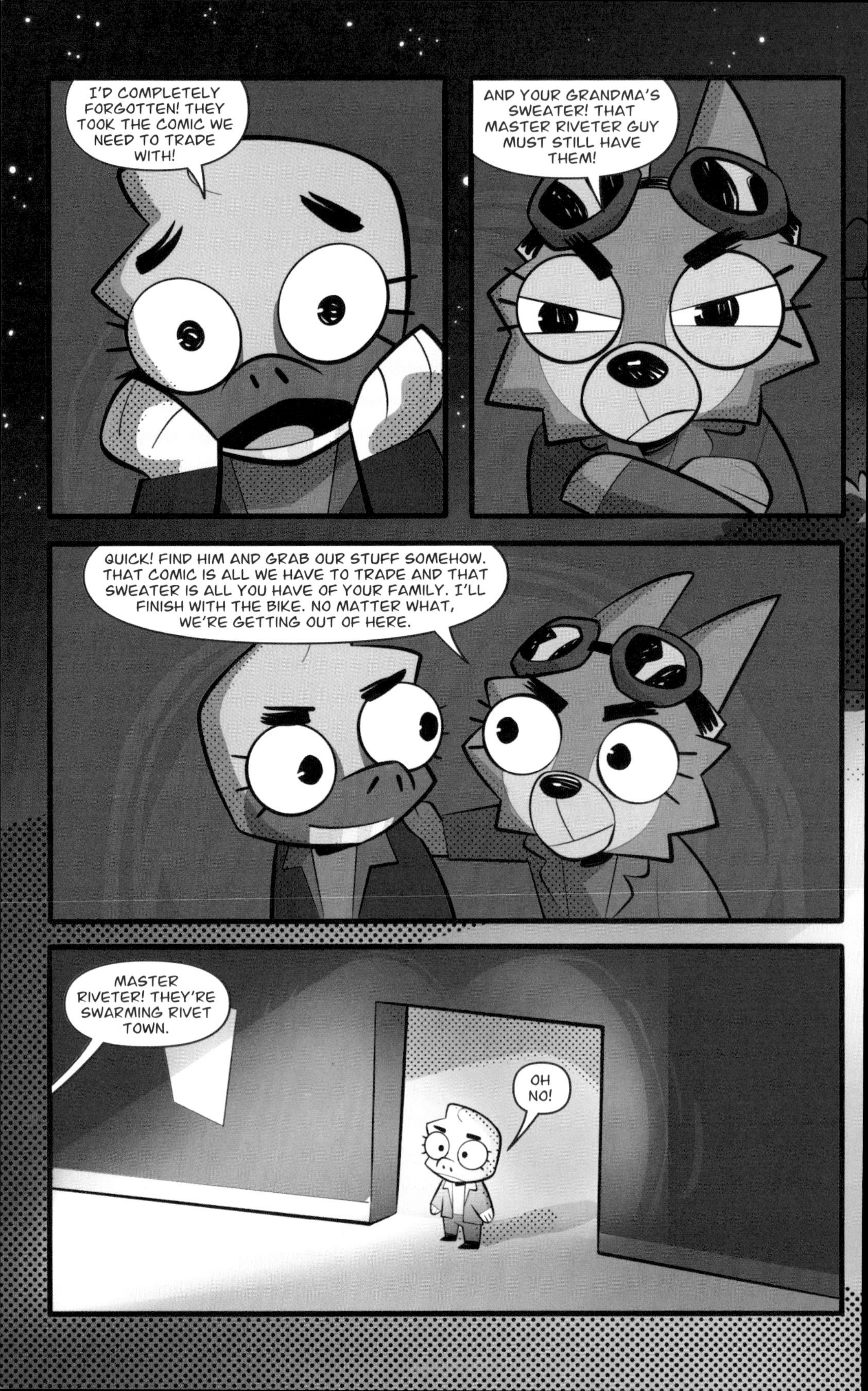
I'D COMPLETELY FORGOTTEN! THEY TOOK THE COMIC WE NEED TO TRADE WITH!
AND YOUR GRANDMA'S SWEATER! THAT MASTER RIVETER GUY MUST STILL HAVE THEM!
QUICK! FIND HIM AND GRAB OUR STUFF SOMEHOW. THAT COMIC IS ALL WE HAVE TO TRADE AND THAT SWEATER IS ALL YOU HAVE OF YOUR FAMILY. I'LL FINISH WITH THE BIKE. NO MATTER WHAT, WE'RE GETTING OUT OF HERE.
MASTER RIVETER! THEY'RE SWARMING RIVET TOWN.
OH NO!

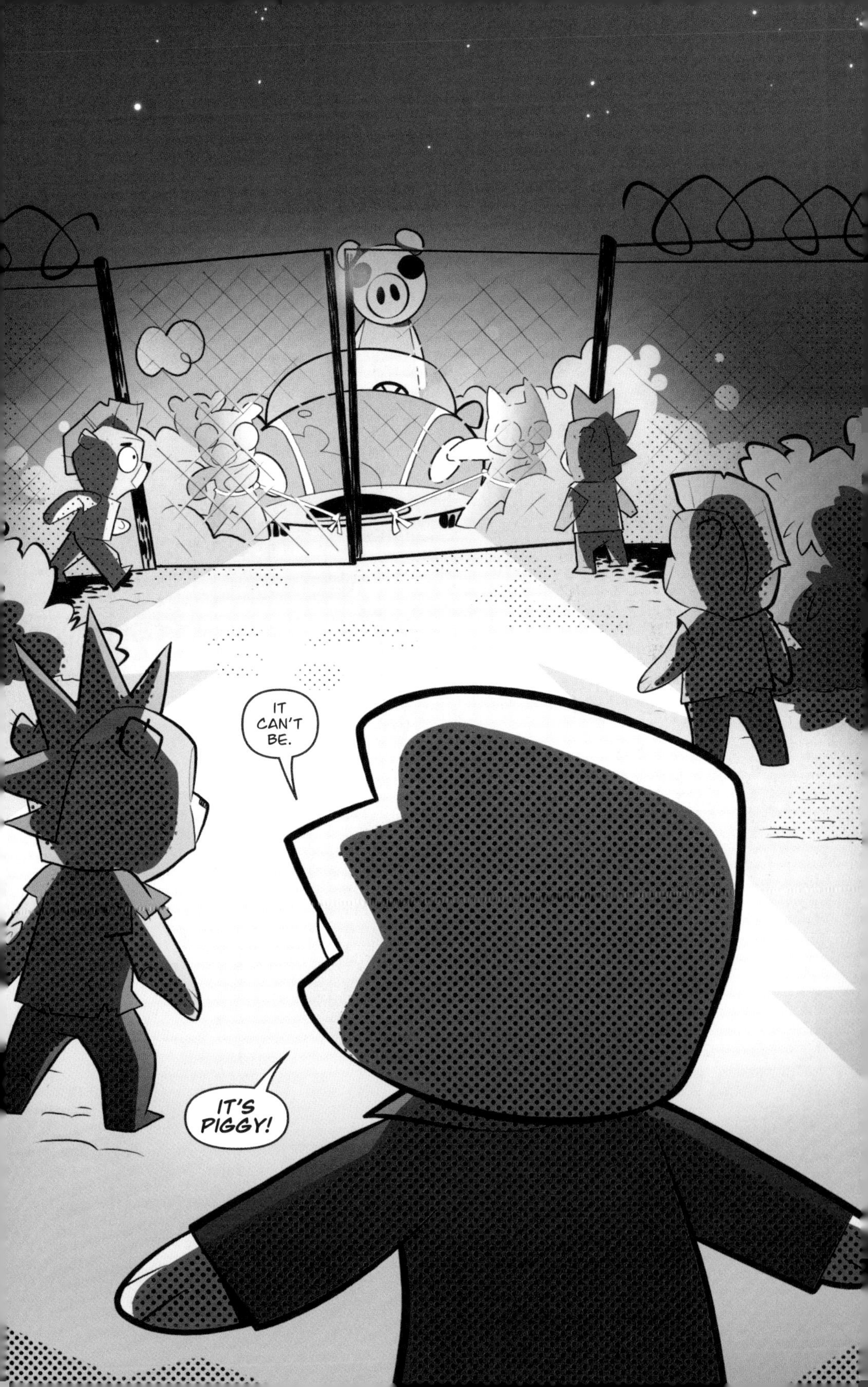
IT CAN'T BE.
IT'S PIGGY!

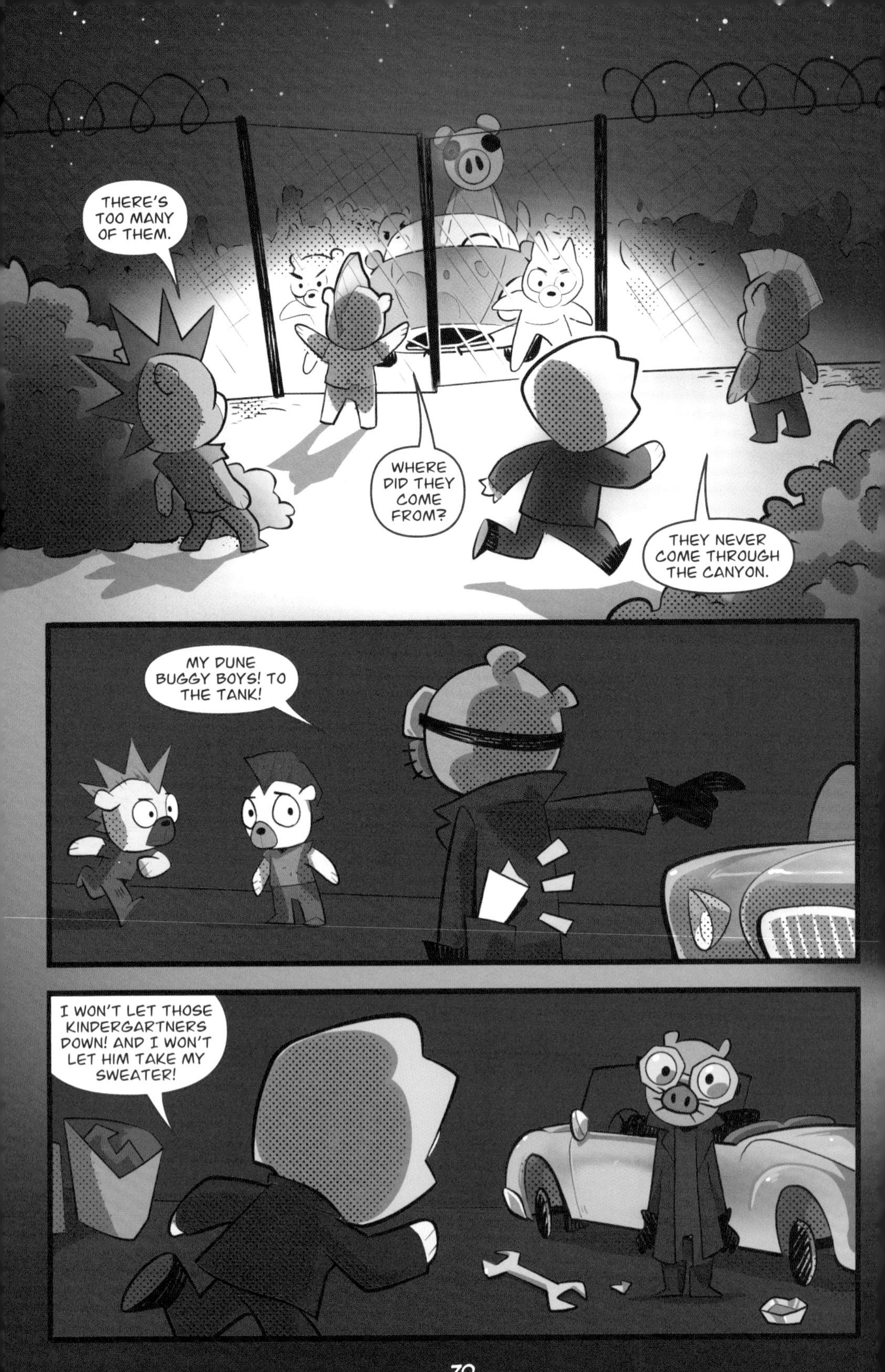
THERE'S TOO MANY OF THEM.
WHERE DID THEY COME FROM?
THEY NEVER COME THROUGH THE CANYON.
MY DUNE BUGGY BOYS! TO THE TANK!
I WON'T LET THOSE KINDERGARTNERS DOWN! AND I WON'T LET HIM TAKE MY SWEATER!

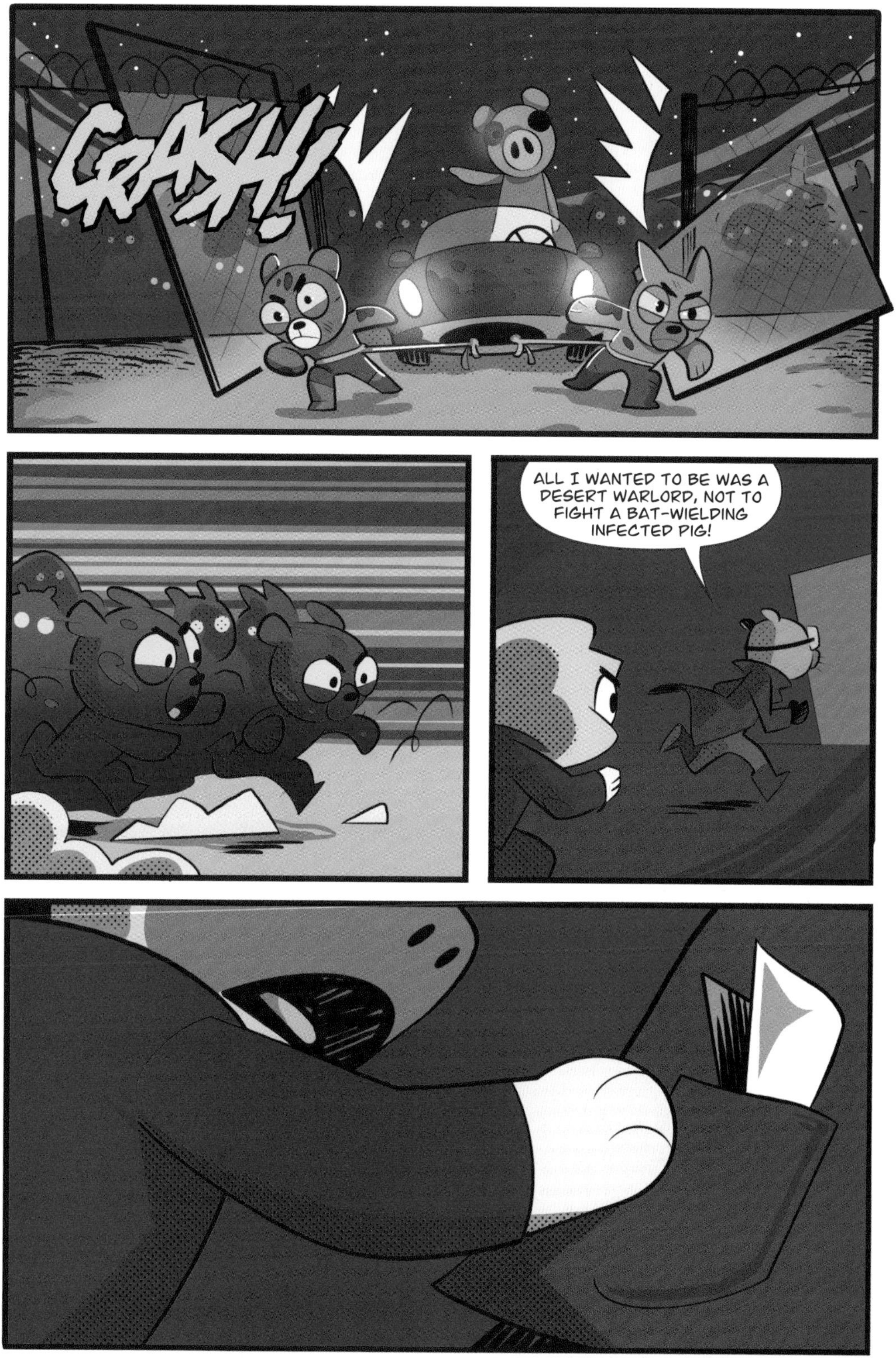
CRASH!
ALL I WANTED TO BE WAS A DESERT WARLORD, NOT TO FIGHT A BAT-WIELDING INFECTED PIG!

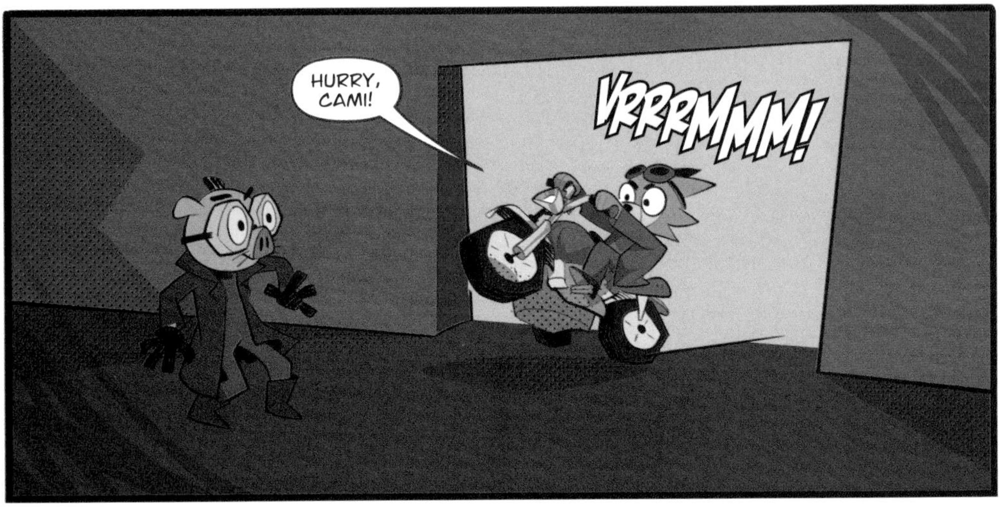
HURRY, CAMI!
VRRRMMM!

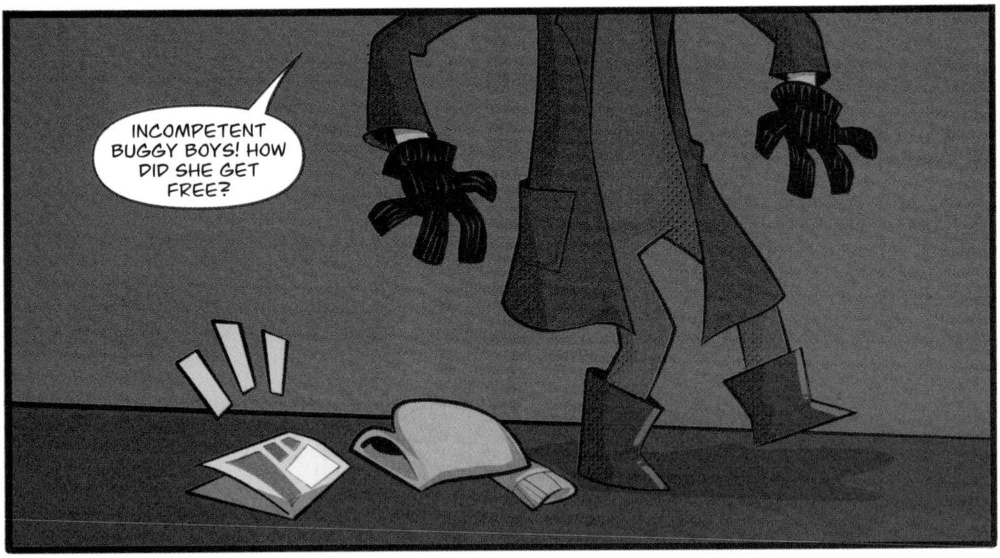
INCOMPETENT BUGGY BOYS! HOW DID SHE GET FREE?

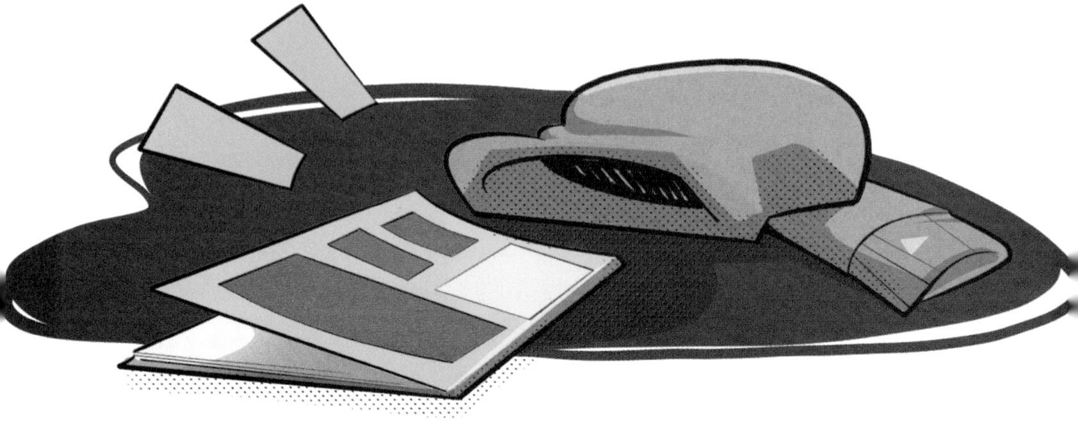

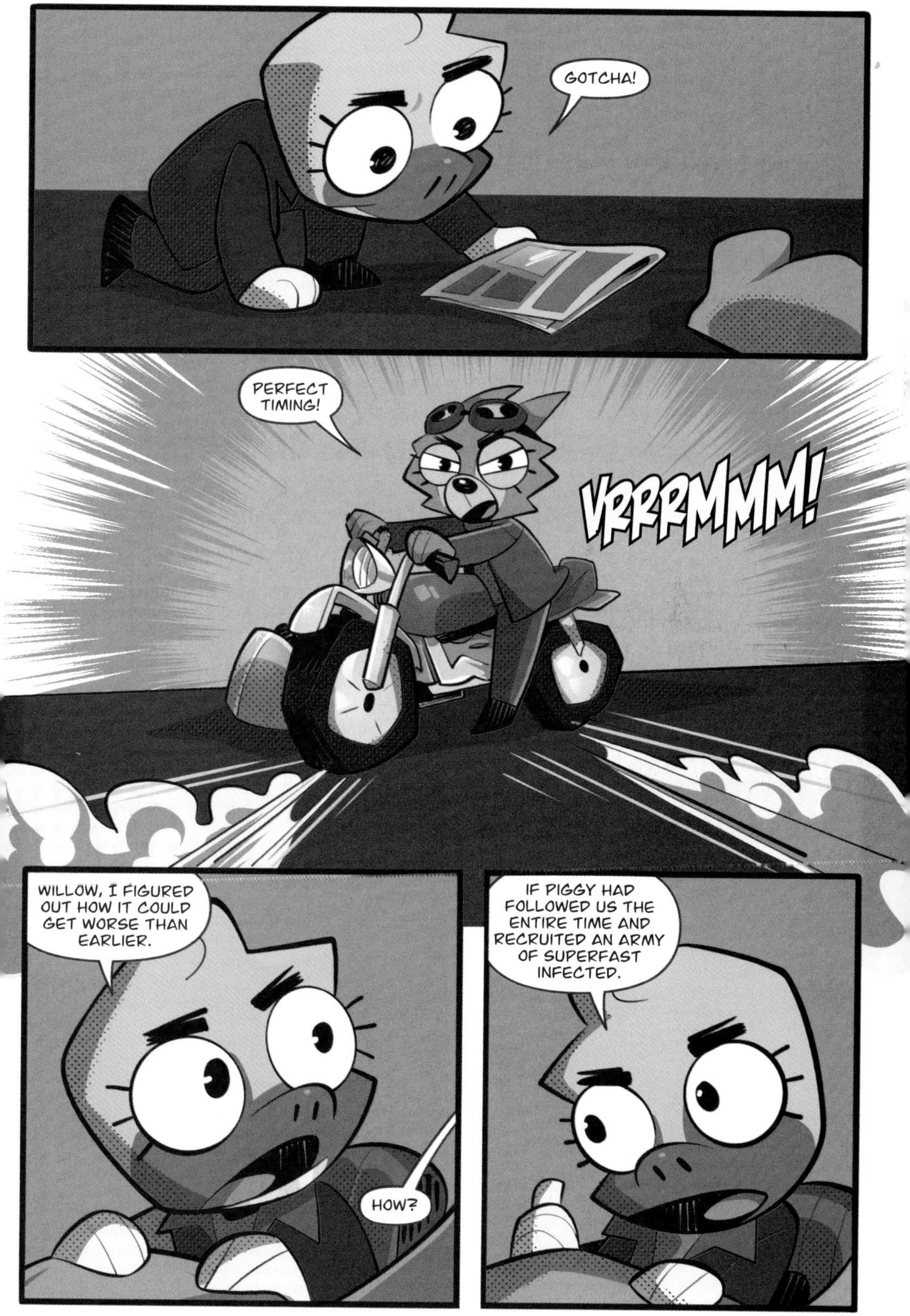
GOTCHA!
PERFECT TIMING!
VRRRMMM!
WILLOW, I FIGURED OUT HOW IT COULD GET WORSE THAN EARLIER.
HOW?
IF PIGGY HAD FOLLOWED US THE ENTIRE TIME AND RECRUITED AN ARMY OF SUPERFAST INFECTED.

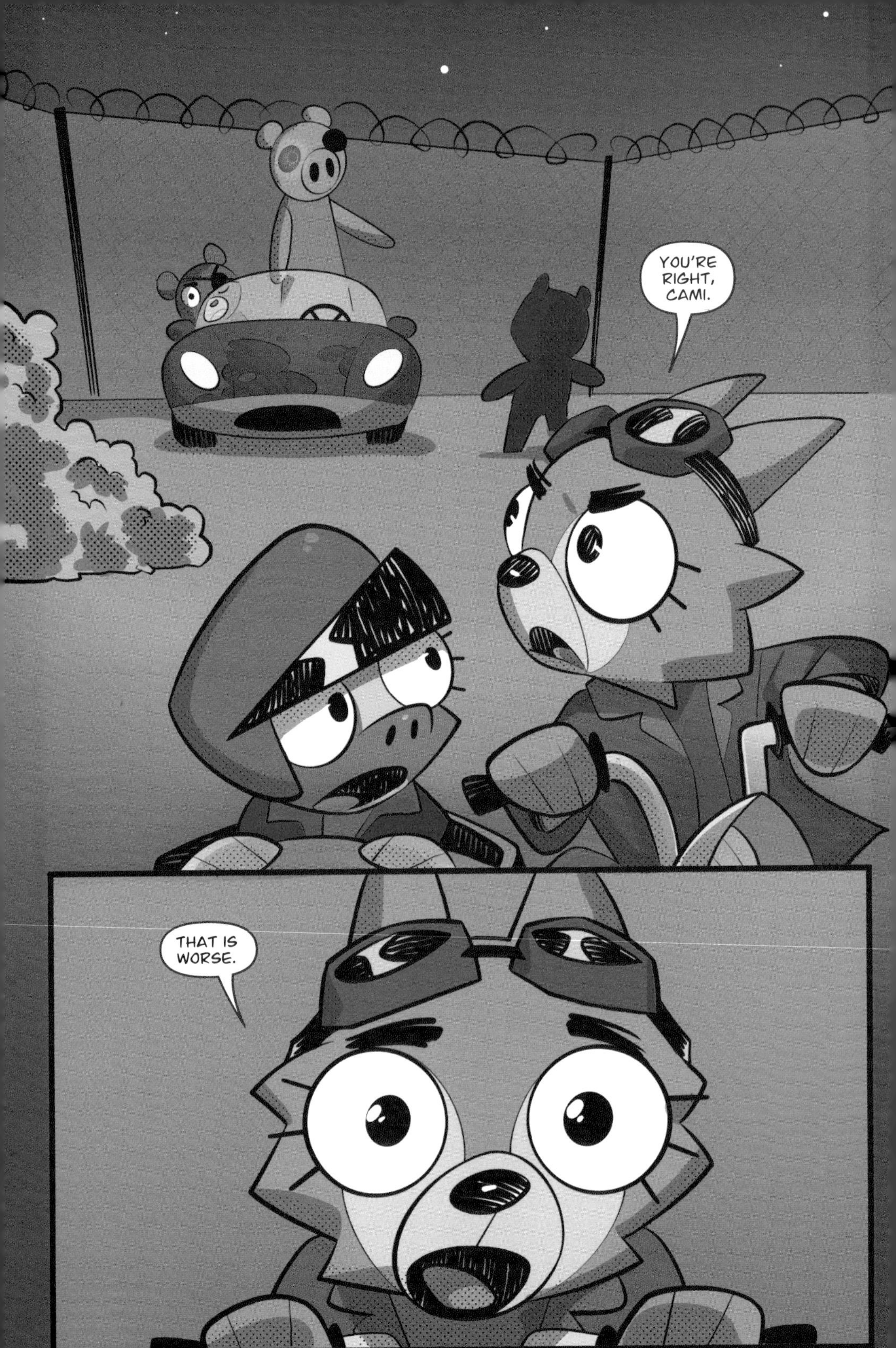
YOU'RE RIGHT, CAMI.
THAT IS WORSE.

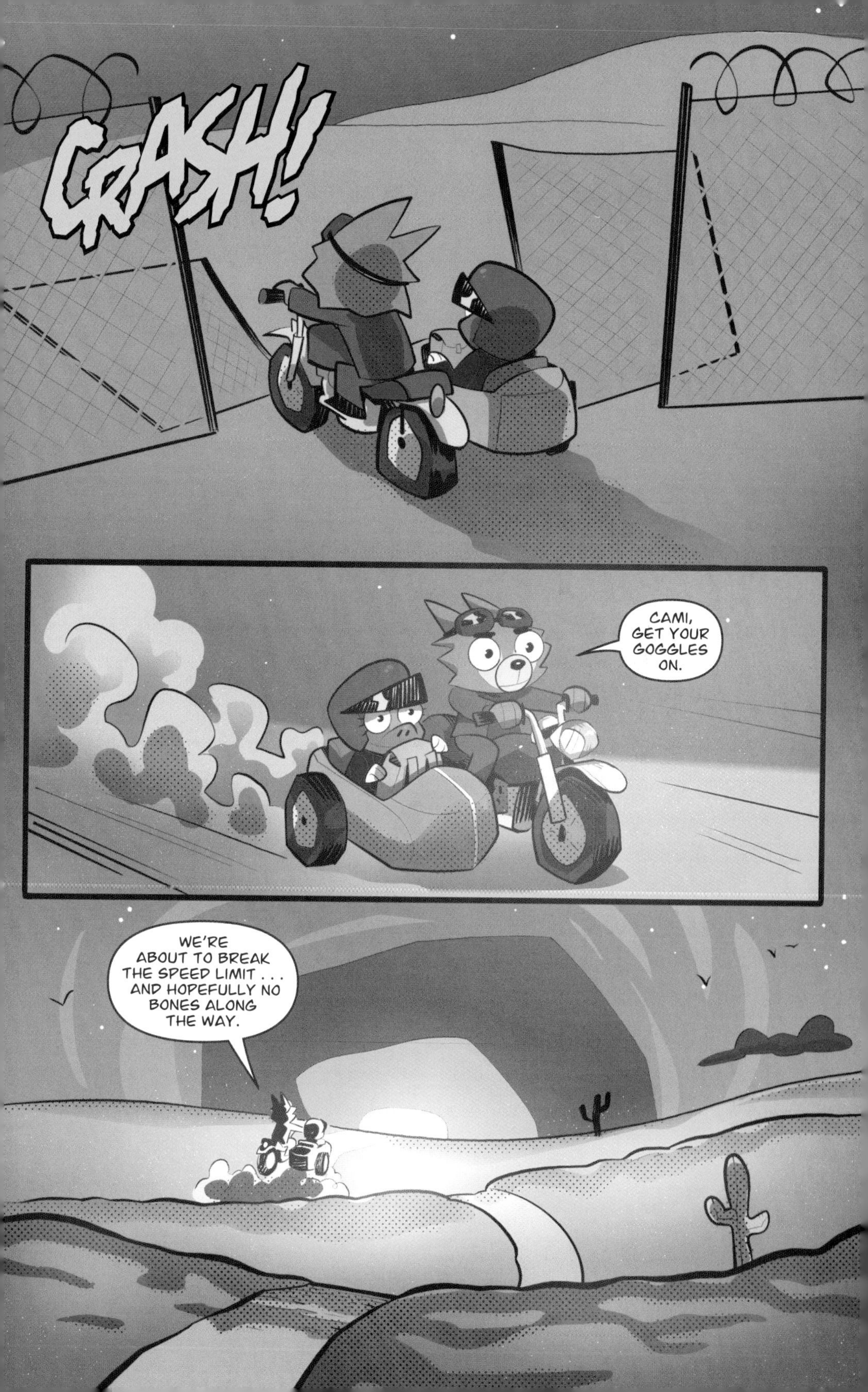
CRASH!
CAMI, GET YOUR GOGGLES ON.
WE'RE ABOUT TO BREAK THE SPEED LIMIT . . . AND HOPEFULLY NO BONES ALONG THE WAY.

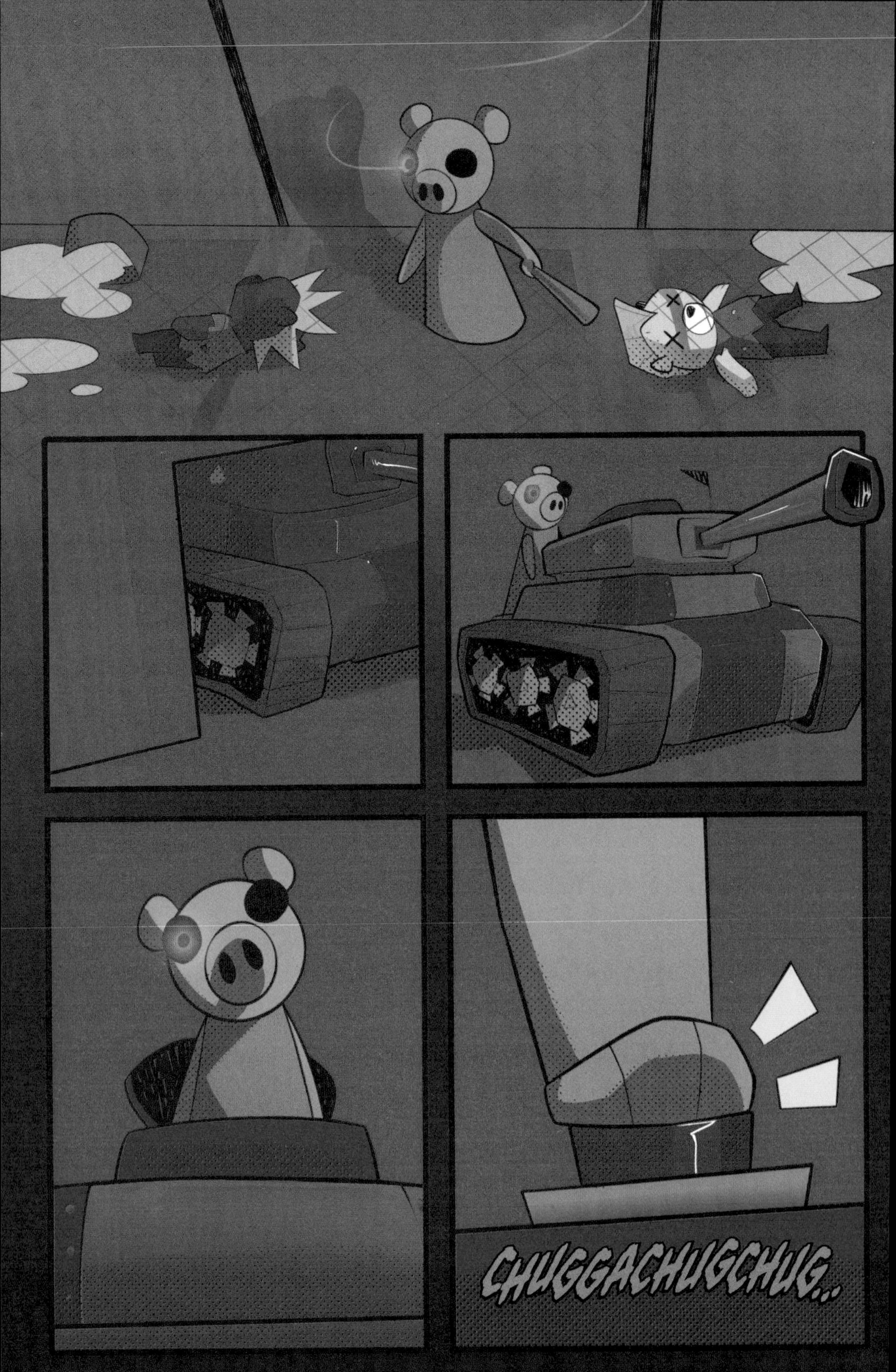
CHUGGACHUGCHUG..

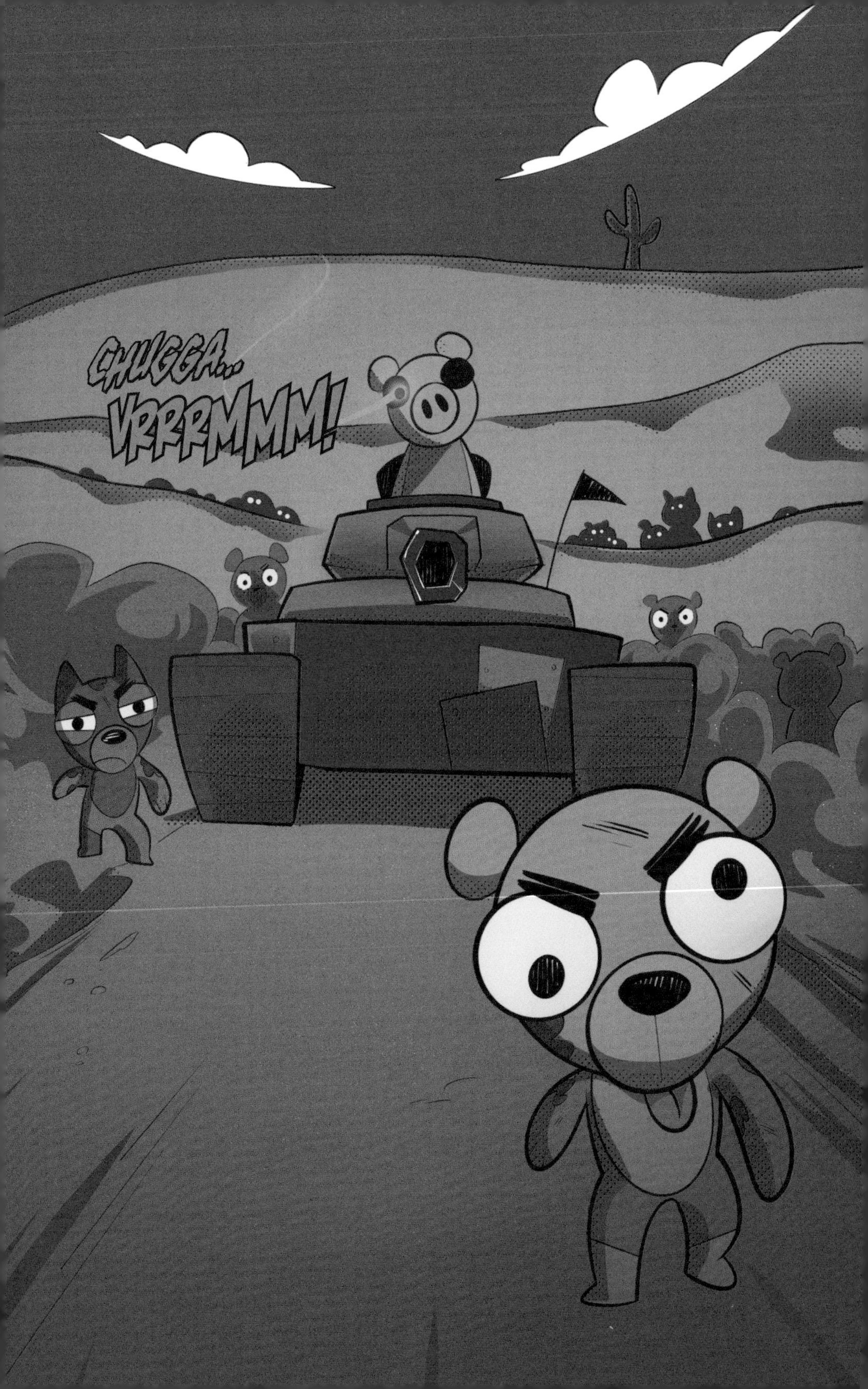
CHUGGA...
VRRRMMM!

# CHAPTER: 4

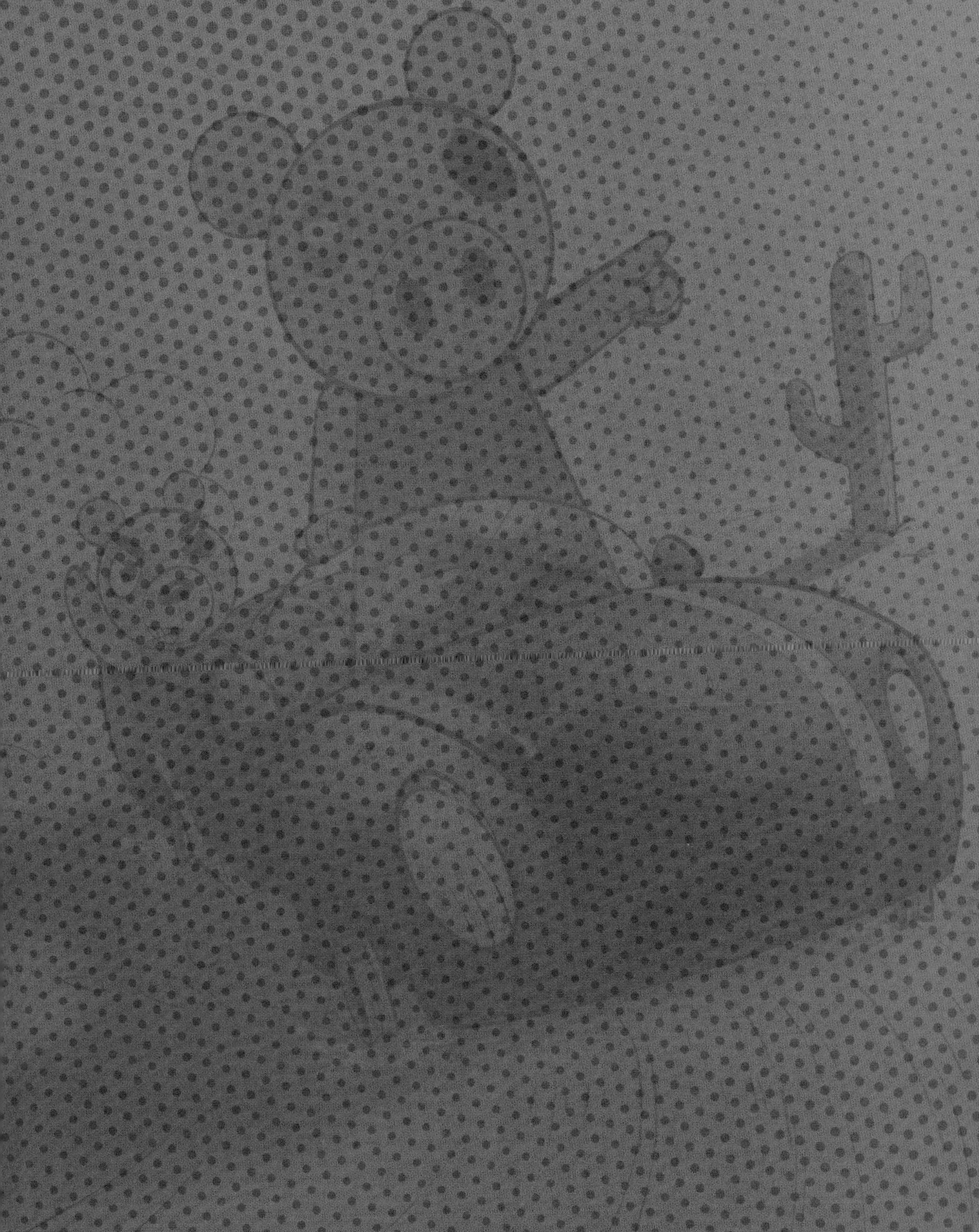

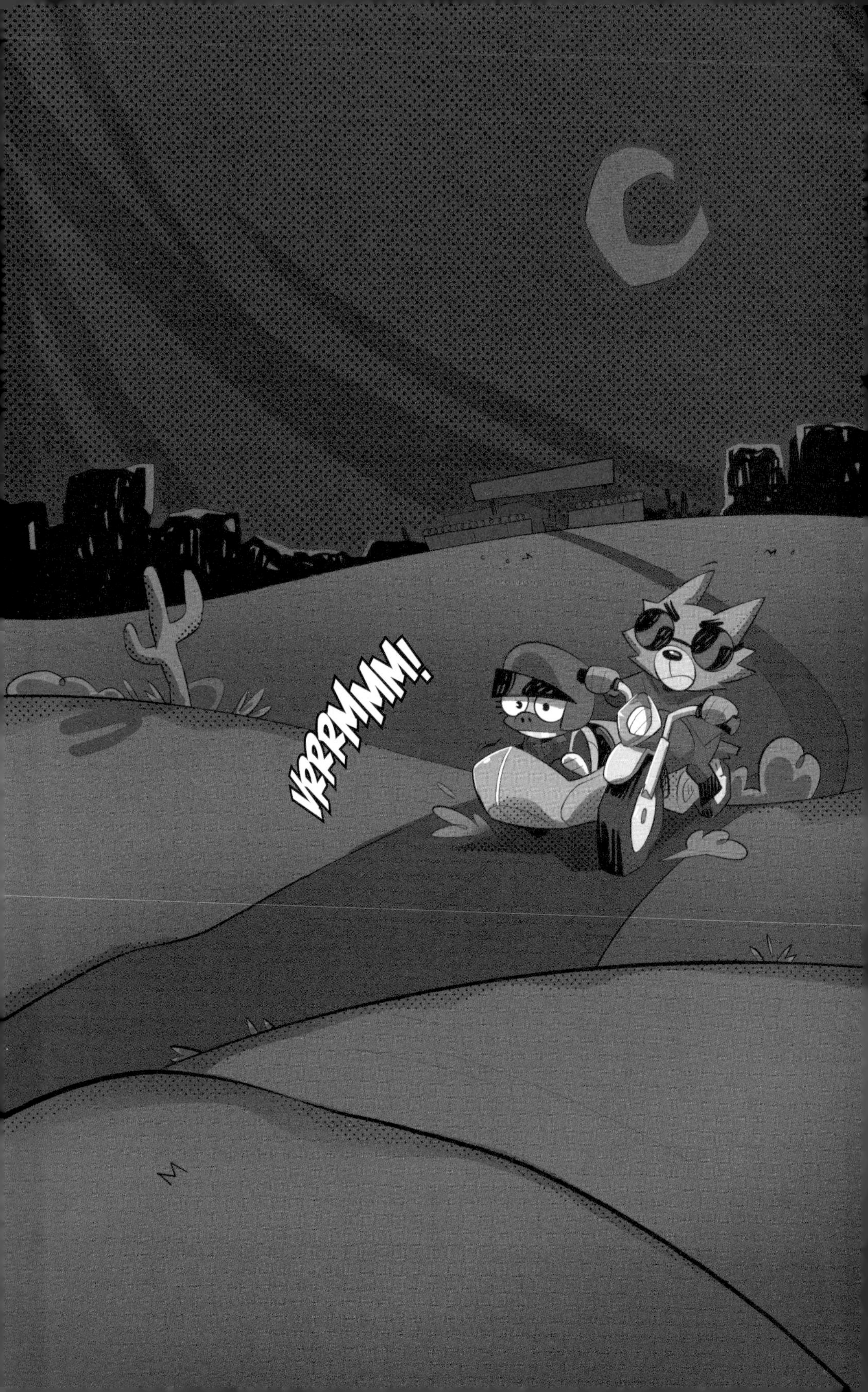
VRRRMMM!

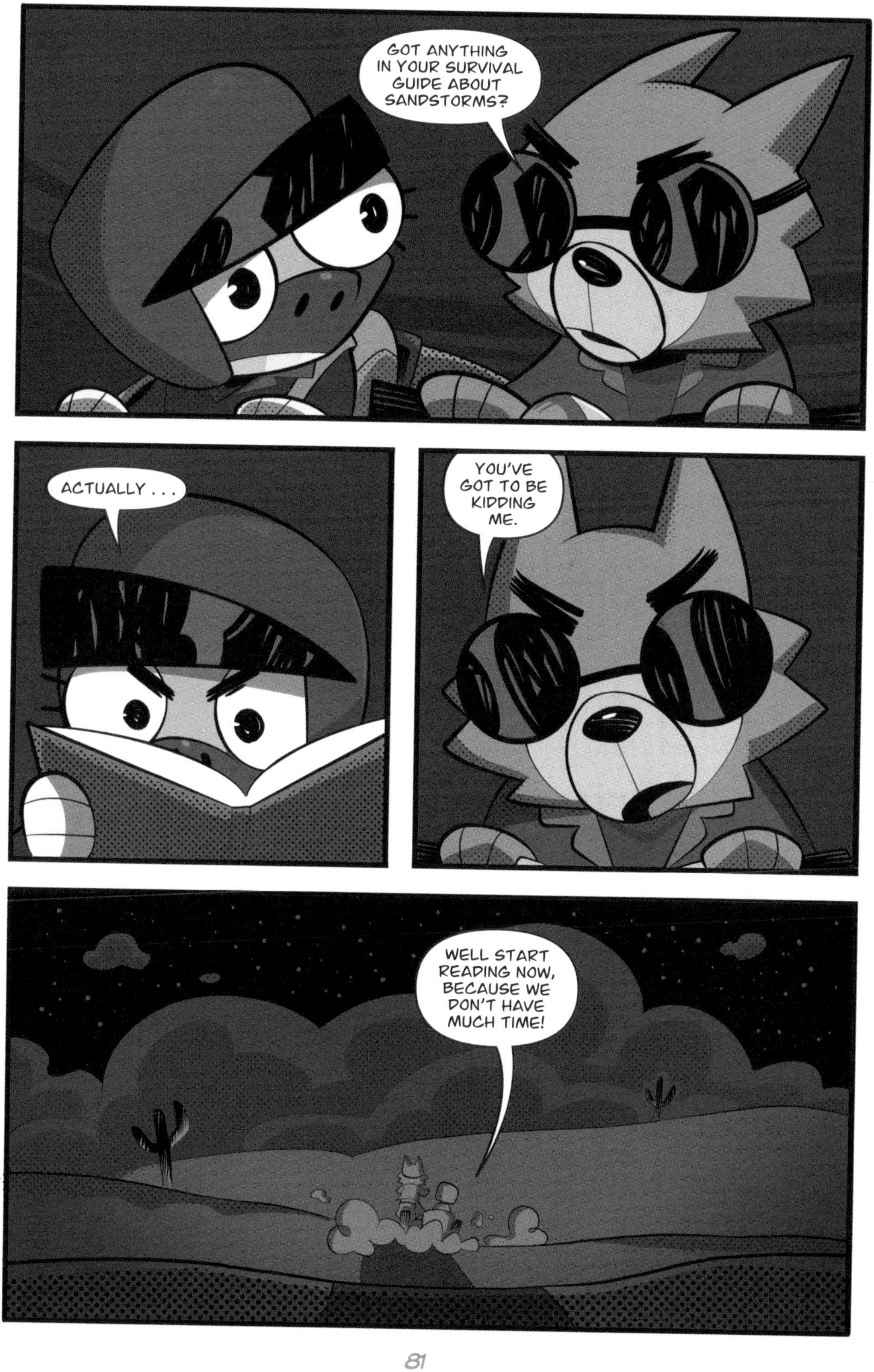
GOT ANYTHING IN YOUR SURVIVAL GUIDE ABOUT SANDSTORMS?
ACTUALLY . . .
YOU'VE GOT TO BE KIDDING ME.
WELL START READING NOW, BECAUSE WE DON'T HAVE MUCH TIME!

# The Silver Paw Survival Tips - Sandstorms

**Tip 1** – Being in a sandstorm is very dangerous, and so all efforts should be made to find shelter fast. If you are caught in one, your primary goal is to protect your lungs. Cover your face with filtering material and pour a little water on the stuff to keep it moist. If you have petroleum jelly, you can also apply it on your face to retain moisture.

**Tip 2** – Next, protect your eyes from sand by putting on goggles or other protective eyewear. It may be harder to see, but keeping your eyes safe is more important than looking cool.

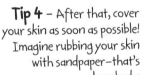

**Tip 3** – We don't think about our ears, but they're another sensitive spot on our bodies that can be hurt by sand. Be sure to cover them, too.

**Tip 4** – After that, cover your skin as soon as possible! Imagine rubbing your skin with sandpaper–that's how bad a sandstorm can get.

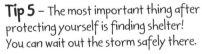

**Tip 5** – The most important thing after protecting yourself is finding shelter! You can wait out the storm safely there.

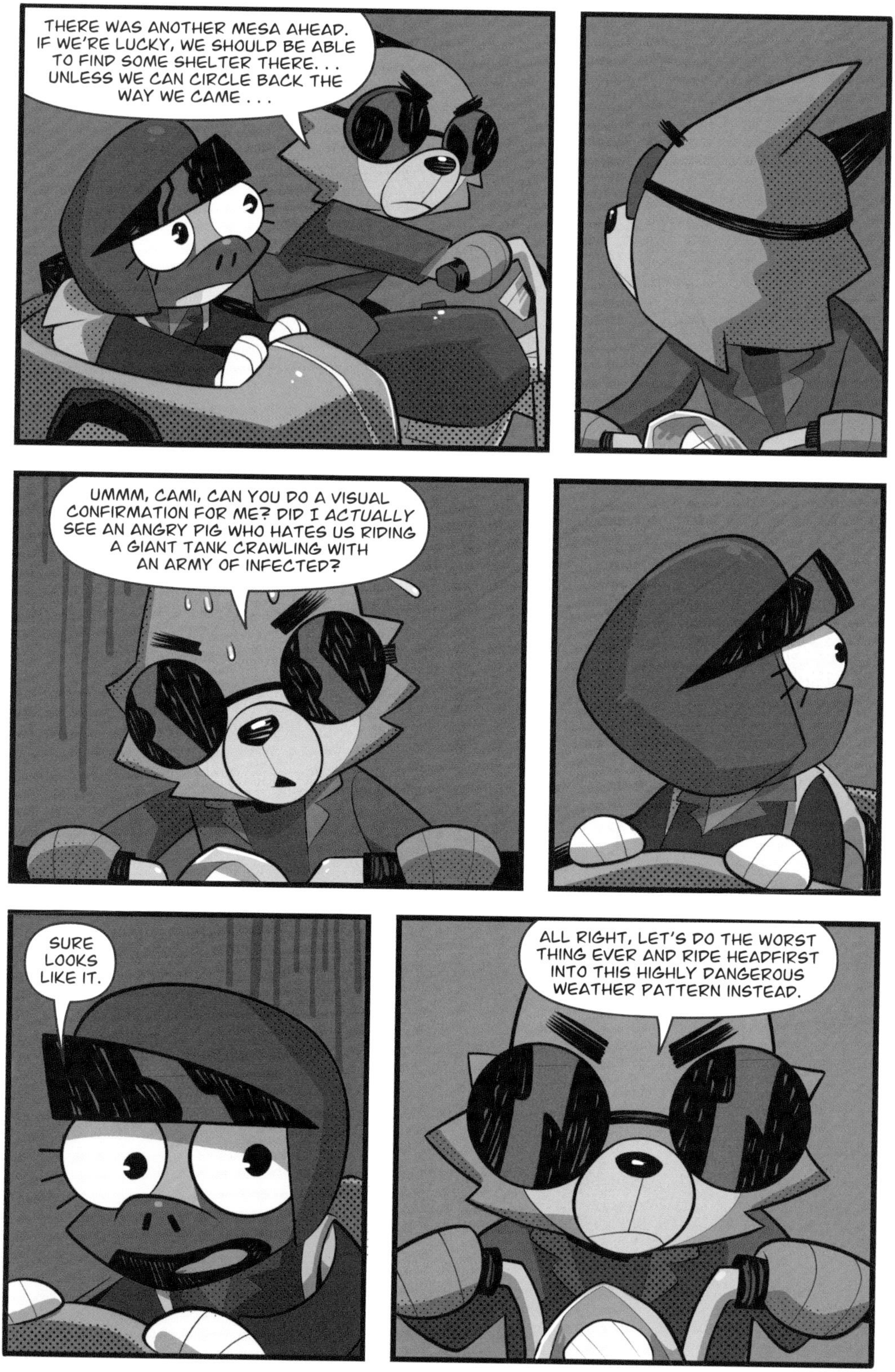
THERE WAS ANOTHER MESA AHEAD. IF WE'RE LUCKY, WE SHOULD BE ABLE TO FIND SOME SHELTER THERE. . . UNLESS WE CAN CIRCLE BACK THE WAY WE CAME . . .
UMMM, CAMI, CAN YOU DO A VISUAL CONFIRMATION FOR ME? DID I ACTUALLY SEE AN ANGRY PIG WHO HATES US RIDING A GIANT TANK CRAWLING WITH AN ARMY OF INFECTED?
SURE LOOKS LIKE IT.
ALL RIGHT, LET'S DO THE WORST THING EVER AND RIDE HEADFIRST INTO THIS HIGHLY DANGEROUS WEATHER PATTERN INSTEAD.

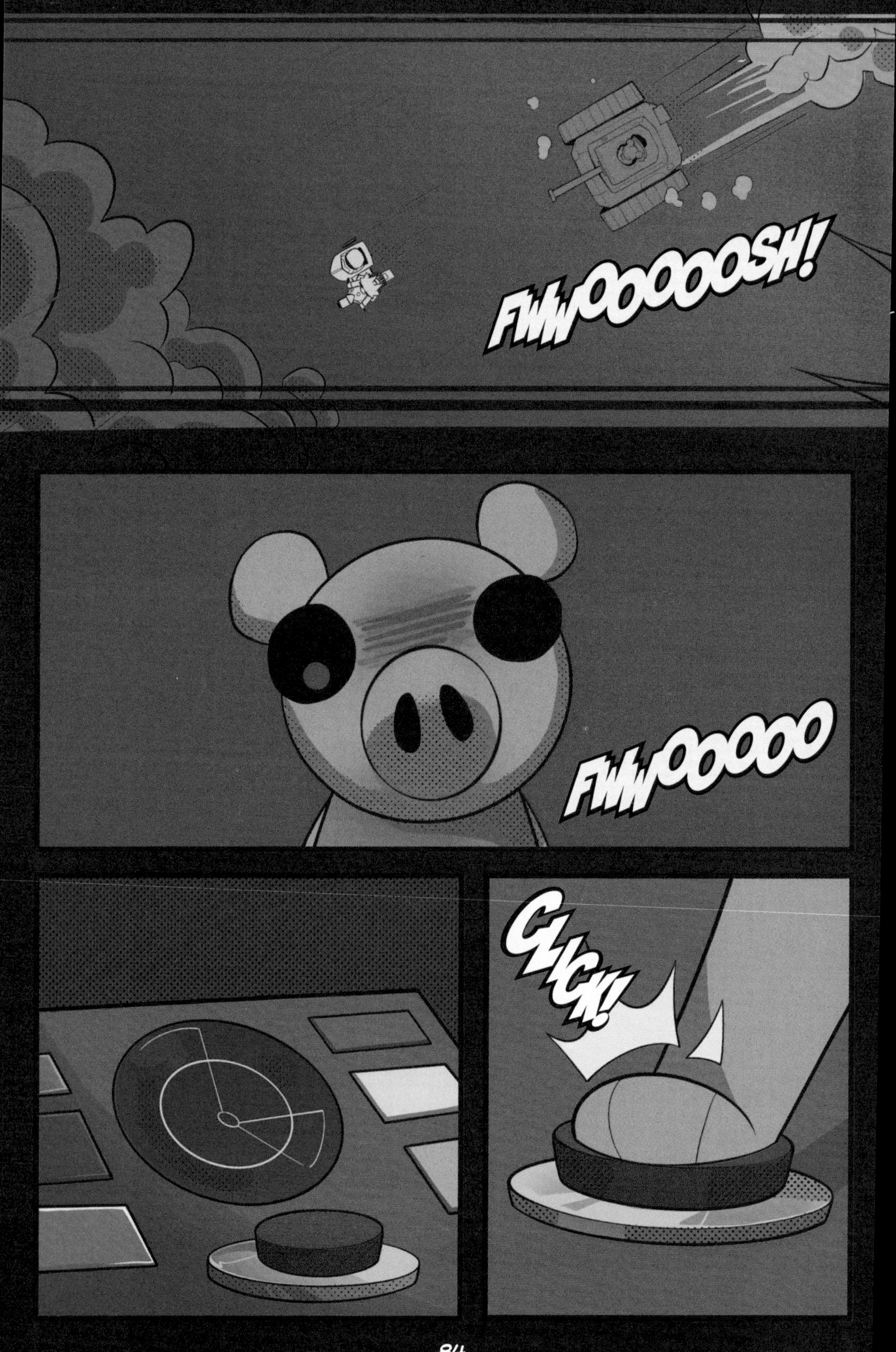
FWWOOOOOOSH!
FWWOOOOO
CLICK!

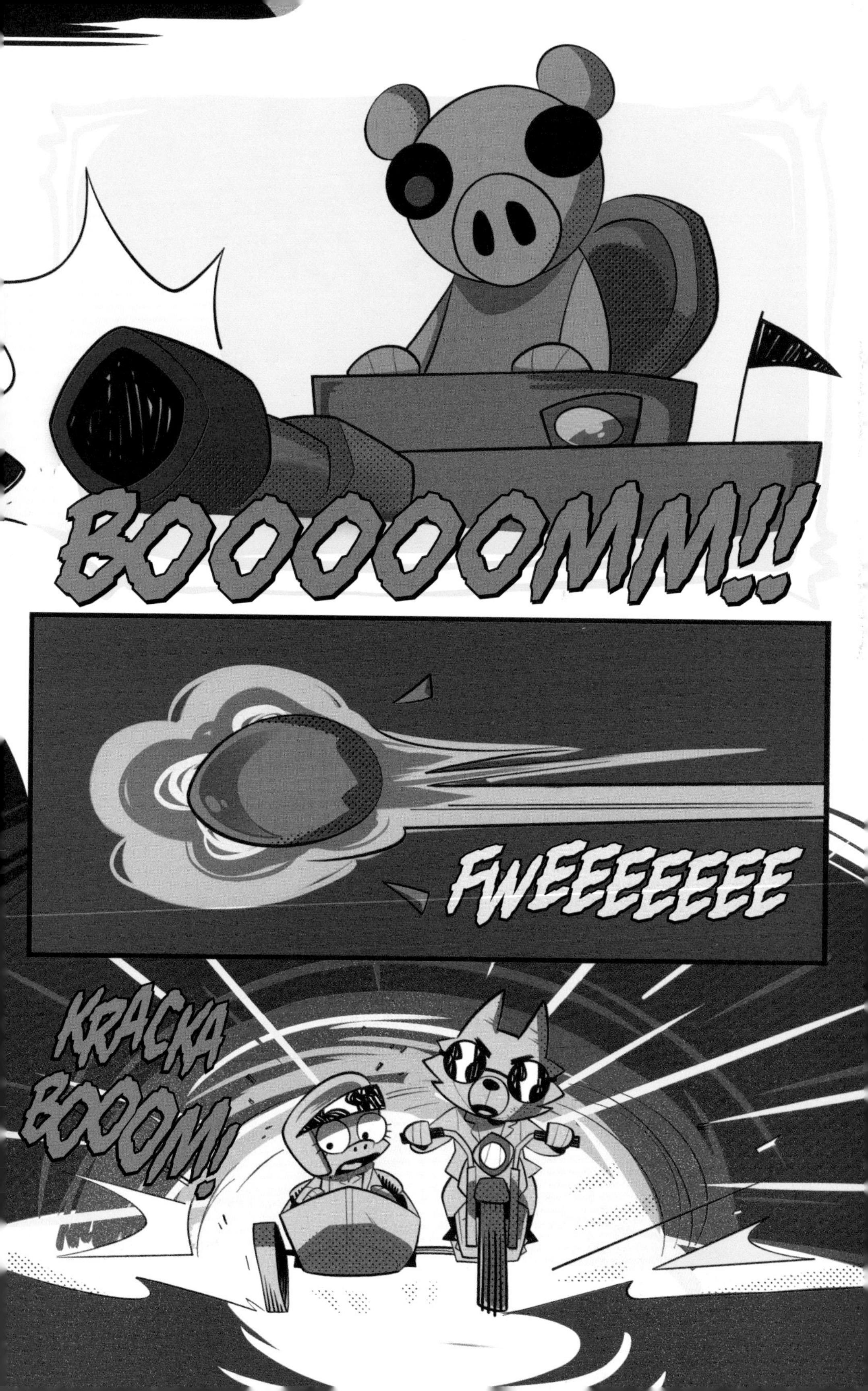
BOOOOOMM!!
FWEEEEEEE
KRACKA BOOOM!

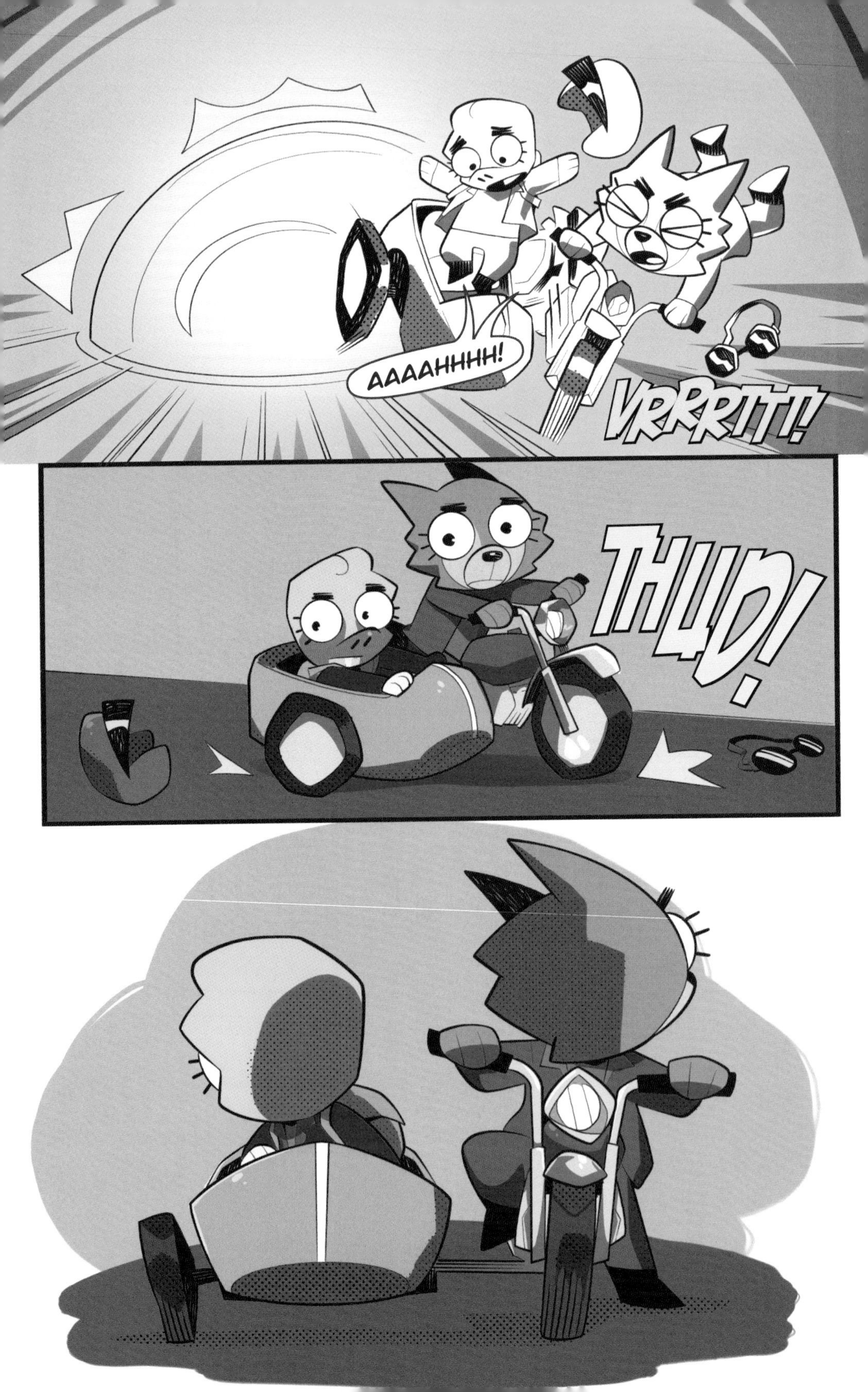
AAAAHHHH!
VRRRITT!
THUD!

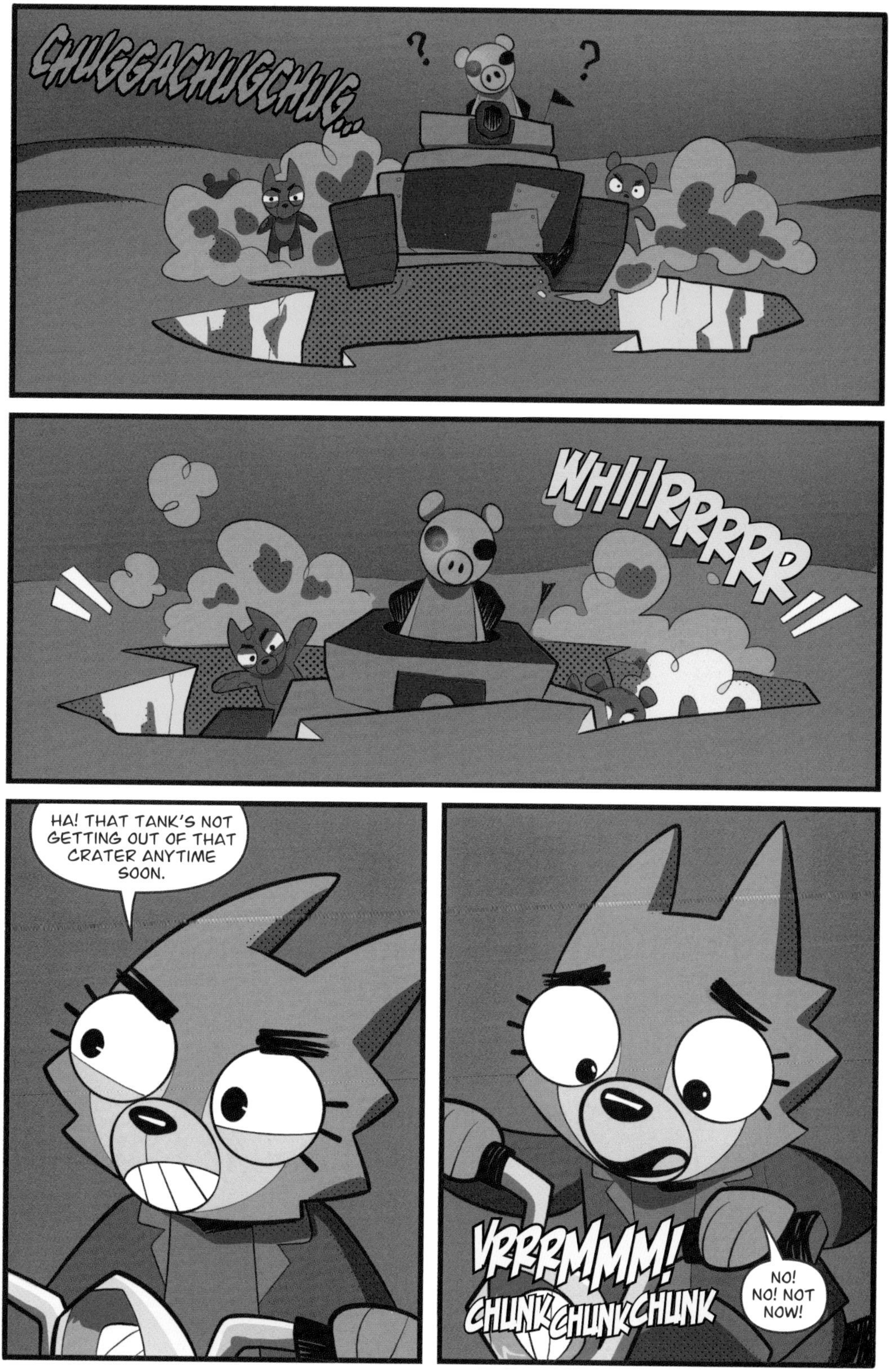
CHUGGACHUGCHUG...
? ?
WHIIIRRRRR
HA! THAT TANK'S NOT GETTING OUT OF THAT CRATER ANYTIME SOON.
VRRRMMM!
CHUNKCHUNKCHUNK
NO! NO! NOT NOW!

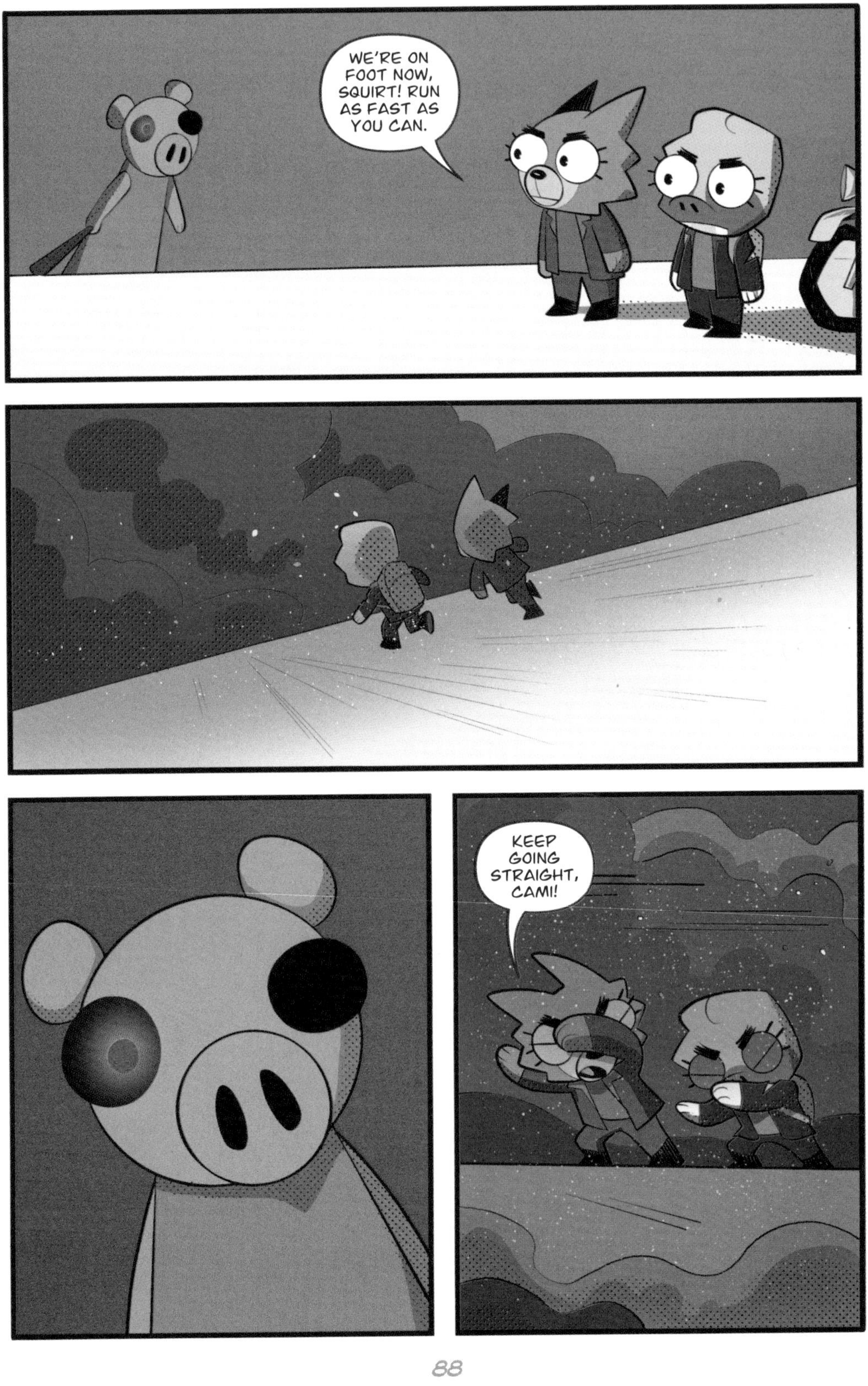
WE'RE ON FOOT NOW, SQUIRT! RUN AS FAST AS YOU CAN.
KEEP GOING STRAIGHT, CAMI!

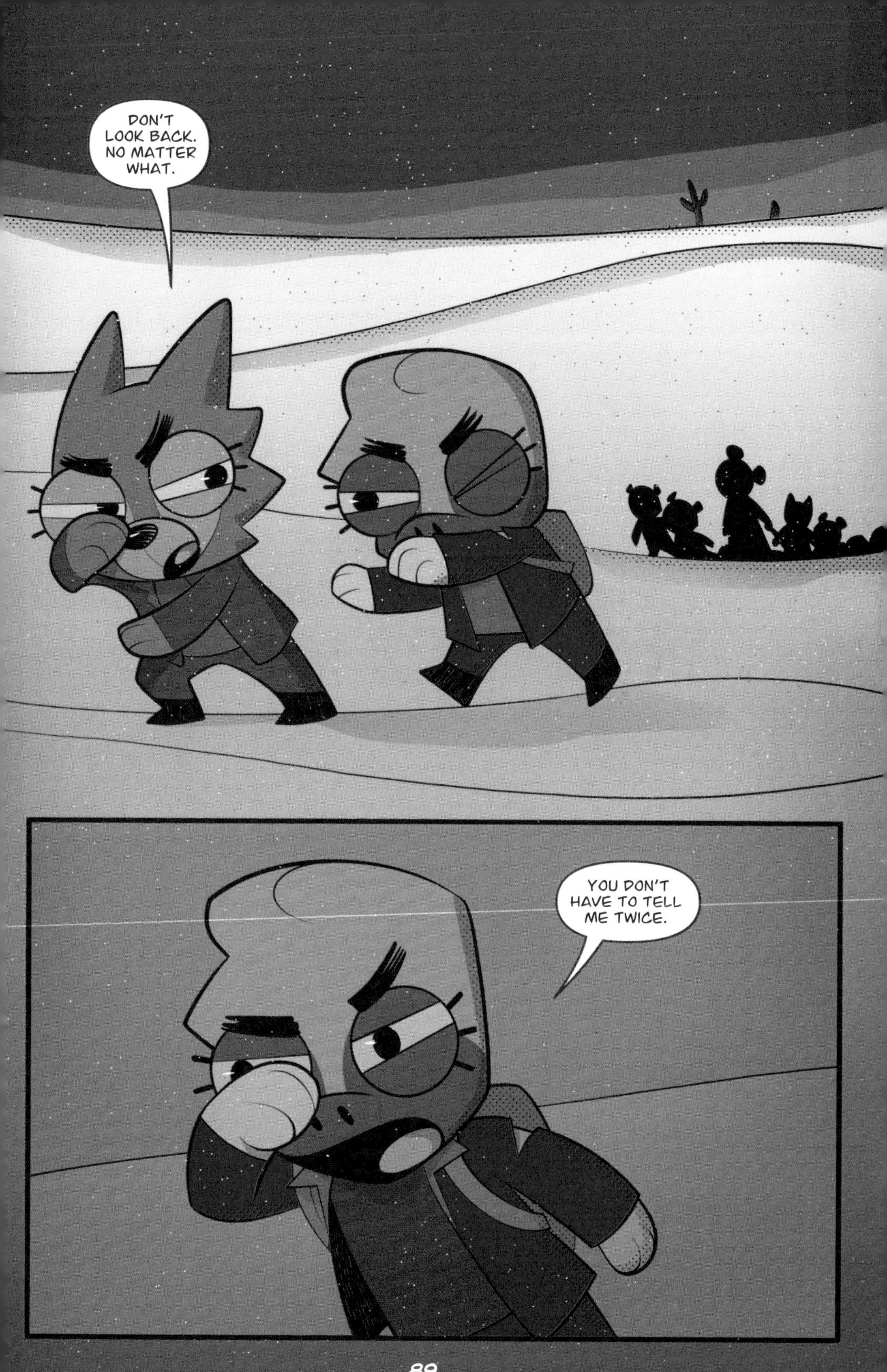
DON'T LOOK BACK. NO MATTER WHAT.
YOU DON'T HAVE TO TELL ME TWICE.

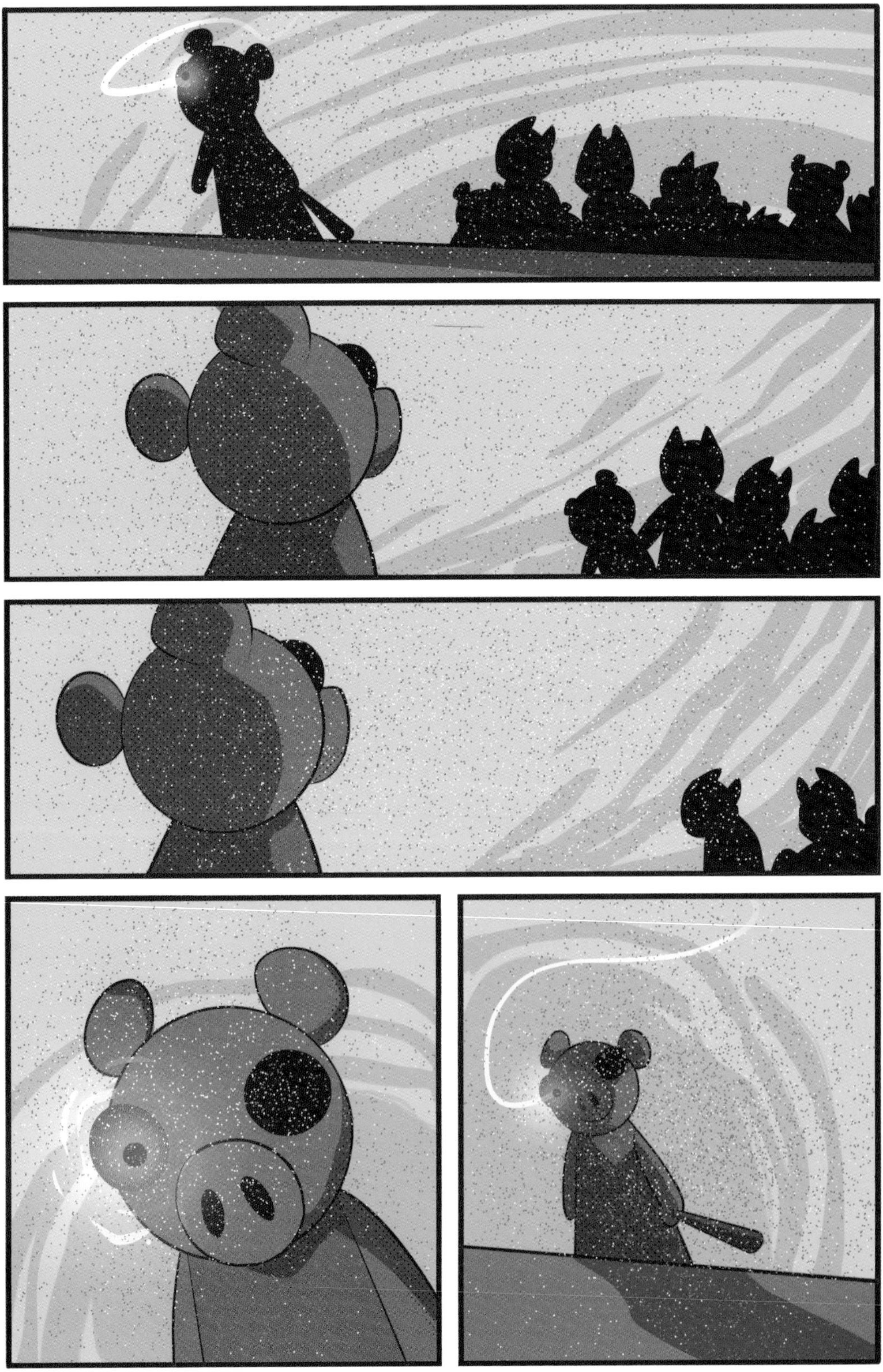

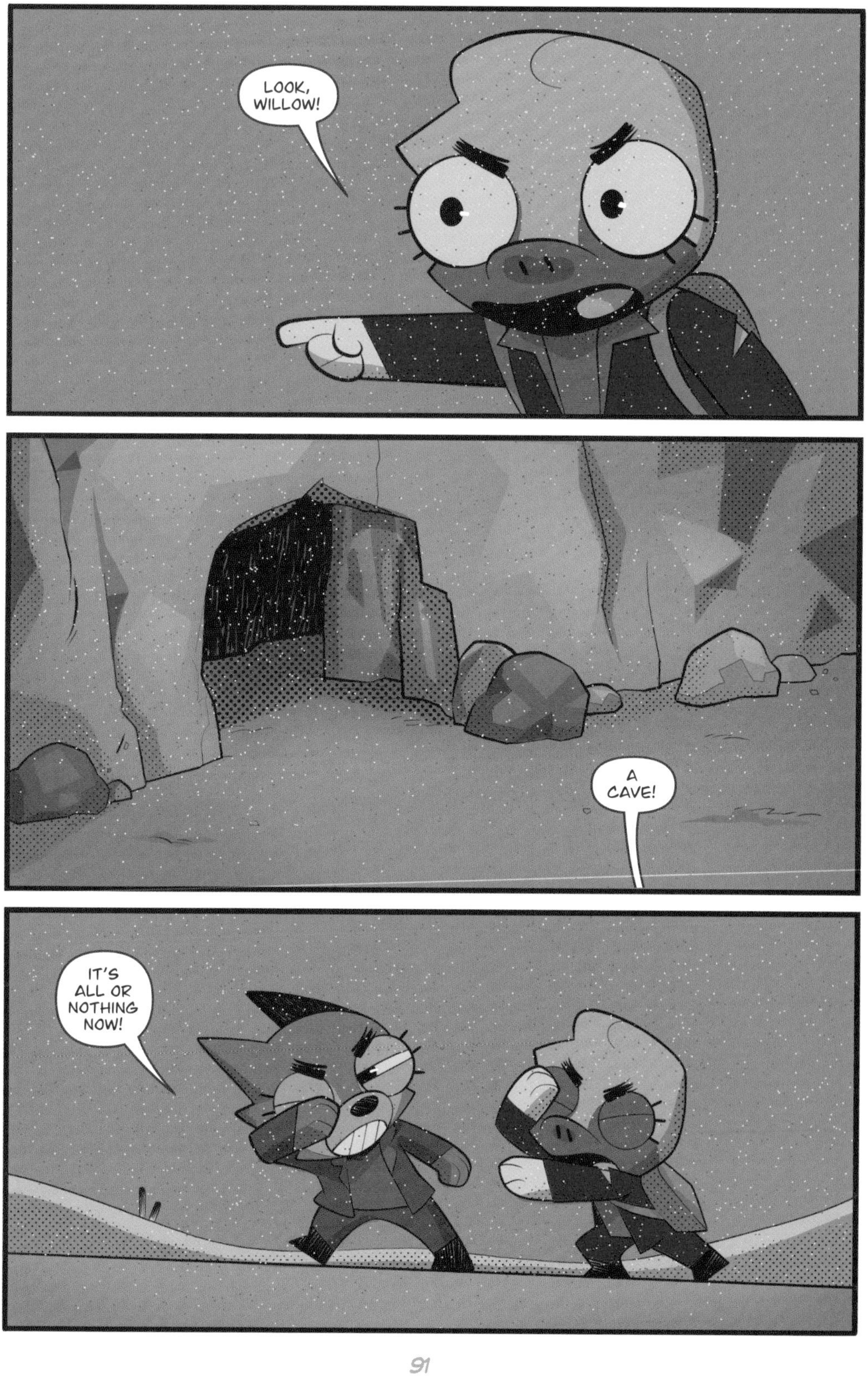
LOOK, WILLOW!
A CAVE!
IT'S ALL OR NOTHING NOW!

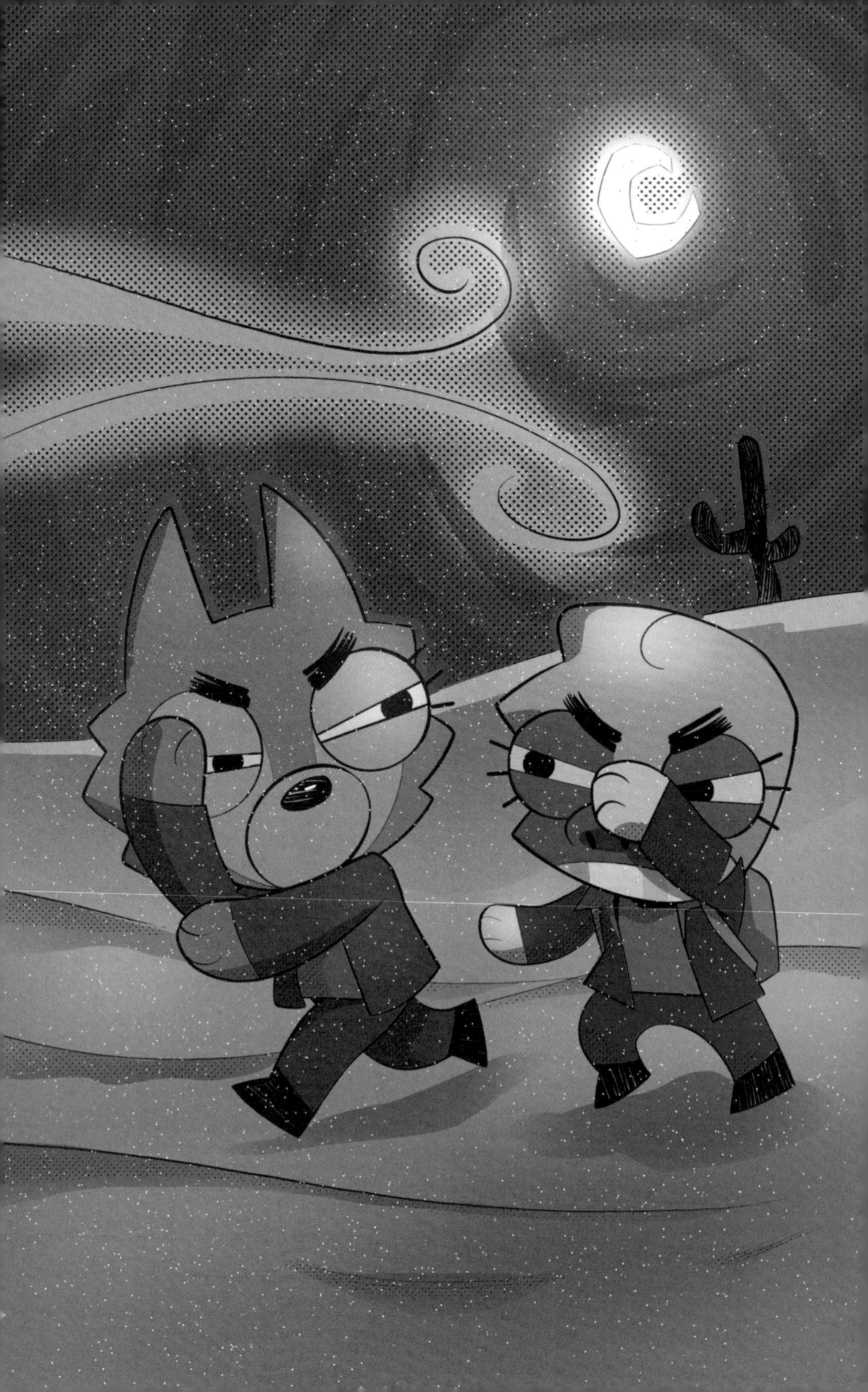

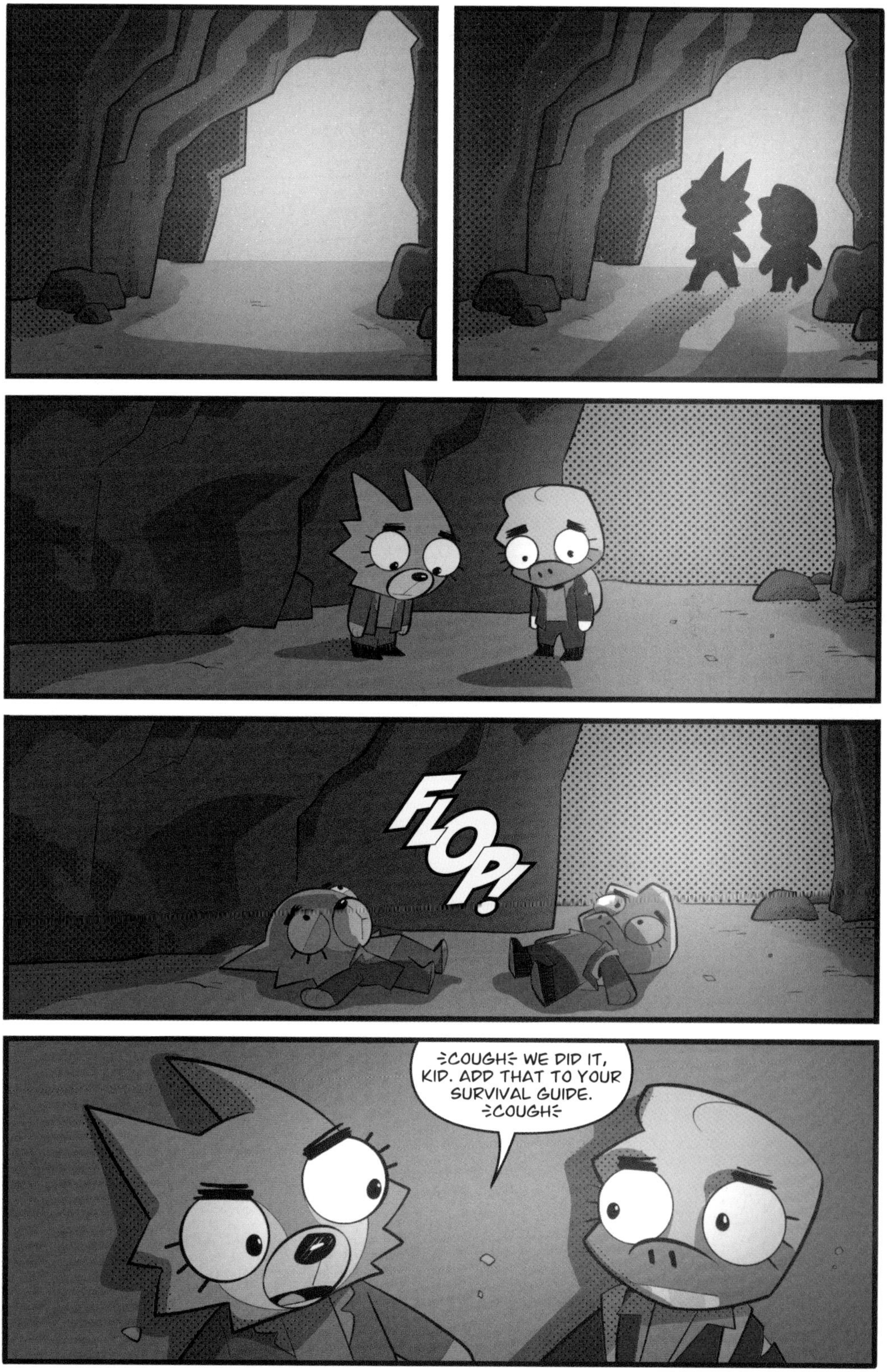
FLOP!
≑COUGH≑ WE DID IT, KID. ADD THAT TO YOUR SURVIVAL GUIDE. ≑COUGH≑

# CHAPTER: 5

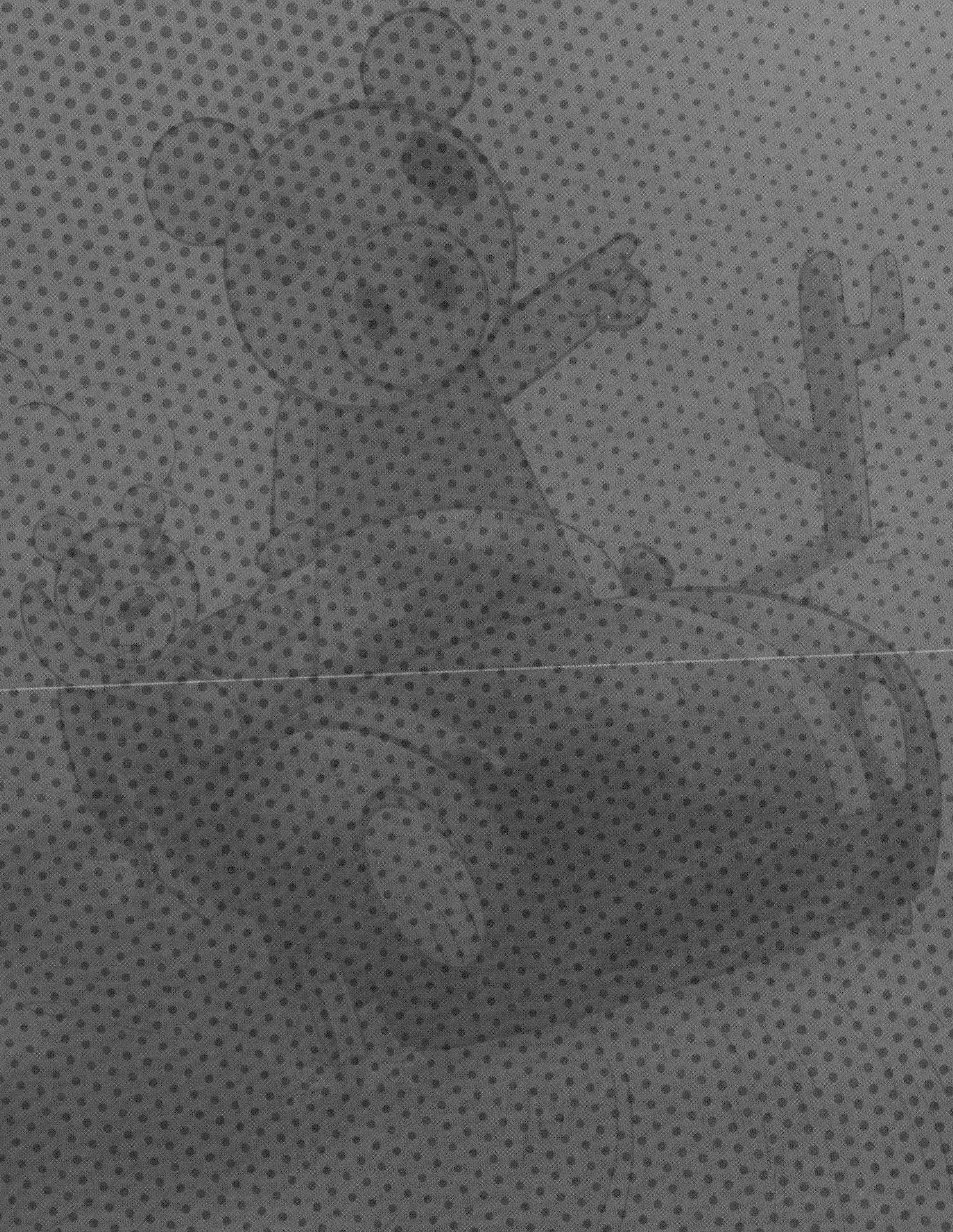

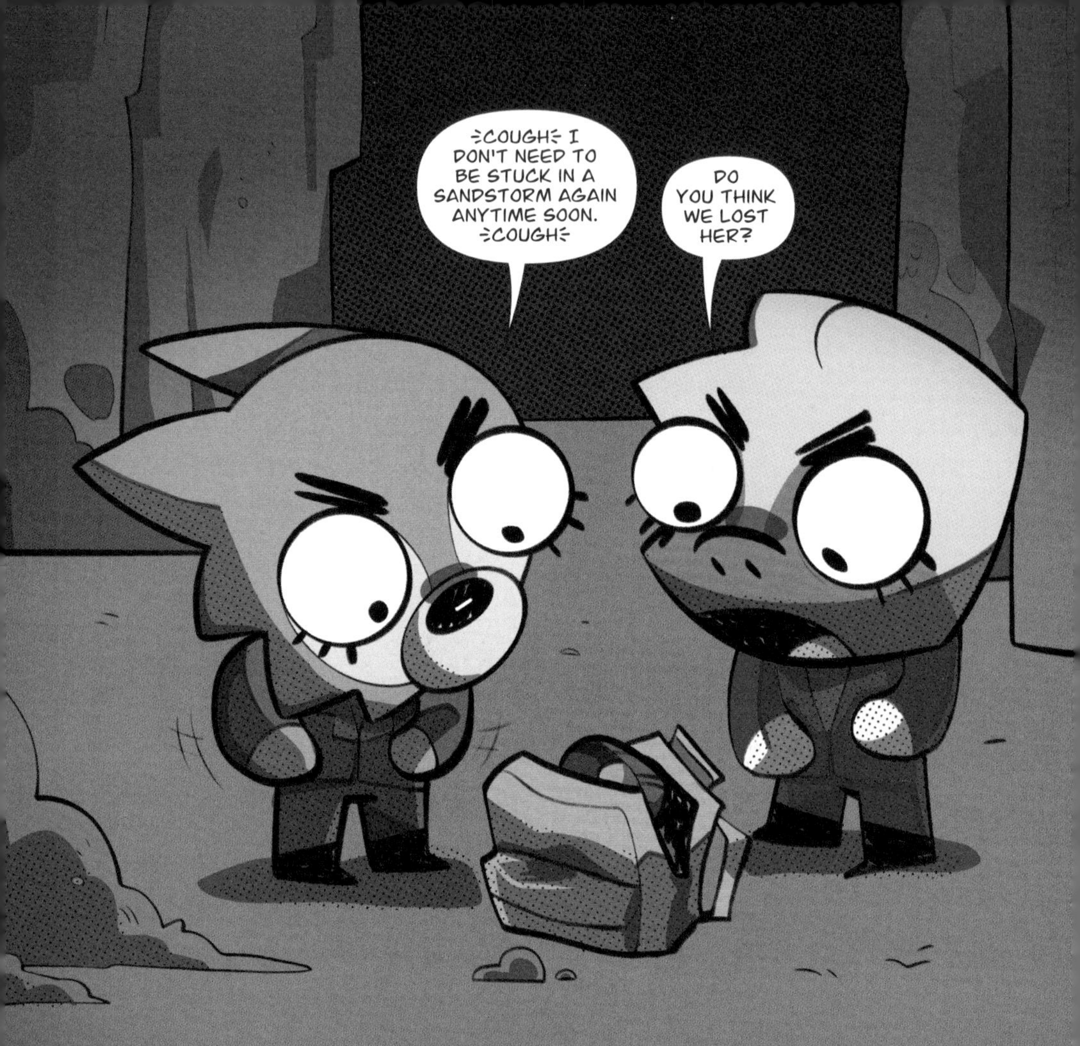

=COUGH= I DON'T NEED TO BE STUCK IN A SANDSTORM AGAIN ANYTIME SOON. =COUGH=
DO YOU THINK WE LOST HER?

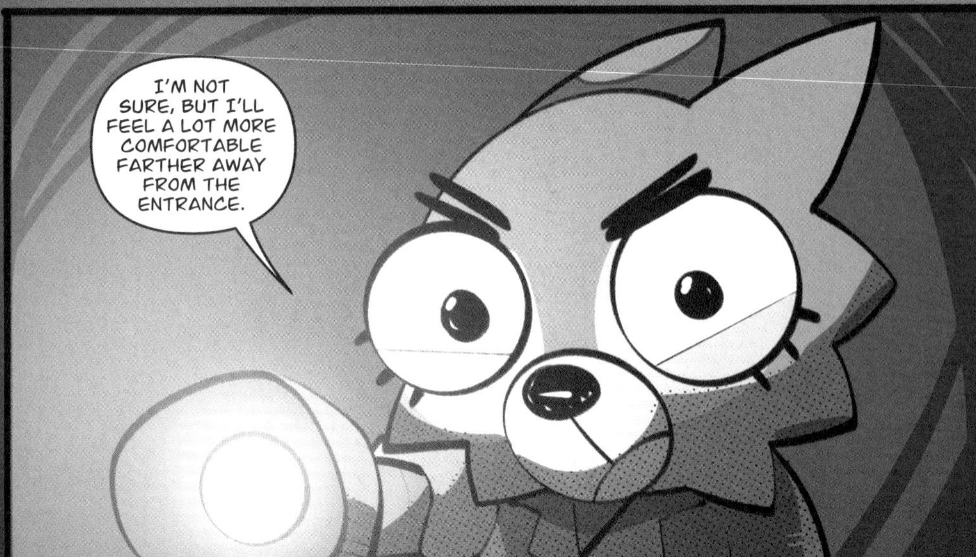

I'M NOT SURE, BUT I'LL FEEL A LOT MORE COMFORTABLE FARTHER AWAY FROM THE ENTRANCE.

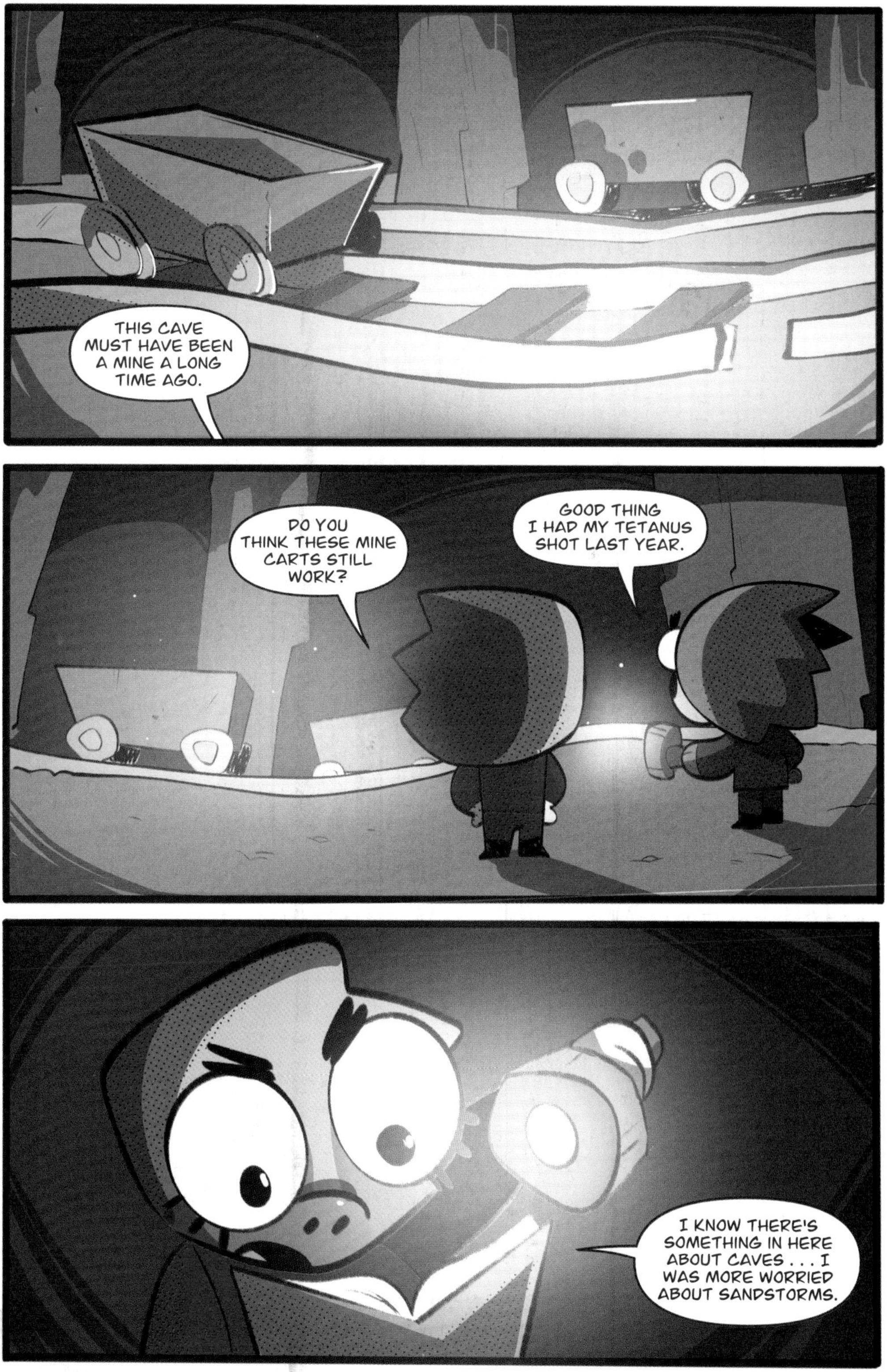
THIS CAVE MUST HAVE BEEN A MINE A LONG TIME AGO.
DO YOU THINK THESE MINE CARTS STILL WORK?
GOOD THING I HAD MY TETANUS SHOT LAST YEAR.
I KNOW THERE'S SOMETHING IN HERE ABOUT CAVES . . . I WAS MORE WORRIED ABOUT SANDSTORMS.

# The Silver Paw Survival Tips - Spelunking 101

**Tip 1** – Spelunking is a fancy word for cave exploration. Exploring caves is a very dangerous activity, so you should never do it alone–always go with an experienced adult spelunker.

**Tip 2** – The most important thing you can take with you is rope, so that you can descend into a cave and pull yourself back out of it. Make sure you have strong rope and good rappelling equipment.

**Tip 3** – It's very easy to hit your head or drop a flashlight in a cave, so wear a hard hat with a headlight to prevent these types of common hazards.

**Tip 4** – Caves can often have little oxygen and contain toxic gases. If you smell gas, absolutely do NOT light a campfire inside and get OUT.

**Tip 5** – And most importantly, always carry a first aid kit in case of injuries when doing dangerous activities.

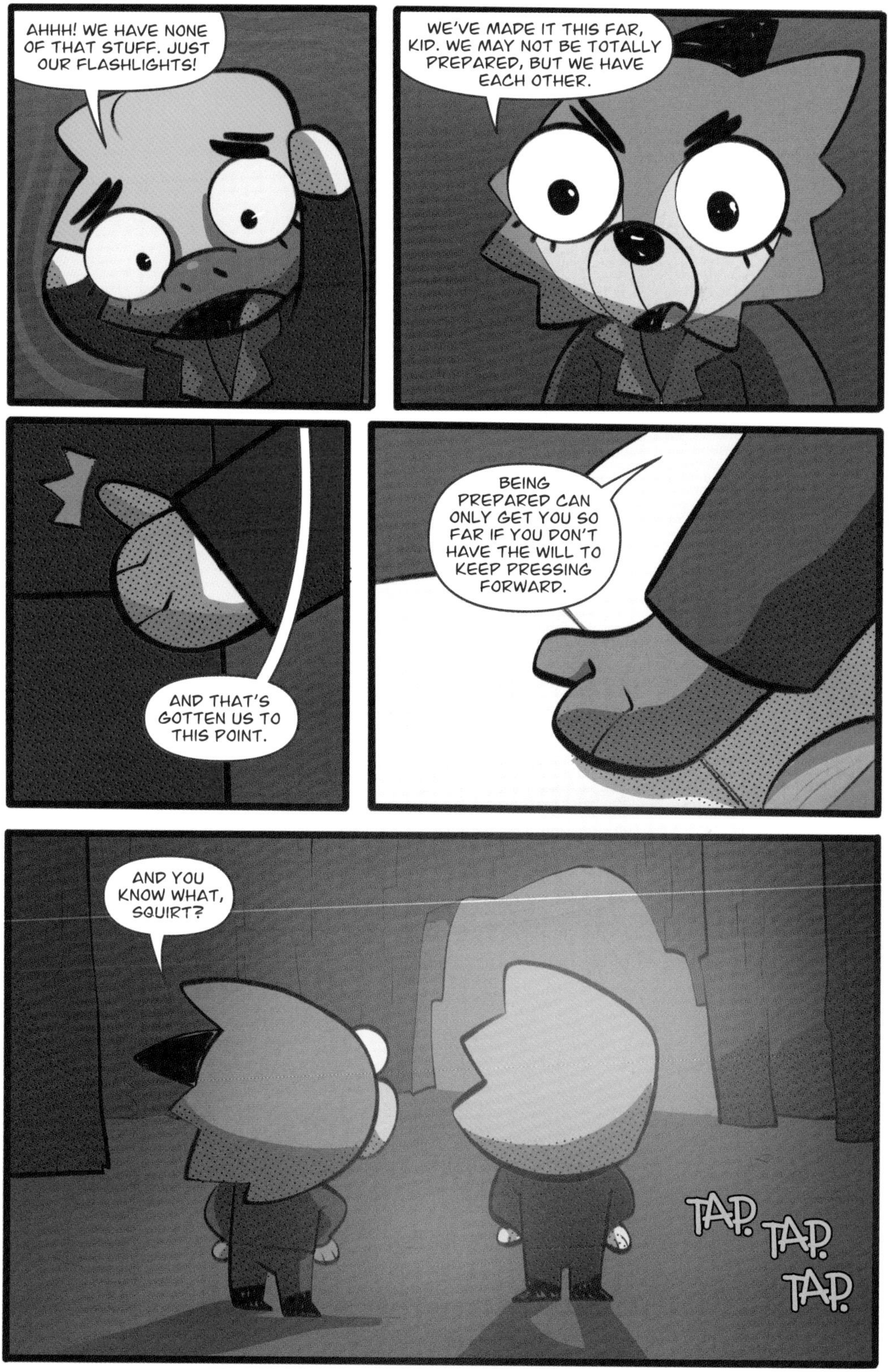
AHHH! WE HAVE NONE OF THAT STUFF. JUST OUR FLASHLIGHTS!
WE'VE MADE IT THIS FAR, KID. WE MAY NOT BE TOTALLY PREPARED, BUT WE HAVE EACH OTHER.
AND THAT'S GOTTEN US TO THIS POINT.
BEING PREPARED CAN ONLY GET YOU SO FAR IF YOU DON'T HAVE THE WILL TO KEEP PRESSING FORWARD.
AND YOU KNOW WHAT, SQUIRT?
TAP. TAP. TAP.

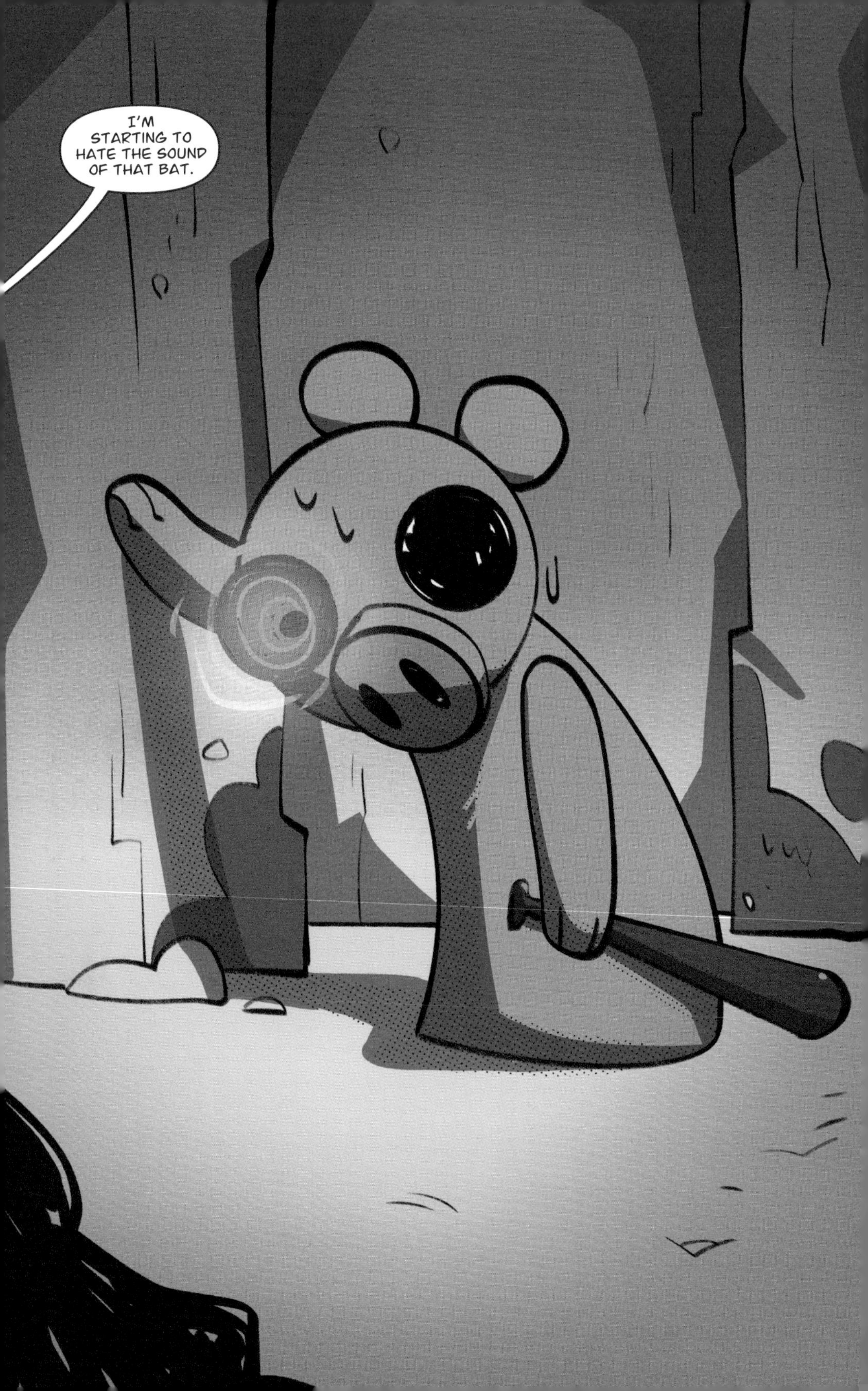
I'M STARTING TO HATE THE SOUND OF THAT BAT.

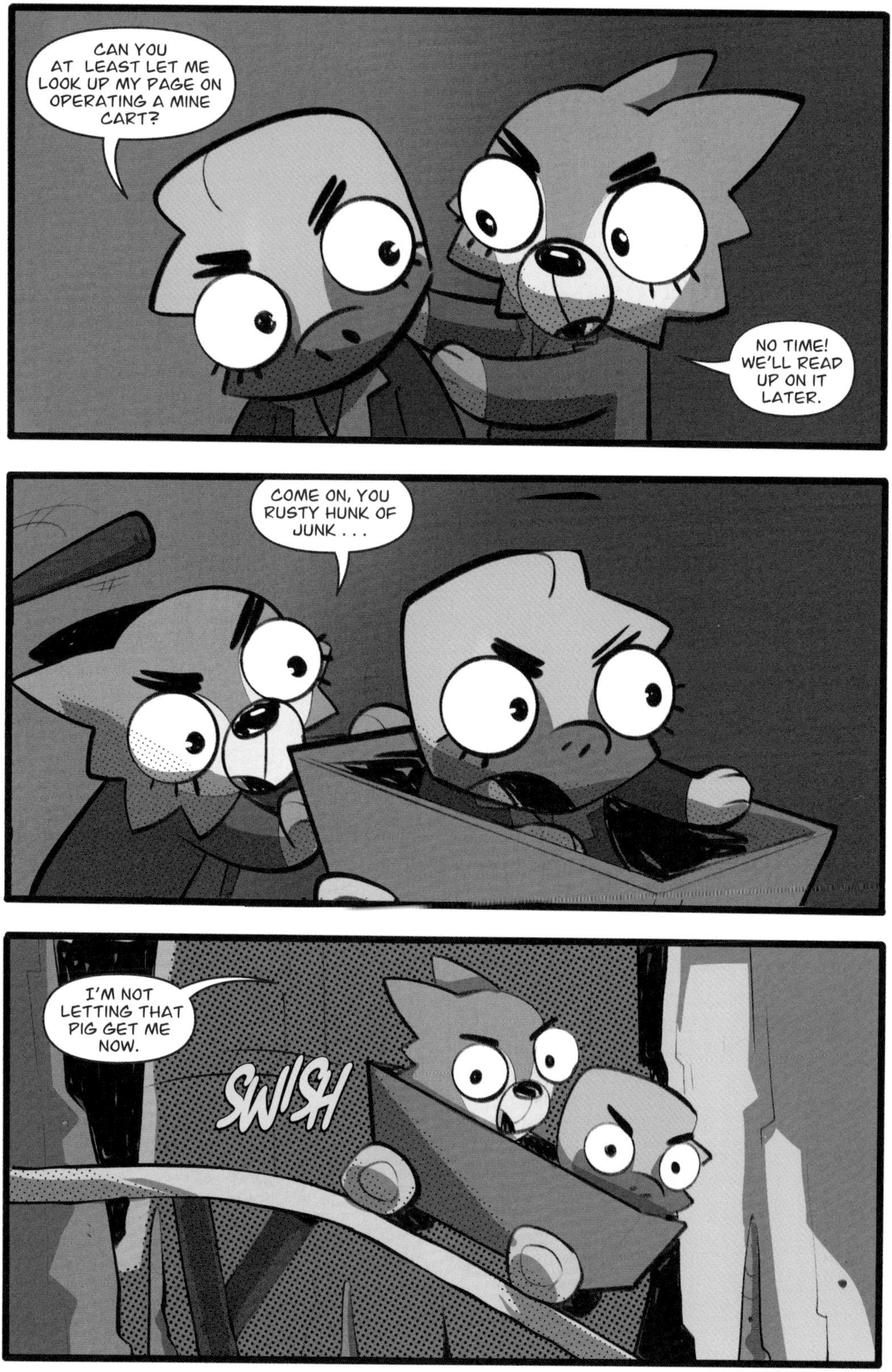
CAN YOU AT LEAST LET ME LOOK UP MY PAGE ON OPERATING A MINE CART?
NO TIME! WE'LL READ UP ON IT LATER.
COME ON, YOU RUSTY HUNK OF JUNK . . .
I'M NOT LETTING THAT PIG GET ME NOW.
SWISH

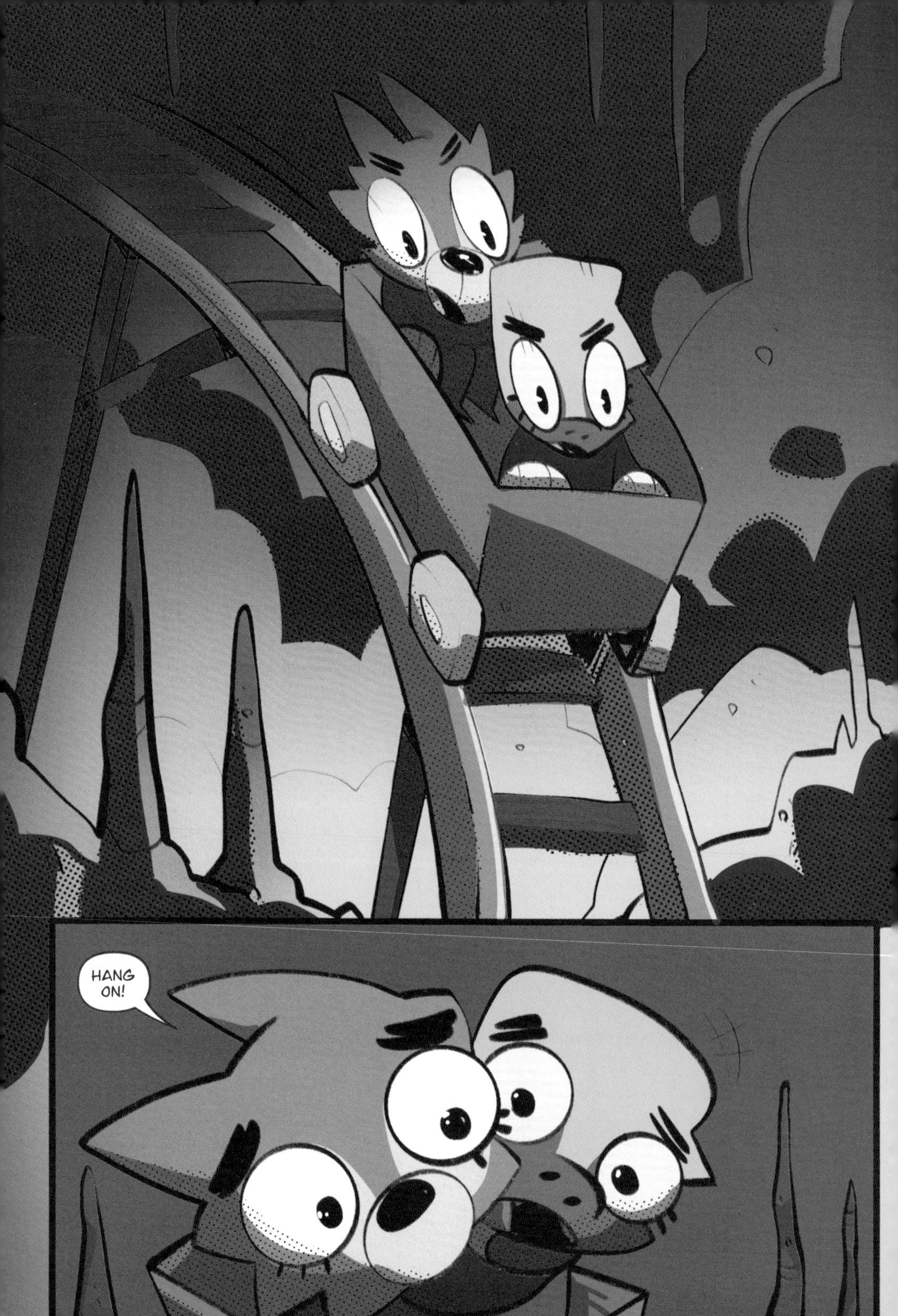
HANG ON!

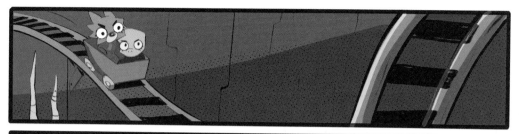

WHO EVEN BUILT THIS TRACK?

I DON'T THINK THEY WERE VERY GOOD AT THEIR JOB.

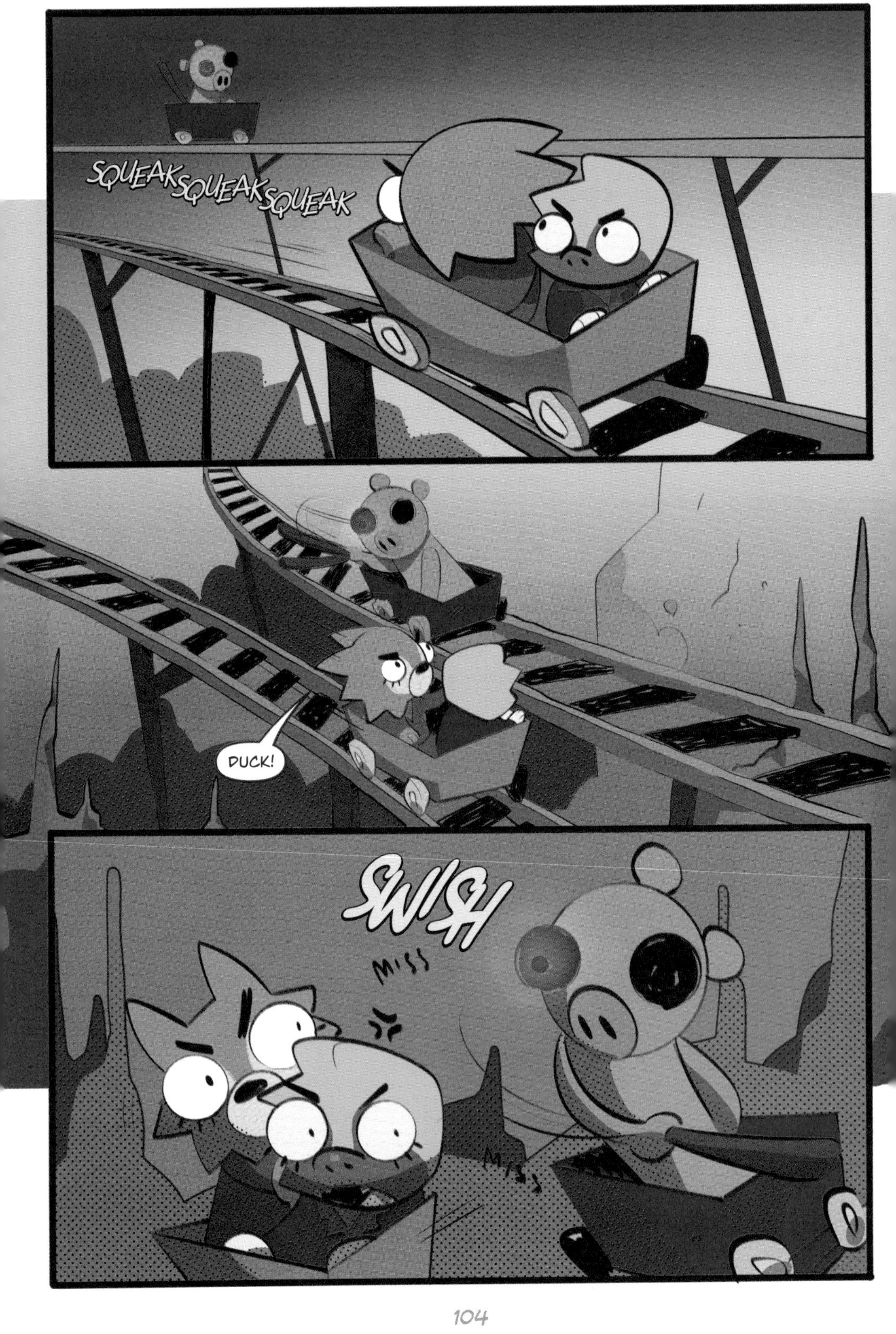
SQUEAKSQUEAKSQUEAK
DUCK!
SWISH
MISS
MISS

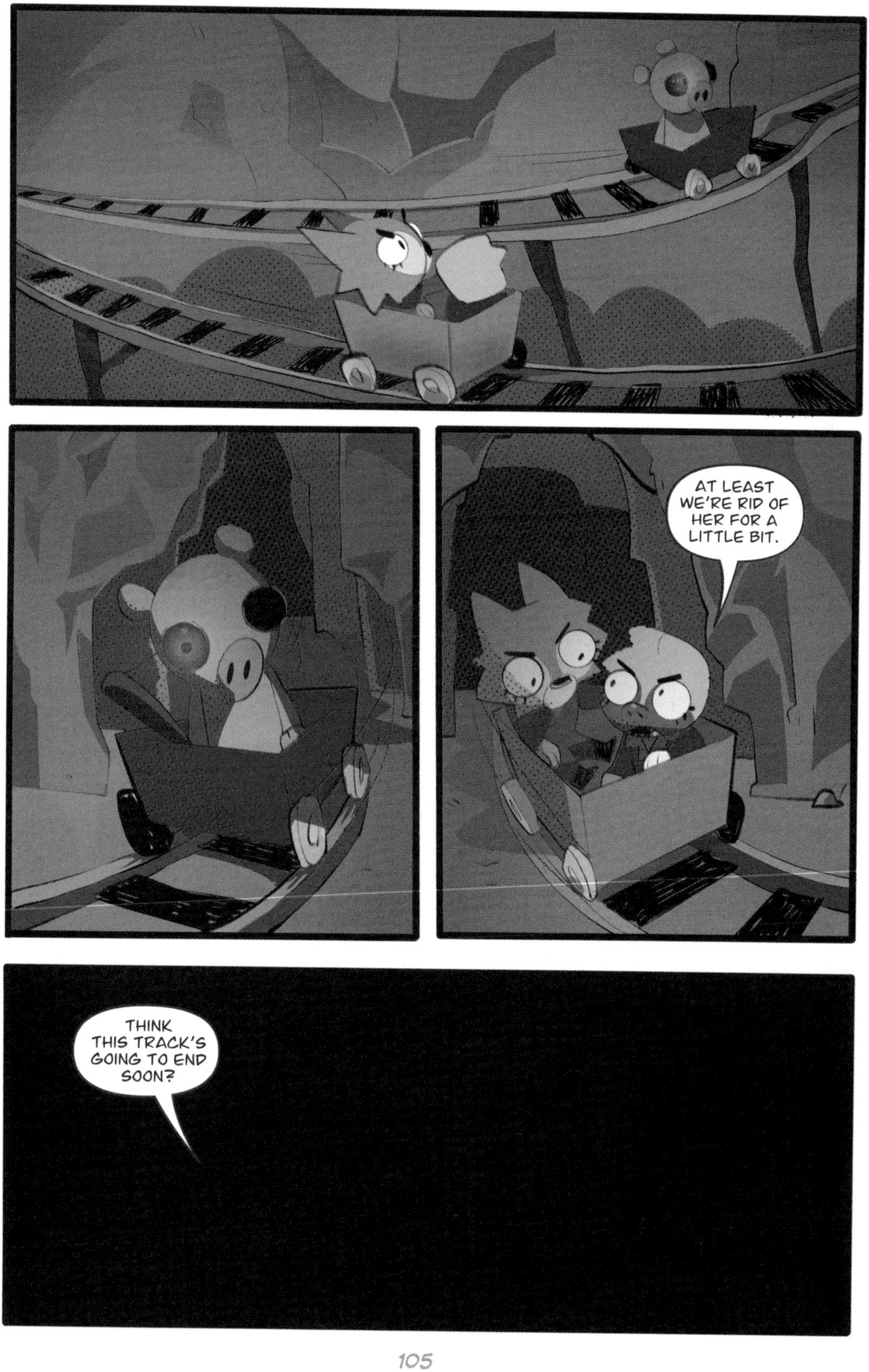
AT LEAST WE'RE RID OF HER FOR A LITTLE BIT.
THINK THIS TRACK'S GOING TO END SOON?

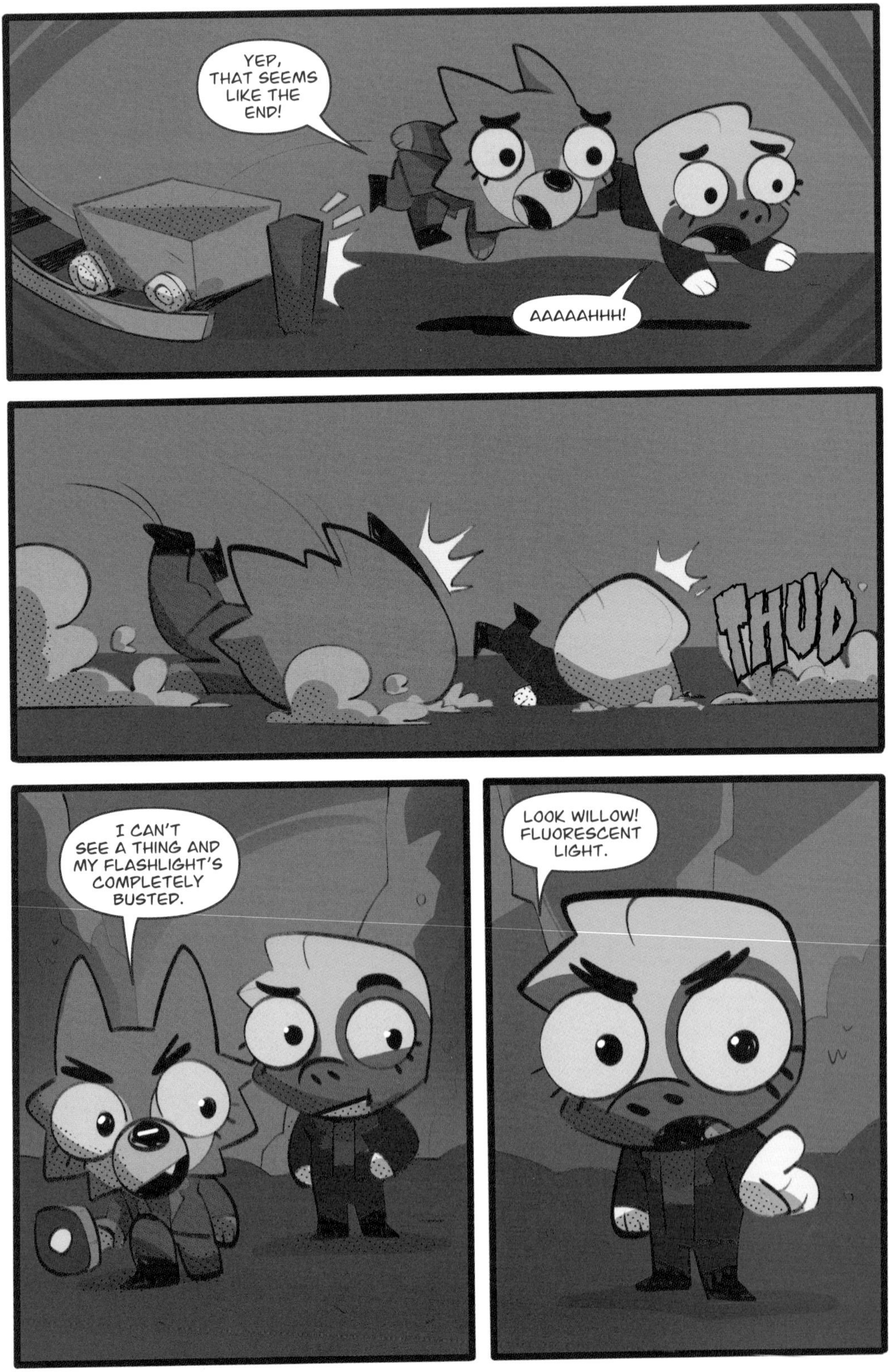
YEP, THAT SEEMS LIKE THE END!
AAAAAHHH!
THUD
I CAN'T SEE A THING AND MY FLASHLIGHT'S COMPLETELY BUSTED.
LOOK WILLOW! FLUORESCENT LIGHT.

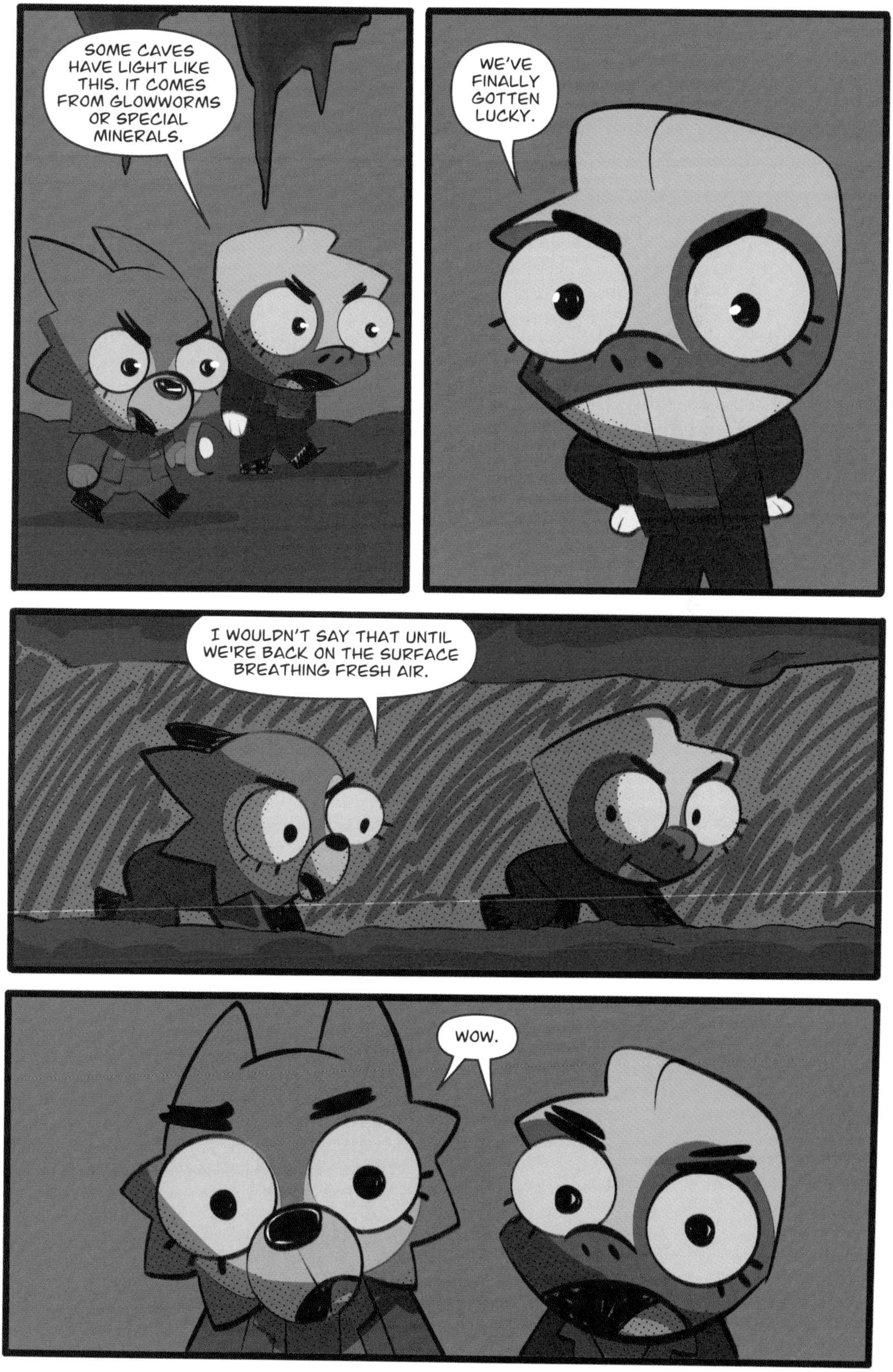
SOME CAVES HAVE LIGHT LIKE THIS. IT COMES FROM GLOWWORMS OR SPECIAL MINERALS.
WE'VE FINALLY GOTTEN LUCKY.
I WOULDN'T SAY THAT UNTIL WE'RE BACK ON THE SURFACE BREATHING FRESH AIR.
WOW.

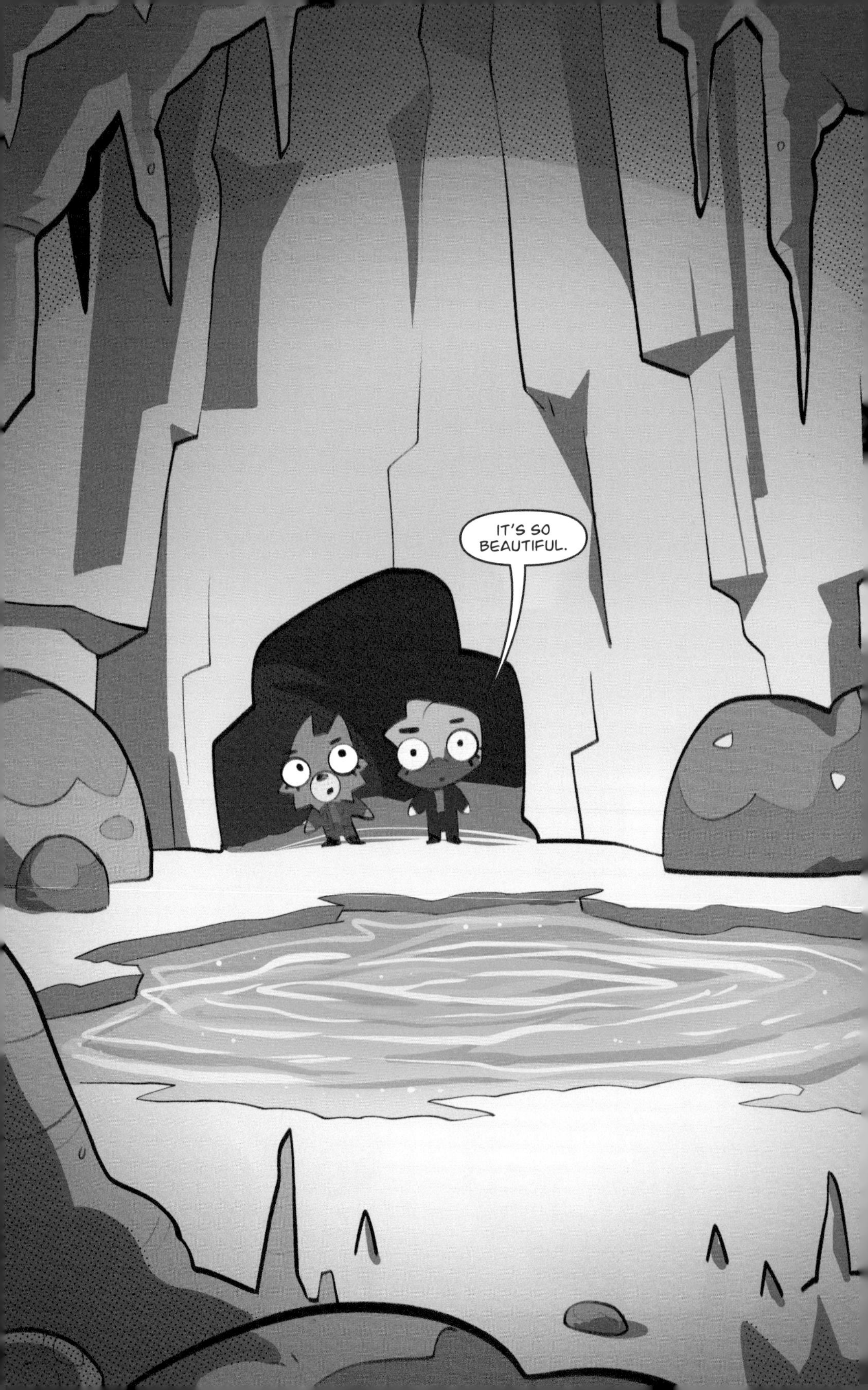
IT'S SO BEAUTIFUL.

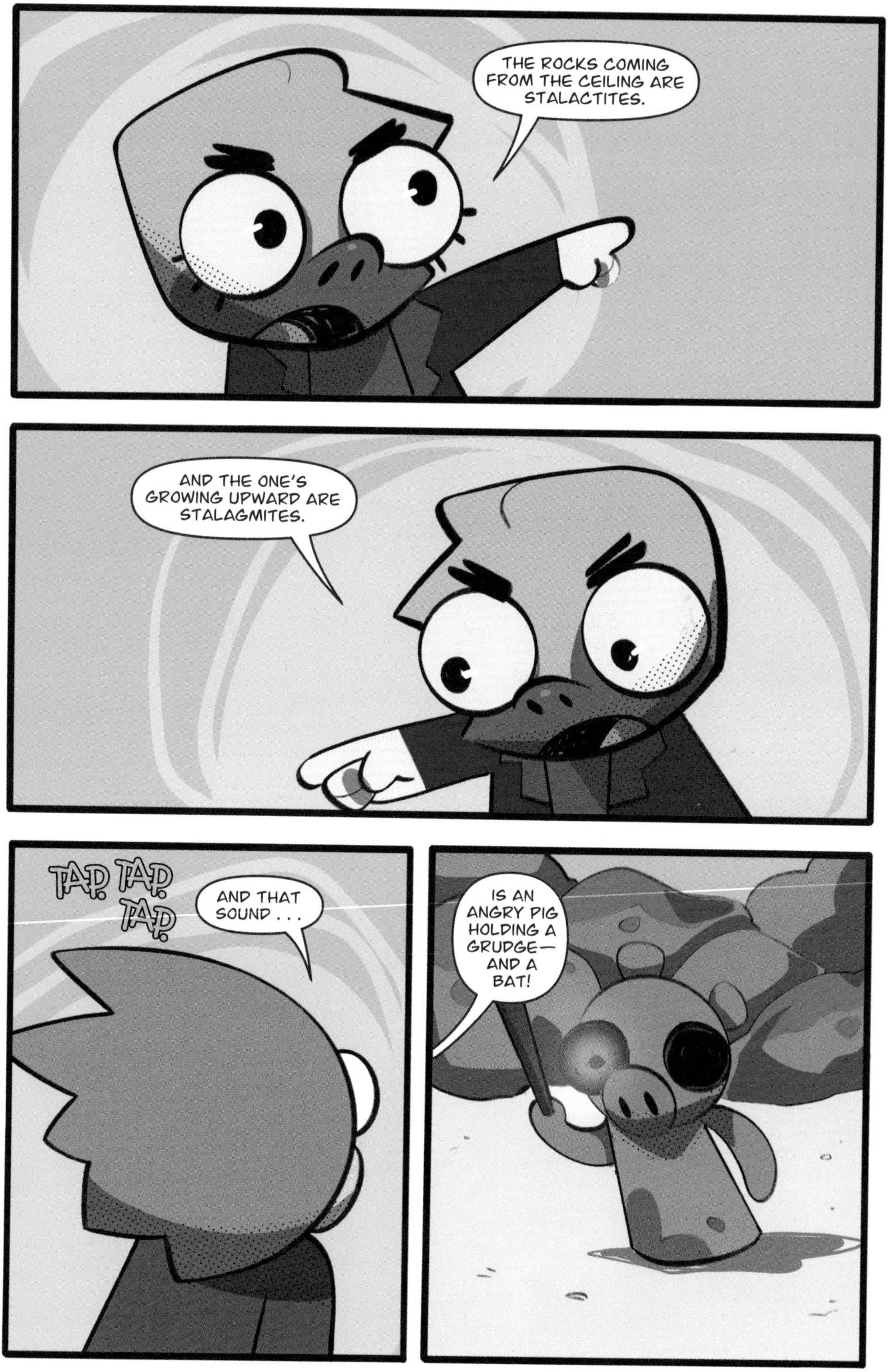
THE ROCKS COMING FROM THE CEILING ARE STALACTITES.
AND THE ONE'S GROWING UPWARD ARE STALAGMITES.
TAP. TAP. TAP.
AND THAT SOUND . . .
IS AN ANGRY PIG HOLDING A GRUDGE— AND A BAT!

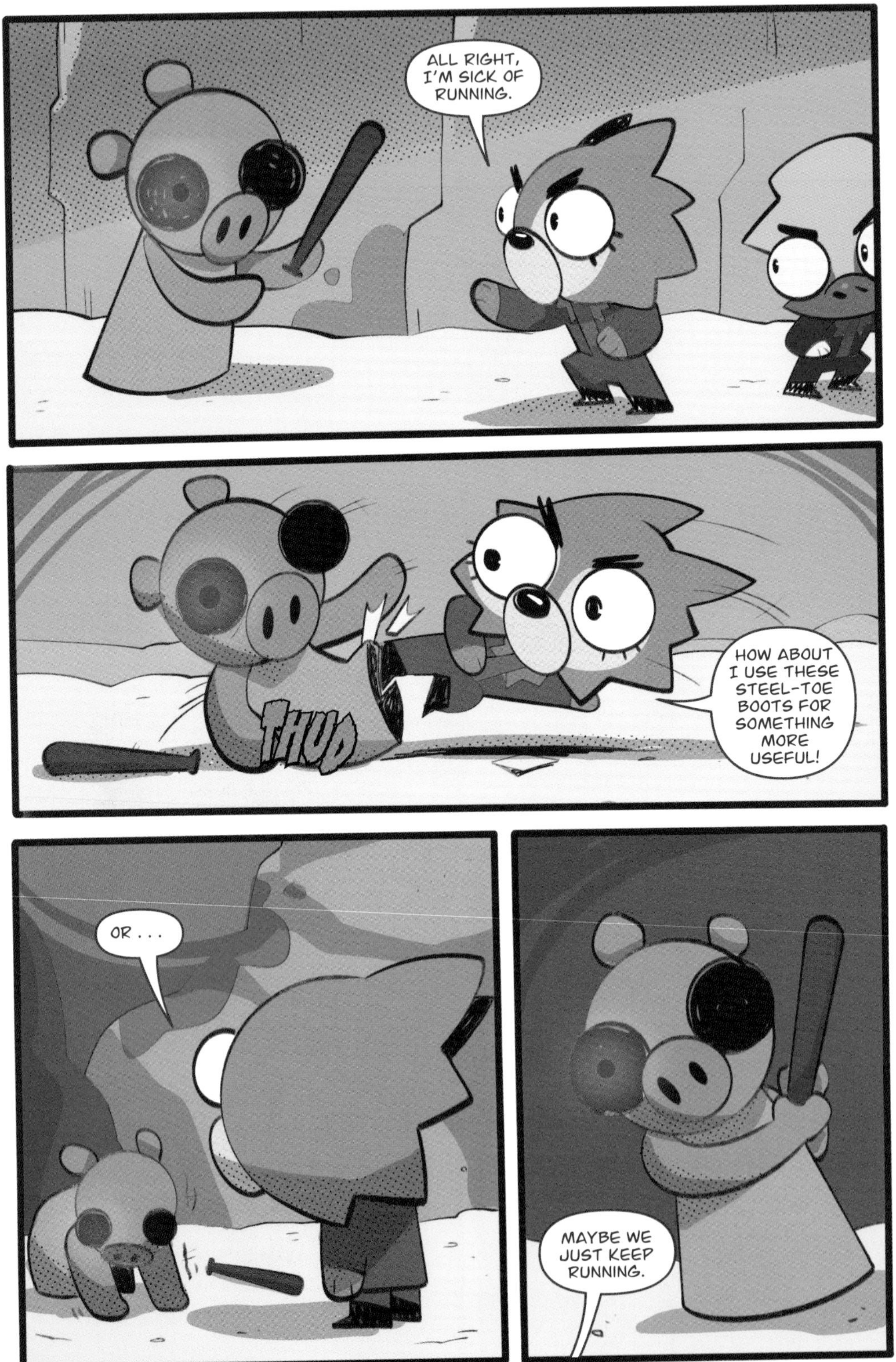
ALL RIGHT, I'M SICK OF RUNNING.
THUD
HOW ABOUT I USE THESE STEEL-TOE BOOTS FOR SOMETHING MORE USEFUL!
OR . . .
MAYBE WE JUST KEEP RUNNING.

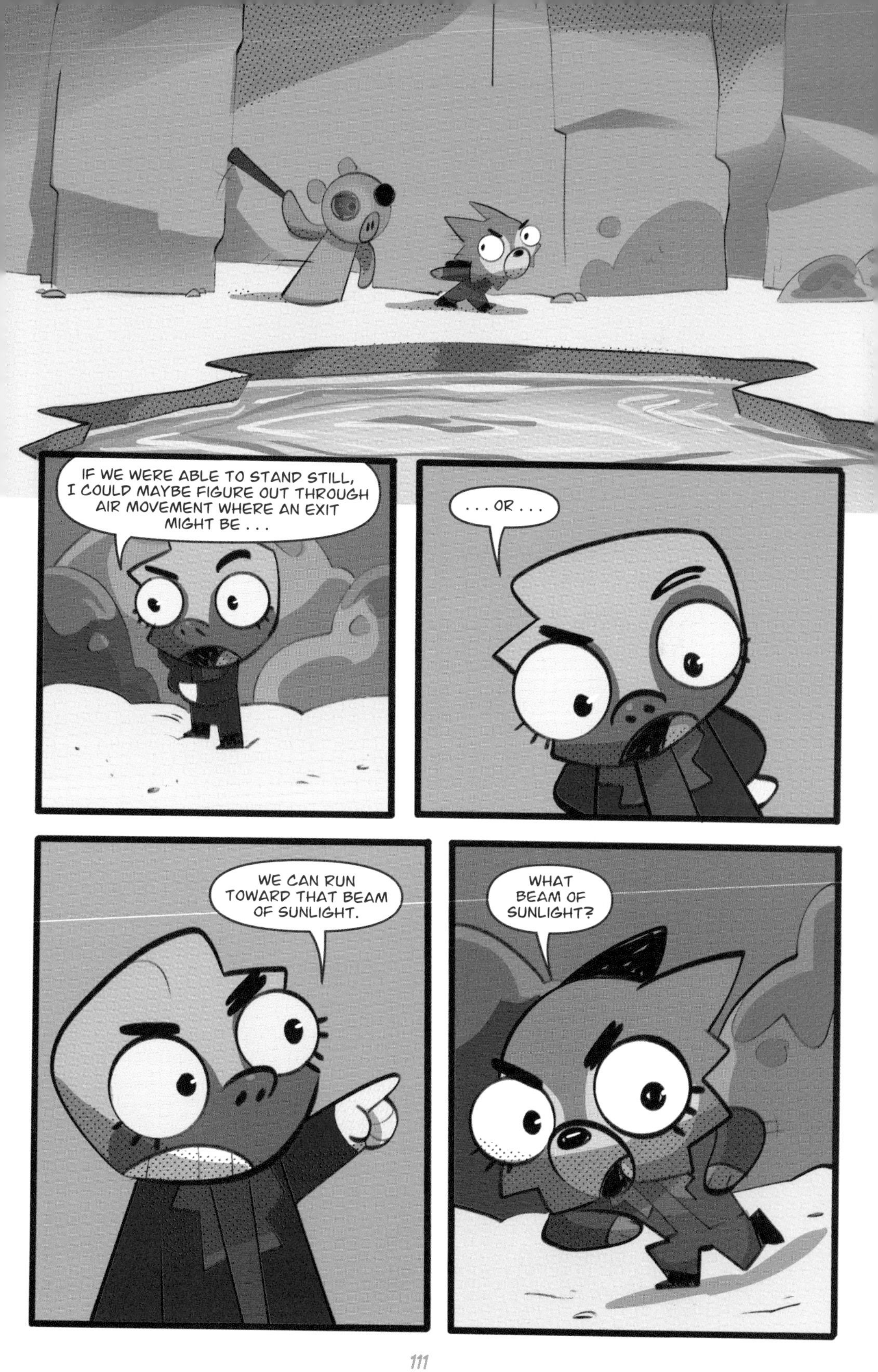

IF WE WERE ABLE TO STAND STILL, I COULD MAYBE FIGURE OUT THROUGH AIR MOVEMENT WHERE AN EXIT MIGHT BE . . .
. . . OR . . .
WE CAN RUN TOWARD THAT BEAM OF SUNLIGHT.
WHAT BEAM OF SUNLIGHT?

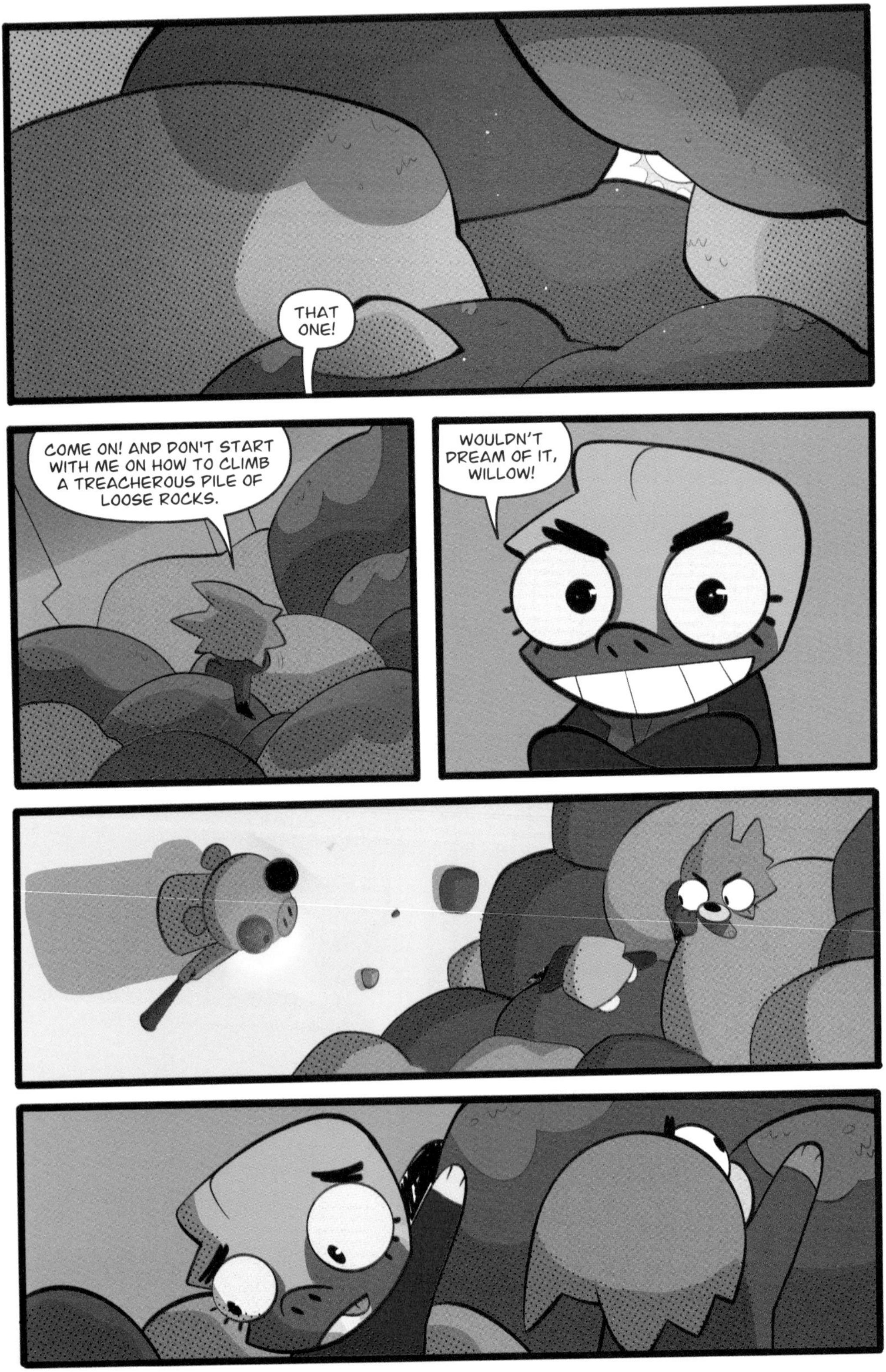
THAT ONE!
COME ON! AND DON'T START WITH ME ON HOW TO CLIMB A TREACHEROUS PILE OF LOOSE ROCKS.
WOULDN'T DREAM OF IT, WILLOW!

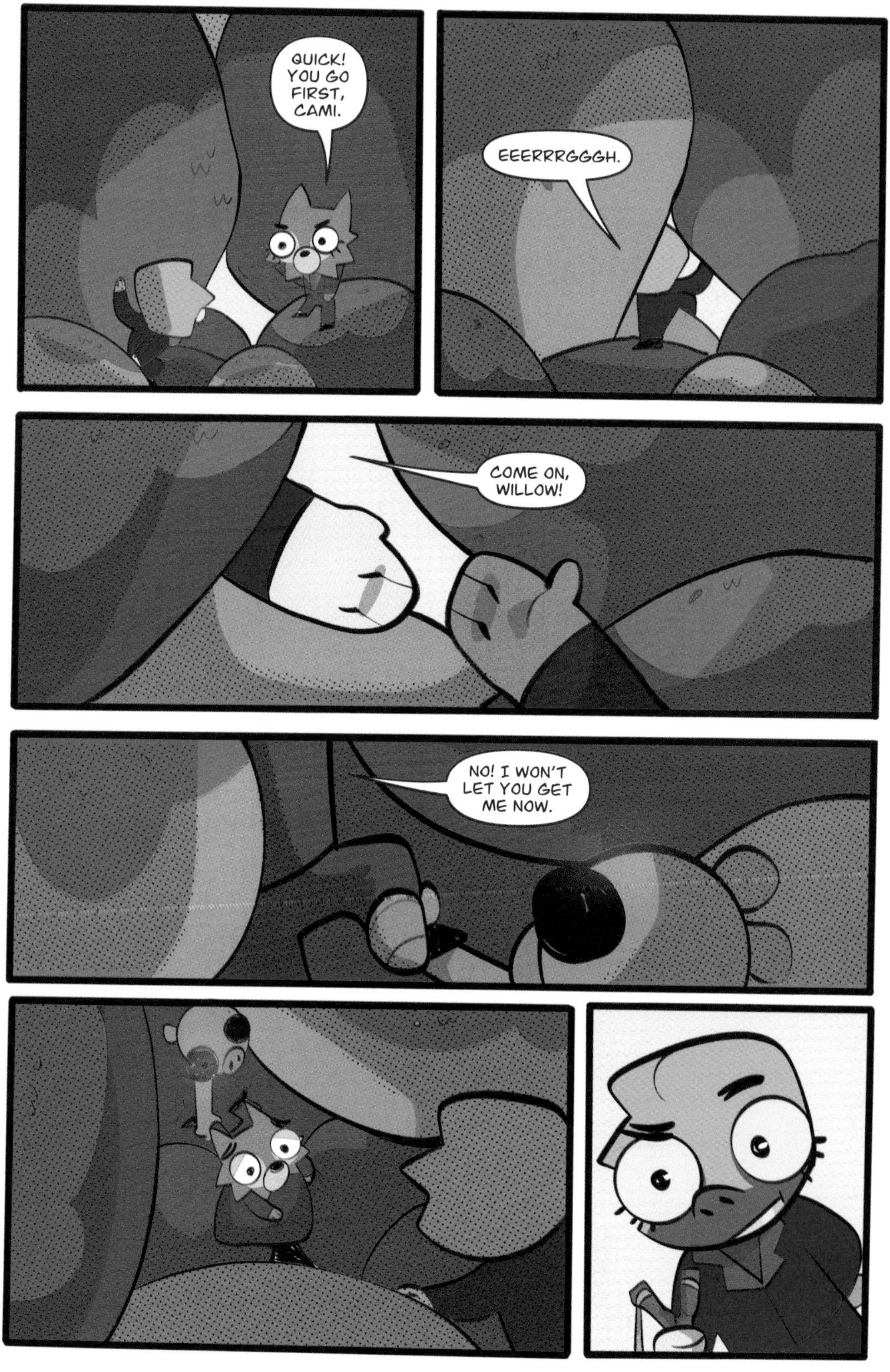
QUICK! YOU GO FIRST, CAMI.
EEERRRGGGH.
COME ON, WILLOW!
NO! I WON'T LET YOU GET ME NOW.

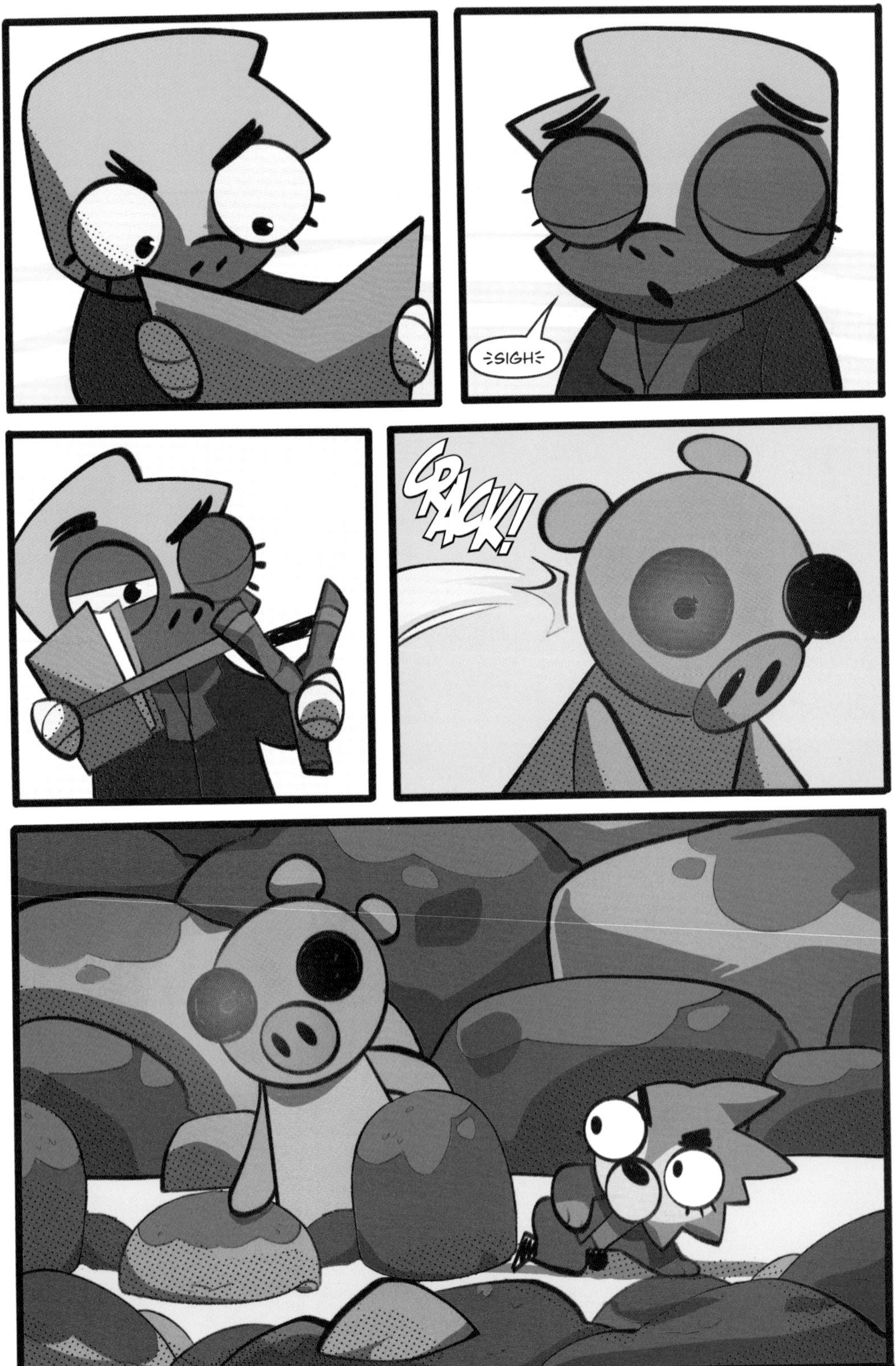
SIGH
CRACK!

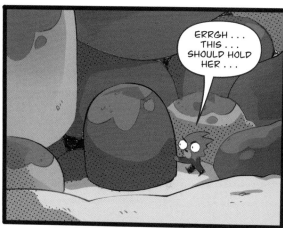

ERRGH . . . THIS . . . SHOULD HOLD HER . . .

YEAH, EVEN SHE ISN'T STRONG ENOUGH TO MOVE THAT THING.

CAMI . . . YOU GAVE UP YOUR SURVIVAL GUIDE.

DON'T WORRY, WILLOW. I CAN ALWAYS WRITE A NEW ONE. AND WITH YOU AS MY FRIEND, I KNOW WE CAN SURVIVE ANYTHING.

AT LEAST . . . MAYBE ONCE WE CROSS THE REST OF THIS DESERT.

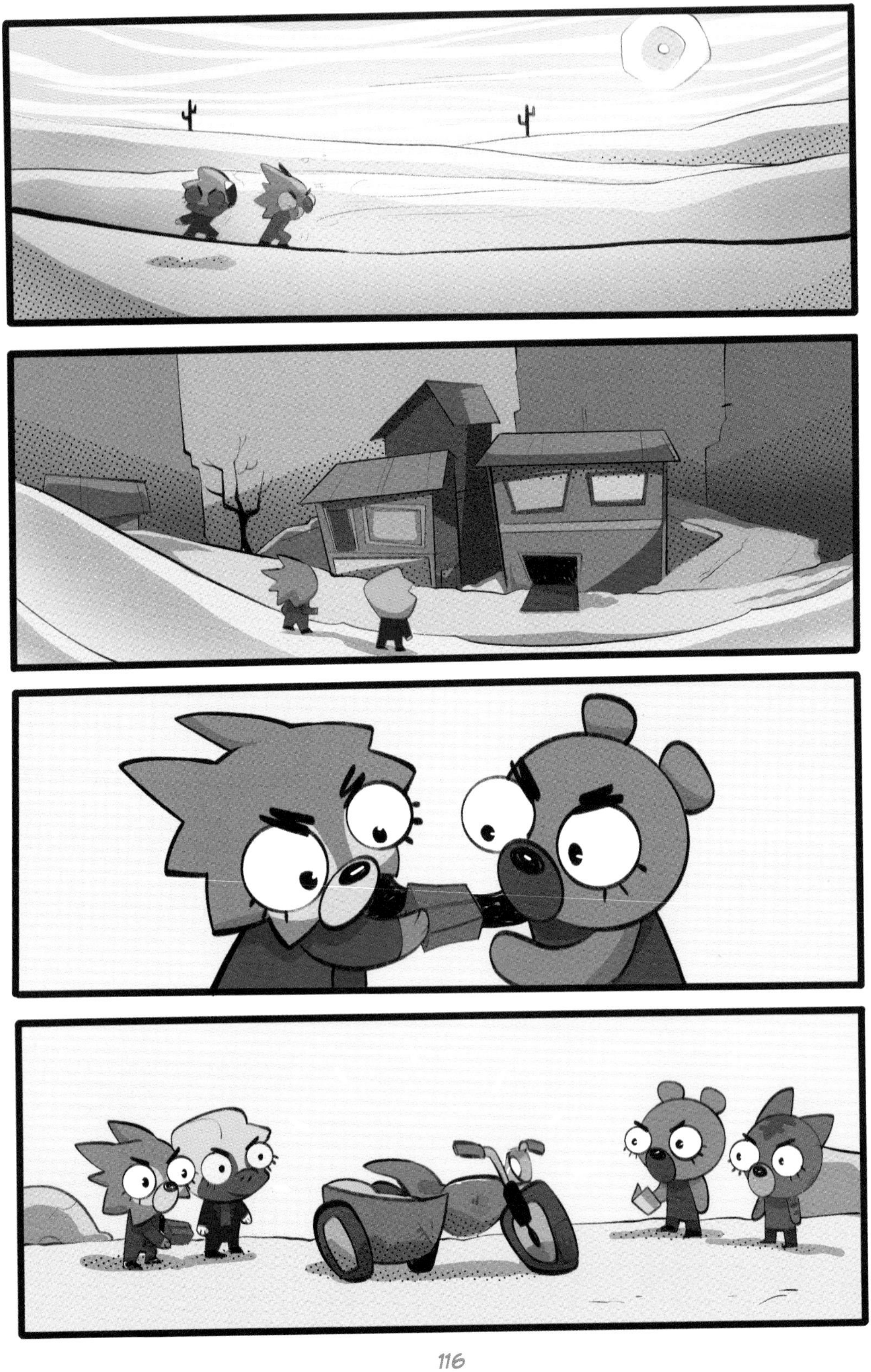

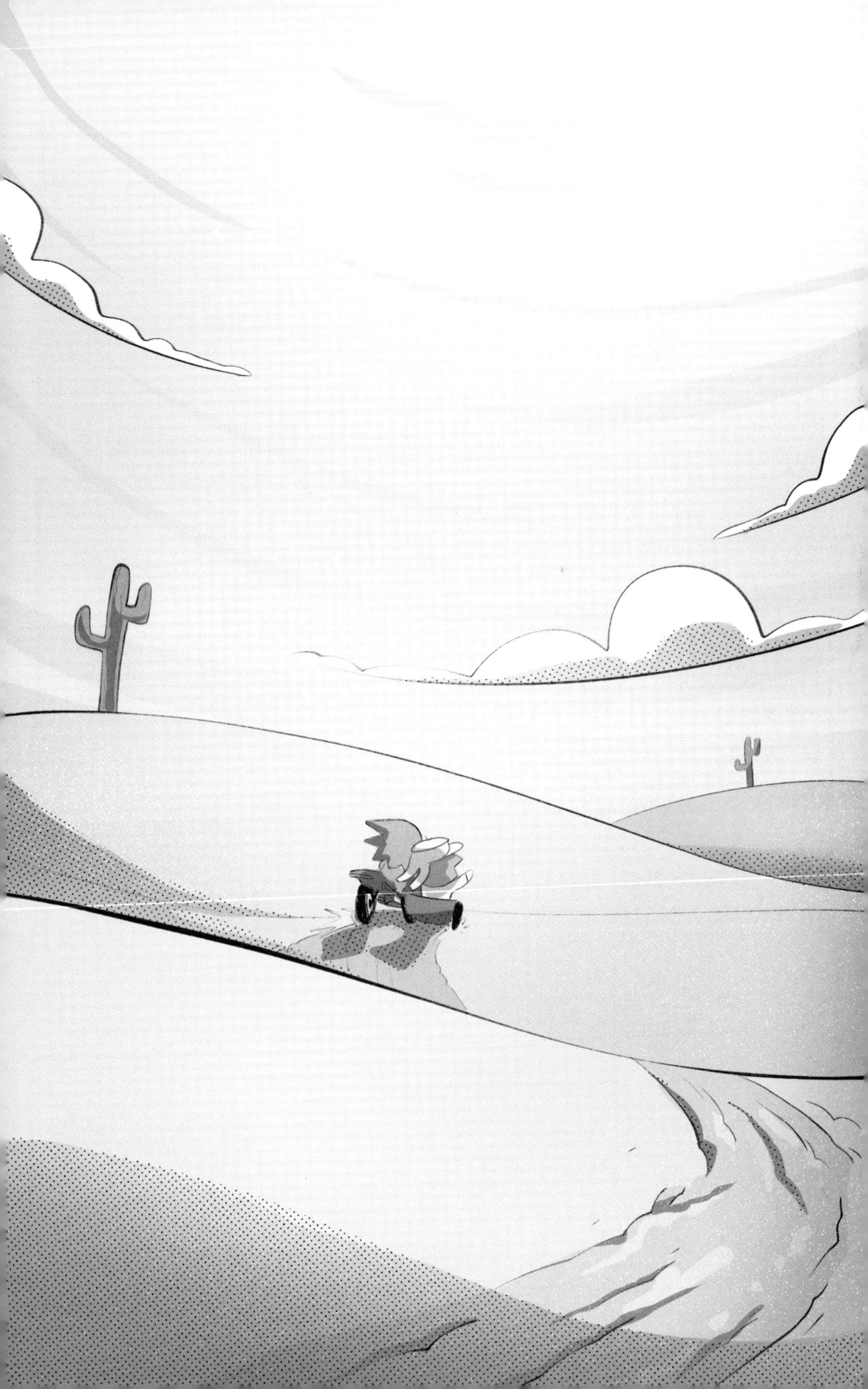

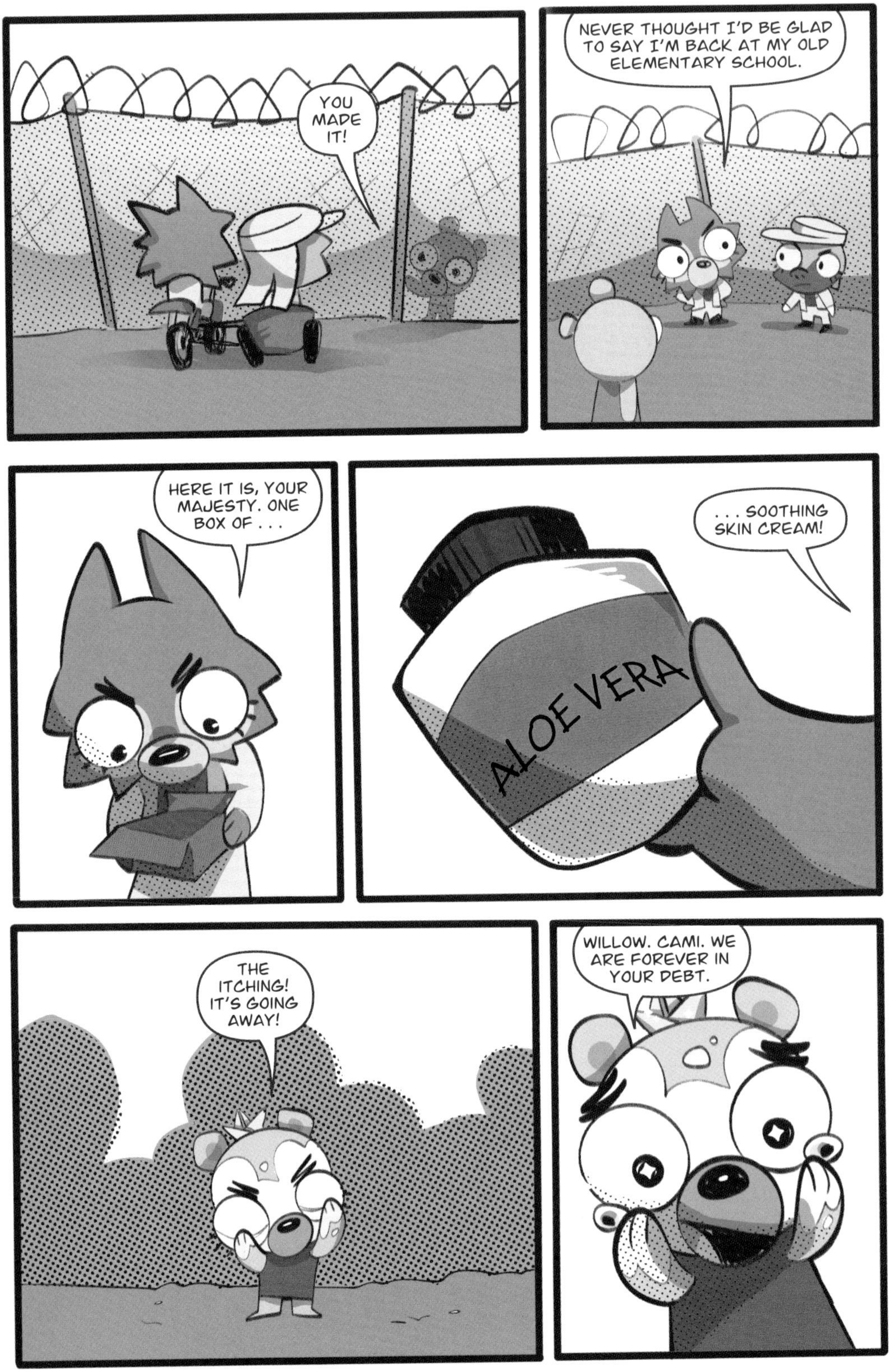

YOU MADE IT!
NEVER THOUGHT I'D BE GLAD TO SAY I'M BACK AT MY OLD ELEMENTARY SCHOOL.
HERE IT IS, YOUR MAJESTY. ONE BOX OF . . .
. . . SOOTHING SKIN CREAM!
ALOE VERA
THE ITCHING! IT'S GOING AWAY!
WILLOW. CAMI. WE ARE FOREVER IN YOUR DEBT.

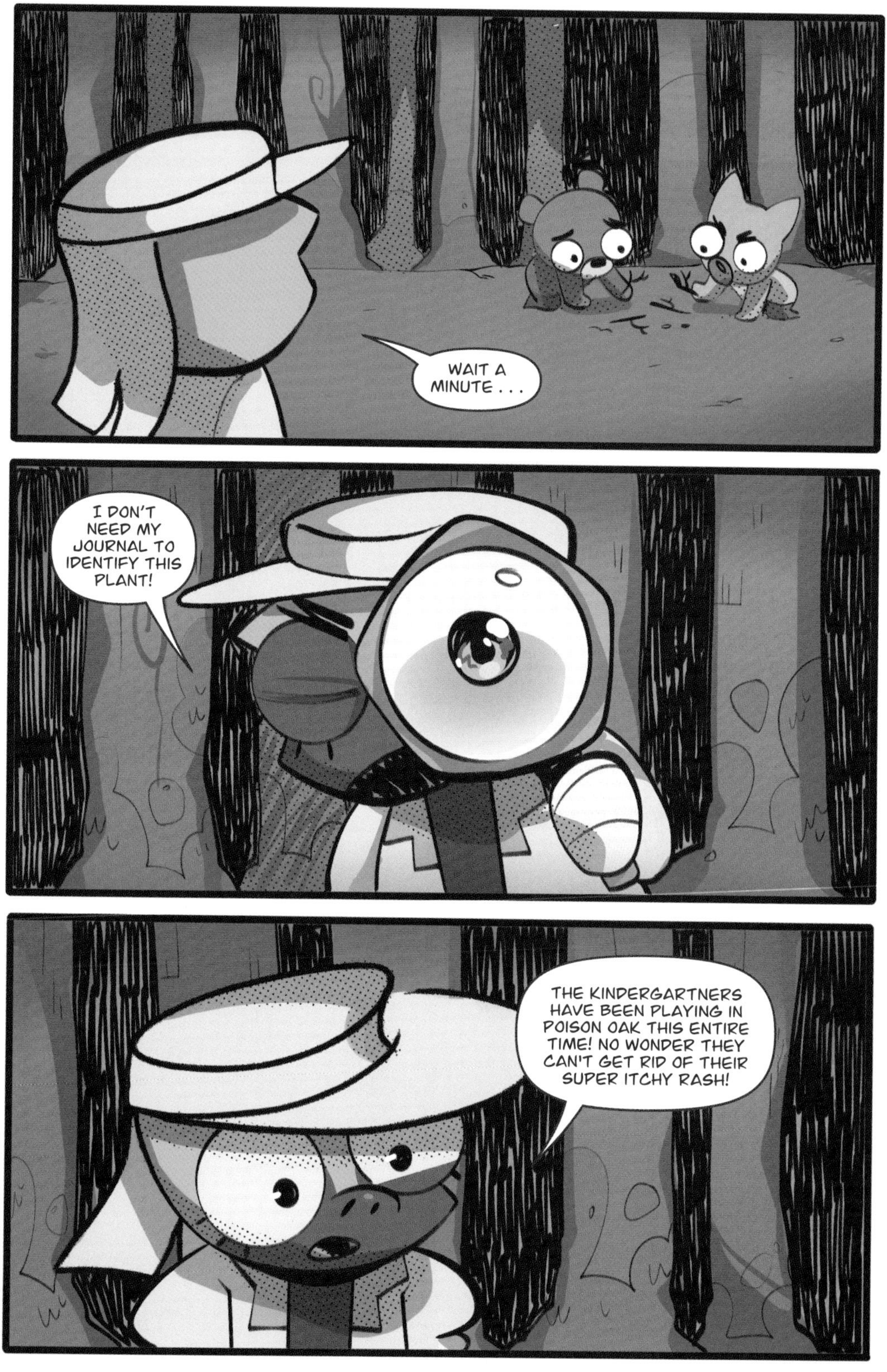
WAIT A MINUTE . . .
I DON'T NEED MY JOURNAL TO IDENTIFY THIS PLANT!
THE KINDERGARTNERS HAVE BEEN PLAYING IN POISON OAK THIS ENTIRE TIME! NO WONDER THEY CAN'T GET RID OF THEIR SUPER ITCHY RASH!

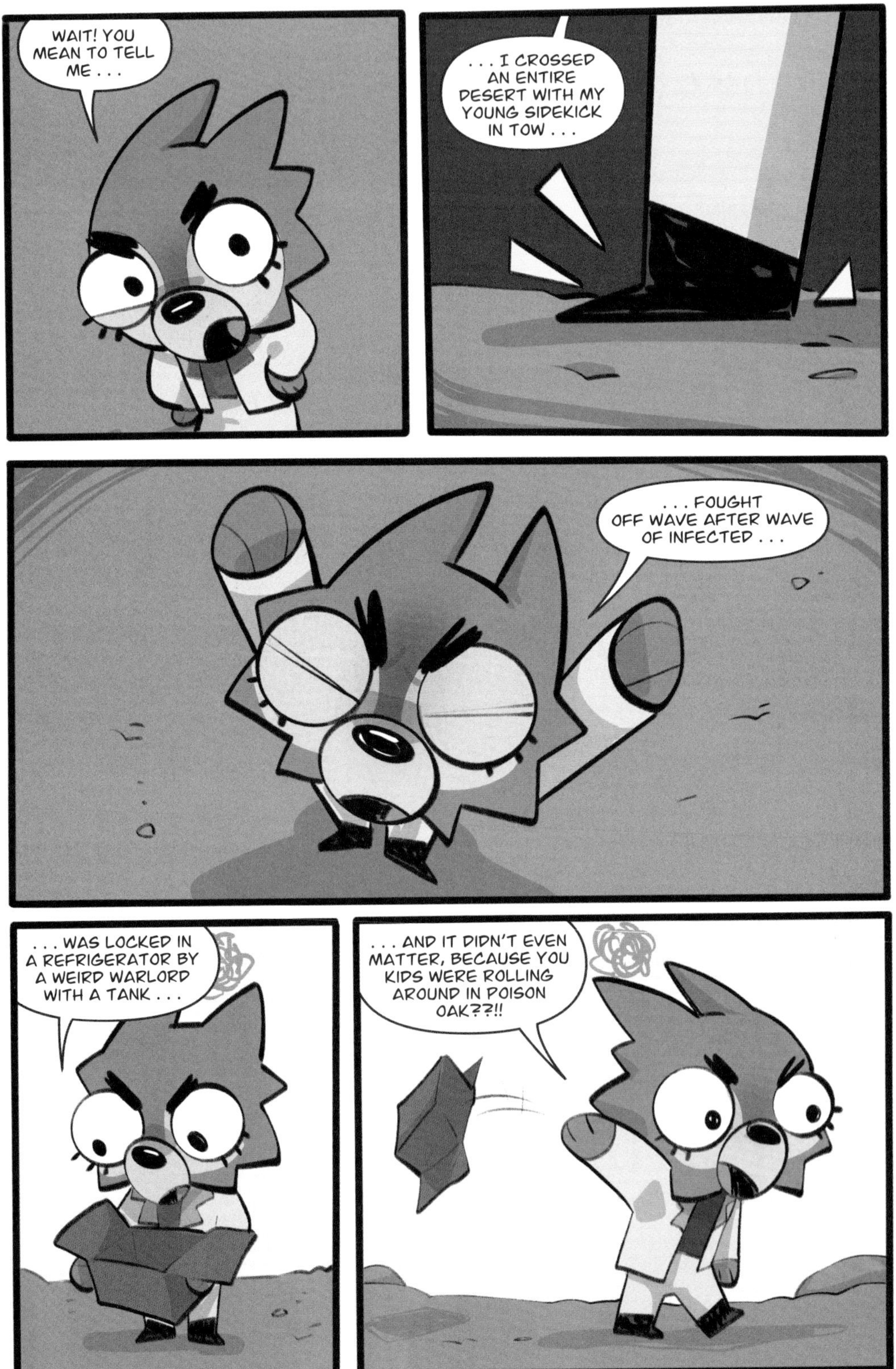
WAIT! YOU MEAN TO TELL ME . . .
. . . I CROSSED AN ENTIRE DESERT WITH MY YOUNG SIDEKICK IN TOW . . .
. . . FOUGHT OFF WAVE AFTER WAVE OF INFECTED . . .
. . . WAS LOCKED IN A REFRIGERATOR BY A WEIRD WARLORD WITH A TANK . . .
. . . AND IT DIDN'T EVEN MATTER, BECAUSE YOU KIDS WERE ROLLING AROUND IN POISON OAK??!!

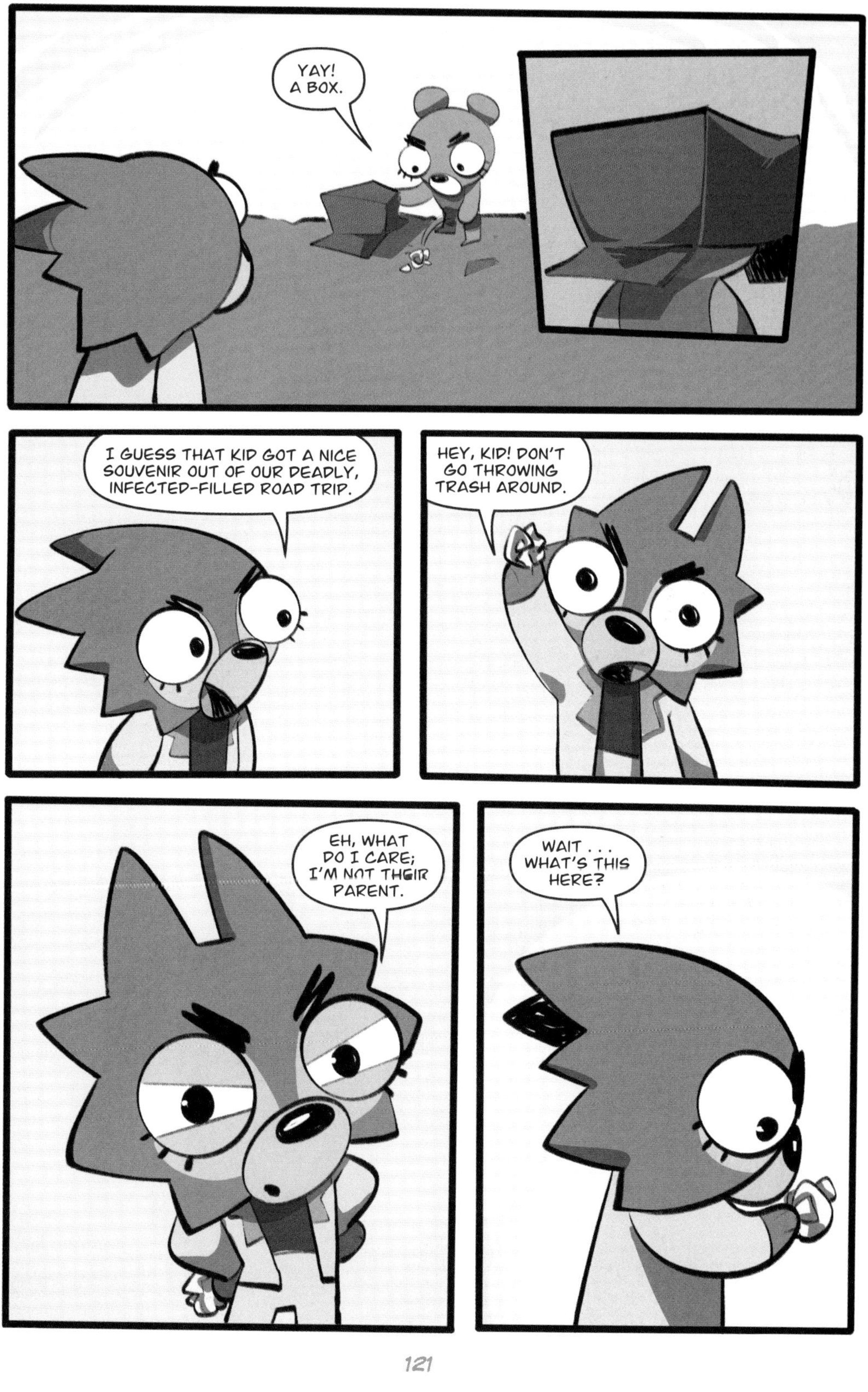
YAY! A BOX.
I GUESS THAT KID GOT A NICE SOUVENIR OUT OF OUR DEADLY, INFECTED-FILLED ROAD TRIP.
HEY, KID! DON'T GO THROWING TRASH AROUND.
EH, WHAT DO I CARE; I'M NOT THEIR PARENT.
WAIT . . . WHAT'S THIS HERE?

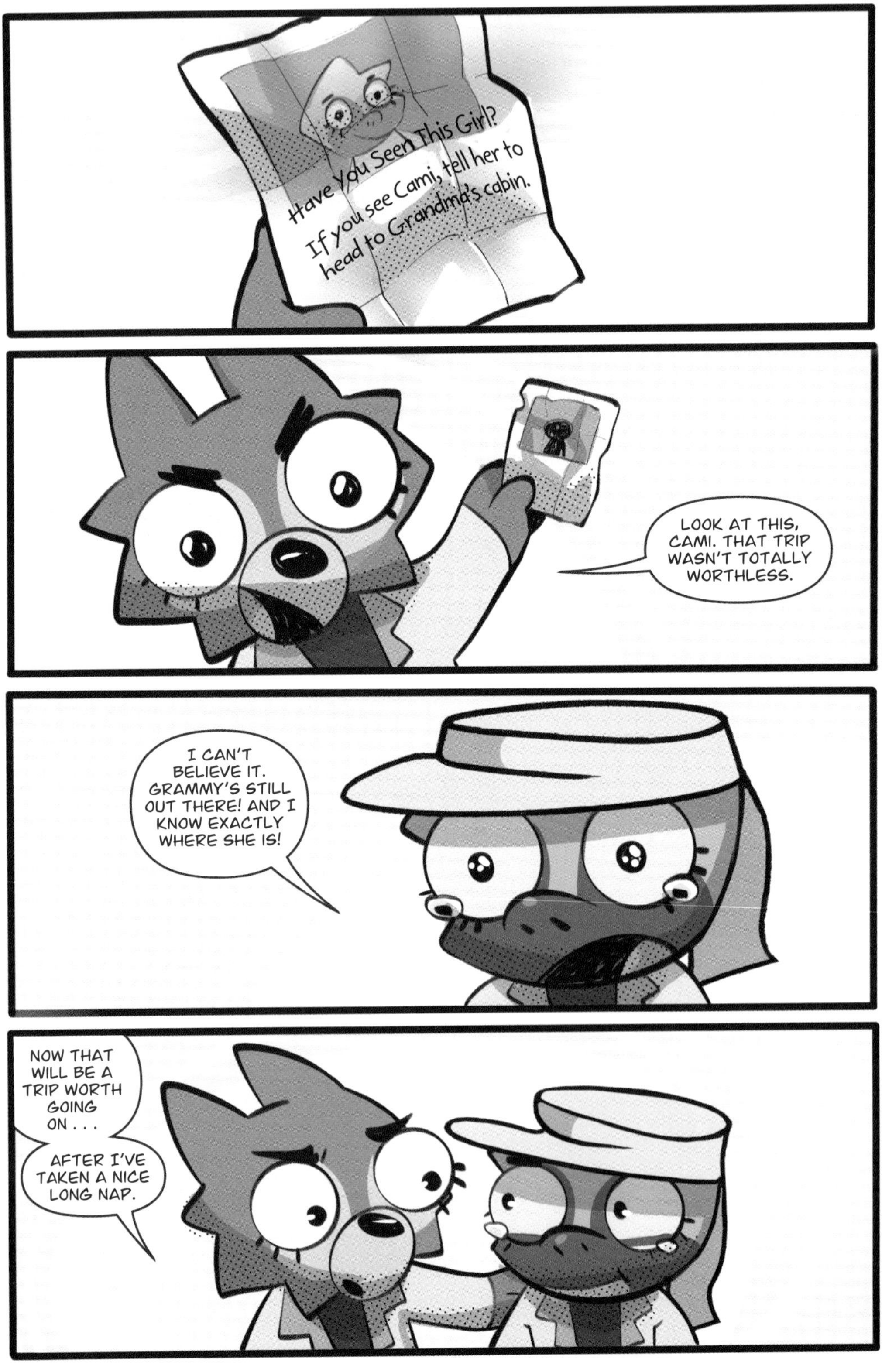
Have You Seen This Girl?
If you see Cami, tell her to head to Grandma's cabin.
LOOK AT THIS, CAMI. THAT TRIP WASN'T TOTALLY WORTHLESS.
I CAN'T BELIEVE IT. GRAMMY'S STILL OUT THERE! AND I KNOW EXACTLY WHERE SHE IS!
NOW THAT WILL BE A TRIP WORTH GOING ON . . .
AFTER I'VE TAKEN A NICE LONG NAP.

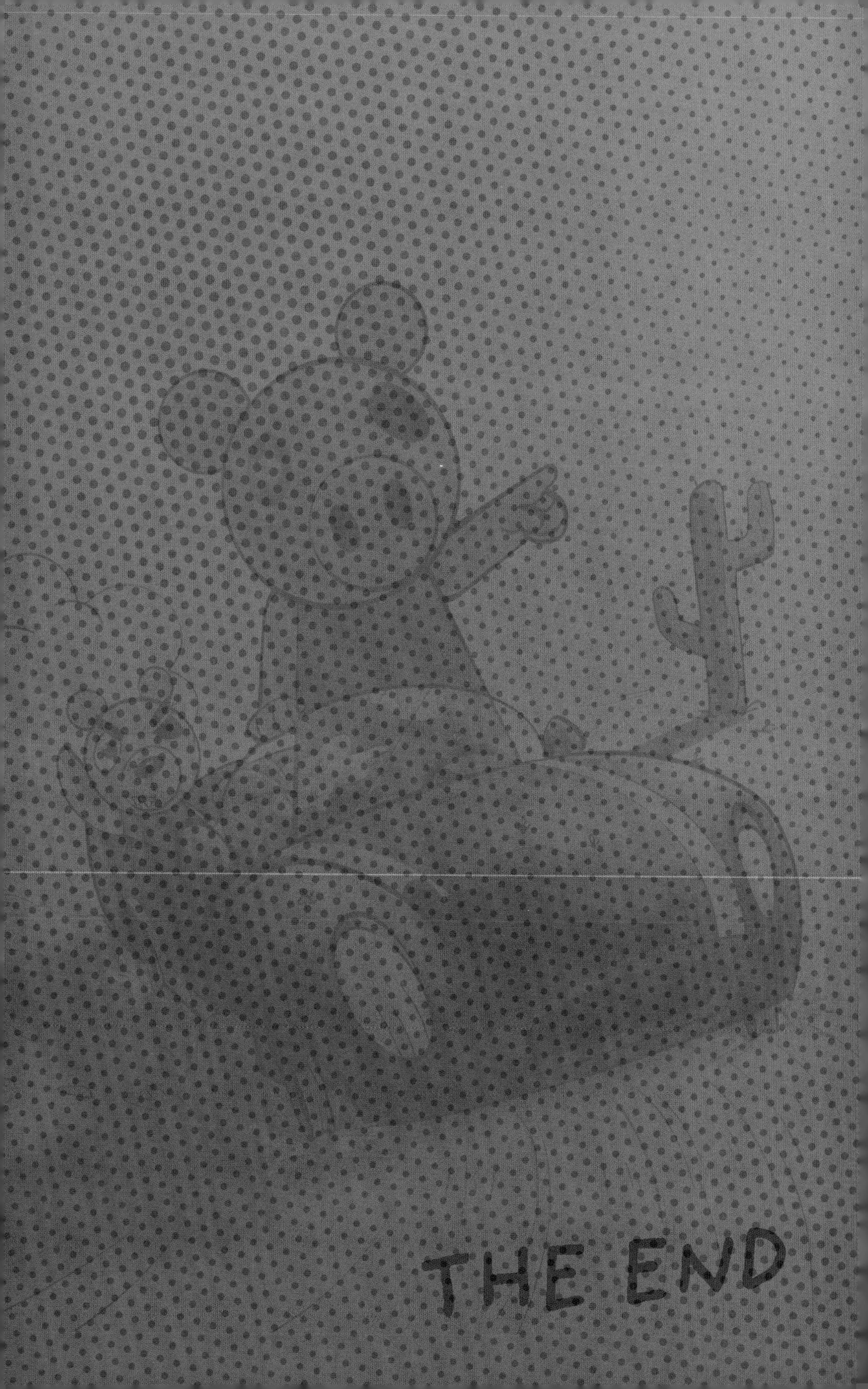
THE END

# PIGGY

## COVER DEVELOPMENT

## Round One: Sketches

AN ORIGINAL GRAPHIC NOVEL
PIGGY
WRITTEN BY VANNOTES
ART BY MALU MENEZES
SCHOLASTIC

AN ORIGINAL GRAPHIC NOVEL
PIGGY
WRITTEN BY VANNOTES
ART BY MALU MENEZES
SCHOLASTIC

AN ORIGINAL GRAPHIC NOVEL
PIGGY
COOL TITLE GOES HERE
WRITTEN BY VANNOTES
ART BY MALU MENEZES
SCHOLASTIC

AN ORIGINAL GRAPHIC NOVEL
PIGGY
COOL TITLE GOES HERE
WRITTEN BY VANNOTES
ART BY MALU MENEZES
SCHOLASTIC

# Round Two: Inks

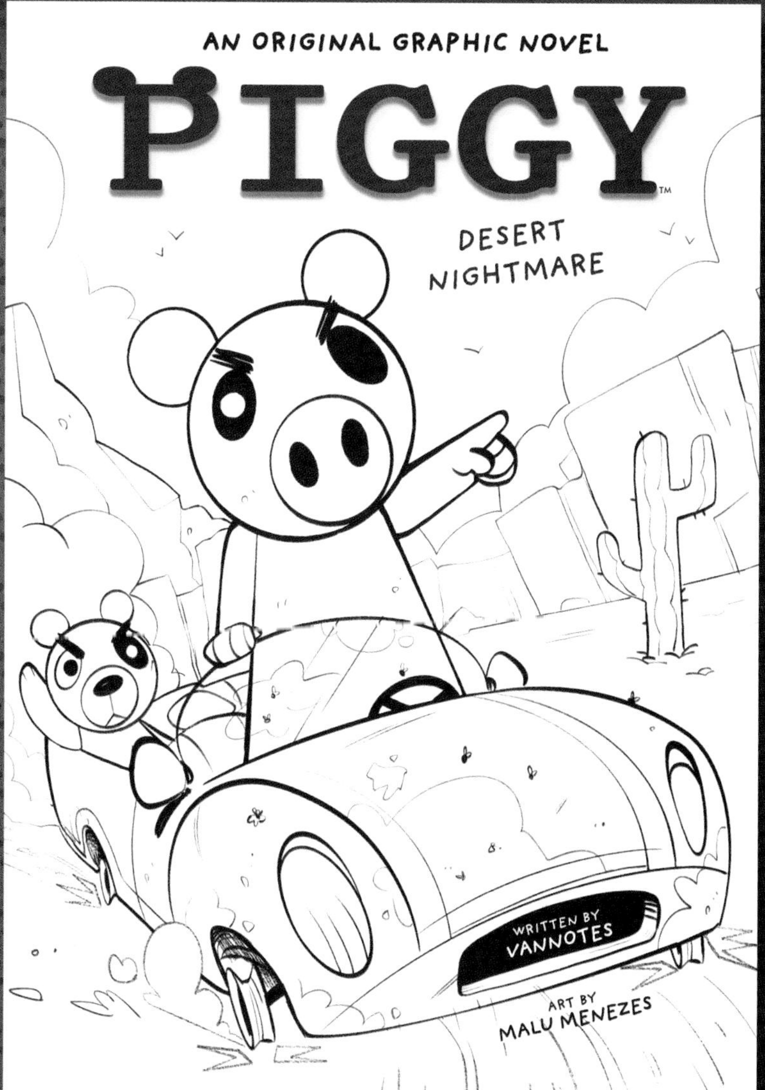
AN ORIGINAL GRAPHIC NOVEL
PIGGY™
DESERT NIGHTMARE
WRITTEN BY VANNOTES
ART BY MALU MENEZES
SCHOLASTIC

# PIGGY
## COVER DEVELOPMENT

# Round Three: Color

## Round Four: Final

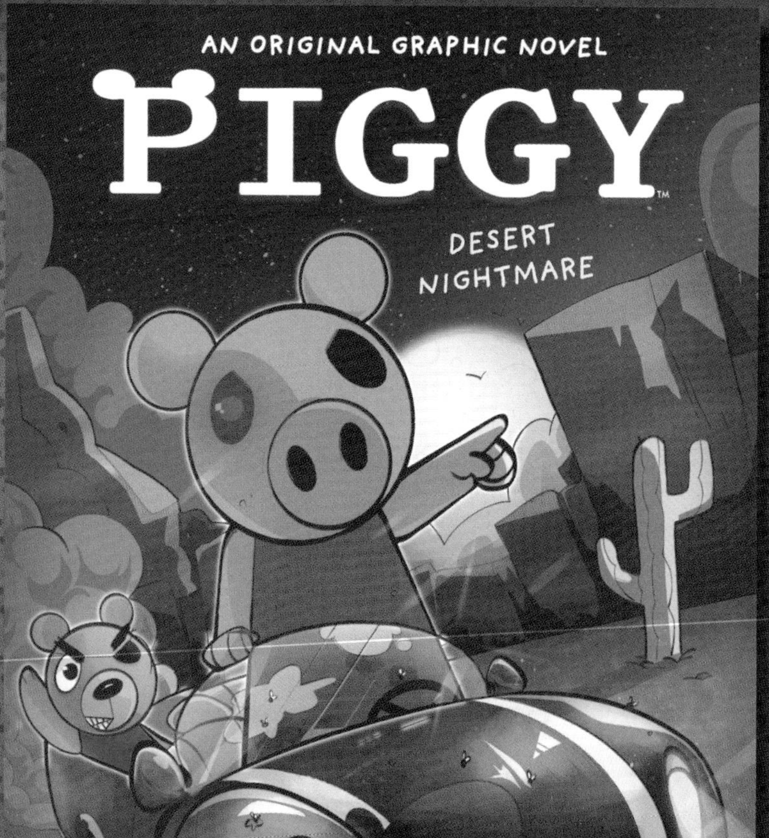

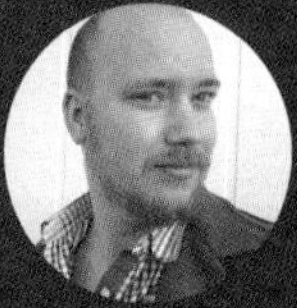

**Vannotes** is a writer, cartoonist, and educator based out of Idaho. Their work includes the *Spy Ninjas Official Graphic Novel: Virtual Reality Madness!*, *Bendy: Crack-Up Comics Collection*, and *Piggy: Permanent Detention*. They received their bachelor of fine arts degree in comic art from the Minneapolis College of Art and Design and their master of fine arts degree in creative writing from Eastern Oregon University. In their free time, they read way too many comics and play far too many video games.

Learn more about Vannotes at **vannotesbooks.com.**

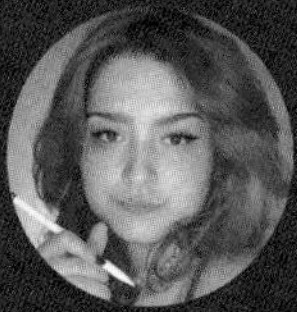

**Malu Menezes** is a Brazilian freelance illustrator and comic book artist who works as a designer, finalist, and colorist in several editorial and comic productions. Before entering the comics business, Malu worked for three years illustrating textbooks, covers, and personal commissions. Soon after, she worked for two years as a tattoo artist of authorial illustrations in small studios in her hometown, Manaus–Amazonas, Brazil. Malu likes indie digital games, reading comics when there are no new games available, and getting new tattoos, of course.

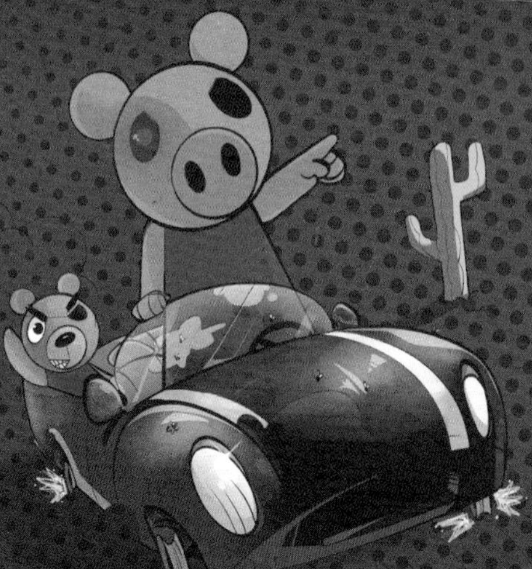